CANDLEMAKER ROW

CANDLEMAKER ROW

Inga Dunbar

SIMON & SCHUSTER

LONDON·SYDNEY·NEW YORK·TOKYO·SINGAPORE·TORONTO

First published in Great Britain by
Simon & Schuster in 1992
A Paramount Communications Company

Copyright © Inga Dunbar, 1992

Simon & Schuster Ltd
West Garden Place
Kendal Street
London W2 2AQ

Simon & Schuster of Australia Pty Ltd
Sydney

A CIP catalogue record for this book is
available from the British Library
ISBN 0–671–71758–8

Photoset in Sabon 11/13
by Derek Doyle & Associates, Mold, Clywd.
Printed in Great Britain by
Butler & Tanner Ltd, Frome and London

For Judith Murdoch

ACKNOWLEDGEMENTS

To the editorial staff of Simon & Schuster
for their patience and good humour,
especially to Maureen Waller who has been in charge of it all.
To her, and to Lucy Parsons, for all their care and hard work
in preparing this book for publication,
I am greatly indebted.

'Here comes a candle to light you to bed,
And here comes the chopper to chop off your head.'

English Nursery Rhyme

1

IT HAD BEEN a gloomy, overcast November morning. Now, shortly after the clocks had struck two, such dim light as there had been trying to trickle down between the tall crowded buildings of Edinburgh gave up the struggle and faded away altogether. Deacon William Brodie hesitated for a moment at the top of Candlemaker Row, peering down into its murky depths. An icy gust of wind blasted up from the Grassmarket, tearing open his fashionable striped duffle greatcoat to reveal beneath it a suit of light clothes, quite unsuitable for the weather and certainly for his surroundings.

Candlemaker Row was a short cut to Michael Henderson's old feed-barn behind the stables in the Grassmarket where he kept his best fighting-cocks, and on the way he intended to visit the Master Candlemaker, George Buchanan, and put a flea in his ear.

He quite forgot that candlegrease always seeped out from the candlemaking shops at the best of times, and now under a layer of ice the steep street was nothing more nor less than a death trap. He didn't notice that nobody was venturing up it; only he, swinging his silver-topped cane, was striding down it, defying it as he always defied everyone and everything, until it was too late.

'Bastard!' he exploded into the darkness, which was fortunately empty, as he landed on his backside. A minute later, his legs whirling under him like the paddles of a windmill, he was down again with so much of his breath knocked out of him that his voice came out in a furious squeak. 'Holy *shit*!' Skidding on and swearing, more by good luck than by good guidance he landed in George Buchanan's doorway. 'For Christ's sake,' he moaned softly while he got his breath back. Then he gathered up his tricorne hat, pulled his dignity and his greatcoat around him and opened the shop door in a very bad mood indeed.

'Deacon Brodie, sir! What can I do for ye the day?' Mr Buchanan rushed forward to greet him, beaming and wiping his hands on an apron that had started out in life made of canvas, but which was now so covered with candlegrease that William Brodie had no doubt it could stand up by itself.

'You can give me another gross of candles, George Buchanan, and see to it that they are not the same as the last lot! No matter how my sister and the maids try to preserve them, they burn out too quickly. And as for my workmen, they are using two each a day now at this time of year. I'm not made of money, you know!'

Mr Buchanan took in every detail of his small, slight visitor's dandified attire, from the cream lace at his throat and his wrists down to the silver buckles on his shoes, and didn't believe a word he said. No wonder they called him 'The Little Macaroni' behind his back. He'd heard them saying it only last week at a meeting in the Merchants' Hall. Yet still, resplendent in his robes and chain of office as the Deacon or President of the Trade of Carpenters, Brodie commanded respect, small though he was. Respect, but not fear, as far as George Buchanan was concerned.

'Och, I remember telling ye at the time, buy cheap, buy dear! The thicker ones last twice as long and they only cost a farthing a dozen more, man! I daresay ye dinna recommend inferior wood to your customers, either?' George Buchanan stood his ground no matter how important his customer. 'Ye wouldna be a Master Cabinetmaker and Deacon of Trades if ye did!'

'That'll be another thruppence, then,' William Brodie grumbled. 'It's all money, money, money!'

'Ay, it's no' easy earning an honest living these days,' George agreed. 'There must be better ways than this.'

To his astonishment William Brodie's face changed as if from night to day. The petulant frown disappeared, and suddenly the Deacon was choking with laughter. 'Oh, there are!' he said.

George wiped his honest face with a red handkerchief and gazed at his customer. 'Ye mean,' he lowered his voice, 'the cockfights? That'll be where ye're going just noo? Away to see yer birds?'

'That's right, George.' William Brodie was still laughing strangely. 'Don't look so solemn, man, it's been almost legal now for the past twenty years! You won't land up in the criminal court if you come to our Mains. There's one tonight,' he added casually.

'The criminal court!' Mr Buchanan's face paled at the very idea.

'I was there this morning. Lord Braxfield was on the bench.'

'My God! Braxie himsel'! Och, tell me about it!' George Buchanan dashed to the far end of his shop and pulled the cloth off a half-barrel. 'Ye're no' in a hurry, are ye?' he asked, filling up two glasses.

'Well,' the Deacon smiled graciously and accepted the glass of ale, 'it was the trial of the three would-be political reformers, George, back from France and talking about revolution.'

'Merciful God! What did they mean, Deacon?'

'They want ordinary folk to have a vote, to be represented in Parliament, to have a say in the running of the country. Sedition, Lord Braxfield called it. Anyway, it all began at nine o'clock this morning ...'

At nine o'clock that morning Robert Macqueen – Lord Braxfield – lifted his wig and made an effort to catch whatever it was that was running about underneath it. Failing in this attempt he smacked the wig back on with an expert bang over his grizzled hair. That sometimes worked. He thought perhaps it had for the moment, and with the skirts of his gown sweeping the boards of Edinburgh's Parliament House he took his seat on the bench.

At his appearance a deathly hush fell over the courtroom. Slowly and deliberately he ranged three bottles of claret on the table before him, and those present hissed like a crowd of frightened rabbits while they counted them. The trial would be over by midday, then. Just in time for Braxie to take the meridian, his mid-morning dram, in one of the taverns. He would have made up his mind already, and with one accord their eyes swivelled to the door the prisoners would enter by, condemned before they were tried, poor devils.

'Weel, weel,' he growled.

'Are ye ready, my lord?'

'Bring them in, man! I havena got all day, ye ken,' he barked, and the three reformers were trailed in to stand before him.

He regarded them for a moment out of powerful eyes set under rough eyebrows, and they gazed back at the Lord Justice Clerk, the most feared criminal judge in Scotland.

He had no patience with them or their cause whatsoever. In his view the landowners were the only ones whose opinions should be regarded. *They* were not likely to flit off out of the country and listen to revolutionary ideas from the likes of the French.

'Hm!' he snorted, and the trial began.

He was on his second bottle of claret and had managed on the whole to keep his mouth shut – except for one or two outbursts in his broad Scottish tongue which, like his thoughts, were short, strong and conclusive – when the man Muir's pleas became altogether too impertinent and too radically persuasive by half.

'There are debating clubs all over France,' he was asserting. 'And if the French can debate the principles of government and representation, so can the British. There is no reason and no law why our society should not be formed in Scotland. We would call it the Friends of the People.'

Lord Braxfield was perfectly aware that Muir was an advocate himself, one of great eloquence. At the same time his shrewd black eyes took in the ripple of agreement in the courtroom.

'And how would ye propose to fund it?' he asked, with feigned interest.

'The skilled workers would subscribe thruppence a quarter, my lord.'

Just as he thought. The skilled workers, indeed. The working class at all, for that matter. What did they know? Without the blue blood of the aristocracy they could not have the brain to begin with. Lord Braxfield stared at Muir coldly.

'Oh ay, ye're a verra clever chiel,' he told him, 'but ye'd be none the worse o' hanging!'

Time went on until another of the reformers, Gerald, actually had the temerity to address his lordship directly. 'My Lord,' he said, 'all great men have been reformers. Even our Saviour was one.'

A horrified Lord Braxfield could see that the argument was beginning to reach ridiculous proportions. Now was the time to nip it in the bud. 'Ay,' he said crushingly. 'Muckle he made o' *that*! He was hangit, ye ken.'

By this time everyone in the courtroom was convinced of the verdict. It would be death by hanging. Braxie was in that sort of mood today with a vengeance, and in a tearing hurry besides. He wasted no time on his summing up, but to their great surprise he didn't don the black cap on top of his wig, for unbeknown to them he had reason to be in a very benign mood that day.

'Fourteen years' transportation,' he passed sentence. 'Ye canna do Scotland any more harm for a while from the other side o' the world,' and in the disbelieving silence that followed when the court rose, everyone gaped at the back of his strongly built figure striding off.

The day was dank, grey and colder than ever when he came out into the Royal Mile with his hands clasped under his coat-tails. The first thing his eye lit on was Archie Johnston scraping the street and then scattering coarse brown salt on it to melt the ice.

'Good day to ye, Lord Robbie,' Archie Johnston said.

'Good day yersel', lad. Noo, when ye get doon as far as Covenant Close see ye make a good job o' it, for I've to go out this afternoon to see a fine lady, and I dinna want to go wi' dirty shoes.'

'Oh, ay? And what time would that be?'

'I'll be leaving at half past two. Ye'll ha'e it done by then?'

'Och, by half past two I'll be at the White Horse Inn, if not right doon to the bottom, to Holyrood itsel'! Ye ken *me*, Lord Robbie. I dinna piss aboot!'

'Hm!' Lord Braxfield continued on his way to Johnnie Dowie's tavern for the meridian since it was now well after twelve noon, the time when all responsible and hard-working Edinburgh gentlemen paused in their business for a little light refreshment.

There he ate some ham, a dish of pease and then a nice beefsteak washed down with a glass or two of brandy. But it was in a gloomy fashion, wondering all the while how he was going to get past his wife that afternoon dressed in his best clothes and setting off in his coach.

'God help me,' he muttered to himself, 'she was in a right bitch o' a mood this morning! If I so much as mention the word Candacraig, there'll be no holding her! Noo, where can I say I'm going?'

An hour later, well fortified, he went home to his house in Covenant Close to face the difficult task of putting on his best shirt and cravat while at the same time diverting his wife, Maggie, clean off the scent.

Somehow he managed it, and at half past two he took his large bag of papers and went out to his coach. Having just bypassed Lady Margaret's cold suspicious stare he now encountered the twinkling, intrepid eyes of his young driver, Walter Thomson.

Walter was a grand lad with the horses and the coach, if a wee bit too adventurous at times, but he got him around the country-side to the regional trials in the so-called summertime through the mud and the mire when no other man could have done the same.

'Noo then, Walter,' he addressed him, 'what's the weather like, think ye?'

'Bad, my lord, and getting worse,' Walter replied with relish. 'The wind's in the north-east, and ye ken what that means. It could easily snow, so wherever ye're going we'd better get there fast.'

'Oot to Candacraig.'

'Then we'll cut doon Candlemaker Row.'

'Weel, I hope ye ken what ye're doing, me lad!'

'Hop in, sir!' Walter laughed and banged the door shut.

He always judged his master's mood by the colour of his nose, and today it was like a strawberry. The old boy had had a few drinks today already, so Walter judged he wouldn't object to a spot of adventure.

The coach trundled up the Royal Mile and then turned sharp left, hovering almost perpendicularly at the top of Candlemaker Row before it made its hair-raising descent.

Inside George Buchanan's shop Deacon Brodie was preparing to leave.

'Hang on one minute, sir! I'll get the shovel and clear a path for ye.'

Deacon Brodie chuckled to himself. George was only clearing a path for him so that he might get a tip for the cockfight tonight. The two men came out of the shop doorway into the merciless cold, George frantically shovelling dirt solidified with wax and ice from before his customer's feet. Step by step they progressed along the little path he was making out to the middle of the street.

'That was a grand story aboot the trial,' George panted. 'I'll send ye the thick candles for the same price as the thin ones ... Ye wouldna have a tip for the Main tonight, would ye, Deacon?'

'Ah, well, you could try the Blackbird or Jean's Fancy,' the Deacon named his two weakest cocks. 'So you're coming to Michael Henderson's tonight, George? Ten o'clock it starts,' he added innocently, turning his head away to hide the wicked gleam in his eyes and catching his first glimpse of Lord Braxfield's coach at the top of Candlemaker Row.

The horses snickered as Walter held them back firmly, the brakes screamed over the cobbles and the coach zigzagged dizzily as it hurtled down to the Grassmarket.

'Get back!' George Buchanan grabbed the Deacon's arm and pulled him back into the shop doorway. 'Man! That was a close shave! It'll be that Walter Thomson again ye ken, Lord Braxfield's coachman. He loves coming doon this way just for devilment. Are ye all right, sir?'

William Brodie smiled one of the enigmatic smiles he was famous for. 'It would never do to meet our Maker thanks to Lord Braxfield, one way or another, would it, George?'

'No fear, God help us all.'

Mistress Buchanan with some of the candlemakers behind her came out to join them at the commotion. They watched the coach slithering down the rest of Candlemaker Row and halting briefly to swing around, skidding alarmingly, into the Grassmarket before it squared up and went on its way.

'Where's *he* going in such a hell of a hurry?' Deacon Brodie wondered out loud.

'Oot to the country. South o' the town by the look o' it,' George Buchanan replied, quite shocked at the use of such language in front of a lady. There had been no hint of it all the way through his tale of the trial in the cultivated Scots one would expect from a town councillor. Now George began to wonder whether Deacon Brodie could swear like a trooper if he had a mind to, and if anyone in Edinburgh really knew the true character of the little man.

'Tell me, why would a lawyer be going out there on such a day?' the Deacon demanded next. 'It can't be to see criminals. It must be to visit one of the gentry, and not too far away either, so that he can get back tonight. Where would that be, George?'

'The only big hoose I can think o' is Candacraig, Lady Susanna Graham's place. I send a lot o' candles oot there.'

'The last time I saw any o' her servants they were saying she's very ill,' Mistress Buchanan said. 'Perhaps she's died, and her wi' no bairns to leave the place to. What will happen to it, then?'

'It'll have to be closed up,' Deacon Brodie said.

'Oh, ay? And *who*'ll get the job o' that, I wonder?'

'As your husband and I have just been discussing, money's tight, Mistress Buchanan.' The Deacon turned to go. 'We must all earn an honest crust as and where we can in this world,' he added over his shoulder with a laugh, 'even if it's only boarding up a house.'

'I never liked that man,' Mistress Buchanan sniffed.

'Noo then, Nellie, give credit where it's due! Apart from being the best carpenter in Edinburgh he's a cooncillor besides, and if he got respectably married he's widely tipped to be the next Lord Provost!'

'He doesn't need to get married, believe me,' his wife said darkly.

'Nellie!' George did his best to deflect her in front of the other candlemakers. 'Cheer up, dearie. It'll be the summer before we know it, and then we'll be away to England to see the bairns again.'

William Brodie cautiously headed on down to the Grassmarket, his hands clinging to the cold stone buildings of Candlemaker Row, and his mind on that snippet of information from Mistress Buchanan. With the Brodie reputation for good workmanship he would be the one chosen to close up Candacraig after Lady Susanna's death. While his workmen were boarding up the windows and securing the doors, he would be inside, going through the house for anything of interest. There could be money there, or jewels. Lady Susanna Graham was fabulously rich. At the very least there might be some interesting documents, and just lately he'd been, well, happening to find interesting documents in houses all over the town. Some day they might be quite valuable. He was making a collection of them.

2

NOW THAT WALTER had settled the horses down to a more dignified pace Lord Braxfield sighed in relief, took some papers out of his bag and began to read them. For twenty minutes he tried his best, until the coach came almost to a stop in order to negotiate the gate in the massive walls of Candacraig.

Then he gave it up with a quivering sigh and put away the papers again, much too excited to concentrate. Why after all these years was Susanna suddenly sending for him a week before Christmas, this particular Christmas of 1786?

Unable to answer the question that nagged him, he sat back to admire the driveway up to Candacraig instead. He liked the way it wound through the trees and then came from a little rise on to a clearing where the great house sat so impressively. A beautiful setting for a beautiful woman, Miss Susanna Marr, as she was when he first knew her.

He had not seen her very often since she had married and become Lady Susanna Graham but oh, when she was young and flamboyant, and the belle of Edinburgh with her flaming red hair! He remembered her in those days, all right. He had been convinced that one day she would marry him. She had said she would; that was why he had had the ring made for her.

He had searched the length and breadth of Edinburgh to find a goldsmith who would make it just as he had designed it, one S joined to the next, and the next, for the initial of her name. When he had put it on her finger she had cried with happiness.

He had never understood why she had disappeared so suddenly after that – to France, of all places, he found out later – and why when she returned and before he had a chance to see her she had married Sir John Robertson Graham, that pale apology for a man; but then of course a wonderful catch as far as immense wealth was concerned.

The coach deposited him under the portico, and a manservant ran down the steps at the front door to conduct him inside.

'Lord Braxfield? If you will give me your hat and your cane, sir, Florence will lead the way upstairs. Her ladyship is not at all well.'

As soon as he set foot on the staircase he smelled apples, the strong smell of apples beginning to decay, and all the way up the smell became stronger and sourer. It was overpowering when Florence showed him to Lady Susanna's bedside, got him seated and then withdrew to leave them alone together.

At first sight she still retained the ghost of her former beauty. It was there somewhere beneath the powder and paint, but she was so thin that her body scarcely lifted the bedclothes. She lay absolutely still, and turned her head towards him with obvious difficulty. As she did so, some of the paint flaked off.

'Dearest Robbie Macqueen,' she said in a faint voice, 'you came after all. I hoped you would.'

'How could ye doubt it?' he asked. 'Yer letter arrived this morning and I took my coach here as fast as I could.'

For years and years his dream had been that she would summon him back some day, remembering how it had been the first time, with her breasts almost out of her gown, an open invitation to any man, his eager hands upon them, the surge of her hardened nipples, her skirts ridden up, her eager moistness and his total fulfilment. Morning, noon and night it went on, those two months before she went away.

It was for the good of her health, so they told him, though nobody in the world looked healthier than Susanna at that stage in her life, thirty-five years ago. To this day he had never understood it.

'Ye always did look like a rosy apple,' he said. 'I could still eat ye, ye witch.'

'Even now?' Her eyes mocked him. 'No, not now, Robbie. What made you think of apples? You can smell them, can't you? But it's not apples, it's my illness, and every day the smell of my own decay is like to choke me. Your rosy apple is rotten to the core.'

She smiled a ghastly smile, more of her powder cracking away from her skin, and he saw that her once-beautiful eyes, like two huge brown pansies, were sunk back into cadaverous cheeks, yellow skin stretched over the bone. Her beauty was long gone, eaten away, and in the shock of it he could not utter another word.

'Poor Florence,' she said. 'She tried so hard for hours to make me look pretty again for you. It was not possible, I'm afraid.'

'What ails ye, Susanna?' he asked directly.

She was just as direct in return. 'It's the trouble you get from going with too many men. I was looking for another Robbie Macqueen, I suppose. I should have known better. There was never anyone like you, darling Robbie, but my past has caught up with me now.'

'But ye're only fifty, lassie! Ye'll get over this,' he said uncomfortably, for her wig had slipped and he saw that there was not a hair left upon her head. Her very eyebrows were only pencilled on.

'I'm dying, Robbie, but I would not ask for that pee-weeing Erskine Caldwell, our own advocate, now at the last minute. I wanted a proper man, one that I could speak to, one who would not be shocked, one who would be discreet.'

She was lying, of course. There was not a more diplomatic solicitor in Edinburgh than Erskine Caldwell if it was a confession she wanted to make, or her will, or both, while he himself did not usually bother with such trivialities. He wondered what was behind all this, for Susanna had always been as devious as she was dangerously beautiful.

'Oh, how I loved you, Robbie Macqueen! I always have. But you were so young in those days, with your way to make in the world before becoming Lord Braxfield! And now here I am ... suddenly the game is over.'

'Na, na. Dinna say that, Susanna. Ye're no' finished yet!'

'Whether I am or not, I must make my will. My husband John

didn't make one. Perhaps he thought he was indestructible. But none of us is, and all this,' she waved her hand weakly, 'must be left to *someone*.'

She wore no rings at all now, he noticed. Probably none of them would stay on her skeletal fingers. 'Ay,' he said, 'but who, Susanna?'

'John Robertson Graham was never man enough to give me a child as you know, and he was the last of his line. Of course,' Lady Susanna scowled, 'there is still Fraser Graham, the biggest thorn in what flesh I have left.'

Yes, Lord Braxfield recalled the old sad story, there was still Fraser Graham. Left an orphan at four months old, the boy had been brought up by his grandfather, Charles Fraser Graham, for the next seven years, and the old Jesuit saying had proved true, indeed it had: 'Give me a child for the first seven years, and you may do what you like with him afterwards.'

In Lord Braxfield's opinion, *all* Fraser Graham's thinking now had its roots in that early upbringing by his grandfather, who was far too free and easy, far too liberal and totally unconventional. When the old man died young Fraser was sent to Candacraig to live with his uncle, Sir John Robertson Graham, who had few ideas of any kind, and Lady Susanna whom he had schooled himself in earlier years to look after conservative interests, and who had possessed enough backbone to see that they were implemented ever since.

The judge sighed. It had turned into a family feud. Young Fraser simply could not swallow his great-aunt's Tory beliefs and prejudices, and so it had continued for the next twenty years. Fraser Graham told him often enough, whenever he took him to task, that he would never go back and live in Candacraig as long as his great-aunt Susanna was alive, and Susanna for her part would not allow it anyway. They were at absolute loggerheads still, for Fraser did not believe in the Establishment as his elders and betters did, young fool that he was.

'Fraser got plenty from his own grandfather, dinna worry. Charles Graham left him a rich young man, even if he left this estate and another huge fortune to his brother, Sir John Robertson Graham – yer husband.' Lord Braxfield ground out the words with no attempt at diplomacy, speaking as he was now to the man's widow on her deathbed. 'Now, *there* was a wee mannie who never did a stroke o' work any day o' his life!'

'Nor any night, either, I can assure you of that,' Susanna agreed bitterly. 'But I always had a soft spot for Fraser, you know, in spite of everything.'

'I'm very glad to hear it, Susanna. His grandfather expected him to become the eventual heir of Candacraig, ye ken. That's why he left yer husband all that money. It was for Fraser – providing ye had no family yersel's, of course, when it would have had to be shared oot.'

Her mouth twisted in a strange smile. 'Well, above all not a pennypiece of mine must be allowed to go to any of my own relations after the way they turned their backs on me.'

'Blood is still thicker than water, Susanna.'

Lady Susanna tried to laugh, but the laugh turned into a choking, rattling cough that seemed to echo through the house, and Florence came running to the bedside. She turned her mistress on to her side and patted her back until the fit was over. Then she gave her a sip of water and straightened her wig and the covers.

'She's very weak, sir,' she said. 'She should rest.'

'Leave us, Florence,' Susanna panted, 'we won't be much longer.' When the maid left, she said, 'Yes, blood is certainly thicker than water, Robbie. That's why you're here. I know Fraser Graham must be considered, that would be only fair. But he's not going to step into all this so easily! There is someone else to be considered, too.'

'Someone else? Who?'

What was she up to? Did she have a trick up her sleeve to get her own back on Fraser? No, his Susanna would not be so vindictive as to cut him out altogether! Lord Braxfield would not believe it.

'I did have a child, once. I was supposed to be in France, but I never got there. I just stayed in London, Robbie, and my daughter was born at the Hornpipe Inn in Narrow Street. I left her there with the friends I made, and all these years I've sent money for her to that address.'

'The Hornpipe? Ye're telling me ye had a bairn in an *inn*?' He gaped at her, astonishment, horror and bitter hurt etched across his face.

'My friends Jack Tarre and his wife Lilian looked after me and the baby, at the time. They had a little girl of their own, and they promised that my child would be brought up as her baby sister. I paid them, of course,' she sobbed, 'but oh, it was so hard to leave her, Robbie!'

Just for one giddy second Lord Braxfield felt his world slipping away from beneath his feet. It was what skating on thin ice must be like, and he had never skated. It was as bizarre as many a night of passion with her had ever been. Every next morning he was never sure if he'd lived through a dream or a nightmare, and now here she was putting him through it again, on her very deathbed.

'And ye never saw the bairn after that?' he stuttered.

'No ... but I never stopped thinking about her, and now it is time to act on her behalf. Hold my hand, Robbie, and write it all down as I speak.'

He took her hand in his left one, and with his other began to write.

Barely three weeks later, early in January 1787, with Fraser Graham the only other person there, Robbie Macqueen stood at Lady Susanna's graveside while the dreary funeral service went on, and it seemed to him that he could still hear her voice so clearly she might have been speaking to him from her coffin. 'Find her, wherever she is, and bring her back, Robbie. It is as much for you as it is for me.'

Whatever she had meant by that he did not know. He was still mystified, although his mind dwelled on it frequently, all through the sudden rush of business in the spring and during the many hours spent travelling around Scotland on his summer circuit.

It was while he was away that Deacon Brodie went to Candacraig. He was to meet Lady Susanna's laywer there at nine o'clock in the morning, and while Erskine Caldwell was making out the inventory with the help of his clerks, Brodie would be supervising his workmen boarding up the windows and making sure of all the locks.

Brodie and his men arrived there long before seven with wagons of wood to carry out such an extensive job. He gave the men their instructions and set off on a solitary tour of the house. Just before nine he arrived in a little sitting-room so exquisitely furnished that he judged it must have been Lady Susanna's own. By far the most interesting piece was a small writing desk. The lock posed no problem to him, and he admired the way its mechanism worked. When the flap came down the drawers jumped open at the same time, although the bottom drawer seemed to stick a little. He smiled at that. When he had time he would take the desk to pieces, convinced that there was a secret compartment in it somewhere, but all he had time for now was a quick search through the papers.

They were household accounts of no great importance. As he was skimming through them he heard the sound of horses and a coach. This room overlooked the drive, and sure enough, the coach was Erskine Caldwell's. He could find no money and no jewellery, but he thought he had cured the problem of the bottom drawer when he snatched out a parchment stuck inside it. 'Last Will and Testament', he read hastily, without noticing that it was only part of a document before stuffing it in his pocket.

'Simon!' he called to his foreman. There was no time to lose. Erskine Caldwell had descended from his coach at the front of the house, and was coming up the steps. 'Help me lift this desk out by the back door into one of the wagons. The glue needs attention. The desk will only deteriorate if it's left here in the cold and the damp.'

Later that night, back at Brodie's Close, they carried it up to one of the spare bedrooms, out of sight. As soon as Simon departed he took the parchment out of his pocket again and studied it. It was ripped, but that didn't matter. The fragment he held told him all he needed to know.

So Lady Susanna Graham had had an illegitimate daughter, had she? Suzanne Gray. And this Suzanne stood to inherit half the fortune! All his poking and prying had borne fruit, after all, for now he possessed the key to it.

Suzanne Gray. In London, was she? The excitement nearly choked him. All he had to do was find her, and he would be the richest man in Edinburgh.

Lord Braxfield was exhausted by the time Walter Thomson

brought him safely home again to Edinburgh. He sat slumped by his fireside, feeling that now he really was all alone in the world without a soul left who really loved him.

The longer he brooded about it the angrier he became with Susanna. She should not have left him in the first place thirty-five years ago, and she should not have left him three months ago for the grave either, with his heart completely broken. Worse still, all she had seemed able to think about in the end was this Suzanne Gray in London, in an inn called the Hornpipe, for God's sake! Why should she, some English madam, inherit one of Scotland's most prestigious estates? He was outraged. She did not even have a name of any distinction. *Suzanne Gray*, indeed! It sounded contrived to him, not a proper name at all. Very like Susanna Graham, in fact. Susanna Graham in disguise ...

His lips curled. So that was it! Susanna had had another lover, had she? She must have gone straight from his own arms and into those of this Suzanne Gray's father, for she must have conceived as soon as she set foot in London. He began to boil with rage and jealousy, even after all these years. When, shakily, he cooled down he forced himself to think logically. His scalp began to prickle as he counted up the dates he remembered from her Last Will and Testament. He counted and recounted, and then in a fever counted again.

Jesus Christ! He poured himself a brandy with fingers that shook so much it dribbled over the fine mahogany of the sideboard. *Jesus! Suzanne Gray could be nobody else's daughter but his own*!

Thirty-five years ago Susanna had had no money, and he had certainly had none, with only a toe on the bottom rung of the ladder of the Law. He understood her dilemma at last. Determined to keep their child somehow, Susanna had fled to London to hide while she had the baby and the secret had been well kept, even from him. She had been a brave woman, as well as full-blooded and loving, and she still loved him, even from the grave. Tears began to trickle down his face.

'What now, woman?' he snapped at Lady Braxfield when, po-faced as ever, she brought in tea and the eternal rock cakes.

'I'll thank ye to keep a civil tongue in yer head, Robbie

Macqueen,' she snapped back. 'A civil tongue ye havena had since the day o' yon Graham woman's funeral! There never was a sniff o' her in the air but what ye were aye in a thundering temper. Ye'd think there had been something atween the pair o' ye!'

He eyed her narrow, barren form angrily. When Susanna was lost to him so long ago he knew he would never love anyone else. Nothing else mattered after that, so he had settled for a woman of means instead.

'Weel, she's dead now,' he growled. 'Let her rest in peace.'

It never occurred to him that his wife might love him just as much as Susanna ever had; perhaps even enough for him to be able to confess to her that he had a bastard daughter somewhere in London. It never occurred to him to give Lady Braxfield the chance. Instead her love was put severely to the test while he continued to mourn bitterly for Susanna, and every night he sat staring into the bottom of his brandy glass as if he might find some answers there.

What ever happened to Suzanne Gray? Had she ever married? What was her name now? Was she even still living, he tortured himself, and, if so, where was she?

3

SUZANNE WAS AT that moment beating her maidservant in Paris. Polly put her fingers in her ears and tried not to hear Caramelle's whimpers of pain. She tried not to listen to Mama's torrent of abuse but the screaming and the thudding just went on and on and on.

'Keep your thieving hands,' thud, 'off my things,' thud. 'Do you hear me?' Mama shouted.

'Yes, Madame. I'm sorry, Madame,' Caramelle moaned. 'I was only looking.'

'Get out! Get out! This is not the first time I've caught you, but it's certainly the last! You are dismissed!'

'Madame Suzanne, I beg you ... I will never do it again. Where shall I go? I have nowhere,' Caramelle sobbed bitterly.

'You can go back to the gutter where I found you,' Mama blazed. 'I've kept you and fed you all these years, but how do you repay me?'

'Only let me stay, and I will work for nothing, Madame.'

There was a pause. 'Nothing?' Mama's voice dropped a little, and Polly knew she would be tempted by that. Uncle Geoffrey had been away on business in England for months now, and there was no money coming into the house. Her mother's lover had always kept them in luxury until now.

At fifteen years of age Polly was more than able to understand Mama's worry and frustration. Uncle Geoffrey expressly forbade her mother ever to try to contact him when he was away in

England, so she was taking it out on Caramelle.

'Very well then,' Mama said. 'But watch out, girl! This is your last warning. Go and get my blue dress, and Polly's to match, ready for the morning.'

'Yes, Madame.' Caramelle went away. Polly lay down on her bed again and Suzanne went to her boudoir, still flushed with temper. When she faced it, it was really Geoffrey she was angry about, and very, very worried. Where was he? He had never left them for so long before, never. Was there another woman? Instinctively that was her first suspicion. No, there couldn't be, not after all they had been to each other for so many years.

She undressed, put on her filmy white nightgown, lay down on the *chaise-longue* in front of the open window for some air, and gradually cooled down. A little smile came to her lips as she allowed the veils of her memory to float away one by one, back to the beginning, to the Hornpipe, to Uncle Jack and Aunt Lilian Tarre, and to their daughter Kate …

How happy they all were in those days! Then all too soon Kate was seventeen and really very plain, with lank dark hair constantly falling down about her round face in spite of every effort to try and curl it. Suzanne was sixteen and as fresh and pretty as a dainty butterfly emerging from its chrysalis.

But Kate loved her as she would have loved a real sister. 'Oh, what's the use?' she would laugh, tearing the hated curling rags out of her hair. 'Suzy, sing us a song! You know she sings like a bird, Pa,' she nagged Uncle Jack once again. 'She should be singing for the customers! You'll be sorry if you don't let her! All the other inns have music of some sort.'

Once he was persuaded to allow it life took a different turn. None of the sailors visiting the inn needed any encouragement to speak to Suzanne in any case, but her singing was a good excuse to talk to her under Uncle Jack's watchful eye.

'Oh, Kate,' Suzanne whispered one evening, 'look at that glorious man who's just come in!'

'Yes. The one with the red hair? He looks like a Norwegian to me.'

'I don't care. Look at his smile! I hope he speaks to us after my song.'

But he didn't wait for the song. He came straight up to her there and then as if pulled by an invisible thread. 'No, I'm not Norwegian. I'm as English as they come,' he told them. 'Oliver Banks is my name. I'm here on shore leave.'

'Shouldn't you be at home with your wife and family?' Suzanne asked boldly, shaking like a leaf in the grip of a strange excitement.

'There's no wife, and no family,' he laughed. 'I'm on my own.'

That night Suzanne sang especially for him, flirting outrageously with her eyes and her mouth and her body. He *must* do something about it after that! Five minutes later she was whispering in Kate's ear again. 'He's asked me to go for a walk with him. If Aunt Lilian asks where I am, tell her a story, any story! Kate, say you will?'

'Oh Suzy … go on, then! But hurry up, for the love of Heaven.'

That October night, out in the dark street, Suzanne felt no cold at all although her gown was low-cut and her arms were bare. The strange excitement which was making her giggle so much also kept her burning hot, and around the first corner Oliver Banks soon put a stop to her giggling. He kissed her thoroughly, and then one thing led to another.

'Ooh,' Suzanne panted. 'Oh, Oliver, yes, yes – do it again!'

She liked it, that was the trouble. In fact she couldn't get enough of it or of him, and after a month of her sneaking out of the Hornpipe Uncle Jack and Aunt Lilian became very worried and suspicious.

'It's all right.' Oliver Banks smiled at them. 'She's promised to marry me when I get back from my next trip.'

'Oh, Suzy!' Kate flung her arms around her neck. 'That's wonderful!'

They were all laughing that night in the back sitting-room when the customers were gone, and Uncle Jack opened a bottle of wine to celebrate.

'When do you go?' he asked Oliver.

'High tide tonight on the *Sea Adventurer*. It's not a long trip this time. We'll be back in April. May at the latest. You won't change your mind before that, will you, Suzy? Promise me.'

After that she and Kate searched until they found the softest white silk in London for the wedding gown. It took Kate three months to sew the gown and stitch on all the little beads around the neck and the hem, but in the end it was a work of art, and April rolled around before they knew it.

'Suzy,' Aunt Lilian said, 'I hope your wedding gown will still fit you if Oliver doesn't come back until May. You haven't had any bleedings, have you, since he went away?'

'No.'

'When was the last one?'

'October.'

'I thought so,' Aunt Lilian said sadly.

April came and went. Then May came and went. One morning Uncle Jack made it his business to find out when the *Sea Adventurer* was expected, and at midday he came back to the Hornpipe with the terrible news that the ship had gone down with all hands in the Bay of Biscay. Suzanne was inconsolable, even when Aunt Lilian told her no strange woman would attend her in July, and that she would deliver the baby herself.

'I've done it before,' she sighed. 'Amongst others, I brought *you* into the world when your dear mother stayed here, but I've told you about that often enough. Your mother is a great lady in Edinburgh.'

'A great lady in Edinburgh! How can she be a great lady when she has a bastard daughter in London? I never saw her, but I hate her, oh how I hate her! Well, soon she'll have a bastard grandchild as well! Someone else to hide away from polite society! Someone else to be paid off for the sake of her reputation!' Suzanne burst out sobbing.

Kate said nothing. She just took the beautiful wedding gown and cut out four tiny baby gowns from it, every now and then a tear falling on the soft white silk. On the fifteenth of July Suzanne couldn't believe that so much pain could be the result of so much pleasure when her own daughter was born.

'What will you call her?' Aunt Lilian asked.

'Olivia Gray. Olivia after her father. Gray after me,' she said bitterly.

'Ho! Not down here, not in this part of London you won't! Olivia's too fancy for here.'

'I know that, so we'll just call her Polly.'

Polly Gray was six years old when a fine, well-dressed gentleman came into the Hornpipe every night for a week, smiling whenever Suzanne got up to sing. At the end of the week he asked her if he could speak with her privately.

'You may, sir, in the back sitting-room, but not, of course, alone.'

'Yes?' Uncle Jack asked the man sternly.

'Your niece has a wonderful voice, sir. I wonder, would she have your permission to follow a career on the stage? Miss Suzy, how would you like to sing and dance on the stage of the Theatre Royal in Drury Lane?'

'The Theatre Royal in Drury Lane?' Suzanne gasped.

'Oh, Suzy ...' Kate sounded apprehensive this time.

'But it's miles away across the city!' Aunt Lilian objected. 'How would she ever get back at that time of night?'

'She would stay with the other girls in lodgings for the season. My wife keeps a sharp eye on them all.'

The family was thrown into an uproar until Aunt Lilian was finally persuaded, and even Kate cheered up a little. Once again Suzanne's life took another turn all because she could sing; she hadn't been in what they called the chorus more than a month when an older gentleman, a man of about forty, called to see her backstage. His name was Geoffrey Fotheringham; he was a married man, he told her at once.

Suzanne stared moodily out of the window. How could anyone resist Geoffrey Fotheringham? Tall, elegant, rich and always laughing, with his fair hair and handsome good looks, *she* certainly couldn't resist him. She was in his arms within five minutes and in his bed before the night was out.

That was the start of it, their wonderful life of ease and luxury, when Geoffrey whisked her and Polly off to Paris to live in his apartment not far from the Bois de Boulogne.

But every now and again he had to go back to London on business. During the weeks he was away she simply couldn't bear it; he would be living with his wife, sleeping with his wife, making love to his wife. The green snake of jealousy writhed and crawled inside her, driving her half out of her mind. It made her do things she regretted later, but she couldn't help it.

In the early days she had tried to put up with it, amusing herself every morning by taking Polly, dressed exactly as she was in miniature, to the park. Then she noticed that many gentlemen lifted their hats to her and looked at her and her little daughter admiringly.

Suzanne admitted it to herself now; it had put ideas into her head. Once, when Geoffrey was away and she was bored to tears and desperately anxious without him, a terrifying thought chased through her mind. He had been deceiving his own wife with her in Paris all these years. He could do the same again. He could be deceiving her with somebody new, somebody younger. What might he be doing now, this very minute, in London – and with whom?

Quivering in panic and desperate for a diversion of some sort she took Polly out walking. They found a coloured girl in a crowd of urchins in the gutter. 'What is your name?' she asked her.

'Caramelle.' The girl's sharp black eyes searched her face warily.

'Caramelle, Madame,' Suzanne corrected her.

'I beg your pardon, Madame,' the girl said, in such faultless English that Suzanne was intrigued.

Most days after that she and Polly looked out for Caramelle. It hadn't escaped Suzanne's notice that a coloured maidservant would be in such contrast to her own fair beauty that it could only enhance it, and before long Caramelle was part of their establishment.

Geoffrey took an instant dislike to the girl. The first quarrel they ever had was over her. He said that if she stayed he would not give such a person one penny in wages, and in retaliation Suzanne flounced out of the room reminding him that she was an independent woman. Money was sent to her from Scotland every month, forwarded by the Tarres of the Hornpipe.

Caramelle certainly relieved the boredom when Geoffrey was away by accompanying them to the park in the mornings and turning more mens' heads than ever in Suzanne's direction. Soon the gentlemen became bolder and left their cards on her little table under the bandstand on their way past. In the beginning she never did anything about them, but she collected them all the same. When any gentleman left his card five or six times she knew he would pursue her further. It was an intriguing game.

For more than a year it had gone on in this fashion, with that little spark of excitement helping her to endure Geoffrey's absences. The hard part came when she had to pay Caramelle six months' wages out of her own money; only now it was impossible.

Suzanne sat up and fanned herself. Just thinking about that girl made her feel hot and uncomfortable again. She hoped Polly was sleeping in this heat. Perhaps she should not share a bedchamber with Caramelle any more.

Oh, it was hot! Even in her sleep Polly knew it was stifling, and there were voices near her bed. There was a man in the room, she was sure of it. Her eyelids flickered half-open and through a gap in the carelessly drawn curtains around the bed she saw a huge black man. He was speaking to Caramelle.

'Oh, Cara,' he sobbed, on his knees with his face buried in her black skirts. 'I can't bear to see you bruised and beaten again.'

'This is a miserable way to live, Choco.'

'I adore you, my sister. You are the only woman in the world I care for.'

'I know,' Caramelle said sadly.

Polly felt very distressed. She tried to cry out, but as always in the world of dreams the cry died in her throat. Chocolat was Caramelle's brother? Did Mama have any idea that Caramelle had a brother and that he was actually in the apartment? Why was he there? When Chocolat spoke again Polly was thoroughly awake.

'You never speak about the past, Cara. Tell me about it now.'

'No! There is murder in it, and terrible cruelty. I will not think about it. I think only of the future. This white bitch Madame Suzanne has never treated me as a human being, a real person. But *one* day ... '

'What will happen?'

'One day she will have to recognize that I am neither a slave nor a dog for her to beat.'

'How?'

'I don't know yet, but I will find a way to get even with her.'

'You found no money in her room? No jewellery we could sell?'

'Nothing, and I got another beating for it into the bargain! No, Madame's money has run out and there will be trouble over it, wait and see.' She started. 'There's the bell! Someone's at the door. You'll have to go.'

Chocolat disappeared from view, and Caramelle stopped only to put on her prim white pinafore before she followed him.

Stretched out on the pink silk *chaise-longue*, Suzanne lifted one of her legs in the air, surveyed the jewelled slipper balanced precariously on the end of her painted toes, and yawned. God, she was *bored*. Her jaws snapped together again when the bell on the front door began to ring, jangle, jangle, jangle. Somebody was determined to come in.

Suzanne was not pleased. When she left the drawing-room for her bedchamber she never liked to have to dress again. Visitors were not welcome at ten o'clock at night. Still, she could not help her flesh tingling a little at the prospect, for who would call at ten o'clock at night unless it was a man?

'It is Monsieur Brodie, Madame,' Caramelle announced.

'Monsieur Brodie? Did he say William Brodie, from Edinburgh?'

'Yes, Madame.'

It must be more than a year since she had met William Brodie in the park, during another of Geoffrey's protracted absences. Brodie was in France on business at the glass-foundries at the time, and upon better acquaintance she found out that he had some strange desires, forever wanting her to do 'French things', as he put it. Blushing a little at the memory she also recalled that he always had money, and a bird in the hand, in her present financial situation, was worth two in the bush.

'Mr Brodie is persistent, Caramelle?'

'He is also quite drunk, Madame. Shall I show him in?'

'Yes.' Suzanne arranged her wrap so that the whole of one leg was exposed right up to her thigh. 'You'd better show him in here.'

She ignored the expression on the maid's face and tried not to grimace distastefully when the horrid little man appeared in the doorway clutching his bag in one hand and a parcel in the other. He reeled in, stinking of drink, and sat on the bed beside her.

'Christ, Suzanne! I've had a hell of a job finding you! It's been so long since I was here last I forgot which street it was! I roamed the park all morning. Why were you not there as usual?'

'Lack of money,' she said pointedly.

'Money! Money, is it?' he roared, pulling out his silk pockets and slamming guineas on the table, showering gold. 'When do I hear about anything else but money, especially from you women? Take the lot, lassie, and come here. You know what I like!'

'Not so fast!' Suzanne said, standing up and moving away to count the money while he tore off his clothes and got into bed. 'Who helped you to find me?'

'Oh, one or two gentlemen I met in the course of business recognized you from my description. They told me you were here. And alone.'

'What?' She clutched the edge of the bedside table. Had Geoffrey heard something like this, too? Was that why he had not returned?

'You needn't faint on me, Suzanne. What's wrong? There's enough money, is there not?'

'There's enough money.' She sighed. 'Let's have some wine first.'

'Och, lassie, I don't need wine!' He threw back his head and laughed exultantly. She had forgotten the sound of that laugh, how it howled and echoed around the ceiling.

'Perhaps not,' she said, 'but I do. Drink a glass of wine with me, and tell me where you've been and what you've been doing.'

As she expected, he was flattered. William Brodie needed no more encouragement to open his bag and show her page after page of boring designs of china cabinets elegantly glazed, and literally hundreds of drawings all neatly annotated in his small narrow handwriting.

None of it meant anything to Suzanne. 'Another glass of

wine?' she asked, smothering another yawn. Not by word or by look did she betray the fact that she wasn't able to anyway as he showed her triglyphs between metopes on a frieze, voissoirs forming an arch on an oriel window and its fenestration.

'And this time I was studying different mouldings,' he told her.

'You're on your way back to Scotland, then?'

'Yes, I sail across to England early tomorrow morning, Suzanne Fotheringham.' He leered, reaching out for her.

Suzanne drew back a little. 'Who told you that was my name?'

'It is, isn't it?'

'No. My name is Suzanne Gray. I am not married to Geoffrey Fotheringham.' The bitterness she felt in her heart about this was evident in her voice, but it was no way to entertain a gentleman. 'What do you need mouldings for?' she asked, trying to look very interested while she refilled his wine glass.

'For the decoration of the ceilings in the houses I refurbish. Never mind that, for the moment. Suzanne Gray, you said? Do you have any Scottish relations by any chance, Suzanne?'

'I might have had. There was a rift in the family long ago. I know of no relations now, I'm afraid. But do go on. Tell me about your mouldings.'

'There are twenty-seven of them here, my dear.' Her eyes glazed over while he showed her the reed, the egg and dart, the bead and reel, the chevron, the dog-tooth, the lozenge, the rosette and the ball-flower. 'Besides,' he brought her to attention again, 'I brought you a present ...' His voice trailed off, and suddenly he was snoring, dead to the world.

Was she glad or was she sorry? For a while Suzanne stood and looked down at the little Scotsman. When he woke up he would rush away to catch the stage to the coast. She picked up the papers scattered over the floor to put them back in his bag, and saw a scrap of what appeared to be parchment stuck in the seam.

Idly, she drew it out, her eyes widening in shock when she saw written on it 'Candacraig, Edinburgh' and 'Suzanne Gray', the only four written words she could recognize. Long ago Aunt Lilian had made her learn them from the letters that came with the money from Scotland every month.

Smiling, she took the scrap of paper and locked it away with the guineas, convinced that she had stolen something far more precious from the little man than the gold he'd thrown at her when he first came in. Another day was dawning when, half laughing and half crying, she crawled into the bed beside him.

He moved at once and suddenly spoke. 'Are you still awake?'

'Yes.'

His right arm burrowed beneath her, hand over her right breast, and held it cupped and full.

'I was no use to you a couple of hours ago, Suzanne!' His left hand stroked her until she trembled. Then he took her hand and directed it towards his manhood. 'He's standing, now.'

'But don't you have to leave? To catch the stage? Besides, is this right, in the morning?'

He giggled in his high-pitched voice. 'In the morning? It's the best time I know.'

'If nobody hears us, then.' She was quivering with desire. 'It cannot be proper.'

'There's nothing more proper than this, a man and a woman in a bed, the one made out to go in, and the other made in to take him!'

He stopped speaking and rolled over her, burying his head in her breasts, his hands stroking the roundness of her belly, his fingers sliding through her fine hairs.

'Now, Will, take me now!' She was as lusty as he was and for the next hour they made love every 'French way' of his whispered requests, while in the room next door Caramelle dozed off and on, wishing they would hurry up. Until she showed the visitor out she was not at liberty to go to her own bed.

Suzanne was smiling lazily when she picked up his parcel. 'Is this my present, Will?'

'Ay, and you deserve it. Open it. As soon as I saw it in the factory outside Vendome it reminded me of you. Who deserves it more?'

She ignored his strange giggling talk while she tore off the paper and held up a flask of perfume. It was made of gilded black glass, fashioned in the shape of a naked woman, from the head which was the stopper down over the delicate shoulders to the pointed nipples, and further down over the slim hips, the mound of Venus pronounced, to the long, straight legs. Just for a moment Suzanne felt oddly repelled, reminded of Caramelle. But the bottle was undeniably magnificent.

'Oh, it's beautiful!' she cried. 'But so naughty!'

'You can be proud of it. The Pompadour has the only other one like it, they said. The King of France gave her it. Think of *that*, Suzanne, every time you use it, and wait for me to come again.'

Caramelle, unseen, crept a little closer to the half-open door. She caught a glimpse of the perfume flask. She had never seen let alone possessed anything so beautiful in her life. Suddenly greed and envy welled up inside her. Her hatred and resentment of Madame Suzanne positively engulfed her as she stared hungrily at what could have been a miniature of herself, fashioned in glass.

'I *will* come back, Suzanne.' Brodie was speaking again, all the time wondering how he could lay his hands on enough money to clear his current debts, for he had persuaded himself that this was the same Suzanne Gray of the document, the heir to the Candacraig fortune. It must be! *Oh, if only he could marry her here and now*!

'You are more of a treasure to me now than ever, Suzanne. Speaking of treasures, did you ever think of coming to Edinburgh? There could be a fortune waiting for you there.'

'In the shape of William Brodie, you mean?' Suzanne asked suspiciously. 'Are you asking me to marry you?'

'As soon as I can give you all that Geoffrey Fotheringham has to offer. At present I am not in that happy position.'

'I'm afraid you never will be, either, not in Edinburgh. That is one city I shall never set foot in.'

Go to Edinburgh! To be branded a bastard, openly this time! No, she would never go to Edinburgh, no matter if the Crown jewels of Scotland awaited her there, after her whole life spent resenting her mother's rejection of her. The bitterness etched on Suzanne's face was obvious to the two people watching her, although neither of them understood the reason for it, and they could not have known what she was thinking now.

That scrap of paper with her name and Candacraig written on it must be worth something. Brodie thought the same, which was why he had been trying to find out what she knew. The 'great lady' in Edinburgh, her mother, could have died. Would she ever have acknowledged her bastard? Suzanne was too cynical to believe it, but all the same perhaps one day she might send Polly to Edinburgh to find out. Nobody would know Polly, after all.

William Brodie was quite satisfied with her reaction to the hint he'd just dropped. She obviously had no idea of any possible inheritance. She would stay in Paris under Geoffrey Fotheringham's protection in the meantime. Long may it last! His own affairs were in such a mess it might take some time to sort them out. But he would have to keep an eye on Suzanne. Liaisons such as hers and Fotheringham's had a way of cooling off, and where might she go then?

As Brodie left Suzanne's chamber Caramelle reeled back, aware that she had just eavesdropped on something of great significance. She saw that Madame had not been looking at the Scotsman's face, and that she had not been listening properly. Madame was a very silly woman. This Scotsman obviously *knew* there was a real fortune waiting for her in Edinburgh.

'Well, well, I always wondered what a black woman would be like.' He leered at her, braying with laughter as Caramelle showed him out.

Suzanne hoped and prayed that Polly had heard none of the disturbance, for William Brodie had certainly disturbed a June night in Paris. He had made a hot night even hotter, in more ways than one. As he went away the sound of his screeching laugh still echoed through the apartment, and worse than anything her mother feared, it burned its way into Polly's very soul, to stay with her for ever.

4

THE FOLLOWING DAY the haze of heat hung over Paris again when Polly stood beside Caramelle waiting for Mama to come downstairs. She felt uncomfortable in the coloured woman's company, but when Suzanne appeared she soon forgot it. 'You look lovely today, Mama.' She kissed her mother affectionately, for Suzanne was a picture in flounces of pale blue satin that exactly matched her large, pale blue eyes.

'Thank you, dear.' Suzanne prepared to open her little blue parasol, sweeping her eyes over her maid critically before they came to rest on her daughter.

There was absolutely nothing to be done about the child's hair; she sighed, and then smiled reminiscently. Oliver's hair had been a few shades darker but, even close-cropped to his head, it had curled. His very beard would have curled if it had been quarter of an inch longer. Well, he had left Polly behind him to remind her of all that, and now here she was with a hundred auburn ringlets like a cloud around her head, and her skin the creamy shade of all true redheads.

But where, Suzanne wondered for the thousandth time, did she get those eyes? They should have been blue, the same as her own and Oliver's; but Polly's eyes were black, under startlingly black slanting eyebrows, and they seemed to be able to see right through you. This morning there were faint mauve shadows beneath them, though.

'You have not slept well, Polly,' she peered into her face.

Then she laid her cool hand on Polly's brow and looked anxiously at the maid. 'Her forehead is hot.'

'Oh, Mama! It is only the weather! It is so hot in that bedchamber of ours. Surely I am too old for a nursemaid now, anyway? Could not Caramelle have a room of her own?'

'We'll see,' Suzanne said distractedly. 'Come, we will go out for the fresh air and have some cool lemonade in the park. That will make you feel better. Now, come along, dear. Already we are late.'

Every morning before the sun became too hot they took the same walk, Suzanne shielding her delicate pink complexion under the frilled parasol which matched her gown, Polly twirling hers, and Caramelle bringing up the rear dressed all in black as befitted a servant.

This morning there was a faint line between her mother's eyebrows, and the sight of it worried Polly. 'Are you all right, Mama?'

'Of course, dear, but like you a glass of lemonade in the shade of the trees would do me the world of good. Thank goodness our usual table is empty.' Suzanne fanned herself and sat down with a sigh. 'Caramelle, go and get three glasses of lemonade. Here is the money. And take your time, it's too hot to hurry.'

'There is something troubling you, all the same,' Polly said when the maid was out of earshot. 'Is it Uncle Geoffrey?'

Suzanne frowned. 'Partly, dear. I miss him, of course, but I miss his money even more.'

'Oh, Mama!' Polly started laughing and then stopped suddenly. There it was again this morning: *money*. The nightmare had not ended after all.

'I'm afraid it is quite serious, Polly. Our money has stopped coming from Edinburgh too.'

'Shouldn't we try to find out what's happened there?'

'No!' Her mother spat the word out vehemently. 'Besides, short of actually going to Edinburgh we could never find out. Ugh! That horrible cold place! I believe it's cold even in the summer!'

'That's no excuse, Mama. It might be that the person who always sent you the money has died and left the rest of it to you. Perhaps they are waiting in Edinburgh for you to go and claim it.'

'Polly,' Suzanne sighed, 'you know I do not like to speak about

Edinburgh. Now, please stop. It was my mother who sent the money because I was born in shame, kept hidden all this time and well paid for it. Do you really think I would go back there now, whatever has happened? Besides, if they wanted me surely they would know where to find me. Has anyone asked?'

'No.'

'Then let us say no more about it, except that that last package sent at the beginning of the year somehow put an even colder feeling up and down my spine. This was inside it, as well as the money.' Suzanne held out a delicate gold ring, fashioned from little Ss all joined together to make a wavy band.

'It's lovely!'

'Lovely, Polly? Never forget that the *only* rings that are lovely have diamonds in them! This is worth very little. You can have it, if you like.' Suzanne smiled at Polly's delight. 'But this is an emergency, Polly. I mean it. I did not tell Uncle Geoffrey that the Edinburgh money had stopped coming. We – had a little coolness about it some time ago. Of course he would not have left us without plenty, had he known.'

When she saw the huge tears welling up in the big blue eyes Polly made up her mind this was not the time to speak to her mother about Caramelle and Chocolat and their conversation of last night. She put a comforting hand on her mother's arm while Suzanne dabbed at her eyes with her tiny lace handkerchief, wondering all the time if her mother even knew that a big black man appeared in their apartment at night. No, she decided, she didn't know, and she mustn't be frightened any more than she was already.

But Suzanne's calculating gaze beneath carefully lowered eyelashes was already sweeping around the other tables. Polly followed her eyes to the dark handsome man, immaculately dressed, sitting alone.

'Monsieur Duval is early today, Mama.'

'Good. Caramelle, put down the tray and take your own glass and Mademoiselle's to that seat over there. Polly –'

'But his face is whiter than ever, and see how he coughs!' Polly whispered when the maid went away.

'We need the money! We must eat. It has come to that. Go and fetch him.'

37

'I'm going,' Polly tossed her mass of red ringlets disapprovingly, but managed a smile by the time she got to his table. It was not the first time she had acted as her mother's go-between, but it was the first time she understood that it was no longer a game; it was deadly serious.

'Mistress Fotheringham?' Monsieur Duval asked when she brought him to her mother's table.

'Do sit down, Monsieur Duval.' Suzanne smiled. 'Mistress Fotheringham sounds so English and so formal! I prefer to be known as Madame Suzanne.'

So Mama was off again. Polly went over to sit beside the maid, leaning back with her eyes closed while the sounds and smells of the Bois suddenly assailed her forcibly, as they had never done before.

She was sharply aware of the clean, green scents of lilac and mimosa bushes beside the seat, of conversations going on all around, of children laughing, of Monsieur Philippe Duval's close-clipped moustache, and what it would feel like to run her finger along the bristles.

Yes, he *was* very good-looking, with his jet black hair, liquid eyes, pale skin and dark red lips. Polly was noticing a lot of things for the first time today, and it felt vaguely uncomfortable. Perhaps this was what grown-ups meant when they smiled dreamily and spoke about springtime in Paris.

Half an hour later she and Caramelle followed Suzanne who was sweeping out of the park, smiling coolly.

'Well?' Polly asked.

'He will come to visit on Friday afternoon, and you must call him Uncle Philippe.'

'Another uncle, Mama?'

'That is impertinent, miss!' Suzanne hissed in her ear, so that Caramelle could not hear. 'He is very rich, and we need the money. With any luck he will be the only trick before Geoffrey gets back.'

Polly cringed. She hated it when her mother talked like that, but unhappily it was the truth, plain and unvarnished. They had to get money somehow, and with that thought a new fear was born. What if she, in her turn, was forced to get it in the same way as Mama?

Oh, why didn't Uncle Geoffrey come home?

Monsieur Duval arrived on Friday afternoon with armfuls of flowers for Mama, a posy of silk flowers for Polly with a bonbon in the heart of each one, and best of all Pompom, a little white dog.

Oh, he was adorable! Polly scampered after him on the blue carpet of the drawing-room. It was the coolest room in the house, for Mama had made Caramelle open all the windows for air and draw the curtains for shade, so that the only places the light got in were the semicircles at the foot of the curtains, dazzling on the stained floorboards.

Polly laughed delightedly. He was such a bad little dog to dampen and darken the fleur-de-lys round the edges of the carpet, and now his paws were up and pushing open the double doors into Mama's boudoir! It was not allowed, especially in the afternoons. Pompom was very, very naughty.

She ran after him and tried to catch him, but he was too quick, a flash of white fur scuttling under the draperies around the bed.

From that minute on Polly forgot all about the puppy, for Mama was not herself. She should have on her nightgown at least, and she should not be bouncing up and down like that on top of poor Uncle Philippe. Mama was making him ill, so that his head was turned towards the door and his eyes were quite blank and staring. They did not see Polly. They could not see anything any more.

Polly felt caught up in the nightmare again, so that she could not speak. She blinked her eyes rapidly and then retreated to hide behind one of the curtains. She did not want to look at her mother any more, but she could hear her through the open door, her sighs and soft murmurings, a silence, a laugh and then her voice talking to Uncle Philippe again. This time the silence was longer. Mama's voice was louder.

'Philippe! Philippe! Speak to me, chéri.'

But there was no answer and a minute later Mama was screaming. 'My God! My God! He's dead! Caramelle! Caramelle!' She came rushing out of her bedroom, sobbing.

Polly was glad to see when she peeped out from behind the

39

curtain that Mama had a sheet draped around her. Caramelle ran into the bedroom. Uncle Philippe lay in exactly the same position as Polly had seen him before. The maid drew down the bedcover and then hastily pulled it back over him again. It settled over the top of him like a tent with a tent-pole sticking up in the middle.

'Heart, probably, Madame,' she said calmly, and Polly detected the cruel note in her voice. 'I have heard of it before when a man is in that position with a woman. We should call a doctor.'

'No!' Mama sobbed. 'The scandal! The disgrace!'

'Then what are we to do with the body?' Caramelle asked.

'The body ... The body ...' Mama repeated the chilling question uncomprehendingly.

'Yes, the body. There will be an enquiry.'

'What sort of enquiry?'

'A sudden death, Madame ...'

'My God, are you speaking about – can you mean that they will say he was *murdered*?'

'Monsieur Duval must have belonged to *someone*.' Caramelle reminded Polly of a cat playing with a mouse. 'They might ask questions. Especially if they see the body.' She glanced at the tent-pole significantly.

'Oh, God! Oh, Caramelle! What am I to do? I cannot have any questions here! I cannot allow anyone to see the body.'

'No. You should not give them the chance. You should get rid of it.'

'But how, Caramelle?'

'I know a way, Madame. It could be done tonight, for a consideration.'

'If you mean money, I have none until Mr Fotheringham comes back.'

'*If* he comes back, Madame.'

'What do you mean?' Suzanne asked wildly. 'Of course he will come back! What do you mean?'

'Monsieur Fotheringham has never been gone as long as this before, has he? In the meantime there are your jewels, and of course there is this apartment.'

Crouched behind the curtains Polly was stunned at such evil.

She had never liked Caramelle. Lately she had bitterly disliked and distrusted her. Now she hated her with all her heart and soul, while at the same time she thanked God that the maid did not know of her mother's hiding places for her best jewels. Only she shared that secret with Mama.

'My jewels, and this apartment? In return for what?'

'My brother Chocolat would help us.'

'I did not know you had a brother, Caramelle. Why have I never heard of him before?'

'When did you show any interest in me or mine, Madame?' the maid asked bitterly.

'Well, I have very few jewels left now,' Suzanne spoke half the truth, 'and the lease of this house runs out at the end of August. I should have had to dismiss you and leave then, anyway, without Mr Fotheringham to renew it. However, that is the bargain. Get rid of the body any way you must, and my few remaining jewels and the rest of the lease are yours.'

'It is agreed, Madame. And where will you go?'

'That is something I will have to think about,' Suzanne answered, and stopped sobbing momentarily.

Caramelle delivered one last slap in the face. 'I wish you to be out of here by tomorrow, you and your brat with you,' she said, and Polly saw that she did so with the greatest satisfaction.

It was different that night, with Mama sobbing softly in her boudoir. She cried and cried until at last Polly fell asleep.

Nobody saw Suzanne Gray rolling up the scrap of parchment she had stolen from William Brodie and pushing it into the empty black and gold flask. Why was Brodie carrying it about with him, she asked herself. It must concern her, and it must be so important that he could not let it out of his sight. She would take it with her to London, but hidden, and think what to do with it later. Thank God Caramelle was too busy helping the big, jet-black man to put the long parcel covered in a sheet over his shoulder to notice her doing it.

Next morning Chocolat came back very early when Mama seemed to be asleep and Polly was pretending. He and Caramelle talked almost in whispers.

'What did you do with him?'

'Threw him in the Seine.'

'You are sure no one saw you?'

'No one, Cara, don't worry. What of the lady?'

'She is badly frightened, Choco. She is going to run away. She won't tell me where, but I could bet it is to Edinburgh.'

'What will happen to you? To us?'

'The rent is paid up to the end of August. We can stay on here as normal so as to avoid suspicion. The neighbours are used to seeing me coming and going. That gives me plenty of time to put my plan into action, but I will need your help.'

'Have I not shown you tonight that I will do anything for my Cara?'

'We are going to be rich, Chocolat, I promise you *that*!'

'We could be rich tomorrow, if you would only do as I ask! Set up a House of Pleasure here. We could call it The Black Tulip. White men would pay more for a beautiful coloured girl like you.'

'I know I may have to sell myself for a while until I save enough money, but don't forget, Choco, I never wanted to be a whore!'

'Enough money? For what?'

'I am determined to get to Edinburgh in the end. That is my plan, for I am sure that's where Madame is coming into a fortune. She will be frightened of all I know about her. It will be easy to blackmail her. She will have to take me in again and keep me for the rest of my life. You too, if you play your cards right.'

'It is too dangerous, Cara. I do not like it.'

'What could be more dangerous than the risk you ran tonight? Besides,' Caramelle's voice dropped even lower, 'if we make a go of it, we might manage a room of your own to take your little boys into.'

'My God, how did you know about that?'

'I know all about it. Don't forget that, Chocolat.' Caramelle's voice was full of venom. 'Just do as I say! There may not be any happiness in this wretched world for me, but I would rather be miserable sitting on silk cushions than on bare boards!'

When Suzanne woke up, Polly helped her to pack a few clothes, but was surprised when her mother insisted on taking her empty perfume bottle. 'I spent all night making these tiny clothes for her, Polly,' she said in a low voice. 'You must pretend she is an old and favourite doll, and give her a name.'

'She's horrible,' Polly whispered back as she dressed the doll. 'She reminds me of Caramelle. What do they always put in black bottles marked with a skull and crossbones? Oh, a name for her will be easy to find, Mama. Poison.'

'I am too tired to argue with you, Polly. I don't care what you call her. Just see that you are never parted from her. *Never!*'

Then came the terrible ride in a hired carriage to the coast with the best of their clothes and Suzanne's hats, with her jewels hidden in the linings, tied up in a few bundles. The driver suddenly stopped just as it was getting dark and refused to take them any further. 'You can go through Rougemont if you like,' he told them. 'Wild horses wouldn't drag me! I'm going back to Paris.'

Cold now, and frightened, Polly followed her mother with their bundles along the one deserted, forbidding street of the village. There were no welcoming lights in the windows and all the doors seemed to be locked.

Half-way along Suzanne pushed open a tall gate which led to the graveyard. 'We can rest in here,' she said grimly, 'nobody will follow us.' They lay down for a few hours on a flat gravestone, huddled together, while the night breeze moaned eerily through the trees that encircled the sacred place.

They got up stiffly at the sound of a horse and cart trundling northwards just after dawn.

'Who are you?' the driver asked. 'You don't belong here. Don't you know that you are in great danger? Strangers never get away from Rougemont,' and he glanced up at the castle on the top of the hill. The rising sun touched its walls, turning them blood-red. 'That's the Château Rouge,' he told them with a shudder. 'That's where the Comte de Rouge lives, the cruellest aristocrat of them all.'

'We are trying to get back to London,' Suzanne said. 'Please help us.' She held out a gold coin.

'Get in the cart, then. Hide under the straw amongst the cabbages. Oh, my God, a black crow!'

As they looked a huge black crow with a broken wing trailed itself across the roadway, its eyes venomous, its beak snapping at them.

'Bad luck,' the man said. 'You'd better hurry. Here are the soldiers coming down from the château already. Don't let them catch you.'

Polly and her mother lay in the bottom of the cart shaking with fear as the soldiers clattered by and the wagon rumbled on its way. They were bruised and sore when the driver helped them out, and with the bribe of another gold coin put them on a ship bound for England.

'Where to now, Mama?' Polly asked when they got to Dover.

'There's nobody left to turn to except Aunt Lilian, Uncle Jack and Kate, dear. To the Hornpipe Inn, Narrow Street, London!' Suzanne told the driver of the first coach they found for hire.

The peace of the countryside had long given way to the bustle of the city of London, even at night, when Polly and her mother became aware that the streets were getting narrower and meaner. Before long the coach stopped. While his mate went up on the roof to untie the luggage, the driver got down and opened the door.

'Is this it, missus?' he asked, looking at the inn doubtfully.

It looked small and dingy when they banged on the door. Polly stood shivering beside her mother while they waited under the inn's sign, which groaned back and fore in the night wind. Polly couldn't remember seeing it before. Now she looked up, struck by the absurdity of it. 'The Hornpipe Inn' was written across the top. Underneath was a picture of a dancing sailor and, down at the bottom, 'Jack Tarre, Prop.' It must be a joke.

Then the door opened. 'God love us! Suzy, is it really you?' exclaimed a stout woman holding up the lantern. A thin young boy stood beside her.

'It's me, Kate. Down on our luck. On our uppers. Can we come in?'

Kate opened the door as wide as it could go. 'Bring in their things,' she told the men.

Kate shut the front door behind them. 'Oh Suzy, I've been expecting you for the last two months,' she said sadly, 'ever since I read the announcement about Geoffrey Fotheringham in the news-sheets.'

'What announcement?' Suzanne asked, while Polly's heart

gave a terrible lurch. Something bad was coming, the black crow's bad luck.

'Oh, my dear. The announcement of his death.'

For two hours after Suzanne recovered from her swoon Kate rubbed her hands, murmured gently to her and gave her cups of strong sweet tea for the shock.

'I feel so bad, Suzy, to have blurted it out like that. You know I wouldn't hurt you for the world. I thought *you* had inserted the notice in the papers. It said he died in London, and I didn't know where or how to get in touch with you.'

'It must have been his wife,' Suzanne sighed. 'We have been waiting in Paris for him all this time, with no money left.'

'And the letters from Edinburgh have stopped, too! Oh my, Suzy! How did you manage?'

'Not very well. That's why we're here. Oh, Geoffrey!' Mama's eyes filled up again. 'He did love me, Kate, and Polly too, like his own daughter. And we loved him, didn't we, darling?'

'Yes.' Polly's black eyes were glistening with tears when Kate put her arms around her.

She had never been a child to show her emotions, Kate reflected. Always quiet, always patient, sometimes even a little sad. But what else could she be with a flamboyant mother like Suzanne? All the same, she believed Polly had a great deal more sense than her Mama had ever possessed. She saw everything with those penetrating eyes of hers, and she kept most of it to herself.

'I can hardly believe it's you, Polly,' Kate said gently. 'It's three years since you were here last. You were only a little girl then, my dear.'

Only three years! What had happened to the Hornpipe in that space of time? Something in the very atmosphere of the place told Polly that in spite of the joke on the sign outside, it was no joke inside. 'Where are Uncle Jack and Aunt Lilian?' she asked Kate now.

'Oh, my dears! So much has been happening! They retired last year and went into the country.' Kate saw them looking at the young boy beside her with puzzled expressions. 'This is Jed,' she said fondly. 'He's deaf and dumb, but he's like a son to me. I speak to him in signs. See, I'll tell him to go back to bed now, that everything is all right, that you are my friends and you will be staying here.'

That first morning, as Polly lay uneasily beside her mother on a makeshift bed in the back sitting-room, the door was suddenly flung open, heavy feet tramped past her head and she looked up into the most brutish face she had ever seen.

Suzanne woke up too and clutched her daughter fearfully while the man passed on through to the bar-room, slamming the other door behind him, angry as well as ugly.

'Oh, Polly! Oh, my God,' Suzanne was moaning as Kate came in with the tea. 'There was a man, Kate —'

'Yes, his name is Brewser.' Kate avoided their terrified eyes. 'He's the cellar-man.'

'What happened to Joe Burton, then?' Suzanne asked. 'He was like one of the family.'

'He left when Ma and Pa retired. I had to get someone else.'

'But why that awful man? Couldn't you have found somebody better than him?' Suzanne hissed, while Polly watched Kate's face going a dull red. 'He was upstairs, too! What was he doing upstairs? Kate —' She paused at last and hesitated as she looked around the dirty unkempt room, so different from what it had been. 'Kate, Uncle Jack and Aunt Lilian did leave the Hornpipe to you, didn't they?'

'The Hornpipe and a tidy sum of money to go with it.' Kate smiled bitterly.

'So what happened?'

'Brewser happened. Like a fool I married him, Suzy.' For a few awful minutes there was a horrified silence before Kate rushed on. 'I did it because I was lonely, and now Tom's run through all my money. He gambles and drinks, you see. Pa never did.' She dissolved into tears. 'The inn is going down. Nobody wants to come here now,' she gasped, 'and most days I do not feel well enough to do the work.'

'The trade must be going somewhere else, then?'

'To the Mermaid at the bottom of the street. You remember it, Suzy?'

'Of course I remember that awful little fleapit! What if we

help you clean up this place? Will that bring the customers back?'

'We could try,' replied Kate as she wiped her eyes doubtfully.

Polly set to with a will and with buckets of water. Kate seemed to be in pain, unable to work at a stretch for long, and for all her brave words Mama hardly knew one end of a scrubbing brush from the other, so it was Jed who toiled silently and steadfastly at her side. He followed her about like a dog, reminding her of little white Pompom, when Polly was doing her best not to think about the dog she had left behind in Paris, or his fate at the hands of Chocolat and Caramelle.

She felt sorry for Jed. His bony wrists had long ago shot out of his tattered shirt cuffs and his knees out of his patched breeches. His boots were holed and without laces and there were no stockings on his legs. She smiled at him, and before the day was done she was beginning to communicate with him by signs and gestures with her hands as she saw Kate doing.

'He's twelve now.' Kate drew the boy to her side. 'Six months ago I found him sleeping in the yard, at the back door, half frozen to death. But you're all right now, aren't you, love?' Jed smiled up at her with all his heart in his eyes. 'Oh, how I wish I could get you another suit of clothes, but there's no money.'

'We are going to get money,' Suzanne promised. Polly knew that tone in her mother's voice. She began to worry.

In the evening they waited for customers. They waited and waited, but only a few strays came in, drank a tankard of ale, stared with dislike at Brewser who was becoming drunker by the minute, and then sloped off.

'They've gone to the Mermaid,' Kate muttered. 'It's all because of Brewser, I know it is.'

'No, it isn't,' Suzanne assured her. 'Geoffrey often used to take me out to the inns in Paris. *Les auberges*, he used to call them. The best ones always had music and beautiful food. That's what's missing here! Music and food.'

'Food? And music?' Kate thought about it and shook her head. 'How could I afford that?

Back in Edinburgh William Brodie was beginning to worry. Perhaps the Suzanne Gray he knew in Paris wasn't the Edinburgh heiress after all. If she were, why had she never been sent for? He had been back home for weeks now, and still there was no sign of her. There couldn't be anything wrong, could there?

He remembered throwing all his papers into his bag when he left hurriedly for his business trip to France. The parchment he'd found in the writing desk was right at the bottom, well hidden. Thank God the bag had never left his side since. He tipped it up now and spread all the papers over his desk, but the parchment wasn't there. It must be! Scrabble furiously as he might, oh God, it was missing!

His heart was beating wildly as he tried to calm down, think straight and remember all his appointments, but his efforts were all in vain. He couldn't remember ever having it in his hand during the whole trip. He had lost it somewhere. It could be anywhere between here and Paris. He felt sick. His whole plan would crumble unless he could find out something about Suzanne Gray from the Edinburgh angle. Well, there was one man who *should* know the answer to that: the man who had done the inventory for Candacraig the same day as he'd boarded it up, Lady Susanna's lawyer, Erskine Caldwell.

Within half an hour Deacon Brodie was waiting to see him, hopping from one foot to the other in his impatience.

'Oh, it's you, Deacon Brodie.' Erskine Caldwell opened his door at last. 'Come inside and sit down. What can I do for you?'

'There's the small matter of my fee for closing up Candacraig, Mr Caldwell.'

'Dear me, so there is. So there is.'

'If it is not convenient …?'

'Nonsense. Sit down while I instruct my cashier.' In a minute Erskine Caldwell was back, obviously affronted at such a blunder of omission on his part. He was prepared to talk. 'I'm afraid the business of Candacraig is going to take a long time to clear up,' he volunteered. 'Fees for this and fees for that are bound to be overlooked.'

'Yes. I suppose there are lots of loose ends to tidy up.'

'Not only here, Deacon, but as far away as London.'

'As far away as London?' William Brodie looked astonished. 'Is there someone there connected with the estate?'

'There *was*,' Erskine Caldwell said guardedly. 'To give you some idea of the complexities of looking after the Candacraig property, for years I had correspondence with a London inn called the Hornpipe. Not that I ever saw it, of course,' he added primly. 'I do not indulge. Ah, Robertson, you have the money?' he asked his cashier who had just come in.

'To the penny,' Robertson snapped, and William Brodie thought they might have been twins facing him, both thin, both bony, with long fingers gripping the money.

'Exactly right,' the Deacon ground out. He could prolong this conversation no longer. And what had he found out? Nothing except the name of some obscure inn in London, and what use that would be he could not imagine. All the same, the next time he was in London he would try to find it.

5

A S SOON AS they got the Hornpipe cleaned up Suzanne disappeared for an hour. 'I have some money now,' she told them all when she came back. 'Brewser,' she smiled at him beguilingly, 'please remain sober tonight, just for me?'

She took him completely by surprise. His ruby-coloured, pock-marked face turned an even deeper shade, but he grinned weakly in reply.

'I want you to go to Smithfield first thing tomorrow for the best meat you can lay your hands on, Brewser. Kate and I will make the pastry. We are going to sell hot food here. Hot pies.'

'And the music?' Polly asked.

'I still have some of my old stage costumes and might be able to squeeze into them.' Polly watched Brewser licking his lips as he ran his eyes over Mama's gown. It did not leave much of her figure to the imagination. 'Then I can sing. But is there no one who can accompany me?'

'I have a squeeze-box,' Brewser rumbled, the first words they had ever heard him speak. 'I was a sailor, once.'

'He can play it, too,' Kate said proudly, with a foolish smile for her husband on her face.

When she got a scowl for her pains Jed got up and marched out. Polly followed him. She knew he was angry by the set of his back, and she knew why. Brewser was tired of Kate. He had his eye on Mama instead, and that could be very dangerous. She sat down beside Jed on the straw on the kitchen floor and held his

51

hand comfortingly, although she felt very frightened herself.

'Is Kate ill?' she asked him in their strange sign language.

Jed's answer, as she interpreted it, made her more frightened than ever. Kate was black and blue all over, according to the boy who felt he was her son. Brewser was very careful to hit her where it didn't show.

The next morning Polly found a blackboard in one of the outhouses in the yard. For a minute she was back with the nuns, learning her ABC, how to read, how to write, how to sew and how to sing, for Mama and Uncle Geoffrey had always left her at the convent when they went away together.

She showed it to Jed, printing on it with her finger and looking around for something to make a mark. He brought her a round stone made of chalk to write the message on the board which she propped up beside the front door of the Hornpipe.

HOT PIES FOR A PENNY
COME IN AND SEE MADAME SUZANNE
THE SONGBIRD OF THE SOUTH.

Later that night, with her vivid hair tucked under a white cap, and in a grey dress to make her inconspicuous, she was helping her mother to dress. Polly put a hand on her arm. 'You sold the jewels you had hidden in the linings of your hats, didn't you?' she accused her.

'All except this.' Mama dropped a gold chain into her hand. 'Put it round your neck, Polly, and string that gold ring from Edinburgh on it so that no one can see it under your dress. It might be important, after all. And even more important, where have you hidden Poison? You have that bottle safe?'

'She is wrapped up in the large pocket of my cloak.' Polly felt the gold ring dropping between her breasts. It was cold and just for a second it made her flesh creep. The very hair on the nape of her neck rose up. 'Mama …'

'Polly.' Mama's soft blue eyes seemed to look straight into her very soul. 'You know why I am doing this, do you not? You understand why I have always kept you at my side, no matter what happened? I love you best in all the world, my darling, but I've made some terrible mistakes. Do you remember that day in the park when we spoke about Edinburgh?'

'Of course.'

'I have been thinking about what you said then, Polly, and I'm sure you were quite right. When the money stopped coming, and that ring came with the final payment, I felt something was wrong. Perhaps, as you said, someone died – my mother. Later I had a suspicion that she must have included me in her will after all. I should have taken you to Edinburgh long ago,' Suzanne sighed, 'but I cannot bear to go. Promise me you will go there one day yourself?'

'I promise. But, Mama –'

'No buts, Polly. Just promise and we'll say no more about it. Listen! There's Brewser starting to play.' Her mother put the finishing touches to the paint on her face, set her lacy hat at an angle and tripped delicately downstairs.

Polly followed her, watching helplessly as Brewser's coarse hands lifted Suzanne up on to the bar counter, his face suffused with lust, and the Songbird of the South began her first song.

After that there was no time to watch. Curious customers came in to have a look, and fortified with hot pies from Kate and the never-ending supply of ale from Polly and Jed, they stayed to join in.

Heavy takings the following week, the return of Kate's smile, a sober Brewser, not even new clothes for Jed at last could remove Polly's feeling that something would go wrong, and it did in the shape of opposition from the Mermaid. Now they had a chorus of three men singing to a penny whistle, and the customers were divided. The takings went down again.

But Mama was not to be outdone. 'Three men put together cannot do what I can do,' she boasted, and drew Kate aside to whisper in her ear.

The sick expression on Kate's face told Polly all she needed to know. 'What now, Mama? You will have to tell me sooner or later.'

'It will be no different from Paris. I had to get money there. I shall only do it once a week. Every Saturday night we will hold an auction.'

'With you as the prize for the highest bidder, Mama? Oh, I cannot bear it,' Polly sobbed, 'there must be some other way.'

'Desperate circumstances require desperate remedies, Polly.

There's *no* other way for me,' Mama said sadly. 'That, and singing, is all I know.'

Suzanne was right. The Saturday night auctions were a spectacular success. In fact they were a success every night of the week, when the men came in either to ogle what they might buy if they had enough money by Saturday, or just to dream about it. The fame of the Hornpipe spread far and wide.

Polly hated Saturday nights, keeping her head down, her hair well bundled up under her cap and her eyes averted from her mother. When the auction was over and Suzanne went upstairs with the highest bidder to a small room which Kate hastily cleaned out for the purpose, Polly refused to sleep up there herself. Instead she shared the kitchen straw with Jed.

One Sunday morning in the early hours they both started up wide awake. Suzanne's visitor was taking his noisy leave, and she was following him down the darkened staircase trying to keep him quiet, especially when his dreadful screaming laugh rang around the ceilings, a laugh Polly would never forget since she had heard it in Paris.

The noise woke Brewser as well. Polly heard him swearing at Kate and thumping around in their room. Brewser hated the auctions as much as she did, and was becoming more and more morose each week.

But morning dawned at last, and Polly and Jed got up stiffly from the kitchen floor and began their chores. Brewser flung out of the house as soon as he came downstairs, quite clearly in a filthy temper. It was a long time before Kate appeared with her eye blackened and her cheek bruised and swollen. Jed hissed like a snake when he saw her.

'My God, Kate! What happened?' Suzanne asked when she appeared. 'What's happened to your face?'

'Nothing. I turned too quickly and ran into the door.' Kate winced.

After that she 'ran into doors' every Sunday morning and each time her injuries grew worse. Jed became very agitated and managed to convey to Polly that Brewser was beating her worse than ever because he wanted Suzanne himself, but Suzanne only laughed when Polly told her. 'Nonsense, dear. He could bid himself if he wanted to. He has the money now. No, no! These things often happen in a marriage. Brewser and Kate will settle down again, you'll see.'

Mama wasn't thinking clearly. She never did when the Norwegian ships were in port, with her weakness for sailors. Now a handsome new one, Leif Johansen, appeared in the Hornpipe that night.

'Oh, my God, Kate!' Suzanne almost fainted at the sight of him. 'Who does he remind you of?'

'I know. If he had red hair he could be Oliver Banks all over again. He looks the same strong, quiet sort. Polly takes after her father.'

'Yes,' Suzanne sighed. 'It's not just the red hair. She has his nature, too.'

'What are you saying?'

'Sometimes, when a daughter is so like her father, her mother simply cannot understand her. Polly is very different from me.'

'She's taller, and she has that brilliant hair. Her eyes are very dark, but she still looks a lot like you, dear.'

'No, that is not what I meant. Kate, you have known me a long time. I suppose I wear my heart on my sleeve ...'

'Well,' Kate laughed, 'we all know when you are in love, if that's what you mean.'

'Not exactly. Geoffrey always used to say I was as easy to read as a book. Transparent. But Polly is different. Nobody ever knows what she is thinking. She plays her cards close to her chest, Kate. She always did, even when she was a little girl.'

'Perhaps that will be a great protection for her, Suzanne. It is not always a good thing to be as open as you are. Perhaps Polly has seen already in her short life that it has led you into a lot of trouble.'

'She thinks a lot. I never did. I just enjoyed myself – and I will again tonight. Just watch me with that sailor,' Suzanne laughed, 'I couldn't possibly resist him!'

Excitement snapped in the air between Suzanne and the big fair man that night. Her eyes danced when she smiled directly at him and the colour in his face changed constantly from pale to bright red and back to almost ashen again.

Polly could not blame her mother. She felt a fierce pang for

Leif Johansen herself, a magnificent example of what a happy, pleasant man should be. Any woman would feel safe with him.

The nearer Saturday came the more the excitement mounted, and the auction itself was a hushed and tense affair. Feelings were running high when Leif won the bidding, and stealing a glance at him when he went upstairs with her mother, Polly could not help noticing that the brightness had gone out of him somehow in the space of a week. He looked drawn, and there seemed to be angry blotches coming out all over his face.

Suzanne lay in her bed long after his departure on Sunday. She was in love again, Polly could tell. Her large china-blue eyes were soft and misty under her drooping sensuous eyelids, and the anguish on Brewser's face could no longer be mistaken.

Ten days went past before Suzanne came down to earth again. Ten days, and still Leif Johansen had never come back. The longer he stayed away the more dispirited she became.

'I need proper powder and paint, Polly. We can afford it now,' she sighed. 'Come with me to buy it,' and after a visit to a theatrical shop they came back laden.

Then one night Suzanne missed a note in her song, and seemed to gasp for breath, but it was hard to judge whether she was ill underneath her thick greasepaint. It passed over, and all seemed to be well until the following Saturday night when Polly knew for certain that her mother was not well at all. Suzanne would not allow her to come in until she had her paint on, and she staggered about as Polly helped her to dress.

By now Kate's good-natured face was battered into a very different shape, and many of her teeth were missing. She held her side constantly, and she no longer straightened up when she walked. Pitifully bent, she was old before her time.

'This is the worst night of my life, Polly,' she wept at midnight, 'the one I dreaded from the very beginning of these terrible auctions. Tom Brewser has won your mother tonight.'

Paralysed in utter horror, Polly could neither move nor speak as they stood watching Brewser stepping jauntily upstairs with Suzanne stumbling behind him. When she was nearly at the top she turned around, making frantic gestures for Polly and Kate to go to her. Then she half fell, clinging to the banister. They rushed to help her. 'Into my room,' she croaked.

Brewser was waiting. He showed no shame, and his smile was a wolf's smile, cruel and triumphant.

Suzanne turned her back to them all. 'I must remove the paint first,' she said. 'Polly, pass me that rag.'

Sobbing and shaking, Polly passed her the rag. What was Mama up to now? Surely she did not expect her or Kate – above all, not Kate, his own wife – to witness this depravity? Brewser himself seemed to welcome it. Then Suzanne turned around, her skin cleaned for the first time for days.

'Dear God!' Kate moaned.

Brewser stood stock-still in the horror of it before he cursed and punched his way out of the room, for Suzanne's face was covered in livid running purple sores which came almost up to her eyes so that she could hardly see out of her swollen eyelids.

'Mama!' Polly screamed.

'Well, Kate,' Suzanne's voice came out thickly, 'I stopped Brewser's little game for you! He won't be back to bother me now, will he? Neither will my sailor boy. He's dead and gone. He left me with something worse than a baby this time,' and she fell to the floor.

'What is it? What is it?' Polly cried as they lifted Suzanne on to the bed.

Kate remained perfectly calm. 'Make that the last time you ever touch your Mama, my poor little Polly. From now on I will attend to her.'

It took only another short week, with the Hornpipe closed down altogether, before Kate shouted to her to come upstairs at once. 'Don't come in, Polly. She is blind now and cannot see you anyway, and she does not want you to see her. But she has something to say.'

'Take the Poison bottle and go to Edinburgh. Go to Candacraig,' were Suzanne's last words.

That night Polly sat with Jed in the straw, as terrified as he was. The boy was shaking, and now and then sobs racked his thin body. She looked down at him, at his black curling eyelashes quivering on his cheeks, and hoped that somewhere he would find a girl some day, a girl who would understand his difficulties, his temper, his passion, and love him for them all.

She was glad he could not hear Kate as she moved about, laying out Suzanne. At last it was done, and she dragged herself to bed. Not long afterwards there was a terrible commotion. It went on for hours, it seemed to Polly. Then she heard Brewser cursing and swearing, his heavy feet going into Mama's room, and soon afterwards blundering downstairs.

He stood for a minute in the dim light while before Polly's horrified gaze he adjusted the long bundle tied up in a sheet he was carrying over his shoulder. It was her mother – it was Uncle Philippe – it was Mama. Every nightmare Polly had ever had fused together in the face of this one, the most shocking of all.

Suddenly Brewser was gone and his burden with him, and Kate was moaning upstairs. Touching Jed's shoulder for him to come with her, Polly rushed upstairs.

Kate's face was battered almost to a pulp. She must have dragged herself out upon the landing. She lay there in a pool of blood, unable to move anything but her hands, and with them she talked now to Jed. The boy cried all the time. Then she gave him something, and bending down he gently kissed her hair, nodded fiercely to her, and ran off.

'Polly.'

'Yes, Kate.' Polly tried to help her.

'No. Don't touch me, dear. Soon the blotches will come out on me. You must not get them, too.'

Polly drew back. 'But, Kate –'

'No, listen to me! Brewser will be back, but not for me. He has left me for dead, although I was dead a long time ago. He will come back for you, since he could not have Suzy. You've got to get away.'

'How could I leave you, now?'

Kate was speaking in short gasps now. 'Let us try to save something out of all this, Polly. Let us try to save *you*. Do as your Mama wished. Go to Edinburgh. The Edinburgh Fly leaves from the Duke of York. Head north out of the city. Anyone will tell you where. Take this money.' She handed Polly a little pouch.

'But what about Jed?'

'Suzy and I pooled all our money. Jed's got one half of it. He will try to get on a ship.'

'He's gone already?'

'Not yet. He has locked the front door and all the shutters from the outside. He is putting down straw all round these old timbers. As soon as Brewser gets back inside the Hornpipe Jed will lock the back door on him.'

'No! Not in here alone with you, Kate,' Polly pleaded.

'I begged him to, and then set fire to the inn. It's the only end for it all. Jed saw it. Can you not see it, too?'

Polly stared at her, too shocked to speak.

'Now go! Hurry, Polly!' Kate began to cry. 'Do it for me as well as for Suzy, love! Quick, before he gets back – or there will be another murder done tonight.'

She fell silent. All her strength was gone. She did not even seem to be breathing, and now there was nothing but a strange, eerie silence throughout the inn. Polly ran out into the darkness, grabbing her cloak on the way, and a long time later, when it seemed she had been running for ever and ever and the grey streaks of dawn were in the sky, she looked back one last time.

Flames were shooting up into the sky, burning her past clean away, and now on the thirteenth of July 1787, two days from her sixteenth birthday, she really was all alone in the world.

6

DEACON BRODIE WAS not the only man in Edinburgh to find himself frustrated at the way Erskine Caldwell was dragging his feet over the Candacraig estate. Lord Braxfield was at fever pitch. His mind was constantly drifting back to Susanna's will, and to Suzanne Gray, his daughter. Erskine Caldwell must have been making the search for Lady Susanna's next of kin, only he was taking a hell of a long time about it. Surely he would have started at the wretched Hornpipe Inn where he had sent the money. What could be the delay, for God's sake?

How was anyone supposed to concentrate on business with all this on his mind? By midday he felt in urgent need of a glass of brandy and something solid to sustain him through this harrowing time, and set off to Johnnie Dowie's tavern. It was crowded, as always, but his eagle eyes spied an empty place. Regardless of anyone else who was waiting he grasped a serving girl by her arm and bellowed at her.

'An inky pinky, my girl, and a glass of brandy! No, make it two, and hurry!'

Then he shouldered everyone else aside, found the empty seat there at the back and squashed himself into it. The man beside him tried to make himself even thinner than he was already and edged away. Lord Braxfield glanced at him and discovered he was sitting next to the very man in Edinburgh he wanted to speak to urgently.

'Erskine Caldwell, by God! The verra man!'

'Good day, Robbie.' Erskine Caldwell coughed nervously. 'I was just leaving.'

'Ye're no' leaving yet, my mannie. I've got a bit o' business with ye first. But what's that ye're drinking, for Christ's sake?' He looked at Erskine's glass with contempt. 'Raspberry cordial? Ye want to drink a glass o' brandy, man.'

'I prefer something lighter, for the sake of my stomach.'

No wonder Susanna had called him that pee-weeing Erskine Caldwell, the judge smiled to himself. At that moment his inky pinky arrived, steak, onions and carrots in a thick gravy served with oatcakes.

'Smell that, lad!' He slapped Erskine heartily on the back.

A nut shot out of the lawyer's narrow mouth, hit the wall in front of them, and ricocheted back into Lord Braxfield's gravy. He picked it out unconcernedly.

'Man, Erskine, ye'll never thrive on nuts and raisins, ye ken. 'But,' he took a gulp of brandy, 'I havena come here today to tell ye how to live yer life.'

'No?'

'I want to speak to ye aboot Lady Susanna Graham.'

'Oh, yes?'

'Noo, dinna purse up yer lips like that at me! I'm no' asking ye for any secrets I dinna ken already. All I want to know is what happened when ye closed up Candacraig after her death. Who did ye get to do it?'

'The best, of course. William Brodie.'

'Brodie, eh?' Lord Braxfield's black suspicious eyes pierced his. 'Ay, just so. He seems to get the job o' closing up all the big houses nooadays.'

'I was very glad of his company, I assure you, while I was going through the papers and the affairs of the estate. Candacraig is a big house. It can feel ghostly by yourself.'

'Of course, ye found her will?'

'I went through every paper myself that day,' Erskine Caldwell said in his reedy voice, 'but I never came across any will.'

Lord Braxfield's fork dropped into his plate with a clatter. Gravy splashed far and wide. 'What d'ye mean, no will?' he spluttered.

'She never made one, as far as I know.'

'Ay, but she did, man! She sent for me to make oot her will. I drew it up for her myself when she was on her deathbed.'

'Highly irregular! She had no business to ask you, and you had no business to do it.'

'Never mind all that! Brodie himself can be trusted, I suppose?'

'*Deacon* Brodie? He is one of the pillars of our society.'

'Hm!' Lord Braxfield fumed. 'So that's why nothing has ever been done to find the heirs! It's a good job *I* know what was in the will. Very well then, Erskine, *I'll* set the ball rolling myself, and that wi' no more delay. Far too much time has been wasted already.'

'Please yourself,' Erskine Caldwell replied stiffly, then rose up and departed.

Lord Braxfield acted swiftly, and the very next morning he walked briskly from his house in Covenant Close to his rooms in Parliament Square, deep in thought.

Of course he should have made a copy of the will, but he had assumed that Susanna would have lodged it with Erskine Caldwell to be kept in a strong-box until further instructions. Now he realized that her only instructions had been verbal and to himself alone. Fortunately every word was branded on his heart in letters of fire, although *that* was no use in a court of law.

So he had made an appointment for that young devil Fraser Graham to come and see him, and it would never do to be late. He intended to be seated behind his desk in his usual regal position of power with his back to the windows so that when the young man sat down the light would shine straight into his eyes.

'Na, na,' he told himself grimly, 'there are tricks in every trade, and I'm too old a cat to be fucked aboot by a kitten.'

Therefore when he opened his door and discovered Fraser Graham already seated, with his long legs nonchalantly crossed on top of the hallowed desk, the wind was taken right out of his sails.

'Good morning, sir.' Fraser uncrossed them and lounged to his feet. 'Your man let me in ten minutes ago.'

'He'd no business,' Lord Braxfield snapped. 'I said nine o'clock, and that's it only ringing now.'

'Oh, I like to be in plenty of time when it's something important ...'

'Ay, lad.' Lord Braxfield sighed and sat down. He was hating every minute of this difficult interview before it even began.

It seemed a pity to him that it had to be with a man so well set up, young and good-looking, with any God's amount of money – but with all the wrong ideas. Fraser Graham had no respect for the Establishment whatsoever. He scorned wealth, with crackpot notions that it was corrupting, that the rich and the poor were too widely separated, and although he was always laughing and rarely thrust his ideas down anyone's throat, there was that element of steely conviction about him that Lord Braxfield detected and bitterly distrusted.

But, alas, he was the only man in Edinburgh with the knowledge and experience to do this work for him now. Fraser Graham, a lawyer himself, had a first-class knowledge of not only the Scottish law, but also the English and especially the French. He visited France so frequently that there were rumours he was taking up with the radicals there.

Very dangerous ...

Furthermore, whenever Robert Burns, the most dyed-in-the-wool Scottish radical of them all, was in Edinburgh, Fraser Graham was never out of his company. Birds of a feather! Lord Braxfield snorted to himself.

'I've got a serious problem, Fraser,' he announced. 'It canna be solved here but it may be solved in London. It concerns a lady.'

'Ah! A lady, in London! The plot thickens.'

'It's no' a matter for levity.' The judge glowered at him. 'It's in connection wi' a will.'

'Oh, yes?'

'Ay. There's a lady in London called Suzanne Gray who has been named in a will, and I need someone to go and fetch her here. It involves a great deal o' money, so I dinna want her told directly until we see if she's the rightful heir.'

'So you need me, is that it? Someone with tact and discretion?' Fraser tried not to smile in the face of Lord

Braxfield's disapproval. 'Of course I'll go. Give me her address and I'll take the next ship out of Leith. I was looking for an excuse to go to France, anyway. I can do my business there and pick her up on the way back.'

'The sooner the better,' Lord Braxfield said.

'Is she pretty?'

The judge was on firm ground at last for the first time during the interview, and wrote down,

> 'The Hornpipe Inn,
> Narrow Street,
> London.
> Props. Jack Tarre and Mistress Lilian Tarre'

on a scrap of paper.

Little did Fraser know that he was going to look for the woman who had the key to the huge estate of Candacraig and could open its doors for him now. She might even share it with him. *Then* he would have to settle down, by God.

'Pretty, did ye say? Weel, considering her mother – I knew her well, a beautiful lady – and then of course her father,' he patted his hair and assumed an expression that Fraser saw to his amazement could only be described as fond, foolish and proud all rolled into one, 'she couldna be anything else! But whether she is or no', me lad, she'll be the bonniest woman in the world to you, I can guarantee it. Wait and see.'

Polly sank down into the inglenook of the Duke of York and leaned her head wearily against its high wooden back. In her mind she was still running, running, running. It seemed that the very windows of this inn were rushing past her still, and she closed her eyes to make them stop. A jumbled blur of pictures raced by in her tired brain. She could not forget the horrific sight of Brewser carrying her mother's body away. Where had he taken it? In despair and grief Polly believed that it must have been thrown into the River Thames.

'*Go to Edinburgh. Go to Candacraig.*'

Those were her mother's last wishes. Polly found herself rebelling against them in spite of her best intentions. Left to herself she would never be going to the cold grey city Mama seemed to believe Edinburgh was, and it was only the same fierce loyalty her mother had always shown her that was making her go there now.

'The stage leaves from the Duke of York. Anyone will tell you where it is,' Kate had said, but she was wrong. Running in what she thought was a northerly direction, Polly soon found out she was chasing through the streets of London haphazardly, sometimes even in circles. She could not keep the direction and most of the people she dared to ask had no idea what the next street was, let alone the next street but one, and the Duke of York was as much a mystery to them as it was to her.

But she had been lucky, in a way, for having told perfect strangers she wanted to get to a staging inn it was a wonder that none of them attacked her for the money she was bound to be carrying. Mercifully none of them did, and when she was almost at the end of her tether, standing in a strange dark street and in tears, a man and his son passing by in their wagon stopped beside her. 'Are you in trouble?' the man asked.

'Desperate trouble, sir.' Polly could no longer disguise it from herself, either. 'I cannot find the way to the Duke of York.'

'Our home is near the Duke of York, and that's where we're going now. Hop up! It's quite a way. You'll have time to have forty winks if you like.'

She got up and the wagon rumbled on into the darkness. It was twenty-four hours since she had left the Hornpipe, but although neither the man nor the boy turned around to look at her, she was too frightened to close her eyes. If anyone robbed her she was finished, for she had a worrying suspicion that it would take all the money Kate had given her for the long journey ahead. She was very tired but still awake when the wagon came to a halt eventually, and the man and the boy climbed down.

'This is as far as we go,' the man said. 'The Duke of York is three miles up that road,' he pointed, 'but the Stage doesn't leave until ten o'clock in the morning. You could rest here for an hour or two.'

'No, thank you, sir.' Polly offered him a coin which he waved away. 'You've given me a good rest, and so much help, but I'll just walk on.'

'You shouldn't.' The man frowned at her. 'Your feet are bleeding. Wait until morning and I'll take you there.'

Something in the boy's face warned her that she had better not. 'Thank you,' she repeated, and forced her stiffening feet to walk and then run along the dark road. She didn't stop running until she found the inn at last and sat down behind a hedge until the new day came in, the doors were flung open and the landlord stood on the threshold scratching his head and yawning. Polly darted out from behind the bush and went up to him.

'I have to get to Edinburgh,' she told him.

He became wide awake at once. 'You have the money?'

'How much is it?'

He told her how much her breakfast would cost, and the journey to Edinburgh. It was as she had feared. Once she paid out the money she had very little left in Kate's little pouch. God alone knew what would happen to her, for she did not.

Here she was, not even having begun the long haul up to Scotland yet, with her shoes in tatters and her feet sore and blistered. She should not have run away from the Hornpipe in these thin slippers – and then the whole procession of pictures began to grind round and round in her head again as she dozed off. Uppermost were the faces of Caramelle and Chocolat. What had happened to them, left behind in the apartment in Paris?

'One old dress!' In disgust Caramelle held up the pink gown to show her brother. 'Madame Suzanne took all the rest.'

'Well, it's torn. Did you know?'

'Why else would she leave it behind? Besides that, it is far too short for me. How can I do the business in this black maidservant's dress?'

'There's no money,' Choco grumbled. 'So what are we going to do?'

'What are *you* going to do, you mean! You have been living too soft lately, Chocolat, while I have been doing all the work.' Caramelle stamped her foot. 'Go and do what you do best! Steal some silk from the stalls in the market – now!'

'But it's dark.'

'That's the whole idea. Nobody will see your black face in the dark. Keep well away from the lanterns. I want red and orange and yellow.'

'To trim a pink dress?'

'The brighter the better. If my customers are old men they will need all the stimulation they can get. And I'll need needles and thread. She has not left so much as a pin.'

The following day Caramelle set to work on the dress, sewing rows of flounces on to the hem, narrower ones on to the sleeves, and the narrowest of all around the neckline which she had lowered considerably.

'You look like some exotic flower,' Choco told her when she put on the altered dress to let him see.

Caramelle's grim expression didn't soften. 'Then the sooner we get to work the better. Go out into the taverns and bring me back some men with money in their pockets. I shall work all night if necessary.'

'And what if any of them turn ugly? It is a dangerous game.'

'No man will dare with you on the premises, Choco. The door of the boudoir will be left half open, and you must stand outside.'

That night they made enough money to live on for the next few days. Choco was delighted when they counted it the next morning, but there was no vestige of a smile on Caramelle's face.

A few weeks later the lease was nearly up on the apartment when at last Caramelle told Chocolat from now on no one else need be admitted.

'We have enough money saved now for our fares to Edinburgh. Think of that, Choco!'

'I *am* thinking about it,' he said gloomily. He did not want to leave Paris.

The wonderful aroma of coffee brought Polly back to life and made her open her eyes again as a serving girl brought scrambled eggs, hot rolls and butter to her table in the corner. The inn was filling up, and outside a family coach was depositing its passengers in the courtyard. She watched them with interest as she ate.

A young man carrying a baby descended first, followed by an older man, stout and homely, holding the hand of his little grandson. A young woman came next leading a toddler, then a girl of about her own age, and last of all a jovial red-faced woman in a plaid cloak, obviously the grandmother, helping the oldest child down.

The young man handed the baby over to his wife and began unloading luggage. Then there were the farewell kisses all round, and the grandmother wiping her eyes with her handkerchief and going back to kiss the baby again, before the young family got back into their coach and it rolled away with hands of every size waving out of the windows. The couple and the young girl picked up their luggage and threaded their way to occupy the other seats at Polly's table.

'My!' the woman remarked. 'What a crowd! I hope they're no' all going on the Edinburgh Fly!' She laid down a round covered basket, a large bag and several boxes on the floor. Her husband laid down even more, and the girl piled her luggage on the top of that. 'Ye don't mind if we sit here, do ye, lassie?' she asked as something of an afterthought, sitting down heavily.

'Please do.'

'Ye're English yersel', then?'

'From London.' Polly smiled. 'Going to Edinburgh, too.'

'Well, that's grand.' The man recovered his breath and smiled kindly at her. 'We can all go together, what do ye say, Ma? The poor lassie looks fair worn out. I'm George Buchanan. This is Mistress Nell Buchanan, and this here is our Margery.'

'They dinna like parties o' three on the coaches, right enough,' Mistress Buchanan informed her. 'They prefer even numbers to fill it up and get the most money they can.'

'It is very kind of you.' Polly sighed thankfully. 'It has not been pleasant travelling alone.'

She drank another cup of scalding coffee and watched the Buchanans tucking into ham and eggs.

'We've been staying with our oldest lassie,' Mistress Buchanan explained, and while she was at it described their whole family lovingly and minutely. 'That's the first time we've seen the baby, the little treasure.' She finished her breakfast and the story at the same time and took out her handkerchief again.

'Now,' Mr Buchanan briskly forestalled more tears, 'we must gather all our things together and be first in the line to be sure of a seat when the Fly comes in. Come, lassies!'

Polly found herself in the corner, next to Margery and opposite her mother and father in the coach, with Mistress Buchanan's motherly eyes searching her face.

'No luggage, miss?' she asked.

'No luggage, Mistress Buchanan.'

'I see. Well yer first lesson is how to address us, if we're to go all the way to Edinburgh together. Call him,' she jerked her head in the direction of her husband, 'Mr Buchanan, and ye can call me Mistress Nell.'

'Just call me Margery,' the girl put in, laughing.

'Thank you,' Polly said. 'My name is Polly Gray.'

'Very pretty, I'm sure.' Mistress Nell's eyes were shrewd. 'So ye're running awa' from home?'

'My mother died and there was no one else left in London.'

'Weel, weel, lassie, that's sad.' Mistress Nell shook her head while Margery's eyes widened to two round blue saucers. 'And you were on foot?'

'A man and his son found me wandering miles out of my way and kindly took me up on their wagon for a mile or two. But yes, apart from that I ran or walked all the way across the City.'

'That's a long way.'

'It *is* a long way. It took all day and all last night.'

'Have ye someone to go to in Edinburgh?' Mr Buchanan asked.

'I believe so, but first of all I must find them.'

'Ay.' He sighed. 'Just so, lassie.'

'It's so hot ye could open a window, George,' his wife requested, and from then on the coach gathered speed through the English countryside, its wheels creaking and groaning over the sunbaked ruts in the road, and further conversation was impossible.

In spite of the drought the fields and trees were so green that Polly's tired eyes felt rested merely looking at them as she sat with her chin cupped in her hands, her gaze fixed on the window. The little hamlets with their thatched cottages were so different from the teeming backstreets of London.

Well, she had escaped after all. The very thought heartened her, and she thanked God for the pale blue sky and the warm sun above, for she had nothing but the clothes she stood up in

70

and her cloak. Her shoes were in ribbons, she had very little money left after paying for her fare – but she was free!

Mile after mile went by while she thought back over her life so far. She tried to recall any conversations she had ever had with Mama about Edinburgh, but they were few and far between. Suzanne had never seen it. She had always become angry when Polly persisted, until shortly before her death when she had told her it was her own mother who had sent her a monthly allowance all these years. Mama's mother – her grandmother – a rich lady in Edinburgh. Her name must have been Gray, Polly decided. There must have been a grandfather, too. Mama must have had a father. Who had *he* been?

Polly had no idea. All she knew was that her mother had been truly happy with Geoffrey Fotheringham and so had she, from the age of six. Her mind went back to endless pictures of him in her memory, all of them happy.

This was very different from being in Uncle Geoffrey's elegant carriage in Paris, where all was gaiety and laughter and going to the Opera – except for that evening when they had taken the wrong turning and found themselves in one of the backstreets, narrow and evil-smelling with a broad stream running down the centre to carry the sewage, and beggars holding out their hands for alms. Polly remembered how frightened she would have been without Uncle Geoffrey. A woman with two ragged, barefooted children poked her head in the carriage clamouring for money, and when she shrank back the woman shook her fist at her and cursed.

'It's all right, Polly,' he had said, calming her down. 'The Porte St Martin is right up ahead. I see it now, and all the coaches and carriages arriving for the Opera. Come, we will look at the lords and ladies instead.'

She remembered next when Mama had allowed her to visit the market with Caramelle, and standing at one of the stalls a man was shouting:

'Soon it will all change! We have had enough! We will rise up against tyranny. *Ça ira*!'

Soon all the market people were muttering and humming.

'Ah! Ça ira! Ça ira! Ça ira!
Les aristocrates à la lanterne,
Ah! Ça ira! Ça ira! Ça ira!
Les aristocrates on les pendra!'

The song, a nonsense of threats against the King and the aristocrats, rattled around in her head for days.

'It doesn't mean anything, does it, Uncle Geoffrey?'

'Oh, Polly! I'm afraid it does, my dear. The King is imposing impossible taxes on all except the nobility and the clergy. The high price of bread falls most heavily on the poorest workmen. Yet when someone tried to explain this to Marie Antoinette, that the people did not have enough to eat, she was so far removed from reality that she said, "Then let them eat cake instead." Now there is a great groundswell of feeling against the monarchy as a result of that statement!'

'Do you mean that the people really will rise up and kill the King and Queen?'

'Revolt? Yes, my dear,' Uncle Geoffrey said sadly. 'I believe there *will* be a revolution, and I for one do not blame the people. Why should they work and toil and still go hungry while all their hard-earned money goes on taxes levied to buy more jewels for Marie Antoinette? But do not speak of this to your Mama, Polly. She is a very delicate lady.'

Every now and then Mistress Buchanan disturbed Polly's reverie, opening one of the round baskets and sharing out apples and home-baked bread and chicken legs, and always the coach rumbled on to the next Stage, and the next, until Mr Buchanan told them that here at this last one they would spend the night.

They descended stiffly, Polly by now hardly able to put her feet to the ground, unnoticed in the flurry when the Buchanans gathered their luggage off the roof and they all went inside. Mr Buchanan found a room for Margery and Polly and one for his wife and himself, and Mistress Buchanan insisted that they should all have a cup of tea before they went to bed. It seemed to Polly that the good-natured family had taken her under their wing, and she was too tired and too sore to feel anything but thankful.

Next day they continued their journey and from her seat at the window Polly watched the country change to a harsher, wilder terrain.

'We'll be crossing the border into Scotland soon,' they told her, 'and that's no' like England, ye ken. It's colder, for one thing.'

It *was* colder with every mile they travelled north, but nothing she could not bear. She was more interested in the Buchanans' language than the temperature, as she tried to interpret it. She was getting used to their sing-song voices, but she couldn't pretend to understand everything they said.

'I wonder why we're stopping here,' Mr Buchanan said hours later when the coach rumbled to a halt and the driver got down to speak to someone who appeared from nowhere at the side of the road.

He stood there with his back to the coach windows speaking to the driver as if he knew him well, as if they were old acquaintances, and she could not help but admire the elegant proportions of his figure, from his fair hair to the breadth of his shoulders and right down the long lean lines of his body. It all suggested power, subtly restrained, and it reminded her ... it reminded her ... Polly's heart leapt up in her throat until she thought it would choke her.

It was Uncle Geoffrey! Oh, thank God! Thank God! Taller and broader perhaps than she remembered him – but tears ran down her face at the sight of him. *Of course* he wasn't dead! She had never really believed that he was, and she wiped her eyes, the nightmare of the past few months rolling away like a huge black cloud.

The door opened and the gentleman got in to join them, easing his large frame into the seat beside Mr Buchanan. The bitter disappointment Polly felt when she saw his face hit her like a sledgehammer. This man was much younger. His hair was the same fair colour but it crinkled instead of lying smooth. She was unaware that her large dark eyes brimming with tears were examining him critically from head to foot, and that they found him sadly wanting. She turned her face away. It was not Uncle Geoffrey, after all, and from then on she avoided his eye as he chatted with Mr Buchanan.

'We'll be coming into Edinburgh in a few minutes,' Mistress Buchanan told her, and started to collect her belongings. The coach slowed down, and then stopped suddenly. 'Just sit still, dearie. We're only stopping here to let Mr Graham off. Wait a few minutes yet.'

'Yes, George,' Mr Graham stood up, continuing his conversation with Mr Buchanan, 'it was a wild goose chase in London, if ever there was one. The inn I was telling you about had burned down a few days before, and there was no sign of Madame. The bird had flown.'

Polly felt the coach spinning round and round in a horrible spiral before everything went black. She had no idea for how long her sojourn into nothingness went on, but when she came back into the world Margery was patting her hands and calling her name, Mr Graham was still there and Mistress Buchanan was bending over her.

'The poor lassie,' she was saying. 'What could be wrong wi' her?'

'Perhaps you should look to your maidservant's feet, Mistress,' Mr Graham said as he stepped down from the coach. 'They look very sore to me.'

7

'POLLY!' MISTRESS BUCHANAN screeched. 'Why did you not tell us? My, my,' lifting up the hem of her dress, 'we'll have to do something about *that* when we get home!'

'That was Mr Fraser Graham,' Margery informed Polly in a whisper, 'going to see his string of horses, likely. He keeps them here somewhere south of the town. Every lady in Edinburgh would give her eye-teeth to marry him, even the ones who are married already. Except me, of course. I want only Jocky Robertson the carpenter's apprentice, although he's never even noticed me.'

The coach rolled on again, this time over a cobbled street, passing huge walls and a massive gate on the left-hand side.

'Holyrood Palace,' Mr Buchanan announced. 'We're here. This is the Royal Mile,' he told Polly. 'Now, now, Nell, there's no need to fluster. Tak' yer time, woman. There will be plenty o' chair men left for us! As for you, lassie, sit still wi' Margery here in the coach until I arrange everything.'

So this was the Royal Mile, famous even so far away as Paris, this narrow winding street on a hill, with the tallest tenements she had ever seen. Twelve storeys high she counted some of them, crowding in on both sides of it, and right at the top Edinburgh Castle crouched like a lion on the Castle Rock. Narrow streets no wider than paths opened off the Royal Mile, and the coach was turning into one of them now, edging slowly through the opening barely wide enough for it, to the little square behind, where it came to a halt.

Facing them was an inn with 'White Horse' written on it in big letters, and a white horse painted on its swinging sign. Mr and Mistress Buchanan got out and it seemed to Polly, sitting there beside Margery in the small square with the tall buildings pressed close together all round, that hundreds of people were running about, rushing here and there, and nearly all of them shouting and waving their arms. She shrank back when a man came up to them and shouted something totally incomprehensible through the window of the coach.

'Don't be frightened of the chair men, Polly.' Margery waved away the men in their tattered tartan and the girls descended from the coach. 'They are very brave men, disbanded from the Highland regiments. They cannot speak English, you see. They are asking us in the Gaelic where we want to go. You're supposed to tell them where –'

They were swept apart in the crowd as the chair men rushed up to them again in another concerted movement, desperate for customers. A grimy hand clutched Polly's arm, a face of wild whiskers mouthing terrible gutturals poked into hers, and panic seized her immediately.

She had nowhere to go. She wouldn't know a place to tell the man to take her even if she had the courage to open her mouth. As it was, her throat was dry, closed up in fear, the Buchanans were lost somewhere in that sea of faces behind her, and then somehow she was out into the dusk of the Royal Mile with sedan chairs swaying past her in all directions.

In a daze she saw that Edinburgh's sedan chairs were not the splendid gilded creations they mostly were in Paris, at least around the Bois. Here they had been painted green a very long time ago and there were only two chair men, one at each end grasping the long poles to lift them up.

Hoping to find Margery and Mr and Mistress Buchanan again she waited forlornly for a long time, hiding from the chair men round a corner, until darkness was falling and men began to light the street tapers with long poles wrapped around with tarry canvas at one end and glowing like torches.

The little pools of yellow light they shed around only cast darker shadows between them, and suddenly Edinburgh became an evil frightening place as the night crept in and the chair men straggled back to be ready for the next coach.

She took to her heels when she saw them coming, up streets and down streets, not stopping until she saw that they were by now deserted. She came to a dead halt, sure that she had been in this particular street before. It was just like London, when she ran around in circles and always came back to the same spot.

'Nowhere to go, have ye, lassie?' a voice cackled in her ear from out of the darkness, and for a second the yellow lights swam round and round in the shock of it. 'Well, ye've come to the right doorway. Every night it belongs to me. I'm Bella. Come awa' in.'

'No! I –'

'Och, dinna worry, lassie. Old Bella'll look after ye. Come awa' in,' the voice insisted, and a hand dragged her into the depths of what seemed like a black tunnel. 'It's no' safe oot there on the street. Come wi' me. See, I've got a light.'

A tiny spark showed Polly that she was in a filthy lobby with a very low door at the far end of it, and it was an old woman who was speaking to her. She wore a long dark cloak which did not fall down straight to the floor but stuck out at a strange angle, and she kept her hood up around a long white bony face.

'I've got some bread and a sup o' milk. Are ye hungry, lassie?'

'No.' Polly shuddered.

'I ken. Just feart. Ye've every right to be, here at the Bow Head.' Bella cackled again. 'Oh, I could tell ye some stories about this place! *Noo then* – will ye look at that great ugly bugger!'

She flared up her light suddenly, and, frozen into a solid pillar of horror, Polly looked down to where the unspeakable squeaking was coming from, straight into the red eyes of a rat.

There was the flash of a blade, a scream, and the rat's head flew off into the darkness.

'Dinna worry. The rest o' them'll smell its blood. That should keep them off for the night, the rats on four feet and the rats on two. That's why I always carry my old friend here.'

Polly saw that as she spoke the old woman was unconcernedly wiping off the blood from the blade of a long sword with her cloak. Then she scraped it back into the hilt she wore at her side over her ragged clothes before allowing the cloak to fall back into place again in its strange position.

Which was she most frightened of? Polly wondered shakily. The old woman, her sword, the rats, the dark – or just Edinburgh? But she must try to look brave, at least, for something told her that Bella would make short work of anything or anyone she despised. 'The Bow Head?' she gasped, when she managed to speak.

'Ay. That's where ye've landed up! I have this place all to mysel', for nobody else dares come here in the dark.' Bella sat down, obviously making herself comfortable for the rest of the night.

'Why not?'

'Sit doon then, and I'll tell ye. What's wrang wi' ye? Is there something wrang wi' yer feet?'

'They're bleeding.'

'Ho! So that's what the rats were after! They smelt yer blood. Tear off the hem of yer petticoat, for God's sake, and wrap them up or else we'll be infested.'

Trying not to cry, Polly bound up her feet with shaking fingers.

'Noo then, wrap yer cloak over the top of them both,' Bella instructed as she doused the light. 'Poor lassie, ye're new to the game, are ye?' Her voice softened slightly.

'I'm new to Edinburgh,' Polly smiled grimly into the pitch dark, finding out already that she was in a city no different from London or Paris, 'and I'm not on the game, Mistress Bella. But what did you mean, nobody dares to come to the Bow Head after dark? Why not?'

'It's because of Major Weir, a great Presbyterian preacher who lived here in this house just over a hundred years ago.'

'Why should anyone be scared of a preacher?'

'Well, you never saw him, did ye? Neither did I, but I used to ken a man who had. Major Thomas Weir was a great tall dark man wi' a grim face and a big nose. He always looked down to the ground and never went anywhere – never even preached withoot his staff in his hand.'

'His staff?'

'Ay, his tall black stick. The old man told me it was carved

78

with the heads of queer beasts. Anyway, he held meetings in there,' Bella jerked her head backwards, 'and the women of the congregation were so besotted wi' him they called him "Angelical Thomas". They used to come here to consult him privately.'

Bella snorted and muttered away to herself for some time before she spoke again. '*Privately*,' she sneered. 'Christ, some women are fools – but he had a gey hold over them, ye ken.'

'You mean –'

'He took ill,' Bella swept on, 'and then it all came oot, everything none o' the good folk could ever have imagined in their worst nightmares. Thomas told them he was a sham, and gave them the story o' his lifetime o' fornication, bestiality – and awful acts wi' his sister. She lived wi' him, of course.'

'Do you mean incest, Mistress Bella?'

'Is that what ye call it? Well, they put the pair o' them into the Tolbooth. That's the prison here, ye ken. At first they thought they were mad, but then they made oot that the Weirs belonged to the Devil. Grizel Weir said the Major's staff was magic. It could walk on its own. She showed them the mark o' a horseshoe on her brow, and told how they travelled to Musselburgh in a flaming coach to meet Satan.'

'What happened to them?' Polly shuddered.

'Ye'd think they would be hung for a pair o' witches, wouldn't ye? But it was for all their other crimes they were put to death, and even as she stood on the gallows Grizel Weir stripped off all her clothes and laughed at the crowd, stark naked, the dirty old bitch. Nobody else ever came into this house again.'

'Well, it was all a long time ago,' Polly struggled to stop the flow of words and obscenities streaming out of Bella's mouth. 'It wouldn't happen nowadays.'

'No?' the old voice laughed strangely in the darkness. 'Then fall asleep now, lassie, if ye can – and dinna be feart if ye hear music and dancing coming oot o' this deserted house in the middle o' the night. I've never heard it mysel' but passers-by have, and seen the fiery coach – *and* heard the Major's staff tapping along that street oot there, straight from the Devil, straight from Hell!'

Bella yawned and within seconds her head fell down upon her chest. She was fast asleep and snoring gently.

The very blackness moved with eerie shapeless forms. There were whisperings in every lift and moan of the night wind outside the doorway. Polly had been frightened before, but never like this.

Then, from a little way off, came the tapping of a stick. As it came nearer and nearer the tapping thundered in her ears, the blood rushed to her head and in a perfect frenzy of terror she got up and ran again in the opposite direction – where to, she was past caring. Just on and on until in the end she was careering down a very steep street.

'It's you, is it, Peter?' Bella woke up sufficiently to make way for the man coming into the doorway at the Bow Head to join her. 'There was a lassie here. Has she gone?'

'I heard footsteps running away.' Peter laid down his stick and rattled his heavy tin mug under her nose. 'Ye got rid o' her then, did ye, Mother? Why?'

'Och, she was no use! She was straight. She won't last long, that one!'

The first fingers of the dawn were etching the sky when Polly collapsed into another doorway, pleasanter than the one before. For one thing it was relatively clean, and for another it felt quite warm in the corner at the side of the door. She had no idea that she had wandered into Edinburgh's Grassmarket. Sometimes she dozed a little, but more often a little noise or the pain in her feet made her sit up again, alert.

She thought the clocks struck five on the morning of her sixteenth birthday, but she was too tired to count before the ceaseless clatter of heavy oven doors opening and closing from a bakehouse somewhere close at hand made her head throb. Her heart jumped into her mouth when she heard light footsteps running towards her. They pattered past her doorway, then hesitated for a moment before carrying on. All the people were getting up. She must get up, too, before she was found out here in the streets like a beggar.

Then came the thudding of iron trays on long deal tables. The bakers must be setting the loaves to cool under open windows, for along with the tantalising smell of fresh-baked bread floury billows of steam pervaded everything, obscuring even the small square of sky at the end of the lobby from Polly's eyes. The sky and the light were getting dimmer and dimmer all the time, and this time the footsteps didn't patter by. They stopped for a few minutes, a hand touched her arm, a voice that might have been Margery's called her name, and then they were off, running again.

Polly came back to the world to see a stern face looking down at her. 'Ye havena been here all night?' Mr Buchanan demanded, Margery goggle-eyed at his side still clutching her basket of floury rolls.

'No. I was at the Bow Head with a Mistress Bella.'

'What?' Mr Buchanan reeled back, scandalized. 'Not that dirty old cratur? Her and that rascally son o' hers who pretends to be a blind beggar?'

'Get oot o' the road, George.' Mistress Nell came panting up and brushed him aside. 'Gi'e the lassie air. Can ye no' see she's faint?'

'Oh, Polly,' Margery asked, 'how did you manage to struggle away down here? We looked for you for hours.'

'Never mind all that,' Mistress Nell said briskly. 'Now then, Polly, did ye no' ken we meant to take ye in? Here in a strange place, and you wi' yer sore feet and all! George, carry her inside! *We'll* look after ye, dearie, here in Candlemaker Row.'

8

THAT FIRST WEEK Mistress Nell set about Polly with
ointments and salves and clean cloths, determined to have
her back on her feet in no time. By the beginning of the second
week she was succeeding, so that Polly was able to help
Margery raid all the trunks in the house for some dresses and
shoes to fit her, for the Buchanans had four daughters although
Margery was the only one left at home now. Not that she was
ever lonely, she explained to Polly. Her parents were mother
and father to her cousins too since their father died, and they
were hardly ever out of the house in Candlemaker Row.

Indeed they were not. Once the three MacAllister brothers,
Fergus, Cameron and Jamie, in steps and stairs between the ages
of seventeen and nineteen, saw Polly, they all three fell
hopelessly in love with her. They did everything in unison,
including that. They even looked like triplets, with their fair
gingery hair, their round blue eyes like their cousin Margery's.
The only difference between them was in their dress. The most
important decision each made every morning was what to wear
in order to out-do his brothers.

But they were charming, pleasant-spoken and merry as they
lounged about in the chairs, their long legs encased in
tight-fitting moleskin trousers under their boots, taking up most
of the floor space while they teased and laughed and openly
admired Polly who sat in their midst wearing a green muslin

gown from one of the trunks, its wide skirt spread out demurely and her feet bare to the fresh air to heal, as Mistress Nell commanded.

'What age are you, anyway, Miss Polly?' Jamie, the youngest, asked.

'One thing none of your education seems to have taught you,' Fergus scowled at him, very much the oldest brother, 'is that you must never ask a lady her age.'

'Oh, I am not old enough yet to mind,' Polly assured them. 'I was sixteen the day I came here, ten days ago.'

'Sixteen must be the prettiest age.' Jamie remained quite unabashed. 'Margery is sixteen as well, and look how pretty she is!'

'Ho! I know what you want, Jamie MacAllister!' Margery said. 'It's your supper. Well, you can sing for it, all of you. It'll be another half an hour yet.'

The MacAllisters needed no more encouragement. 'We'll sing a few of Robbie Burns's, then,' Cameron announced. 'After all, he *has* written the best love songs in the world. Come on, boys, we'll start with "Ye banks and braes o' bonnie Doon".'

Polly did not understand all the Scottish words they were singing, but she thought the tunes were beautiful, and very often sad.

'He hasn't only written love songs, you know,' Cameron told her when they paused for breath. 'Here's one that means a lot to us,' and they began to sing:

> 'The rank is but the guinea's stamp;
> The man's the gowd for a' that.
> For a' that and a' that,
> A man's a man for a' that.'

The more they sang of that song, the more chilling Polly found it. Something in the words reminded her uncomfortably of 'Ça ira'.

That evening, after they left, the Buchanan family settled round a low fire and chatted before they went to bed. Mr Buchanan shook his head over their nephews. 'Oh well,' he sighed, 'the young rascals are clever enough to get through their degrees with the least possible study anyway, I suppose.'

'It's not them we're needing to worry about,' his wife told him. 'It's Polly. My goodness, dearie, why did you not tell us it was your birthday?'

'Oh, it was not important!'

'Poor child, and you wi' no mother! Your mother would have given you a present.'

'But you have given me so many presents since I met you, Mistress Nell! Dresses and shoes, and bed and board, and nothing but kindness!'

'The dresses and shoes were all cast-offs, anyway. I would feel better if we could give you something that really mattered, Polly.'

Something that really mattered ... Mama was dead, that was what really mattered, Polly thought. The only thing left now was to carry out her wishes. Although she had accomplished the first part of her plan, to get to Edinburgh, she had no clear idea what to do next. There was a man here in this town who knew a great deal about her mother. He probably knew about her, as well. But with her hair constantly hidden underneath that white cap her mother always made her wear, with any luck he might not recognize her – especially if she had another name instead of Gray.

'There *is* something, if you do not think it too impertinent, Mistress Nell.'

'Tell us just the same.'

'Are there a lot of Grays living in Edinburgh?'

'It's not a common name here,' Mr Buchanan answered. 'Not Gray. Now Graham is a different matter.'

'But you do know one or two by the name of Gray?'

'There are two seamstresses, sisters.'

'Whatever ye do, dearie, have nothing to do wi' those two!' Mistress Nell protested. 'They've got plenty of money, but that's all they've got! No manners, no pleasantness, no kindness of any sort!'

'I ken o' one old man,' Mr Buchanan said doubtfully. 'But he might be dead by now.'

'Och, there's bound to be more than that,' Margery put in. 'I'll try and find out.'

'You see,' Polly hesitated, 'I would rather the people I am

looking for did not know who I am just yet, so please don't tell anyone.' Mr Graham had given her a desperate fright on the coach when he spoke of an inn burning down and a 'Madame'. She did not want another shock like that. 'I would rather look them over for myself first, perhaps under another name.'

There! It was out, what had been worrying her for days ...

Mr Buchanan looked thoughtful. 'Well,' he said, 'everyone knows we go south to see our family every year. Probably they will take it for granted that ye're some relative of ours.'

'Ay.' Mistress Nell beamed. 'Polly Buchanan, a distant relative, staying with us after a bereavement. It's half true, anyway. What do you think, Margery?'

'It sounds fine to me,' Margery said.

Polly sighed with relief. So far, so good. Now, what next?

Fraser Graham was strolling around the Grassmarket when he met the MacAllister brothers going in to the White Hart.

'A hair of the dog, Fraser?' Fergus groaned.

'At this time in the morning? Where were you last night?' He accompanied them to a table.

'At the cockfight, betting on Deacon Brodie's birds. Of course we lost money.'

'How does he manage it?' Cameron asked. 'He always seems to make money while everyone else loses it.'

'Are you sure he bets on his own cocks?' Fraser asked. 'He's a very cunning little fellow, you know.'

'He wears two hats,' Jamie said suddenly, and they all gazed at him.

'He wears two hats? Listen to that! He's still drunk, the little bugger! Now what do you mean by that, he wears two hats?' Fergus asked.

'One by day, and one by night,' Jamie said. 'That's all I know.'

'Yes.' Fraser frowned. 'You could be right.'

Jamie might just have stumbled on the truth, he thought. The Deacon did a lot of his work by night, after all. What else might he be doing at the same time – or was he the impeccably honest tradesman he appeared to be? Fraser made up his mind to investigate the Deacon much more thoroughly.

The brothers were on their feet. 'We're off to have some coffee at Candlemaker Row,' Jamie informed him. 'Come on, Fraser! Come with us. The Buchanans have brought back such a pretty girl from London.'

'Oh? What's her name?'

'Polly.'

'Polly?' He remembered the Buchanans calling that little maidservant of theirs Polly when she fainted in the coach. 'Polly what?'

The brothers looked at each other vaguely and shook their heads. 'Polly Buchanan, I suppose,' Fergus said as they reached the house and went inside to find Margery and Polly in the sitting-room.

'Of course I've seen you before,' Fraser said when Margery introduced him to her, and she looked into his lazy green eyes under their drooping eyelids.

'Yes,' she said coldly, 'when you mistook me for a maidservant.'

'No lady with the spirit to match that hair of yours would stay offended for long because of that little mistake,' he said. 'No, it must have been something else I said that day to make you faint. Now, what was it?'

'I assure you, sir, you did not offend me in the least,' she said hastily, for his green eyes were now turned full on her, and she realized resentfully that far from not being able to see, this man saw too much. 'Sometimes the spirit is in the right place, but the flesh is weak. It was the pain in my feet that made me faint.'

Very much on her guard, Polly reminded herself that she was being cross-examined by the man who had actually spoken the word 'Madame' and had found an inn in London which had just burned down. It couldn't have been the Hornpipe. That would be too much of a coincidence. All the same, she would have given her back teeth at that moment to find out.

'They did look very sore,' he agreed. 'You must have travelled a long way on your feet before they were in that state.'

It was none of his business. It was nobody's business, except her own, and from that minute she swore she would give none of her secrets away. The best way to do that was to say nothing.

'You have come here to stay, Miss Polly?' Fraser tried again.

It was a delicate question. 'In the meantime, Mr Graham.'

'In the meantime?' Mistress Nell came bustling in with the coffee, and caught the tail-end of his question and her answer. 'For a long time, we hope. Margery has been missing her sisters so much.'

A tiny crease appeared between Polly's eyebrows. Try as she would she could not help frowning a little. She simply could not stay in Candlemaker Row for much longer. She would have to go about the business she had come to Edinburgh for – and Fraser Graham had noticed her hesitation, damn it ...

Mercifully insensitive to the tension snapping between the two of them, Fergus interrupted. 'What was it like in Paris before you left, Fraser?' he asked. 'We hear there are riots every day, and the people hate the King.'

Once again Polly heard little alarm bells in her head. Paris? He had been in Paris? Why? The inn burned down, the search for 'Madame' and now Paris?

'If you are going to speak about politics we shall go right upstairs,' Margery warned. 'They are so boring.'

'Nonsense, Margery, it is the only way to pass the time of day.'

'Do you not work at anything?' Polly made a great effort to detach herself from Fraser Graham and smiled at the MacAllisters.

'Of course we do, worse luck,' Jamie said. 'At the university – that is, when we get the time to go.'

'Shouldn't you be there this very minute,' Fergus frowned at him, 'now that the coffee has cleared your head?'

'We should all be somewhere else,' Cameron grinned, 'but we'd rather be here with Aunt Nell.'

Mistress Buchanan tried to look disapproving and failed miserably. 'Coffee, Mr Graham?'

'Fraser, please, Mistress Nell. Much as I would like to, I shall have to refuse this time. I'm afraid I must go.'

'A very nice gentleman,' Mistress Nell observed when he left.

'He's very clever,' Jamie assured her.

'Hm! He would need to be, to follow all the rubbish *you* were speaking this morning.' Fergus kicked his foot and Cameron frowned at him.

That night Mr Buchanan read his news-sheets, his slippered feet up on a footstool, while Mistress Nell and Margery took up their sewing.

'Do ye sew?' Mistress Nell asked Polly.

She shook her head and smiled, remembering all the hundreds of painstaking little stitches she used to have to sew at the Convent the times Mama had left her there and gone off with Uncle Geoffrey. The Sisters were good and kind to her, and taught her to read and write, but to sit still and push a needle out and in cloth for hours meant just that – sitting still for hours – and Polly was itching to get out now and begin her quest.

'My fingers are all thumbs.' She shook her head and said good-night.

In bed she got to grips with her problem. Perhaps Mistress Nell and Mr Buchanan just wanted her to stay there and be company for Margery. It was beginning to look very like it, and that was a situation she must squash immediately, before it got out of hand. Company for Margery! It sparked off another idea before she went to sleep.

Next morning her lips were compressed into a determined line when she breakfasted early with Mr and Mistress Buchanan. Margery, she knew, would not be up for another hour.

'I would stay here with you for ever,' she told them, 'but today I have made up my mind to find work.'

'That's easily remedied,' Mr Buchanan said. 'Ye can come and work for me in the shop. Margery often helps out when we're busy.'

'Ay. Go wi' him, and see,' Mistress Nell encouraged. 'We'd rather ye stayed here, Polly. Margery would miss ye now.'

Inside the candlemaking shop the heat and the smell of the tallow were overpowering. Stone pots crowded the work-benches, men and women were pouring the heated wax into the pots, tying lengths of wick to sticks and dipping and redipping them into the wax until the candles were as thick as they wanted them to be, and then dangling them from sticks above their heads to harden and dry. Hundreds of finished candles hung from the roof. Two men were filling boxes with hundreds more to sell.

It took Polly less than two minutes to make up her mind this was not for her, stuck in a crowded shop, in the heat and the smoke and the smell. She would never meet the people of Edinburgh that way. It would be a hit or a miss if anyone called Gray ever came to buy candles there, and anyway it seemed that only Mr Buchanan himself served the customers.

He might forget himself if anyone named Gray *did* come in, and call her out in his well-meaning way to meet them. No, it could all end in a dreadful muddle. She would have to get out. She would have to do things her own way and find everything out for herself in private, especially Candacraig.

'Oh, it's a wonderful shop!' she said carefully, back in the Buchanans' house.

'It's no' bad.' Mr Buchanan tried to look modest.

'Your workers all have such neat fingers, though. I could never manage to do their work, not like Margery can.'

'She's a grand little lass.' Mistress Nell beamed. 'She can turn her hand to anything, can Margery. Sewing, cooking, baking – anything.'

'Yes,' Polly agreed, 'but I will have to try work of a different kind. You see, what I do best is read.'

'You can read, Polly? Oh my, very few men can do that, never mind women!'

'So perhaps I could be a companion to some lady. I could read to her, write all her letters for her, help her with her accounts and entertaining. I would be better at that.'

'Oh, Polly! Well, if ye're determined, let me see where ye could go ... Of course, there is always Miss Jeanette Brodie, but ...'

'But what?'

'Oh, she and her brother have a beautiful house. And he is such a fine cabinetmaker that he's the Deacon of that trade. They live in the Lawnmarket.'

A beautiful house, owned by a Deacon. In the Lawnmarket. Wasn't that up near the Castle? People like that were bound to move in society, and a companion would have to accompany her mistress wherever she went. Oh, if only she could be so lucky!

'It is a brother and a sister, then?' she asked, hoping to find out more about them before she plunged in. 'Deacon Brodie and his sister, Miss Jeanette Brodie?'

'Ay, that's right, and very important people they are. William

Brodie inherited the business from his father who was a Deacon before him. The very close they live in is called Brodie's Close, ye ken. He's a toon cooncillor, and some say the man to be the next Lord Provost of Edinburgh.'

'What sort of a man is he, Mistress Nell?'

'A wee dandy, always beautifully dressed.' Mistress Nell pursed her lips.

From that Polly deduced that she did not like the Deacon. However, it was his sister who might be needing a companion. What work she might have to do was not important, anyway. The object of her exercise was to find out quietly what she could about the people here in this town who may concern her. 'And his sister, Mistress Nell?'

'Och, she's no' a bad wee soul! It's just that she has become a little strange lately, and canna keep a maidservant or a companion for longer than a week.'

'Well, I could try.' Polly tried not to sound too eager. 'How do you get there?'

'I'll tak' ye mysel',' Mr Buchanan offered reluctantly when he was told about it. 'We'll give ye a week, and then I'll be up to Brodie's Close to take ye back, wait and see. I'll shut the shop early tonight, at seven. Get yersel' ready by then, lassie, and we'll go.'

At half past six Fraser Graham managed to find the time to call at Covenanter Close, and stood sighing on the doorstep. It was always the same after he'd been away for a day or two. The pressure of business in his law practice built up to such a pitch that he was forced to work all day and well into every night to catch up with it again.

It was a forlorn hope that Lord Braxfield might be at home this early. If he wasn't, Fraser reminded himself that he would have to make a point of seeing him tomorrow morning in Parliament Square, at the meridian at the latest, for he still hadn't reported his findings to him yet.

He rang the bell and waited again. Lady Braxfield was bound to be at home. Above all he must not let it slip to her that he had been as far afield as London looking for a woman on her husband's behalf. The Braxfields were notoriously at odds. She would never believe the woman was a client. At that point the door opened a slit, and the unkempt head of a maidservant poked out.

'Is Lord Braxfield in?' Fraser asked pleasantly.

'Nah,' said the girl and closed the door in his face.

Well, well, Fraser thought, as he turned away and got up into his coach again, surprised that Lord Robbie would tolerate such a person under his roof. Things between him and his wife must be even worse than usual.

He was still thinking about it when he descended into the Grassmarket and drove around once or twice. The dusk was only beginning to fall, and it was too early for all those who frequented the drinking dens and taverns of the town. He might as well go home and catch up on his paper work, and he set the horses to climb up Candlemaker Row.

The clock on St Giles was ringing seven when Margery stood with Polly in the doorway of the shop waiting for Mr Buchanan. Daylight was fading fast, the candles were beginning to glow and a coach was coming up from the Grassmarket. The man inside it shouted to the driver to stop just as Mr Buchanan rushed out, still wearing his greasy apron.

Fraser Graham got down. 'You are going somewhere, ladies? May I be of any assistance?'

'Oh, Mr Fraser, sir!' George Buchanan grasped his arm in his relief. 'I was to take Miss Polly up to the Lawnmarket at seven o'clock, but owing to an oversight an important order for the toon cooncil was missed. I'll ha'e to work late now, to get it ready for tomorrow morning.'

'Of course I'll take her.' Fraser smiled. 'It will be my pleasure. And you, Miss Margery?'

Mistress Nell came out, as distraught as her husband. 'No, Margery must help us, sir. Now remember, Polly, if ye dinna like it, come right back here. Goodbye, dearie.'

Polly hugged Mistress Nell and watched her run back into the shop in a distracted fashion. Then she hugged her friend.

'Oh! Whatever have you got in your cloak pocket, Polly!' Margery exclaimed.

'Thank goodness you reminded me, Margery,' she said, handing over the perfume flask to her friend. 'I should keep this in a safe place. Will you look after it for me?'

'What is it? A doll?'

'Made of glass, so don't drop her. Her name is Poison.'

'*Poison*! Oh, I'll miss you, Polly!'

Fraser Graham handed her into the coach, and she waved back at the Buchanans for as long as she could see them. 'They have been so kind to me, Mr Graham,' she explained to him.

'And now you are leaving them, Miss Buchanan?'

She jumped a little at the sound of her strange new name. 'Yes. I did not feel I could impose on their hospitality for ever. I may have found work, you see, if I succeed in my interview this evening.'

'You did not like me calling you Miss Buchanan just then, did you?'

'How could I dislike Buchanan? It was my father's name,' she invented swiftly, 'and of course the name of dear Uncle George who has been so kind to me here in Edinburgh.'

'Both older men. But perhaps you prefer older gentlemen?' Something in his tone stung her. 'How old?'

'How old are you, Mr Graham?'

'I have never met a lady so direct as you. Twenty-eight. Is that about right?'

'Oh, no,' Polly said, thinking of Uncle Geoffrey. 'Much older than that. I have observed that the older they get the gentler and kinder gentlemen seem to become. The younger they are the more they tease.'

'Oh, dear! But I am heading in the right direction, would you say?'

Polly regarded him out of clear dark eyes. 'It is kind of you to take me in your coach, sir,' she agreed.

'Then, in return, will you call me Fraser? And permit me to call you Polly?'

She glanced up at his lean face. Perhaps she had not known him long enough to permit such familiarity, and he was only trying her out. In the light from the dim streetlamps she saw the lines etched from his nose to the corners of his mouth, and suddenly felt sorry and ashamed of her suspicious thoughts.

Twenty-eight was an age of responsibility, it seemed, with cares and worries. Was he not making himself responsible for her now? He need not have bothered, she thought, in her present state of anxiety as the coach turned left.

'Yes,' she said. 'I like Fraser for a name. It is strong, and it is Scottish. Where are we now?'

Fraser tapped on the side of the coach to make the driver stop. 'I forgot that you do not know Edinburgh. We are in the Royal Mile. It is all one street, but different parts of it have different names. You remember where the Fly came in, down at the bottom at Holyrood Palace? Next it's the Canongate. Further up it changes its name to the High Street; further up still it becomes the Lawnmarket; and right at the top there, where you see the Castle, it is called the Castlehill.'

'I did not understand that exactly until now.'

'When I was a child I was taught that the Royal Mile is like the backbone of a herring, one mile long, and the little closes running down from it on either side are the fine bones. When we turned left at that big church called the Tron Kirk just now, we were entering the Lawnmarket. Where is it in the Lawnmarket that you must go, Polly?'

'To Brodie's Close. To the house of Deacon Brodie.'

'To the house of Deacon Brodie?' Fraser repeated slowly and heavily.

Why was it that the night became a little darker, a little colder, and the noisy bustle of the town seemed to recede into a strange hush?

9

THERE WAS A distinct chill in the atmosphere now, both
outside the coach and within it. Fraser glanced down at
Polly doubtfully. 'Deacon Brodie's house?' he asked again.

'Yes, to Miss Jeanette Brodie,' she said. 'I am to be her
companion – or so I hope.'

'Brodie's Close!' Fraser shouted to the driver, and after that
the silence went on. It continued while the coach rumbled on a
little way, then stopped gently. The driver got down and they
descended the little steps soberly.

'Is there anything wrong?' Polly asked.

'No, nothing.' Fraser smiled immediately, too immediately to
convince her. He had been debating something in his mind, she
was sure of it, before he shook his head like that and answered
her so quickly. 'This is Brodie's Close. Come, through this
opening here.' He bent his head, and she followed him into the
darkness lit only by one faint taper.

When her eyes became accustomed to the gloom she made
out a turnpike staircase. 'Is it up here?'

'This is the stair. But I will come with you to the door, for I
don't suppose you know how to tirl the risp?'

She shook her head as they climbed the spiral staircase. They
were now standing before a massive oak door, remarkable for
its curious and elaborate workmanship. Polly stared at it. It did
not seem to have a bell-pull or a knocker. Then she saw that a

small serrated bar of iron was screwed perpendicularly to the door jamb.

Fraser grasped the ring hanging down from it and pulled it smartly up and down several times. It produced a harsh and grating sound. 'The young bloods come out of the ale-houses at night looking for some sport,' he said, 'and God knows the Royal Mile has plenty of ale-houses. I daresay the MacAllister boys have all had a turn at stealing the knockers and the bells off the doors in their time!'

Polly knew that he was only trying to still her quivering nerves. Then from inside the door they heard the sound of faint movements.

'Someone's coming,' Fraser whispered. 'Prepare yourself. Sometimes Miss Brodie looks a bit strange considering she can't be thirty years old yet, but I am sure she will be very nice.'

They heard the key turning in the lock on the other side, the sound of heavy bolts rattling back, top and bottom, and then at last the door opened to reveal an old woman wearing a white pinafore. She looked questioningly at them both.

'We've come to see Miss Brodie, Mistress Mattie. Would you kindly tell her Fraser Graham is here with a lady to see her?'

'Come in, and I'll see what she says.' Mattie ushered them in and opened the door of a room which made Polly gasp. 'Wait here, if you please.'

She felt dwarfed under the high ceiling of the room. In the fireplace a log fire burned brightly, its flames lighting up the wood panelling of the walls. Tall candles waited in the silver candelabra, one at each end of the mantelpiece, and drew her eyes to the chimney-breast itself where a large picture of the 'Adoration of the Magi' had been painted directly on to the centre panel.

At the two furthest corners of the room behind the projecting chimney-breast she saw the first steps of little staircases spiralling to the floor above. The whole room would have been like a hall, had it not been for the rectangular rosewood table with its matching chairs which occupied so much space.

'Mattie's been with the family for years. She was here in their mother's time – old Mistress Cecil,' Fraser had time to tell her before Mattie's feet came pattering back on the parquet floor which glowed the colour of honey in the soft light of the fire.

'Miss Brodie will see you now,' she said, and led them along a passage. 'She's in here, in the parlour.'

As soon as she set eyes upon Miss Jeanette Brodie Polly knew that here was a sight she was unlikely to forget as long as she lived. A tiny doll-like figure rose up at the entrance, and after a pause during which her eyes inspected Polly from top to toe and then all the way back again, she began to toddle towards them.

She wore a satin brocade ball-gown in a most violent shade of purple, its huge skirt tucked and ruched ornately and so widespread that she must have been wearing panniers to support it. Her overskirt, tucked up at the sides, was of scarlet, although her little slippers peeped out, one bright green and the other blue, from under her swaying skirts.

Ribbon rosettes adorned her sleeves from shoulder to elbow in random colours, and gauze and feathers floated round her neck as she walked. Her hair was piled up over a wire frame, greased and heavily powdered, and in her hand she was carrying a large fan which shed more and more feathers with every step she took.

Polly stared at her, dismayed. Everything the little creature was wearing was much too big for her and much too slack, and the overall effect of her incongruous appearance was more that of a wizened old lady, rather wandered in her wits, than that of a woman not yet thirty years old. It was a pity that her fair colouring was drowned like this. Her wide grey eyes were pretty, and by far her best feature.

'Well, Mr Graham,' she said, 'who is this you have brought to see me?'

'Miss Polly Buchanan,' he said smoothly, 'the niece of Mr George Buchanan. He was coming with her to introduce her to you when he was detained. I happened to be passing by at the time.'

'I see ... and where is it you come from, Miss?'

'London, Miss Brodie.'

'What a very delightful dress! The London fashion, I'm sure! Do turn round and let me look at it. As you can see, I am a great expert on fashion myself.'

Polly suppressed a wild desire to laugh. 'Yes, I can see that,

Miss Brodie,' she managed to say quite soberly, turning round slowly while the tiny hands stroked the blue silk of one of Margery's gowns and made stabs at it, like little fluttering birds.

'Mistress Buchanan thought you might be wanting a lady companion.' Fraser strove manfully to pin her down.

'Yes, yes, I *do* need someone,' she said vaguely. 'There's no one to talk to, you see. The Deacon must attend to his business, so I am left alone a lot.'

'Oh,' Fraser said. 'What exactly would you be requiring her to do?'

'No cooking, of course. Mattie is the cook. But anything else.'

'Anything else?' Fraser looked very disapproving. 'Do you mean housework? Like a maidservant?'

'The maidservant we had left a few weeks ago.'

'Then,' Fraser stood up, 'I'm afraid we have been wasting your time.'

'I'm sorry, Miss Brodie,' Polly said gently when she saw tears in the little lady's eyes. 'I am no use at housework or cooking, you see. But I could help you with your letters and appointments, escort you wherever you wish to go, help you to entertain your guests, read to you and' – she had a sudden inspiration – 'of course, recently from London myself, keep you right about the latest fashions.'

She had struck the right note with that last statement. Miss Brodie looked at her with more enthusiasm when she said it. But she chose to be awkward.

'I can read, you know,' she said almost belligerently, so that Polly knew for certain that she could not.

'Of course, Miss Brodie.'

'I am thinking about whether I shall engage you.'

'You are thinking about engaging a maidservant too?' Fraser asked. 'And what about the wages?'

'Oh, the Deacon sees to all that! I believe he pays Mattie every half-year. The workmen are different, naturally. They have to be paid every week. Most of them are family men, you see, Miss Buchanan.'

'Yes. It is so important to keep down expenses in the home,' Polly agreed, 'and it is so much easier when you keep accounts.'

Miss Brodie's defences crumbled away altogether with that

last remark. 'You know how to do that, too? Well, Mr Graham,' she turned to Fraser, 'Miss Buchanan would come to no harm here, staying with us.'

'Well,' Fraser said doubtfully, his green eyes looking at Polly anxiously, 'perhaps not, providing she was not made into a skivvy.'

'I will see about another maidservant at once.'

'What do you think, Miss Polly?' Fraser asked.

'I think I should be happy here, Mr Graham.'

'When shall I fetch her back, then, Miss Brodie? Tomorrow?'

'Oh no.' Miss Brodie clutched Polly's arm, as if fearing she would disappear. 'I need her now! She can begin now!'

'Of course I can,' Polly said.

'But where are your bags?' Fraser asked.

'I'll run down to Candlemaker Row and pack a few things tomorrow.'

'I'll see you out then, Mr Graham,' Miss Brodie sped to the door and held it open for him, and then almost ran through the dining-hall to the front door. 'I thought he would never go,' she told Polly breathlessly when she fluttered back. 'Now, you must call me Miss Jeanette, and I shall call you Polly. I see you wear no decorations except for that gold chain?'

'It was left to me by my mother. She died recently. That's why I am here, Miss Jeanette.'

The little face crumpled suddenly.

'I have lost my dear Mama too. I know how you must feel, and it is very lonely. I still miss her dreadfully, and then, to make it even worse, two months ago our dear sister Jacobina moved away.' Miss Jeanette tried to control herself. She made a tremendous effort to smile, patting her hair into place with a pathetic little gesture.

'You see, we were always a very close family, Jacobina and I particularly. We were always together either in this house or hers, for she and her husband Matthew Sheriff lived not far away in the Royal Mile before they moved away to the New Town.'

Polly wondered where this New Town was. To judge from Miss Jeanette's despair it must be a hundred miles away.

'So now they are both gone, my mother and my sister,' Miss

Jeanette was sighing now, 'and my brother is out so much about his business. Oh yes! I have been very lonely, very lonely indeed ...' Polly smiled encouragingly, and the little lady brightened. 'But now it will be different, will it not? We shall have so much to talk about, and I shall teach you all I know about the art of dressing. Let me explain the finer points of my attire to you now.'

Surely she did not dress like this every day? To sit alone? But as Miss Jeanette prattled on Polly realized that indeed she must. There was a footfall outside the door, and with a sinking heart she remembered there was still another member of the household to meet tonight. She wondered what she might expect of him.

The door opened and Deacon Brodie stepped into the parlour, dispelling all her misgivings at once. He was dressed immaculately in cream-coloured broadcloth, his black cravat with its gold pin setting off his white frilled shirt to perfection. His fair hair shone silver and his eyes crinkled boyishly at the corners when he smiled at her.

'We have a visitor, Jeanette?'

'Miss Polly Buchanan, Will. Fraser Graham brought her to see me an hour ago, since George Buchanan was detained. George is her uncle. She has lately come from London, and she has agreed to stay as my companion. It was like a bolt from the blue.'

'It must have knocked my sister sideways, this bolt from the blue,' he smiled, 'because she has not told you yet that I am Deacon Brodie, the master of this house and my trade, and a town councillor – but not as grand as all that when you get to know me. You must not be put off by the whitewash of my dress.'

'Oh, Will!' Miss Jeanette protested and turned to Polly, proving that she had not picked up some subtler meaning in the Deacon's words. 'Don't worry about his light clothes, dear. I have them sent out to a washerwoman. But why are you home at this time of day, Will? It is very unusual.'

'It is only for a minute to collect something from my room. I will see you both later, then, for supper?'

Polly saw that his eyes were grey like his sister's, wide-set, but there was a sparkle in them that hers lacked, a merry brilliance infinitely disturbing, and somehow infinitely out of place.

She was still trying to define it two hours later when they went into the dining-hall and sat down, three of them at one end of the long table in the beautiful room. The candles on the mantelpiece had been lit, and more were placed upon the table where they flickered and glowed and softened even Miss Jeanette's garishness.

But she could not define it, any more than she could decide why he had used such a strange word as 'whitewash' to describe his own appearance. She frowned, thinking that surely it implied some sort of cover or disguise? Some sham or form of concealment? False colours, like windows whited so that no one could see through them?

The previous hour had been spent talking to Miss Jeanette, or rather listening to her, on one of the subjects so dear to her heart.

'Our dear sister Jacobina has been married to Matthew Sheriff for some years, you know. Of course, she is a lot older than I am. They are very rich, they have no children, they live in a large house and have many servants. Oh, dear – that reminds me ...' Miss Jeanette rang her bell and after a few moments Mattie appeared at the door.

'Mattie,' Miss Jeanette said, 'this is Miss Polly Buchanan, come to be a companion to me.'

'Oh, yes,' Mattie sighed. 'Another one.'

'Tomorrow we must engage a maidservant, someone to do the cleaning,' Miss Jeanette rushed on. 'Do we know of one?'

'I'm sure I'm pleased to hear it.' Mattie sniffed. 'I'm getting too old to do all the work around here. And no, we do not know of one offhand, but leave it to me to have a girl here by twelve o'clock tomorrow. Now I will go and dish up the dinner.'

The mussel brose was delicious, yet Polly could not eat much of it, and when Mattie brought in the roasted chicken and Deacon Brodie carved it with a flourish, she tasted only a few morsels. It was the same with the lemon syllabub, which as a rule was one of her favourite desserts.

'You will have your meals with us,' Miss Jeanette said. 'Mattie likes to eat alone. There have been a lot of girls trying to fill the post that you have taken up today – all of them quite unsatisfactory – and she says she cannot bear any more of them chattering away while she is having her meals. But you are not eating, Polly!'

'It is only the excitement of the day.' Polly smiled. 'The food is excellent.'

'Dear old Mattie,' Deacon Brodie said. 'She is getting on in years now, but my sister will not part with her. We do not allow her to do anything other than cook nowadays, except to act as Miss Jeanette's personal maid ... when necessary.'

There it was again, not only a downright lie according to Mattie's statement but also some delicate double meaning above Miss Jeanette's head. But it evaporated in the atmosphere all around him of confidence, cheerfulness and great good humour, spiked with an elusive mischief as he laughed and jested his way through the meal.

At the end of it Polly was forced to confess herself uplifted, cheered and very flattered. Outrageous they might be, but the Brodies were kindly with it, and the Deacon himself so very amusing and stimulating. She had never met anyone like him before.

'You must be tired now,' Miss Jeanette said to Polly when he excused himself and left the room. 'You have had a long day, and come into a strange new world compared with London. I will ring for Mattie to bring you your night-candle and show you the way to your room.' She shook her silver bell again and within minutes the old woman was at the door. 'Fetch a night-candle for Polly, just this once. By tomorrow she will know her way around. I am not quite ready to retire myself yet, Mattie. I would like a word with my brother.'

'I'll stop him on the way out, then.'

'We won't need anything else tonight, Mattie dear. Good-night.'

'And Deacon Brodie?' Polly asked when she had departed. 'Does he go to bed at ten o'clock too?'

'Oh, dear me, no. Very rarely, if ever,' Miss Jeanette replied with a sigh. 'Often he has business only starting at this hour. So many places to go, so many people to see, and so many of them tradespeople requiring maintenance or repairs of their premises, which they have not had time to discuss until the day's work is done and the evening meal is over! Sometimes he does not get back home until the early hours. I am so glad you spoke of this, Polly.'

'Yes, Miss Jeanette?'

'Because I could have neglected to warn you, without such a reminder, that you may hear doors opening and closing, foot-steps in the middle of the night, and become frightened. It is nothing more than my brother returning from his night business. I do not even notice it now, myself.'

'Then I shall say good-night, Miss Jeanette,' Polly said when Mattie reappeared with a candlestick in her hand.

'We have not had much chance to talk, dear,' said Miss Jeanette, 'but it will be different tomorrow. That is, if you like it here. You will stay, won't you?'

Polly smiled into the anxious little face. 'Yes, I will stay.'

'I hope you sleep well, then. Good-night, Polly.'

William Brodie came back downstairs to sit with his sister in her parlour, dressed in the dark clothes he always wore for his 'night business'. He brought a bottle of claret with him, poured out two glasses, and sat twirling his own between his fingers, contemplating the wine in it along with this new girl in the house, this Polly. Polly. Funny – but she reminded him of someone. Who?

'What do you want, then?' he asked.

'Do you *have* to go out every night, Will?'

'Oh, it's not all work at nights, you know, Jeannie! Sometimes if I've the time I have a game of cards with three new friends I've made lately.'

'In Clark's Inn, I suppose. Could you not bring them home to play here, Will? We could do with some men around the house.'

Jeanette Brodie thought of all the nights she'd cried herself to sleep since James Leslie had disappeared into the wilds of Aberdeenshire. She had thought he would marry her, and that at last she would know the beauties of a man, and not long afterwards she would have a baby. But it had never happened and now at her age it was almost too late. Oh, if only she could meet some men! Her brother filled up her glass again.

103

'Not these men.' He laughed. 'You'd never give these men house room. Smith, Brown and Ainslie are rough, not your sort at all.'

How did he know who might be her sort? Just about any sort would do now in her desperation. She often discussed the facts of life with her sister Jacobina. She knew that other women had the same strong desires she had, desires that nearly drove her mad. She had heard the young maidservants creeping along the top corridor to her brother's room in the middle of the night, to offer themselves. Sooner or later their bellies would start to swell and she would have to dismiss them.

She knew that most gentlemen wandered away from home at nights – all except for Jacobina's husband Matthew Sheriff, of course. Most gentlemen had tremendous urges it took more than one woman to satisfy. If only one of them would wander into this house ... God knew she dressed herself up enough every day to attract such a man. Any man. Not that she told Jacobina *that*, of course.

Jacobina would be shocked. She always concluded their talks grateful to God that Will seemed to have settled to their father's business. It provided a home for Jeanette and work for Matthew Sheriff, who was an upholsterer, and so she agreed grudgingly that Will must be allowed a little freedom.

'No, it's not that, Will.' Jeanette sighed now. 'You never bring them here because you think I don't know you play for money. But I do. I turn a blind eye to your gambling, and to your fighting-cocks out in the yard.'

'Christ! I hope you don't think that's all I want out of life! A game of cards and a few cockfights? I get sick of work, work, work, Jeanette, all day long, all night long! Drink up, now!'

Jeanette did not believe he worked all night long. She was convinced he consorted with women, but Jacobina would not allow her to voice such an immodest suspicion.

'I don't understand you, Will. Father loved his work. Why can't you? After all, you were the only one of us he educated. He sent you abroad! He gave you everything, even the business in the end.'

'What else, and me the only son? That's the law in Scotland,'

104

he said indignantly. 'Believe me, he wouldn't have if he could have got out of it. He hated me as much as I hated him. Sometimes I wish he had left me a poor man and spent his money on a whore instead! Then I wouldn't be tied to this place and a life of damned respectability.'

'Oh, Will.' Jeanette began to cry, and he poured more wine into her glass. She picked it up and drank, too upset to notice she was doing it.

'It's true,' he said, ramming it home. 'I live for my nights of freedom when I can have fun and sprees and enjoy myself with my friends!'

'Sprees? What kind of sprees?'

'Every kind,' he shouted. 'Every kind of devilment a gentleman can think of!'

'What does that mean? What else besides the gambling and the cock-fighting?'

'Where's the excitement, where's the danger in that, for God's sake? A man must live dangerously now and then up and down the Royal Mile – or die of boredom!'

'It's just as well it's only me you're talking to, Will Brodie. You'd better watch your tongue in front of other folk. If I didn't know better, if I didn't know that our father left you well-off, that kind of talk would make me think you were one of these burglars that everyone speaks about from morning to night.'

'Would it, now, Jeannie?' He laughed uproariously, as if dismissing such a ridiculous suggestion.

An even worse suspicion took its place. 'Oh, Will ... you don't mean ... *women*? Why don't you marry?'

'Marry?' He was beginning to get really angry now. 'Don't be a bloody fool, Jeanette. No man has to marry in Edinburgh. There are plenty of women here just begging for a man's favours without that.' He jumped to his feet impatiently.

'Oh, won't you stay and talk to me? Do you *have* to go out tonight?'

'You know I do! I always do!'

'Don't go angry then, Will. Please.'

'Oh, Jeannie, Jeannie,' he put his arms around his sister, 'I'm not angry. Can you not see that I hate myself and the life I live here? Sometimes I wish I could run away.'

'But you won't, dear brother? You'd never leave me here all alone?'

The tears were running down Jeanette's face now, and William Brodie smiled at her smudged cheeks and her wig all awry without a single pang of conscience. He couldn't have her interfering, and that was all there was to it. He had to have peace of mind, to know that she was safely in her bed every night, out to the world and out of his affairs.

'Not if you behave yourself and keep turning your blind eye, dearie. Now, it's time to send for Mattie. You look as if you're ready for your bed. Take the bottle with you.'

Polly followed Mattie back through the dining-hall again and up one of the little staircases at the rear. The flickering flame of the candle lit up the hand-rail. She marvelled at how it curved with the wall, round and round. No tree trunk ever grew in such a curve, and yet as she slid her fingers along it with every step she could not feel a single joint. The landing was dim, and the dust on it, which she hoped the new maid would banish tomorrow, showed it was disused.

Inside her room Mattie lit more candles from the flame cupped in her hand and then departed with a muttered good-night. In the candlelight the room sprang to life, large and well-furnished with an unusual arched window. She went to sit on the upholstered seat fitted under it and looked down on the scene below.

The view of Edinburgh by night was even more exciting than by day. The streetlamps made yellow pools in the darkness and showed up the chair men still running with the sedans, only now they all had their curtains closed. She dreamed of who might be in them, and where they might be going. The caddies were still hard at it, running errands for people, some with letters in their hands, some carrying pails of water, and all of them watching each other. She had no doubt they all knew each other, and most of Edinburgh's secrets.

To her right the massive shape of the Tolbooth loomed before St Giles's Cathedral. Prisoners were locked up in there. A few ghostly lights wavered within the small barred windows on the ground floor, so there must be a few inside tonight. She shuddered and looked away to the street beneath her window and watched the people passing by. Her attention became drawn to the figure who had darted out on to the pavement directly below.

If he had been dressed in white, she could have sworn it was Deacon Brodie, but this man was all in black, and, besides, his hair was dark, what she could see of it under his tricorne hat. He took a step into the pool of light under a streetlamp, and she saw that it *was* Deacon Brodie, after all.

He seemed to be a man of secrets, a man who would take a long time to get to know. She sat for a few minutes after he melted into the darkness and wondered why he had changed into dark clothes to go out at night to conduct his business, until it dawned on her that she would do exactly the same herself, especially if she did not want other people to know what she was doing.

The bed was cold and she suspected rather damp when she lay down in it, and she could not sleep. A thousand impressions drifted through her mind. It was only four hours ago that she had left Candlemaker Row and the Buchanans, and only three weeks since she had left London and the Hornpipe and a life that seemed a long, long way away now.

Only three weeks! If she hadn't made up her mind to do as her mother wished she would never have known the Buchanan family existed, nor the Brodie family, nor the MacAllisters, nor Fraser Graham, either. But now here she was, by hook and by crook in a strategic position to find out what she wanted to know about Mama's relations, if there were any.

She tossed and turned, for sleep would not come. The Lawnmarket was hushed now, and the silence unnerving. The street noises of a few hours ago had kept her company. This quivering silence was much louder. It pressed in on her, heavy with little rustlings and whisperings she could not quite hear, and perhaps only imagined. She remembered that she was all alone up here; that if the door of her bedchamber were somehow opened, no one would know, and if she screamed out, no one would hear her, and her flesh crawled in the black night.

There was a spate of burglaries in Edinburgh just now. The newspapers were full of it. The burglars could be prowling up and down the Royal Mile at this very minute, or smashing a window to get into somebody's house. She got out of bed and shot the bolt across her door, and afterwards lay shivering and straining her ears far into the night, but there was no sound of tinkling glass, no footsteps creaking up the staircase, no whispered voices, and no hand upon the handle of her door.

She was being silly and fanciful. All the same, a night spent in a graveyard with the dead had held none of the terrors that filled her tonight, with living people all around her. Eventually she grew drowsy, and her last conscious thoughts were for the Deacon. He was not what she had expected him to be at all. She conjured up his neat, slim figure and his handsome looks, and yet felt somehow disappointed. It was just that she had expected him to be more solid, since he was so highly respected; perhaps with a look of severity, or solemnity, under the weight of his many arduous commitments.

She found it hard to reconcile his impression on her with all of that. But still, she thought with a sigh as she turned over and finally went to sleep, she had seen him with her own eyes, so industrious, and so late at night.

10

DEACON BRODIE SLAMMED shut the front door of his house, locked and double-locked it behind him and stood for a moment at the top of the turnpike stair just savouring the darkness. There wasn't a happier man in all Edinburgh than he was at that moment! There wasn't a happier man in Edinburgh every night when the darkness came down and he could put on his black clothes.

He had everyone fooled. Jeanette, Jacobina, most of the shopkeepers of the town, they all believed he was so industrious! They never questioned why he changed his white day suits. They all took it for granted that crawling about in shop premises by lantern light measuring up for repairs and renovations was a dirty job. Of course he would put on dark clothes which wouldn't show the dirt.

So he had them all fooled! The truth was he changed more than his clothes when the darkness came down. He changed his whole character. He was a different man. Now the real adventures could begin and the utter boredom of his days could be forgotten for a few glorious hours.

He was as free as a blackbird, he laughed softly to himself, as he stuffed his bunch of keys into his pocket and felt immensely satisfied to feel the velvet of his mask already there. Ah! Then he had forgotten nothing, if the opportunity to use them arose! He was all set for a night of pleasure, and in Edinburgh there was every kind of pleasure that a gentleman could possibly want.

Like a shadow he flitted down as far as the Canongate and off
it into a maze of filthy back streets, up an unspeakable stair and
so, after a series of raps and tappings previously arranged and
precisely echoed from the other side of the stout pine door, into
the upper room where the Hell-Fire Club was meeting for an
initiation ceremony.

There was nothing he liked better than an initiation ceremony
when some young man set out to convince them of his sexual
prowess, the one condition of membership. Usually it was a
story of fantasy. Only rarely was it true, but so long as it was
even remotely credible and, more importantly, it gave the
members the vicarious thrill they were seeking, that was good
enough.

Tonight there was a full house. Everyone was there, pressed
together along benches at the long trestle tables filling the room.
There were bottles of claret and ale, and whisky jars passed
back and fore amongst the men. The chatter grew louder by the
minute and the laughter heartier as the jokes became more and
more lewd.

Already the large room was filled with smoke, and it was very
hot. Nevertheless, William Brodie lit the first of a bundle of
cheroots he'd managed to slip into his pockets when last in
Sandy Plugg's shop. He was more than interested to see that the
nervous young man about to be initiated that night was none
other than Jocky Robertson, one of his own apprentices, and
Jocky was just finishing the oath, scarcely heard above the
Hell-Fire Club's roaring approval, the clapping of their hands
and the stamping of their feet. It gave Jocky any encouragement
he still needed to embark on his story.

'It was one day last week in the course of my work,' he said,
'that I was fitting airtight drawers for a rich customer who shall
remain nameless, but of course is very much older than his
wife.'

Everyone cheered, William Brodie loudest of all. He loved
stories of old men cuckolded. In some way it gave him a feeling
of revenge for the way his own father had kept him down, and
so short of money that there was no chance of ever getting
married – until, thank God, he had died.

He cast his mind back to a certain establishment which had

required new shelves and airtight drawers for tobacco. He remembered screwing the brass handles on them himself. Until now he had forgotten that Jocky was the lad he had sent to do most of the work of fitting them into Sandy Plugg's shop.

'The wife never left me alone,' Jocky continued. 'She was forever touching me when her husband wasn't looking. In fact, gentlemen, to be plain, she was forever touching me up! My poker was always at attention!'

'The little bastard,' the Deacon muttered under his breath, recalling Wilhemina Plugg's generous curves, and found his own poker was standing to attention, too.

The louder the thumps of approval, the harder Jocky Robertson pressed on, sweating, with his story. 'At last I could ignore her no longer ...'

William Brodie looked across at Sandy Plugg the tobacconist. Everyone else was looking at Sandy Plugg, too, for they all knew who had had drawers recently fitted into his shop. When the cheering erupted he woke up sufficiently to open his mouth and laugh, and after each gulp of whisky his face grew redder and redder until now it was an alarming shade of ruby. Clearly, Sandy was too far gone in drink to have any idea that the story was about his own wife. Sandy was, as usual, as drunk as a lord.

'She inveigled me upstairs,' Jocky said, warming to his theme and very quickly afterwards arriving at its obscene climax. When he did, William Brodie befouled himself and revelled in it.

'Ho! Ho! Ho!' cheered the members at the top table. 'Ay, Jocky, you're in,' they laughed. 'A worthy member o' the Hell-Fire Club.'

It was well after midnight when they all poured out again into the Canongate, reeling about or standing in groups unable to tear themselves away from each other, and any ambitions Deacon Brodie might have had of doing a spot of breaking and entering were soon abandoned. All the same, the night was still young – so now where?

He couldn't go to Ann Grant, wife to him that she was in all but name. For one thing, she would pick up his clothes and brush them and fold them, and then she would see the stain on his breeches, drying out white now. She wouldn't say a word, she would never reproach him, she would only hold out her arms to him, love him and afterwards let him sleep like a baby on her soft white breast.

And in the morning he would have to face their three dear children, look into his favourite daughter's clear innocent eyes and try to explain why he hadn't been to see them for such a long time.

No. He longed for something more *exotic* … which took his thoughts back to Paris and the most exotic woman he had ever known. He had traced Suzanne again, after a long search, and when he was ready he would go to London and fetch her back here to Edinburgh to claim her fortune. By that time she would be his wife and the money would be as good as his. It was his ace in the hole, his last resort, his insurance against a rainy day.

But in the meantime he was still stuck here in Edinburgh, still desperately short of money, and still savagely needing a thoroughly bad woman tonight. His thoughts turned to Jean Watt. Yes, there was always Jean Watt.

He made his way further up the High Street until he came to Libberton's Wynd and unlocked her door.

'Who is it?' she called out from her bed.

'Who were you expecting?' he asked with a frown.

'Ye could have been a burglar!'

'When did burglars have keys? How many keys are there to this house, anyway?'

'Two, and ye ha'e the other one. Ye ken that fine, Will Brodie. And I kent it was you all along. Stop talking! Ye'll wake baith oor bairns! Are ye sober?'

'Of course I'm sober. I wouldn't be much use to you otherwise, would I?'

'Well then, what are ye waitin' for?'

She rolled back the bedclothes with one hand and lifted up her nightgown with the other so that all her dark beauty was exposed, including her rouged nipples. William Brodie swore, tore off his clothes and scrambled down over her. 'Jean Watt, you're a witch, a beautiful witch! Who's your man?'

'Only you, Will! I swear it!'

He woke two hours later when the sky was beginning to turn grey and put on his clothes again. Before he swung his cloak around his shoulders he took two cheroots from the bundle and left them under the pillow. Jean Watt would be quite happy with that. As for her two boys, he mused as he noisily opened the door of his own house, he had never really believed that either of them was his.

Polly didn't know what it was that woke her so early that morning. It could not be five o'clock yet, for it was only the first light of dawn. The sudden barking of dogs, a man shouting and windows flung open told her the town was waking up, anyway, and she lay still for a while and listened to the voices of the early caddies and the chair men calling to each other as they slithered and cursed through the night-rubbish on their way up to the Lawnmarket to meet the Glasgow coach and the carriers from Inverness.

The light was still thin when the scavengers arrived next, trundling their barrows and grumbling at their work. She could hear their shovels grating against the cobbles. This upper part of the Royal Mile was kept respectably clean at least, for it was from here that most travellers and visitors caught their first glimpse of Auld Reekie.

Now she could open her window and let in the fresh air and the sounds floating up from below. Then the whistling and the tramping feet began down in Brodie's Close. She leaned out to watch the cheerful workmen going down to the timber-yard at the far end of it, and soon she could hear their saws in the workshops and smell the sweet clean scent of the sawdust from the wood.

When they had all gone in she went back to bed and lay propped up on her pillows. She was wide awake now, and still the questions of the night before persisted in her tired brain. As the daylight grew stronger she could see the interior of the room more clearly. Her eyes roved from one piece of meticulously crafted furniture to the next, from the huge carved wardrobe, the marble-topped washstand, the bow-fronted chest of drawers, the exquisite writing desk, right round to the dressing table so elegantly glazed, its wood faced with perfectly matched mahogany, its fretwork as delicate as lace.

Her eyes came back to the writing desk, and she frowned. Somehow it seemed quite out of place amongst all the other heavy furniture. It was so dainty.

The spent candle, its grease thickly rivuleted upon its plate, lay on the little cabinet beside her bed, and remembering last night a great sense of loneliness rolled over her once more, and a dejection too much like a foreboding to shake off.

She would never make a good companion to anyone at this rate, she thought, making her gloomy toilet. Not to anyone, and certainly not to Miss Jeanette Brodie, who looked as though she needed more support and bolstering up than that afforded by the hoops and pads and whalebones which held her together at present.

Polly had no clear idea what would be expected of a good companion, anyway, but instead of admitting that she had taken this position on false pretences she tried to imagine what she would expect of such a person herself. Someone who was sparkling clean and bright, to begin with; someone capable who could be relied upon in any situation, even to take charge; someone diplomatic, who would not cause trouble, and most important of all someone who was cheerful, pleasant and calm at all times. It was a tall order, but she was determined to succeed and to allow no one to dislodge her from her fragile foothold in Brodie's Close.

Mattie was there when she got down to the kitchen, and the fire was blazing up. 'Sit in at the table and eat your porridge,' she said. 'I've got the fire going. It's a wee bit nippy in the mornings, even though it's still early August.'

Surprised and cheered by this reception Polly discovered she was really quite hungry after all. The porridge had just the right amount of salt in it, and the milk was as she liked it, fresh and frothy, and ice-cold.

'That was lovely, Mistress Mattie,' she said, getting up.

'Sit still a minute, lassie, and ha'e a tassie o' tea with me so that I can tell ye what ye have to do.'

A *tassie*, Polly thought, as Mattie poured it out. That was directly from the French word for a cup – *une tasse* – and that was something else she would have to guard against. She must never admit to speaking that language. She must cover up her French connection. Nobody must know anything about her. Not yet.

114

'First of all, breakfast,' the cook was saying. 'Ye can have it every day wi' me in here, since ye're no' a lassie to chatter, I'm glad to see. I serve Deacon Brodie – Master Will, as he likes to be called at home – at eight o'clock sharp in the dining-hall,' and after a little pause Mattie added in a voice heavy with meaning, 'no matter when he gets home after his night business.'

'Oh ... and Miss Jeanette?'

'Miss Jeanette never appears before eleven.'

'She doesn't get up until then?'

'That's when I get her up,' said Mattie primly, as though she could have said a great deal more, but thought better of it. 'So ye need be in no hurry.'

'Oh, Mistress Mattie, I'm so glad you were the first one I saw this morning! I feel better already! Would I have time to run down to Candlemaker Row for a few things? It wouldn't take long. I have very little.'

'Ay,' the old woman smiled, 'on ye go, lassie. By the time ye get back I'll ha'e a maidservant here. Her name's Jess and she's too shy to speak, but she's a good worker if I say so mysel'.'

'Oh! You know her already?'

'She's my niece from the country. All ye ha'e to worry about is that ye're ready to call on Miss Jeanette by half past eleven.'

'It's very drab down here, Mistress Mattie.' Polly frowned. 'If they had painted it white it wouldn't have been so dark.'

'God bless ye, lass! All the leftovers of paint from the important rooms upstairs are always put into a large pot, mixed together and used for the servants' quarters! We are used to it. Only the kitchen is painted blue. Master Will says it keeps the flies away. It's something in the blue paint that does it. Poison, I expect.'

'That is a very clever idea, Mistress Mattie.'

'Master Will is a very clever man,' the cook said, and again there was that trace of cynicism in her voice.

'I'd better be off, then,' Polly said. 'This little door – is it a back door to the house?'

'It is that. It's used by the servants and the trades. You'll be going out and in by the front door most of the time, of course. But go this way just noo, and see. Ye'll find a gate, and that leads into the Close.'

Polly sped down the Royal Mile and into Candlemaker Row, reminding herself all the way to look cheerful when she got to the Buchanans' or else they wouldn't let her go back.

'Here, have a couple of nightgowns,' Margery went upstairs with her to raid the trunk again, 'and here's a pretty dress for daytime, grey and white. This is an old green dress I grew too fat for – at least my bosom did! Oh, I wish I could go with you, Polly!'

Polly wasted no time. After assuring Mr Buchanan and Mistress Nell that she would come back again soon, she took her small bundle and ran back to Brodie's Close, entering the house the way she had left, by the back door.

Sure enough, Mattie had the girl Jess there and in harness already. She stood at the deal table in the middle of the room with a lemon skin which she was dipping in salt and silver sand in one hand, and a copper pan she was cleaning in the other. When she looked up her expression was grave and timid, but Polly could see that all her movements were quick and deft.

'This is Miss Polly, Jess,' Mattie said.

The girl only smiled shyly and didn't open her mouth as she returned the pan to the side of the open fire ready for cooking, and then tested the heat of the separately fired ovens for baking which occupied most of the right-hand side of the kitchen. Dust-proof straw baskets filled with hand-picked coal stood beside them.

'I'd better go upstairs with these things, then,' Polly said, and while she shook out the dresses and put them away she found her early morning conversation with the cook had given her plenty to ponder over.

So Deacon Brodie often didn't get home until breakfast time? Mattie seemed to have her own ideas about that. Certainly it did not seem very likely that the 'night business' went on until seven or eight in the morning. What was he doing? Where did he go? And Miss Jeanette ... she retired so early and she slept so late. Why was it that the brother required so little sleep, and his sister so much?

Polly washed her face again and changed into the pearl-grey gown, admiring its frosty white collar and cuffs, and half past eleven was ringing on St Giles when she tapped lightly on the parlour door.

116

'Come in,' said a voice from the bedroom beyond, and as Polly walked through it her nose detected a strange odour, a fusty, fruity smell that she could not identify. The bedroom door opened suddenly.

'She's ready now,' Mattie said.

Polly followed the old servant in through the door to the bedroom. In here the heavy odour was even stronger, with a sharper note, like vinegar. 'Good morning, Miss Jeanette. You are well, I hope?'

'Perfectly well, my dear. It takes me a little time to come to myself in the mornings, that is all. Now that I am, you may make up the bed, Mattie.'

'Na, na, Miss Jeanette,' Mattie said. 'The new maidservant is here. She's the one to make the beds, remember.'

'Oh? What is she like? Fetch her here.'

'This is Jess Aitken.' Mattie came back within minutes with the girl. 'She doesn't say much, Miss Jeanette.'

'Well, that's one good thing, I suppose.' Miss Brodie dismissed Jess with a wave of her hand. 'Try her out for a week then, Mattie.' Then she returned her attention to Polly. 'My mind has been concentrating on gloves today,' she said vaguely.

'Gloves?'

'Yes, it is gloves today. Every day, rain or shine, I make a point of going to the shops and the Luckenbooths on some small errand – as long as the money lasts, that is. Today it is a white ruffled shirt for the Deacon, and gloves to match my new gown.'

'A white ruffled shirt for the Deacon?' Mattie snorted. 'Will Brodie must ha'e twa dozen o' them up in that cupboard o' his! He's no' needin' another white ruffled shirt! Any money ye ha'e would be better spent on a new gown for yersel', Miss Jeannie.'

'Did I show you my latest gown, Polly?' Miss Brodie asked, completely ignoring this outburst.

'No, I don't think you did, Miss Jeanette.'

She would not have believed that Miss Brodie's day gowns could be even more disastrous than her evening gowns, but it seemed they were. The startling effect of their colours in the strong daylight made them seem worse, for today she was attired in brown striped with dashing, clashing shades of red and orange, which only served to emphasize the unbecoming flush on her cheeks. Polly had thought her mistress to be of a sallow complexion, but she was far from sallow this morning.

'How do you like it, dear?'

Well, at least the new gown was all one colour, she saw with dismay. It was a muddy navy-blue, entirely unadorned. 'It will be a useful day-gown when it is trimmed, Miss Jeanette,' she answered as tactfully as she could.

'Oh, what did I tell you? I am never wrong with the fashions!' her new mistress cried happily. 'And the *trimmings*! They are so exciting, are they not? How shall we arrange them?'

'Perhaps it would be a good idea, as you thought, to start with the gloves. A pretty shade of bright blue?'

'That is certainly what I thought myself, dear.'

'Then you must have been reading the article on ladies' fashions in the *Courant* last week, Miss Jeanette. Do you remember what it said about dyeing lace to match?'

There was a warning cough from Mattie, and when Polly looked across at her the old woman was frowning.

'No, I don't believe I did,' Miss Jeanette said off-handedly. 'But yes, we will go out and find some blue gloves to begin with. Are you ready? Will you be warm enough with just that little shawl around your shoulders?' Without waiting for an answer she led the way to the front door where she grasped a long walking-cane, silver-topped and betasselled, from the box of canes which stood in the corner.

'Now let us be off,' she said. 'It is such a lovely day.'

They walked out under the carved stone of the archway to Brodie's Close and into the milling uproar of the Lawnmarket, Miss Jeanette taking up most of the pavement with her wide-hooped skirts and the even wider angle of her walking-cane, scattering oncomers to right and to left.

The people looked at her, openly grinning. It seemed that Miss Jeanette Brodie was not so much a character as a figure of fun, and to Polly's own surprise she began to feel angry and then very protective of her small eccentric mistress. She made up her mind then and there that she would try to make some changes to help her.

'First for the meridian,' Miss Jeanette said, sweeping into one of the coffee-houses which seemed as numerous as the taverns in the Royal Mile.

'That is a custom here, Miss Jeanette? I'm afraid you will find me very ignorant about Edinburgh ways. What is the meridian?'

'Oh, my dear, I shall be happy to teach you! At midday the gentlemen go to the taverns for a "cauld cock and feathers" – that is, a gill of brandy and a bunch of grapes, or perhaps something more substantial. We ladies go to the coffee-houses and drink a cup of coffee. Everyone who is anyone in Edinburgh takes the meridian.'

Polly could not help noticing that Miss Jeanette's coffee had an aroma quite different from her own. She had not needed to order it. It was served at the table as soon as they came in, and brought back vividly the strong smell of drink that had seemed built into the very walls of the Hornpipe.

It was having a very beneficial effect on the lady, anyway, dispersing the mottling in her cheeks and putting a sparkle in her eye. She was alert now, and anxious to be off to the Luckenbooths.

They passed Mr Creech's bookshop on the way, where all the distinguished men of Edinburgh were foregathering as usual, many of them lawyers spilling out of Parliament House in their wigs and gowns. One of them, she saw with a start of surprise, was Fraser Graham, looking severe and businesslike.

'They call these men the "literati", you know,' Miss Jeanette whispered, pointing discreetly. 'Look, there is Adam Smith. Mr Creech is about to publish his book called *The Wealth of Nations* which is supposed to be a very important work. And that old man over there is David Hume who wrote *The History of England*.'

'So they are mostly writers who come here every morning, Miss Jeanette?'

'They have literary breakfasts, so I believe. The people here call them "Creech's Levees". Robert Burns was here a few months ago, so I daresay we will be seeing a new book of poems from him shortly, and then he'll be back.'

Polly listened with one ear. A few yards away just out of earshot Fraser Graham was buttonholing a formidable old man, and whatever he was saying to him was agitating him very much.

*

119

'I thought I would catch you here.' Fraser Graham put out his hand to detain Lord Braxfield in the milling crowd in Parliament Square. 'There has not been the time to come and report my findings in London until now.'

'Get on wi' it, then, laddie! Henry Erskine's over there talking to Iley Smith, and I'm needing a word wi' them both.'

'There was no Suzanne Gray at the Hornpipe Inn. In fact, there was no Hornpipe Inn. It had burned down a few days before I got there.'

'What?' Lord Braxfield turned pale. 'Were there any survivors?'

'They found two bodies. They believed one to be that of a Kate Tarre, the landlady, and the other that of a Tom Brewser, the cellar-man. Some people I spoke to said they were a married couple.'

'Was there no word of Suzanne Gray at all, man?'

'There was a Madame Suzanne who used to sing there. They called her the Songbird of the South. It seemed she disappeared before the inn burned down. Then one old woman gave me a clue which led to Paris, where I was going anyway.'

'Paris? Good God!'

'Eventually I tracked down the apartment that Madame Suzanne had lived in, but the only people in it were a coloured man and a coloured woman.'

Lord Braxfield looked more and more horrified as the tale unwound. 'Who were they?'

'Caramelle and Chocolat.'

'Caramelle and Chocolat? What sort of names are those, for Christ's sake?'

'They give themselves fancy names in the brothels of Paris, Robbie. However, money is the language everyone understands – it loosened the woman's tongue. She spoke very good English. The man was too terrified from start to finish to open his mouth.'

Lord Braxfield turned back into Parliament House, Henry Erskine and Iley Smith forgotten. 'Come inside and tell me the whole story again,' he groaned.

'The woman Caramelle said she had been a maidservant to Madame Suzanne – before she left in a hurry, after some scandal.'

'What impression did ye get, Fraser? D'ye think this Madame Suzanne is still living?'

'I got the impression that those two think she is, although they don't know where. Now, sir, to change the subject, and since I have this chance to speak to you alone at last, why has the Candacraig estate not been settled?'

'Erskine Caldwell canna find a will.'

'Perhaps she never made one. In that case it will come to me.'

'What makes ye think that, laddie? She spoke to me about making her will! And she had relatives on her own side, ye ken.'

'She would never have left *them* so much as a kind look!'

'Weel, weel, we'll ha'e to give it more time, Fraser, and see what turns up,' Lord Braxfield said sadly.

As Fraser left the room he looked back and saw that the judge's head was sunk in his hands.

Lord Braxfield was in the deepest despair. It was a long time before he looked up again. 'Oh, Susanna.' He sighed aloud. 'What are we going to do now?'

11

MISS BRODIE GUIDED Polly round every single stall in the Luckenbooths. She marched up and down the lanes between them examining all the goods, and it soon became obvious that it was such a pastime of hers that she noticed any tiny change from the day before.

Fraser Graham came out of Lord Braxfield's rooms and stood watching them for a minute before he casually wended his way towards them.

'Here is the stall I want you to see, Polly,' Miss Brodie was saying. 'Look at all the gloves! Leather and lace, and even silk!' Eagerly she picked out a pair, paid for them, and handed them over to Polly for inspection as they walked away.

'But you wanted blue, Miss Jeanette, and one is green and the other grey. It is an odd pair, and you have not waited for your change, either.'

'Oh. Does it matter, dear?'

'Yes, of course it matters.'

'Well, go back and see to it for me. I will go on down to Mr McCreadie's shop in the High Street to look out a shirt for my brother. Being a deacon is very important, you know. He must look the part.'

Miss Brodie darted off and Polly was left with the gloves in her hand, wondering what that last remark meant. 'He must look the part.' So many of the Brodies' remarks reminded her uncomfortably of a masquerade, somehow. She made her way back to the glove stall.

'Well?' demanded the woman in charge, when Polly showed her the odd pair and reminded her of the change. 'What of it? She wouldn't know the difference anyway! She can't see the colours, and she can't read the prices.'

So that was it. Everyone knew this, and was quite blatantly taking advantage of her. How much was Mr McCreadie cheating her out of at this very moment for the Deacon's shirt?

'Perhaps she cannot,' Polly replied, looking at the stall-holder with flashing black eyes, 'but I can.'

The woman sniffed, preparing to be awkward.

'And so can I,' said a man's voice behind Polly's back. 'I can count, Molly Simpson, and I have been watching the whole performance. What are you going to do about that?'

'Oh, Mr Graham, sir,' the woman said. 'I did not see you.'

'No?' He smiled grimly.

'No, sir, and I did not see Miss Brodie's change until now! It must have slipped down here.' She grovelled in her box under the counter. 'It was blue gloves, wasn't it?'

'You will kindly permit Miss Buchanan to choose the gloves she requires.'

'Please do, miss. And if you will forget my mistake, I will forget the price – seeing as it's you, sir.'

Polly selected a pair of blue gloves and he held out his hand contemptuously. 'Just give me the correct change, Molly Simpson, and you will not tell me what I must forget. I will forget nothing, least of all that this stall is banned in future for the ladies of my family and close acquaintance. There are plenty of other glove stalls for them to go to.'

Still angry he marched Polly away, leaving Mistress Simpson shrilly protesting her innocence behind them. Polly was just as angry, and not only with Molly Simpson. She snatched her arm out of Fraser's.

'I could have dealt with that woman myself, you know, Mr Graham.'

'Fraser, we decided. Oh, I daresay you could, at that. Anyone watching the way you were tossing that red hair of yours could see that! And anyone unlucky enough to receive a glare from two such angry black eyes could see it, too! But then Molly Simpson knows me, and until this morning she didn't know you.'

All the time he was speaking he was wondering uncomfortably who it was she had reminded him of so strongly at that market stall. There was something in the set of her jaw when she was angry, there was something in the way her strong eyebrows came down in a frown over those eyes ... The strange thing was, it was not a woman. Miss Polly Buchanan had many of the characteristics of some man of his acquaintance.

'Then I suppose I should be grateful to you,' Polly said coldly.

She wasn't grateful at all, he could see that. Well, she would have to be taught some lessons for her own protection if she was going to live in Edinburgh. She was too young to be on her own. 'Why isn't somebody here with you?' he demanded sternly.

'Oh, I am not alone. Miss Brodie is not far away. She went on to Mr McCreadie's shop.'

'Then you will permit me to escort you to her there.' He put his hand under her arm. 'You should not be out here alone. Do you understand me? Ladies do not go abroad alone, ever, in Edinburgh. Not even in daylight.' Her heart sank. His expression had not changed since they left the stall in the Luckenbooths. It remained cold and uncompromising.

'It could have been some ruffian standing behind you at the Luckenbooths. As it was, that woman in the glove stall had no intention of giving you or Miss Brodie any money back. Edinburgh is just another city like London, although perhaps not so big, and you must know by this time that there are all kinds of wickedness there.'

Indeed, some he had never even dreamed of, Polly reflected. 'I must learn to stand on my own feet here, as I did there, but it is very kind of you to go to all this bother.' She sighed as they progressed down the High Street almost to John Knox's House.

'What's the matter?'

'There is nothing wrong. The Brodies are a little strange, that's all.'

'You should not be working for them. George Buchanan has told me he did his best to persuade you to stay in Candlemaker Row, and I had no idea that Brodie's Close was our destination when I took you in my coach, or else we should not have set out.'

'You're all making too much of it, I am sure. The Brodies seem quite amusing people to me so far.'

Then Miss Jeanette appeared in the narrow doorway of Mr McCreadie's shop in extreme difficulties. She could not bend her hoops and hold her parcel and her cane at the same time, and when the cane clattered to the street Fraser sized up the situation at a glance. 'Allow me to take charge of your parcel, madam,' he said, picking up the cane while Polly rushed to help her with her skirts.

'Oh, thank you, sir. Polly, dear, what is the answer to this?'

'We must have lighter, narrower hoops put in your dresses, Miss Jeanette. These are far too big for you.'

'And you, Mr Graham? You must have thought I was my dear Mama when you called me madam. You may call me Miss Jeanette.'

'I beg your pardon,' he said gently, 'but, you see, it was your cane which confused me. It is the older ladies who generally walk with them, is it not? Of course I see now it is you, Miss Jeanette, as young and as pretty as ever. Shall I carry it up to the Lawnmarket for you, and escort both of you home again?'

Somehow, Polly did not think Miss Jeanette would be taking her walking-cane out again, and for that she heaved a sigh of relief.

'I believe Mistress Scott is to have tea with you, not this Saturday afternoon but next, Miss Jeanette?' Fraser asked.

'Such a very nice lady!' she fluttered. 'But how could you know, sir?'

'I have known the Scotts for years. Mistress Margaret asked me if I would escort her to your house. Neither young Walter Scott nor his father will be available on that date.'

'When you do, you must come in with her.' Miss Jeanette glowed up at him.

'I have sent for the two dressmakers, Polly,' Miss Jeanette said a day or two later when Mattie was screwing up her hair under her wig, 'with a message to bring narrower hoops. Much narrower.'

'I am sure they will suit you much better, Miss Jeanette.'

'I have been thinking about what your friend Mr Graham said, and he is quite right. I have been living and dressing too much in the old style, the style of my Mama.'

'Yes?'

'And I have been taking special notice lately when we have been out. The ladies are not wearing their hair so high, nor have I seen it powdered.'

'No,' Polly answered warily. She had a feeling that here was thin ice. All this was of supreme importance to Miss Jeanette. 'But is that because of the powder tax, perhaps?'

'Perhaps. Anyway, I have been thinking it is time for a change, but I am afraid I cannot make the change myself.'

'Is there any way that I can help you?'

'You were speaking the other day about the fashions reported in the news-sheets.' Miss Jeanette looked away as her colour heightened. 'There must be dozens of news-sheets from the weeks gone by in this house. Of course, it would be no use to go back any further than three months, would it?'

'Then you would like me or Mattie to look them out?'

'No, Polly. You see, Mattie cannot read the dates on them, can you, Mattie?'

Mattie shook her head.

'Perhaps if you could go through them yourself, dear? I just feel there is some urgency. I do not think any one of my gowns is quite right.'

Polly could hardly believe her ears. Miss Jeanette had from the first been proud of her fashion sense. Then there *was* something else on her mind, and it was worrying her to distraction. That must be why she was forcing herself to concentrate all her energy on her gowns by day and, Polly was quite sure now, drinking herself to sleep by night.

'Read out some of the ideas to me, Polly,' Miss Jeanette said. 'You will stay with me when the dressmakers arrive, will you not?'

'Of course I will, Miss Jeanette.'

Polly read the fashion columns out to her and she drank them in like a parched garden when the rain finally came, the ideas in them evidently brand new to her.

127

Half an hour later it did not take the seamstresses long to realize that their days of palming off just anything on Miss Brodie were numbered. As Polly had expected, they stood rooted to the spot at the sight of the garments piled up on the bed. They were sisters, she judged from their faces, and she didn't like the look of either of them.

'You are going somewhere? You require another gown?' the older one asked when she recovered herself.

'No. Miss Brodie feels there is something wrong with every gown you see there,' Polly said quietly. 'I know it, you must have known it, and now she knows it too. She has difficulty with colours, and naturally that has made it even more difficult to interpret the latest fashions from the news-sheets. It is a pity that you did not realise that too, and discuss them with her at the time.'

'Oh, but we knew she could not ...' The younger sister stopped short upon a warning look from the other.

'Well, we must try to put these gowns right,' Polly said, 'and since you knowingly made such expensive blunders, of course it is your responsibility to put them right free of charge. We would not like the Brodie family's influential friends to know about this, would we? It could do your business so much harm.'

She kept very calm while she delivered these criticisms in a firm but pleasant tone, and her gaze did not waver.

The older woman shuffled her feet uneasily, still scowling. 'I don't know,' she said.

'The workmanship is good.' Polly held up one of the offending dresses. 'Would it not be possible to take the gowns with the prettiest materials, unpick them altogether and then make others in the modern fashion, all in one colour?'

The sisters exchanged looks.

'Well, there would be plenty of material,' the older one said slowly.

'How pretty this cream satin could be!' Polly hoped her job of gentle persuasion was nearly over. 'Imagine it beaded with pearls from that dark green!'

'We could manage to do something with most of them.' The younger sister was becoming infected with Polly's enthusiasm.

'Could you really, Miss Gray?' Miss Jeanette asked

anxiously. 'In time for the outings and balls of the coming season?'

Miss Gray!

'And, of course, put in even smaller hoops than those you have brought?' Polly put in.

'We will be back on Friday with at least one remodelled,' they promised when Polly ushered them to the front door.

'I'm sorry I did not know your name is Gray until I heard Miss Jeanette saying so,' she said conversationally.

'Oh yes. Constance and Patience Gray. Unusual for Edinburgh, but then you see our father was an English sea-captain,' the older sister told her a little loftily.

'Are there many Grays in Edinburgh?'

'None, spelled G-R-A-Y, like our name. The rest are the Scottish name, spelt with an E. Why?'

'No reason. I thought it was a nice name, that was all.'

To Polly's relief the women went away smiling. The outcome of that afternoon's work could have been very different.

'How old do you think I am, dear?' Miss Jeanette asked her when Polly returned to the sitting-room.

'Not old at all, Miss Jeanette. You must be the baby of the family, perhaps not much older than I am myself.'

'Now then, you must not flatter me.' She smiled sadly. 'But it is true I am not yet thirty ... I always wanted to look older than I really was.'

'Why?' Polly asked, wondering if the truth might be coming out at last.

'To be like Mama. She was so kind, and yet so strict, you know. She would not have allowed any recklessness or loose talk or wild ideas! Of course it is in the nature of men – my brother,' she stumbled, '– a little gambling, a little gaming! She said we women must expect such things. Yes, Polly, this was a happy home as long as my dear Mama was alive. Is that not so, Mattie?'

What was she trying to say? Was she referring to the Deacon, one of the most respected men of the town?

'But I am not made of the same stuff as she was, my dear, so there is no use in trying to take her place any longer. I have *tried*, God knows I have tried, but Will, my brother ... Oh, pay no attention to my ramblings! The point is, I wish to be myself again, and to look my own age. I have a life to lead, too. Do you agree with me, Polly?'

'With all my heart. We could start by washing your hair to get all the powder out of it, Miss Jeanette. Then it must be brushed until it is dry so that it shines again – but Mistress Mattie is the expert with hair,' Polly said carefully.

'I should be,' Mattie sniffed on the way out to get hot water, but Polly saw that she was pleased. 'I've been doing it since she was a bairn.'

It took most of the day and endless basins of hot water to wash the grease and the powder out of her mistress's hair, but when Mattie brushed it dry and tied it back with a ribbon Miss Brodie looked ten years younger already and even got up early on Wednesday to go out for the meridian.

By seven o'clock on Friday evening Miss Jeanette's excitement had transmitted itself to the whole household. It ran like tongues of quickfire through the corridors and passages and stayed to quiver in the air. The first of her new gowns had arrived, and the evening meal that night must be special so that she could show herself off to her brother.

Polly dressed in Margery's pale green gown, with rose-pink velvet ribbons slotted in and out of the ruffles about the neck and elbows for the occasion. As soon as she put it on she had an uncomfortable feeling that perhaps it was a little too low-cut for her. Margery had been right; it *did* display too much bosom, but even if she had possessed anything else to change into it was too late to do anything about it now.

William Brodie was waiting in front of the log fire when she went downstairs. When she entered he stood up in his coat and trousers of light grey, the coat lined with white silk, and his cuffs and ruffles of cream-coloured lace. His eyes glittered when he saw her.

'A glass of wine, my dear?'

'I have never tasted wine, sir. I am used to lemonade.'

'A small glass of this will do you no more harm than lemonade. And call me Will, please. Sir and Deacon are terms for outsiders.'

'I shall call you Master Will, I think.'

The wine had a pleasant, fruity taste. After she swallowed it the fumes rose to her head to give her a strange, happy sensation, one almost of unreality, and it was at that heady moment that Miss Jeanette chose to make her entrance.

The door of her sitting-room opened noisily, and they heard her pattering along the passage. She, too, seemed part of the unreality when she stood for a moment framed in the doorway, so dainty, so young and so changed.

Polly glanced at the Deacon, but instead of the admiration she expected to see his face registered amazement, disbelief and a shocked dismay all at the same time.

The seamstresses had taken the cream-coloured gown to pieces, trimmed it with seed pearls and made it up again. The pearls nestled in tiny rosettes of lace so that they resembled dewdrops on pale roses and the whole effect was pure, feminine and very charming.

'Oh, Miss Jeanette!' Polly said. 'How very pretty you look!'

'Thank you, dear. Do you like it, Will?'

But Deacon Brodie's face was sweating, and his voice was like a whiplash when he spoke. 'These dressmaking bills will be the ruination of me! How much did *that* cost? Where is the money to come from? Tell me that! Where is the money to come from?'

His last words were delivered in a mixture of a shout and a despairing scream, and it trembled through the room. Polly, shocked and horrified, saw that Miss Jeanette might crumple to the floor.

'It did not cost a penny,' she said swiftly. 'The dressmakers are having to alter all her gowns because of the terrible mistakes they have made with them, and since the fault was theirs Miss Jeanette will not have to pay any more.'

'Oh, well ... Well then, Jeannie, that's a different story,' he said, wiping his face with his handkerchief. 'It is delightful. Whose idea was all this?'

'It was Polly's.' Miss Brodie quivered. Her face was still very white. 'She carried it out. I am sure I could not have had the courage.'

'She has brains, then, as well as beauty.' The Deacon was trying desperately to recover the ground he had lost. 'I must say, it makes you look years younger.'

But as they sat down to dine Polly felt a shiver of unease. It was the thought of the money spent which had enraged him, and yet he appeared to be so rich. He dressed like a dandy himself. 'The Little Macaroni' was his nickname, as she had learned after joining his household.

If he had made a mistake, he was determined to erase it from their minds. He was laughing, gently teasing his sister now, and she was happy again, dimpling up at him, so very relieved.

Polly had to remind herself that only a few minutes ago he had been white-faced, shaking with anger, on the verge of violence. She concluded that she did not know him any better now than she had a week ago.

Then he was joking and flirting with them both and enjoying himself enormously. His mood was so infectious that Polly's doubts evaporated like bad dreams, and she did not know if the exhilarating feelings she was experiencing sprang from the wine or from the daring compliments he was paying her, for as soon as he smoothed his sister's hurt feelings he turned to her young companion in the pale green gown with that wickedly low neckline. He could not keep his eyes off it, or her.

Polly confined her gaze to the Deacon's hands which were occupied so skilfully with the carving knife and fork. They were strong, with short black hairs on the backs of them, and the fragile cream lace at his wrists only made them seem stronger and more masculine.

Mattie was in attendance as usual. She took the plates from him, serving the first to Miss Jeanette and the next one to Polly. Then the Deacon helped himself to some mutton, and poured more wine into his own glass and his sister's.

'The mutton is very tender,' he directed his remark and his smile at Polly, 'and we have hearty appetites in this house. Even with your slender waist, my dear, I am sure you have a healthy appetite, too?'

The sly mischief in his voice alerted her. He was not referring to food. She decided to ignore it.

'So far as I am aware, it is average, sir, although the Buchanans complain a good deal about it.'

'But then, perhaps your palate has not yet been stimulated?'

132

His meaning was as plain as his fascination with her neckline. Polly shivered again, and tried to shrink a little inside her gown. 'We must see what we can do about *that*.'

Mattie removed the oval plates in stony silence, Polly's hardly touched. There was something in the air, something that made it impossible for her to eat.

'And now for the spiced peaches, my favourite dessert,' Deacon Brodie smiled, as Mattie set down Polly's plate before her with the very tiniest thump.

'A peach for a peach!' He laughed easily into her eyes.

The candle flames bent sideways in the wake of Mattie's agitated scurry around the table. As they guttered momentarily and cast pools of darkness before they straightened up again to burn brighter than before, Polly saw Deacon Brodie's eyes glowing, an imp dancing in each one.

They found a response in her at last. He was so droll and amusing, Deacon Brodie with his teasing! In spite of herself Polly laughed and sparkled, able finally to give as good as she got.

After Mattie came to take Miss Jeanette to bed, Polly could have sat there all night listening to his silver tongue. At first she was on her guard, reminding herself that that same silver tongue could fork like a snake's and hiss out venom. But he had such a way with words, such a way of telling a tale, that gradually she became fascinated, and before long she was listening to the story of his life.

He had never wanted to be a cabinet-maker, but his father had forced him to follow in his footsteps. All he had ever wanted to do was go to sea and visit other lands. Instead, his life faded into a dismal twilight, shackled to a carpenter's bench.

It was the coming of the Theatre Royal in Shakespeare Square at the other end of the newly built North Bridge almost twenty years later which had made his life worth living again – especially when *The Beggar's Opera* was performed. 'Do you know it, Polly?'

She shook her head.

'It's the story of another Polly,' he laughed, 'Polly Peachum, a girl of the London underworld, and Macheath the arch-criminal, in a wonderful topsy-turvy world where every value is reversed, every man has his price – every woman too – and prisons and all authority are for escaping from. Oh, the excitement! Oh, the contrast to humdrum Edinburgh where you are too well known and too little appreciated!' He sang a snatch from it, gazing into her eyes all the while. 'Oh, it is magic, the purest magic, is it not, Polly?'

She was so captivated by his pleasant baritone, his charm, his humour and his warmth – if a little doubtful of the message behind John Gay's sprightly words – that she was forced to agree, and it came as a douche of icy water over her when Mattie reappeared with her night candle and stood stubbornly waiting to escort her upstairs.

The Deacon laughed lightly. 'I would be leaving you soon, anyway, for it is nearly time for my night business to begin.'

It was not so much that he was leaving, although that was disappointment enough, as it was the hot, elated glow in his eyes when he said it which disturbed her so much. It was not the look of a man going soberly to work. It was more the look of a man who was going out to some illicit but infinitely pleasurable rendezvous. With whom, she wondered, when she heard him slipping out of the house.

While he waited in Clark's Tavern for some unsuspecting strangers who liked a game or two, William Brodie drank a few pints and fingered the handmade dice in his pocket. He was short of money again.

An hour later at the height of the gambling when he saw that his companions were becoming quite merry, he surreptitiously changed the dice. Shortly afterwards he was on a winning streak and the whole atmosphere at the table changed. He soon found out that the men he was playing with were not the out-of-town country bumpkins he had taken them for at first. Silence fell in the tavern when one of the farmers got up angrily, scraping back his stool on the stone floor. A minute later he had William Brodie pinned in the corner and the other two farmers were searching his pockets. There was a howl of anger when the genuine, unloaded dice was found.

'I did not put it there! Someone else did! One of you!' William Brodie yelled.

One of the men punched him on the chin, and while he was still reeling from that another took up the stool he had been sitting on and struck him a blow to the side of his head. He lay there, poleaxed, and immediately a brawl broke out around him. It seemed that every man there had a grudge against his neighbour. When he came to, William Brodie crawled unnoticed out on to the street, staggered to his house and somehow opened the front door.

Polly heard the crash from upstairs, then silence, then the sounds that came so shockingly out of the silence, the screams and wild sobbings. They went on and on, punctuated by a woman's terrified voice. She had her dressing-robe on, the bolts shot back and her door open all in one movement, and arrived down in the dining-hall at the same time as Mattie.

'What is it? What is it?' she cried, when a terrible sight met their shocked eyes. Miss Jeanette was bending over her brother, who was lying just inside the door on the honey-coloured floorboards in a pool of blood.

12

'HE'S DEAD!' MISS Jeanette sobbed wildly. 'Look at his face!'
Mattie lifted her hysterical mistress off the body of her
brother and bent over him herself. The Deacon was still
breathing, but unconscious, his face hideously grey, and blood
poured out of a deep gash under his right eye and dripped off
his chin to soak his cravat and his waistcoat.

'Dead drunk, ye mean,' she said wearily. 'Polly, help Miss
Jeanette back to her bed while I get cold water and soft linen to
clean the wound.'

Polly helped Miss Jeanette back to her bedchamber and when
she returned she took the basin and the cloths from Mattie's
shaking hands.

'I am getting too old for this, Polly,' the elderly woman said.
'*He's* not going to come to, tonight. We'd better put him to
bed.'

'We will never be able to carry him upstairs, Mattie!'

'I usually have to drag him. He's always too drunk to feel a
thing, anyway. But this time I must undress him first. His
clothes are in a terrible state.'

The stench in the room, in spite of its high airy ceiling, was
indescribable. The Deacon's clothes were covered with slime
and purpling stains and something even more unspeakable than
all of that.

They took off his top clothes and Mattie flung them in a heap.
'We will burn the lot,' she said. 'Nobody can be expected to

wash the likes of that. Now, go upstairs to his room and get him some fresh underclothes. It's up the other stair from yours and the first door on your right. Dinna worry, lassie. I've dressed and undressed him since he was a boy.'

Daylight was flooding in now through the twin skylights in the roof and Deacon Brodie's bedchamber was illuminated. Polly paused uncertainly on the doorstep and gazed around at this large room which was filled with the finest furniture she had ever seen.

Here was the space to display it. She saw bookcases filled with gold-tooled leather books, wardrobes inlaid with mother-of-pearl, and rich brocades such as she never knew existed.

She opened drawer after drawer, all cedar-lined, all piled with the finest linen laid over with tissue paper, and could not bring herself to disturb any of it. Then she discovered a nightshirt tucked away under the pillows of the massive four-poster bed and was retreating with it when her eye fell on something so completely foreign in a room furnished to such a degree that she was halted in her tracks. It was an old cash register, big and black and ugly. What was it doing there?

Down in the dining-hall the evil smell had nearly gone now that Mattie had removed the Deacon's foul garments. Quickly and expertly she pulled the nightshirt over him.

'How is the wound now?' Polly asked.

'Stopped bleeding. Let's try and get him up the stair.'

Cautiously they raised him to a sitting position and put his arms around their necks to drag him upright. He was surprisingly heavy for so small a man. Step by step they heaved him up the staircase, his feet dangling and his head lolling until they reached the four-poster bed and together they lifted him on to it, dead to the world.

'Why does he have that old cash register up here, Mistress Mattie?' Polly whispered.

'I don't know. Perhaps for a keepsake. It was his father's.'

'How does it work?'

Mattie touched one of the buttons. A great deep drawer flew open and Polly thought that if the register had been a keepsake, a relic of great sentimental value, then it had been cruelly desecrated, for now instead of coins it held diamond rings, plain gold rings, seals, brooches, crosses, earrings, buckles and even silver teaspoons, all cleverly hidden away as a thief might hide them.

Mattie drew in a deep breath and her face went very pale. 'We had better go to bed ourselves now, lassie,' was all she said.

Polly went to bed, her face as pale as Mattie's. What was happening to her? Were her feet to be forever bogged down in a morass of the sin and corruption of other people? In a perfect mire of drink and vice and filth? For there was no doubt that Deacon Brodie – the respectable Deacon Brodie – had been fighting drunk that night in some hell-hole of the town. And there was every likelihood that those were stolen goods he had up there in his cash register.

The following Saturday Mistress Scott arrived promptly at four o'clock, escorted by Fraser Graham. After not seeing him for a whole week and more, once again Polly was struck by his resemblance to Geoffrey Fotheringham both in looks and size. She saw at a glance that he was not in his usual gentle-serious mood. Today his smile was maddening, and before she managed to free her hand from his firm grasp Deacon Brodie came into the sitting-room like a merry March wind, dry and cool and sweeping all before him.

'So it is our little companion you have come to see!' His eyes took in the scene. 'She is an inspiration, is she not, Mistress Scott?'

Mistress Scott inclined her head graciously, but there was a tiny frown between her eyebrows. Polly did not dare to glance at Fraser Graham, who had squeezed his large frame into one of the dainty silk tapestry settees. She thought in his present mood he would be enjoying this.

'Yes, we are very happy to have Polly here,' Miss Jeanette agreed, 'and so glad you have come to see us. You must forgive my brother. He does *so* love to tease.'

'How is it that ladies can contrive to look ten years younger each time we see them, while we just grow older, Deacon?' Fraser smiled at Miss Jeanette.

'Ladies were deceivers ever, Mr Graham.'

'Yes, I am amazed at how well you look, Jeanette.' Mistress Scott swept into action with the air of a woman determined to keep the party polite, before he had a chance to quote anything else.

'A few little changes,' Miss Jeanette said airily while she dispensed the tea and Polly went round with the shortbread. 'We must move with the times.'

'Indeed,' Deacon Brodie put in, 'and they are wicked, wicked times, are they not?'

Mistress Scott took his words at face value and launched into her favourite topic, the disgrace and the shocking decadence of the day. Miss Jeanette and Polly sat a little more upright, nodding their heads sadly as she gave vent to her feelings.

'Mark my words,' Mistress Scott finished, 'it is not over yet, not by a long chalk! We are due for another of these scandalous burglaries any minute now! And, in fact, if I didn't disapprove so much of my son Walter's fantasies, I would be inclined to agree with him, that there is a master mind behind each and every one of them!'

The Deacon choked suddenly, and coughed and laughed at the same time.

'Please excuse me,' he begged breathlessly, wiping his eyes with his fine lace-edged handkerchief.

'Something gone down the wrong way?' Fraser asked sardonically.

'You have not caught a cold, have you, Will?' Miss Jeanette looked at him anxiously.

'No, my dear. But I must ask you all to excuse me now. Business is pressing.'

'Must you go, Will?'

'Yes, Jeannie. The town council will not wait.'

'And what can possibly be on the agenda today, Deacon?' Fraser asked. 'On a Saturday?'

'As a matter of fact it is a little invention of my own, to be considered urgently at an extraordinary meeting,' he admitted modestly, 'but too indelicate to mention at an afternoon tea-party.'

'Nonsense!' Mistress Scott was as forthright as usual. 'It must be terribly important. Tell us.'

'Then, much as it grieves me to mention such a thing, it is the new gallows, madam, with a trap on the floor, so that the terrible and ultimate penalty our criminals must pay may be a more swift, a more certain and a more humane affair.'

An eerie silence fell on the sitting-room. Polly did not dare look up. The subject was one which haunted everyone day and night, all week long. On Sundays the ministers constantly thundered from the pulpits reminders of the wages of sin, as she had found out every time the Buchanans or the Brodies took her with them to the church. It seemed to be their favourite theme.

Mistress Scott was the first to break the silence. 'You're a good man, Deacon Brodie,' she said soberly. 'Edinburgh has long been fortunate in its town council, the good men chosen to look after our interests. But that was one aspect of crime which I must admit I had not thought deeply enough about, to have the proper compassion for the wrong-doers.'

Deacon Brodie bowed over Mistress Scott's hand and departed, still smiling.

'Oh dear, I wish he could have stayed long enough to hear the real purpose of our call,' she said when the parlour door closed behind him, 'but, naturally, he is included in the invitation to join my little party at the Theatre Royal on the twenty-second of next month, Jeanette. So is Polly, of course.'

It was so unexpected that Miss Jeanette sat with her mouth open. Polly could scarcely believe her ears. That Mistress Scott should even contemplate such a den of iniquity as the theatre! The kirk condemned it bitterly.

'As you will know I am a Christian woman,' Mistress Scott went on, 'but it does not follow from that that I agree with every opinion our ministers of the Gospel try to impose on us.'

'Hear, hear,' Fraser agreed.

'The best and most famous actress of our land, Mrs Sarah Siddons herself, is coming to Edinburgh to perform *Venice Preserv'd* by Thomas Otway! The whole of Edinburgh will come to a standstill when she arrives!'

'Oh, how wonderful!' Polly could not help exclaiming with her eyes shining.

'The twenty-second of September, did you say?' Miss Jeanette took up her engagement book from the table at her side and flicked through its blank pages. 'Yes,' she said at last, 'I believe we could manage the twenty-second,' and made a great show of marking in the date.

'And perhaps afterwards you will both be my guests at Fortune's for an oyster supper?' Fraser asked.

'But we will see you at the Theatre Royal first, Polly.' Mistress Scott smiled and turned back to Miss Jeanette. 'She is about the same age as young Walter, you see. He will be there, too. They could entertain each other, I'm sure, while we older people sit together.'

Smiling quietly, Fraser Graham ushered her out into the early evening, and Polly was left feeling a little disappointed. He had not said that he would be at the Theatre Royal himself. That meant she would not get the opportunity to speak to him alone, should he happen to sit beside her, for now she had made up her mind to ask him next if he knew anyone in Edinburgh called Gray. He was a lawyer, wasn't he? Lawyers were supposed to know everything.

Then there were the MacAllister brothers to consider after that. They would know a lot of people at the University. At all costs she must keep one foot in the Buchanan camp while she had the other in the Brodies'. How firmly, and for how long, depended on the Deacon. She did not intend to clean up any more messes he got himself into, that was certain. She did not think Mattie would either, for it was plain to see that the old woman was becoming more and more disgruntled every day. That disgraceful affair when they had to put him to bed may have been the straw to break her back. Or was it the discovery of the contents of the old cash register? In any case, Mattie had changed since that night.

In spite of all this Polly still found it hard to condemn the Deacon outright. This very afternoon he had told them about the new gallows he had designed, and the town council of Edinburgh in all its majesty would scarcely buy something so important as that from a rogue.

Later that same night William Brodie sat alone in Dawney Douglas's tavern in Anchor Close. Although his eye was healing it might not be prudent to go back to Clark's until the scar fell off. He sighed and wondered gloomily how he had ever managed to get through the ten thousand pounds his father had left him, but get through it he had – except for a little nest-egg put by for a rainy day – and very swiftly and easily, too. Well, there was no use crying over spilt milk. Besides that, it was taking a few pints to wash away the bitter memory of the council meeting earlier.

Oh, of course they accepted his design for the new gallows. They even voted to install it right away. But as usual they were grippy with the citizens' money, and they had not paid him nearly enough. It strengthened his resolve to bolster his resources in other ways.

Oh, God, it was always this wretched chase after money! It went grinding on week after week while he tried to pay his workmen with one hand and fulfil his other commitments with the other, while all the time debts piled up behind him. He was spending his life chasing his own tail. How was he ever to get back Suzanne at this rate? All he longed for now was another great pile of money like his inheritance.

He'd made keys for every house he had ever worked in, and lately when he got the time he watched the movements of the occupants, especially at night. If he established that they went out on a regular basis, then in he went. But mistakes could happen, like the night the old lady he thought was dead sat up and screamed when she saw him at the foot of her bed.

And that fool of a Mistress Ballantyne! A few weeks ago, on Friday night, he saw her and her husband driving away in their coach. The house was still in darkness when he unlocked the back door. It had seemed easy – until a great black shape, all teeth and fur, came hurtling at him. Christ! How was he to know they kept a bloody savage dog? No, a better way was the one he was planning for tonight, if his companions ever arrived, and he fell to considering them.

There was George Smith. Although he was an Englishman, Smith was the only one of his gang he really trusted. Then there was Andrew Ainslie, a friend of Smith's. 'I know he's a moaner and a groaner,' Smith persuaded him, 'but he's a good look-out man.'

'He's a bloody whine all right,' the Deacon agreed. 'Well, I hope he doesn't let us down.'

143

But it was John Brown who worried him most of all, in spite of being the most daring and useful member of the team. John Brown had escaped the law of England after being sentenced to seven years' transportation for theft. He had been caught once. William Brodie could never get rid of a niggling little feeling that Brown might be caught again, and so land them all in it.

They arrived at Douglas's together. That was a mistake for a start – the Deacon frowned – even if the tavern was the darkest one in Edinburgh. But they drank a few more pints while they went over their plan. Leaving it as late as they could, they each took their leave one by one so as not to arouse suspicion.

The bell of St Giles was ringing one o'clock in the morning when they met together again outside the University, and Brodie produced four black masks. After some persuasion the other three put them on.

'Now, George,' he said to Smith, 'here's a pair of pistols for you.'

'Have you got yours?' Smith asked, tucking them into his belt.

'You're mad, the pair of you,' Brown said. 'You never told us you would be armed. If we're caught, we could swing for it.'

'We'll only be caught if we stand around and talk like this,' Smith said. 'Get on with it, Will!'

Brodie led them to the outside gate at the back of the University. It was a solid pine door, heavily studded.

'Christ!' Ainslie sniffed and whined, 'we'll never get through that!'

'Shut up, Ainslie!' Smith smacked him, and opened the gate in less than a minute with his picklock.

'Follow me,' Brodie whispered.

Hissing at each other to be quiet they tiptoed in single file along the corridor until they came face to face with the library door, which was much more solid than the outside gate had ever been. This time Smith had no success.

'The bugger won't turn, Will.'

'Let's go,' said Ainslie, 'before we waken the whole town.'

'Go then,' Brodie said. 'If you do you'll get nothing.'

Ainslie stayed, moaning, while Smith struggled with the unyielding picklock. Brodie alone remained calm.

'There's nobody here, the place is deserted. Do you think I would come on a job like this unprepared? Stand back, the lot o' ye!'

He took a short crowbar from under his cloak and levered it between the keep and the lock until the wood creaked and crushed. Smith put his shoulder to the door and smashed it open. Then they all stood stockstill and listened, their hearts in their mouths, for two minutes, three, four, five. Nothing happened. Nothing moved. There was no sound.

'This way,' Brodie said, and led them to the glass showcase in the middle of the room. Locked away inside it was the silver mace, huge and gleaming. 'What did I tell you?' he whispered. 'Solid, it is! It'll be worth a fortune melted down.'

Smith put his cloak over the glass and gave it a tap with the butt of his pistol. There was a tinkling sound, and then they were all handling the massive silver mace and guessing its weight.

'How do we get it out?' Ainslie asked fearfully. 'That bloody great poker! Everyone will see it!'

'I'll put it under my cloak and carry it upright. Help me to wrap the cloak well round it, the lot o' ye. Now,' he added when it was secure, 'form a guard around me, for I'm defenceless like this.'

Not another word was spoken until they were out of the University again and the gate was pulled to.

'Where are you going to hide it in the meantime?' Brown asked.

'Down at Michael Henderson's in the Grassmarket. He's the one man in the whole world I can trust. You can all come with me, and then we'll split up and go our separate ways. But go slow, boys! This thing's rubbing up against me! I'm a man in my prime, ye ken!'

Ainslie giggled hysterically, and Smith smacked him again on the way down to the Grassmarket. Half an hour later, with the mace disposed of, Brodie was exultant. The other three were well away, and he walked back up the Bow Head too excited to think about going home. It was a night for his dearest Ann. She would understand. She would look after him.

She did. It seemed a long time since he had been with her last, and he could not get enough of her. At last he fell asleep with the morning sunlight coming in through the curtains. She kept their children in the next room as long as she could, and at seven o'clock she eased herself out from under him, stark naked, and put on her clothes.

Next she picked his clothes up off the floor, shook them and folded them neatly. When she came to his cape, the weight of it led her to discover the two pistols in the pockets and she stood gazing at them in absolute terror before she woke him up.

'Come back to bed, Ann. What's wrang wi' ye? Ye've never said no before.'

'Why are ye carrying pistols, Will?'

'Gentlemen must these days, dearie. The Royal Mile's a dangerous place lately.'

A great shudder ran through her. 'It's the first sign o' bad luck in all our years together, Will.'

'Fetch in the bairns and I'll show ye some good luck, then.'

The door burst open at that moment and the children hurled themselves on to the bed with cries of 'Father! Father!'

'We miss ye so, Father,' said their oldest child, Cecil, aged eleven. 'Why can ye no' come oftener?'

'Oh, I love ye just the same,' Brodie assured his favourite child, whom he had named after his own mother, Mistress Cecil Brodie. 'I've got something for ye, never fear, for I think aboot ye all the time. Gi'e me a kiss, sweetheart.'

'I'll give ye a kiss first, and then sing our new skipping song for ye. Are ye ready?'

'Let me hear it then, darling.'

> 'I'm a braw wee man,
> A bonny wee man,
> Sweet as sugar candy.
> Macaroni is my name,
> Macaroni Dandy …

'Father, why do they call ye "The Macaroni"?'

'Do they?' He laughed. 'A macaroni is a man who is always beautifully dressed,' he said as he unwrapped a handkerchief in front of their eyes.

Out came a gold locket for Cecil, a brooch for her little sister Jeannie, a silver teething ring for baby Billy, and last of all a ruby and pearl pendant for Ann herself.

Oh, he was a braw wee man, her bonnie wee man – but how was she to fill the bairnies' mouths wi' food when he brought trinkets instead o' money? Ann shook her head and smiled indulgently. The ruby and pearl pendant would be the first thing to go.

13

O N MONDAY EVENING Polly and Miss Jeanette heard the slam of the front door when the Deacon went out. Polly picked up the new *Edinburgh Evening Courant* which was lying on the table by the window. 'Would you like me to read you something?' she asked.

'I wish you would. It's too early to go to bed yet.'

'There's a notice here in big black letters –

By the Right Hon. The
LORD PROVOST, MAGISTRATES AND COUNCIL
of the City of Edinburgh:
Whereas, on the night between Saturday and Sunday the ninth and tenth of September current, some wicked persons did feloniously break open the doors of the library of the University of this city, and steal the UNIVERSITY MACE. A reward of TEN GUINEAS, to be paid by the City Chamberlain, is hereby offered for the discovery of all or any of the persons above mentioned, or of any person in whose possession the said Mace shall be found.
Edinburgh, September the eleventh, 1787.'

But there was no comment. Polly glanced up, a little surprised, and it was as though an icy hand clutched her heart.

Miss Jeanette's face was a study of horror. It was entirely drained of colour, and her eyes so darkly shadowed beneath that they seemed twice their normal size – enormous, stricken and utterly terrified.

'What is it? Oh, what is it?' Polly jumped up, scattering the newspaper in all directions.

But Miss Jeanette could not speak. She gasped for breath and turned a little blue. Polly searched frantically on the table beside her, under her engagement book and the pencils and the collection of handkerchiefs, until she found the little bottle that she knew was there somewhere.

She waved the smelling-salts under Miss Jeanette's nose until she gasped and choked and the tears poured from her eyes. But her colour was returning. Polly gave her a few minutes to recover. 'Can you speak now? Is that better? Can you tell me what is wrong?' she asked anxiously.

Miss Jeanette groaned and shook her head, leaning back in her chair with her eyes closed. After what seemed an eternity she opened them at last. 'Never, never speak to me again about these terrible burglaries,' she gasped. 'I am so sick and tired of the people who come in here and speak of nothing else. Even Mistress Scott was at it! And now they are in the newspaper! It is too much.'

'I would not have upset you like this for the world, Miss Jeanette. Shall I fetch you a cup of water?'

'No. Tell Mattie to come. She will know what to bring.'

Polly fled to the kitchen. Mattie nodded, her lips tight, when she heard the message. 'I'll come right away,' she said, wiping her hands.

Polly was at a loss as to what to do next. Perhaps she should go back to the parlour in the meantime. She went back noiselessly towards the door she had left open in her haste, but on the threshold she stopped short.

Miss Brodie was standing with her back to her, holding the *Courant* up to the light with hands that trembled pitifully in agitation. The page was opened at the notice about the burglary, but the newspaper itself was upside down.

Mattie brushed past with one hand concealed in the folds of her apron skirt; from the sad look she cast Polly it was obvious that her hand was clasped round a bottle.

*

As September progressed Miss Brodie remained tearful and downcast, very much like the weather. For days Jess had been forced to dry all the clothes on ropes stretched along the kitchen ceiling which meant the ironing had to be done in the evenings. Polly could no longer bear to see the maid struggling on her own, and often gave her a hand.

She should have been trying to cheer her mistress, but to tell the truth she much preferred the maids' company anyway, for no matter how hard they worked nothing was right so far as Miss Jeanette was concerned, and it was fast becoming a very unhappy household.

The crisis came at six o'clock one Saturday evening, when Mattie was hard at it cooking for Sunday and Miss Jeanette rang her silver bell to summon Polly to the parlour.

'You carry on wi' yer ironing,' Mattie said. 'I'll go. I'm wanting a word wi' her ladyship anyway,' and shortly afterwards there was the sound of raised voices from the parlour.

'What now?' Polly asked the cook when she returned to the kitchen.

'She has dismissed me.'

'Dismissed you? No! She can't have done, after all these years!'

'She has.'

'The Deacon will not allow it, Mattie.'

'I dinna really care what the Deacon says. I want to go, anyway.'

'If Mattie goes, I'm going with her,' said Jess, with the longest speech of her career in Brodie's Close.

When Mattie departed early on Monday morning, taking Jess with her, there was a break in the weather. It became bright and clear, and all that was in Polly's head was the washing. She would be able to get it out on the lines at last, but as she folded the clothes into the basket she took another long hard look at her situation.

At this rate she was not getting the chance to set about her own business. Anyway, it was never part of the bargain that she should be doing the washing at all. Fraser Graham had pressed Miss Jeanette hard about that, as she recalled, and for a few moments her thoughts drifted away from the problem at hand to him.

But when she stepped outside the back door and marched down the long path with the basket under her arm she asked herself a question: this beautiful house she had so longed to enter – was she trapped in it now, slaving for a sullen, thankless woman and her strange brother?

Something would have to be done about it ... A loud squawk in her ear, a rattling of wire and the violent beating of wings seemed to underline her rebellious thoughts when she drew level with the cock-pens on the way down past the workshop, and she stopped to gaze at the creatures.

There were four of them, snapping viciously with their cruel beaks at anyone who passed, all bad-tempered and arrogant as they stalked about and all staring at her with their beady, bloody little eyes before they hurled themselves again at the flimsy wire netting holding them in.

Polly gave the cage a kick in retaliation, and at once the fighting-cocks screamed at her, clinging to the wire with their murderous spurs of steel. She kicked the cage again. It made her feel better, especially when she was on the outside.

'Shall I open the door and let you take them on yourself?' a laughing voice asked, and she turned around quickly, almost colliding with a young man with a dark mischievous face and very blue eyes. 'Who are you?' he asked familiarly. 'Are you the new maidservant?'

'Certainly not. I am Miss Brodie's lady companion.'

'Hm ... hanging out the washing? Are you staying here?'

'Why?'

'Because I could be a help to *you*.' He grinned wickedly.

'Yes, I can imagine.'

He had the cheek of the devil. Polly knew all the ways he would want to help her, all right. Or any woman, come to that. But he was very attractive. Blatant sexuality stared out of his eyes.

'Well! What's your name, then?'

'Miss Polly, to you. What's yours?'

'Jocky. Jocky Robertson.'

Ah, so *this* was the Jocky Robertson of Margery's dreams!

On the whole Polly couldn't blame her. But more importantly the seeds of a new idea were planted in her brain.

'Well, Jocky Robertson, since you're here, you might as well help me to hang this lot out.'

'I'm supposed to be earning my living, you know,' he said, and began to string the washing on the line. 'I work here.'

'Oh, yes? What at?'

'Carpenting. This is my last apprentice year.'

It was the same Jocky Robertson, all right.

'You might be seeing a new maid here shortly.' Polly smiled and took up the empty basket.

'She won't be as pretty as you – pretty Polly!'

'Prettier! Wait and see.'

Polly had no intention of trying to manage without Mattie, and she deliberately made no meals and did not even set the table. Driven by hunger after the sparseness of yesterday's meal, Miss Jeanette was sure to come to the kitchen to find out why. She did, early in the afternoon.

'When are we going to have something to eat, for pity's sake?'

'I wish I knew, Miss Jeanette. Mattie will be sorely missed.'

'Then she should not have said those things she did about my brother! *I will not have it*! Do you hear me? I will not have it!'

'Of course not.' Polly remained calm, but her heart sank even further. It seemed, living with Miss Jeanette every day, that she was becoming more and more agitated. She thanked God she had kept from her the news of the latest robbery, this time from the silk merchants Inglis and Horner.

'Are there none of yesterday's cold collations left? What is there to offer the Deacon when he comes home?' Miss Jeanette darted to the pantry and began to rummage around.

'I'm afraid you won't find anything in there. There is nothing left.'

'Then where is the next meal to come from? Someone will have to go out and buy some meat or a hen and cook it.'

'That will be when you get another cook, Miss Jeanette. Unfortunately, I have never been able to cook, myself. Can you?'

'Of course not!'

'Then what are we going to do?' Polly waved her arm around

to indicate the sea of ironing festooning the kitchen. 'Even if I could cook, I would never have the time to do it.'

'I will have to get another woman, I suppose. Goodness knows where I shall get her from.'

'Candlemaker Row,' Polly said promptly and tried to keep the triumph out of her voice. 'My cousin Margery Buchanan is an excellent cook. She would come *today*; she has nothing else to do.'

Miss Jeanette leapt at the suggestion like a drowning woman clutching at a straw. 'Send a caddy down for her, then. Better still, get the chair men to go for her,' and sighing in relief Polly went out into the Royal Mile to find a sedan.

'Oh, thank you, dearest Polly!' Margery was flinging her arms around her an hour later. 'Show me the workshops first! Show me where Jocky works!'

The Deacon had gone out on his night business, Miss Jeanette had gone to bed, no doubt with a bottle, when Polly relaxed a little in the glow of the kitchen fire after Margery went back home to Candlemaker Row for the night.

She was tired out, for she and Margery had worked very hard to catch up with the housework, but still she was not ready for bed. Greatly daring, she lit another candle to add power to her own so that she could look over some of the news-sheets, unread for so many days, waiting in the pile to light the fires in the morning.

She took up the *Caledonian Mercury*, four pages of closely printed news dated several days ago, and snapped it open to a scandalous headline.

A DISGRACEFUL BRAWL

In Clark's Tavern, Fleshmarket Close, last Friday night over crooked dice in a gambling game, it is understood that the mysterious perpetrator dressed all in black disappeared from the scene, but not before receiving a horrific blow to his eye, the scar of which should make him instantly recognizable.

Well, lots of men received injuries to their eyes, perhaps by falling or some other accident, Polly tried to argue with herself, but her heart had sunk to her boots. She wanted to believe that the mysterious man could not have been Deacon Brodie, not in a brawl like that, but she knew perfectly well that it was. However, the next headline was enough to drive the worry even of that clean out of her head.

THE GHOST OF THE ROYAL MILE

Although the citizens of Edinburgh have long been acquainted with numerous tales of this apparition, only one person so far has reported an actual sighting.

'Miss Philemena Sproat, aged eighty-one, of Morocco's Land in the Canongate, was awakened in the early hours of Friday morning with a draught on her face, and saw something black in the shape of a man at the foot of her bed, whereupon she sat up and screamed.

'The apparition seemed to float out of the open window, then turned around and shut it, and to her horror waved its hand at her. Miss Sproat's recovery from a long illness has suffered a further setback

Polly shuddered as she read it. Anybody peering down the shadowy ill-lit wynds and closes of the Royal Mile might readily believe a ghost walked there. She did, for one ...

'Your cousin Margery has such a beautiful complexion, like her mother before her, Polly,' Miss Jeanette said the next day, almost restored to her former nervous, twittering self. 'What do they put on their faces to achieve it?'

'Nothing, Miss Jeanette. It is not what they put on the outside, it is what they put into the inside that makes the miracle.'

'What do you mean?'

'The Buchanans have a secret recipe. They make a most refreshing drink from lemons. Mistress Buchanan swears it clears away all the poisons in the body in just one week. They drink nothing else.'

'Oh.'

'I believe Margery has made some this morning. Shall I go and see?'

'It's too late for me now.' Miss Jeanette sighed. 'For some reason my skin has gone all blotchy and dull.'

'No, it's never too late. Why don't you try the lemonade for a week and see? I'll ask Margery to put it on the table for you and me instead of wine. I'll go and speak to her now.'

'Quick, Margery!' Polly said in the kitchen. 'Make some of your lemonade. I've told Miss Jeanette it will clear her complexion in a week, and she believes it. If we can keep her off wine and spirits for that length of time it is bound to improve her.'

No news from the outside world of Edinburgh town was good news, and gradually Miss Jeanette became calmer. Her chatter was all about their impending visit to the Theatre Royal and what she should wear. Every night for the next week she went to sleep sober, and every day encouraged by Polly she gazed into the mirror to watch the transformation.

Once again she was taking a great interest in her appearance, and her bad days were becoming fewer and fewer. Saturday turned out to be one of her very best days since Polly had known her, and together they came in smiling from their daily visit to the Luckenbooths, carrying their small parcels.

'It is still only four o'clock,' Miss Jeanette said. 'Just in time for tea.'

But before she had time to summon her Margery was knocking on the parlour door. 'There is someone to see you, Miss Jeanette.'

'I am not expecting anyone. Who is it?'

'It is a young gentleman. He would not give his name. He says it is to be a surprise.'

'Oh? Oh well, then,' she patted her hair a little frivolously as though young men came calling on her every afternoon and it was a thing of very little consequence, 'you had better show him in.'

'Here he is, miss,' announced Margery as she ushered in the visitor a minute later.

'Oh!' Miss Jeanette shrieked with delight. 'Oh, it is you, Jamie! I never thought we would ever see you again! Polly, this is a dear friend, Mr James Leslie.'

'And you are prettier than ever, Jeannie.' He bent and kissed her lightly.

Tall of frame and narrow, with a heavy black beard and gangling legs, Mr Leslie shook Polly's hand and stood smiling at them shyly. 'I have finished the job in Aberdeen,' he said, 'and have come back to work with Matthew Sheriff again.'

'Bring three cups instead of two, then,' Miss Jeanette directed the hovering Margery. 'You will take some tea with us, Jamie?'

'I was hoping to arrive in time for tea, my dear. Fortunately there were no delays on the Aberdeen coach.'

'Oh, so this is your first port of call?'

'After six months, one week and four days?' He looked directly at his hostess and Miss Jeanette blushed very attractively. 'You knew it would be, for apart from being as cold as charity, it was very lonely up north.'

'Yes. It has been very lonely here, too. That is why Polly came to be a companion to me.'

'Ah, I see.'

'I don't think you do, Jamie. I cannot bear to be alone,' Miss Jeanette added with a catch in her breath, pouring the tea from the little silver pot and then filling it up again from the jug of hot water which Margery fetched, all eyes and ears.

Polly took the cup from her trembling hand and gave it to Mr Leslie.

The trembling spread to Miss Jeanette's voice. 'When you left me I did not have a friend in the world to speak to, although Polly has helped these last few weeks. But I suppose you will be going away soon on another job?'

Polly hastily offered Mr Leslie a slice of Margery's fresh-baked honey cake.

'You cannot imagine how I have looked forward to this moment, Jeanette,' he said. 'No, I will not have to go away again, not in the immediate future at least. My aunt Mistress Scott has asked me to join you all at the theatre on the twenty-second, and I was able to accept her invitation without any hesitation.'

'Oh, indeed. So you went to her house first after all.' Miss Jeanette looked ready to cry.

'No.' He smiled calmly. 'I had the good fortune to meet her out here in the Lawnmarket on my way up from the coach.' He set down his cup carefully on the table. 'But what is the matter,

Jeannie? You were never touchy like this,' he said, rising up and going to kneel beside her chair. 'Yes, I am back now, and you can talk to me, dear.'

Polly set down her teacup beside his and got to her feet. 'May I be excused, Miss Jeanette? I shall tell Margery to leave the tea-things until you ring, shall I?'

'Very well, dear,' her mistress said distractedly.

Mr Leslie had his arms around her almost before Polly left them alone together, and she couldn't help overhearing a little of what Miss Jeanette was sobbing to him.

'Oh, Jamie! I've been so worried ... It's Will. I'm sure he's mixed up in some very bad things.'

'Hm!' Margery said when they had been working together a day and a half in the house in Brodie's Close. 'They may have *said* old Mattie was here only to do the cooking. Believe me, she must have had a lot more to do than that, many a time, at the rate Miss Jeanette dismisses her servants.'

'Such as?'

'Emptying the pots.'

'Well, fortunately she was persuaded to take on a young girl to help Mattie towards the end. One woman cannot be expected to cook, clean, wash and do everything else required in a house of this size. But when Mattie left, so did Jess.'

'So what are we to do, Polly? I can think of many girls who would come to be a maid here!'

'Name one who would come immediately.'

'Annie Begbie, in the Grassmarket.'

'Leave it to me, then, Margery. I won't go into the dining-hall tonight. That will sound a few alarm bells, to begin with. Instead, you and I will empty all the pots. It's the second drum, isn't it?'

'Yes. The first drum at eight o'clock is the signal for the shops and Luckenbooths to shut, and for the customers and the shopkeepers to hurry home while the going is good. The second drum is for the gardy-loo. Have you ever done it before, Polly?'

'No.'

'Well, you'd better learn. You never know when you might have to do it yourself sometime if I'm not here to help.'

'It would be terrible getting through the days here without you now, Margery. The nights are bad enough, after you leave.'

'Well, you know Pa ... he wants me home by nine o'clock to set his mind at rest, he says. Little does he know that it is not one of the MacAllister brothers escorting me.'

'Oh, Margery! It's Jocky Robertson, I suppose?'

'Ahhh, Jocky ...' Margery went off into a rapturous trance while they were standing at an open upstairs window with the dirty pots and pails around their feet. The terrible smells that came up from them did not seem to affect her rapture in the least, until at half past eight the second drum sounded and she sprang into life again. 'Gardy-loo!' she shouted, and flung out the contents of the first chamber-pot into the Royal Mile below. 'Now, you do the next one.'

'Gardy-loo!' Polly's turn came next with a bucket of filthy water, and so they went on emptying all the pails and pots in company with everyone else in the street until at last they could shut the window again on the stench.

In spite of it, Polly could not help smiling to herself, to remember that in Paris they shouted 'Gardez l'eau'. 'Gardy-loo' must be the Scottish corruption of it, but she dared not tell Margery the joke. That would be giving too much of her past away, and one careless slip of Margery's tongue might do untold, and so far unforeseen, damage to her cause.

'That's Miss Jeanette ringing her bell for you! You'd better go, Polly.'

'Did you enjoy your meal?' Polly asked her when she got to the sitting-room.

'It was excellent, as you would have seen had you been here. Why, pray, were you not at the table? A companion is supposed to be a constant companion, not part-time.'

Polly smiled inwardly. Miss Jeanette had fallen straight into the trap. Ever since Mr Leslie had appeared she had been in a better temper. Now she was preparing to become angry again. Polly swung into action immediately.

'Yes, Miss Jeanette, I missed the meal. But it was either your excellent dinner or dirty chamber-pots, that was the choice. In the same way as Mattie, Margery cannot be expected to get through all the work here single-handed. I decided to help her with the dirtiest job in the house.'

Miss Jeanette was too affronted by this plain talking in her sitting-room to reply. She waved her scented handkerchief before her nose weakly, and Polly could almost see her mind working. She could not afford to lose her new cook or her companion, either. 'You mean we require another maidservant. My brother is not made of money, you know.'

'As Mr Graham explained when I came here, that sort of work is not part of my contract. It is the first and last time I shall ever attend to the gardy-loo. It is not what Margery is here for either – although both of us help out with many another job voluntarily. She is here to cook.'

'Yes, well ... I suppose we shall have to get another girl from somewhere, then.'

'Immediately, if you want your slops removed.'

'Where could I find one at such short notice, anyway?'

'Leave that to me. Being a lady's companion also means taking worries of that sort off her mistress's mind.'

'Yes.' A smile lit up Miss Jeanette's face again. 'You are a very good companion to me, Polly. I'm sure I don't know how I would manage without you. Oh, *do* come and have another little peep at the dress I shall wear to the theatre!'

The theatre; Polly was as excited at the prospect as her mistress. She had almost forgotten what going to the theatre was like. It seemed so long since she had last been in one. Lately Paris was constantly on her mind. She tried to concentrate only on its happy memories, but try as she might its dark secrets intervened.

14

THE HOUSE SEETHED with excitement all day on the twenty-second of September. Mr James Leslie arrived far too early at six o'clock to escort Miss Jean and Polly to the theatre, and was dumped unceremoniously in the sitting-room by a distracted Margery.

'Wait here, if you please, sir,' she said, and thrust the *Courant* into his hand. 'As you will see from the advertisements, the play does not begin until half past seven, and the ladies have not even started to dress.'

Mr Leslie subsided on to a settee with a quiet smile, and the preparations continued. After they helped Miss Jeanette to dress, the girls got out Margery's best silk gown from its box; it was peach-coloured with little bows down the front from the neckline to the hem. Margery fastened Polly into it, tied her hair back with the peach silk ribbons to match and adjusted her evening cloak around her shoulders.

'You'll be the belle of the ball,' she assured her. 'Now, Polly, lift up your skirts, and don't trip on the staircase going down.'

The Deacon was in the dining-hall when they reached the bottom, dressed in the dark suit for his night business. Margery rushed off to attend to the final touches of Miss Jeanette's attire.

'You are not coming with us tonight then, Master Will?'

'You know me, Polly! It's *The Beggar's Opera*, the wickedness, the excitement – or not at all!'

Polly forgot him and everything else in the rowdy, perfumed, heady atmosphere of the Theatre Royal as soon as she entered it. The people were not in their seats, but laughing and moving about among their friends, shouting and throwing orange skins at each other, and bursting into laughter again. Anything was possible in the theatre.

She found herself seated next to young Walter Scott on her right, and on his right Mistress Scott sat next to Mr Leslie and Miss Jeanette. On Polly's left there was an empty seat next to the aisle. She supposed it had been reserved for the Deacon. Then the lights dimmed and the play began.

For the next hour all of Edinburgh was enthralled and enchanted by Mrs Sarah Siddons. Her voice rang to the very rafters, every word as clear as though she spoke to each one of them.

Some time through it Fraser must have taken the empty seat beside Polly so silently that she was not even aware of him until the curtain came down for the long interval.

'Oh, she is magnificent!' Polly said, and Fraser smiled at her enthusiasm.

'She *is* magnificent!' Walter Scott agreed. 'For she has breathed fire into a story that is decidedly weak.'

'Weak?'

'We all know what will happen, do we not, right from the start? But her acting is so supreme that it does not matter. She makes the story unimportant. I suppose that is why she has been called back here for a demand repeat performance.'

'You have seen *Venice Preserv'd* before?'

'Oh yes, two years ago – didn't we, Fraser?' Walter Scott turned his back a little on his mother to include him in the conversation. 'I thought it such a poor story then that it made me more determined than ever to write my own some day, much better than that,' he finished on a lower note. 'I dare not let my mother hear me. She does not approve of writing.'

'He has shown me his *Guy Mannering*,' Fraser whispered into Polly's ear. 'Some day he will be a great writer. Keep talking to him. His mother is watching.'

Polly turned back to Walter Scott again, and a sharp movement behind her and an indrawn breath distracted her momentarily. She was in time to catch a glimpse of a figure in black rising up and seeming to float away. She was left with the impression that it might have been a woman, but then as the figure disappeared into thin air a much more uneasy notion took hold of her imagination.

Had she just seen the ghost of the Royal Mile? Was that why she suddenly felt surrounded by this black, pulsating aura? No, that was no ghost she had just seen out of the corner of her eye ... In fact, if this had been Paris and not Edinburgh, she could have sworn she was in the presence of Caramelle.

But here amidst the noise and the colour and the excitement of the Theatre Royal these were silly, superstitious ideas, easily dispelled.

'I knew those two would get on well together, Jeanette,' Mistress Scott said after a glance around at Polly and Walter.

'It was an inspiration of yours, Mistress Margaret,' Miss Jeanette agreed, and then since apart from Mr Leslie her brother was uppermost in her mind, 'Poor Will!'

'Is there something wrong with him?'

'Oh, no.' Miss Jeanette sighed as the lights dimmed again. 'I just wish he could have been here with us tonight, but you know how conscientious he is. While we are enjoying ourselves here, he is out on his night business as usual. I only hope he is happy, that's all!'

The dark willowy figure emerging from the Theatre Royal into the pitch-black street intrigued Deacon Brodie also. He could distinguish no face under the hood, and there was a cold, rushing feeling as it whispered past him. He too could have sworn it was a woman. He thought it was the long skirts of a cloak which made the whispering sound – and then before his very eyes it simply disappeared into the night.

The ghost of the Royal Mile? He smiled at the mere idea. The Royal Mile was *his* territory, and he had been doing very well up to now, 'walking through walls', as they put it in the news-sheets, terrorizing the gullible people of Edinburgh. He was the only one who could; he was the only one who possessed all the keys to that mystery. There would be no more ghosts here to queer his pitch if he could help it.

*

Walter Scott insisted on sitting next to Polly again when Mistress Scott and her party boarded their coaches after the play to go to Fortune's in the High Street for one of their famous oyster suppers.

They all walked into the darkness of the Stamp Office Close and entered the tavern, suitably impressed when Mistress Scott told them this was the meeting-place of the Poker Club, a most remarkably brilliant set of men which included Hume, Robertson, Blair and Fergusson, to name but a few.

After such an introduction it was all the more surprising to Polly to find that the Oyster Cellar of Fortune's was a dark cavern of a room, dimly lit by cheap tallow candles, whose only furniture was one large rough table at one end of it around which were seated other ladies and gentlemen. It was covered with ashets of oysters, pots of porter and jugs of lemonade.

'They've kept our seats,' Fraser said, manoeuvring himself beside Polly as the Scott party managed to squeeze in, and immediately, as if by some signal, the fun began – the vivacious conversation, the repartee, the laughter and the applause. The strangeness of the cellar and the dim light added to the atmosphere. It was so dull and mean and crude that it was the perfect foil for so much brilliance, and even in that company Fraser Graham shone and sparkled.

The fiddlers who had come in unnoticed and sat in one corner seemed to sense when conversation was waning and struck up a reel.

'I wish I could ask you to dance with me, Miss Polly,' Walter Scott said with a wry smile, 'but my game leg prevents me. An illness in my childhood left me with one leg much shorter than the other.'

'I'm so sorry! And even sorrier now that the music has begun you cannot tell me any more stories. Your mother is waving to you. I think she wants you to join her.'

'Yes,' he sighed, and limped away.

Now the room burst into life. The ladies fluttering up and down the formations of the reel were like butterflies in their dresses of silk and satin.

Then Fraser Graham was advancing towards her and

bowing. 'Will you do me the honour of dancing the next reel with me, Polly?' he asked.

'It will be a pleasure,' she said.

'May I fetch you some lemonade in the meantime?'

She frowned, but nodded her head. The oysters had left her quite thirsty but she would rather he had just talked to her.

There was a twinkle in his eye when he returned. No doubt he had been making up something to tease her with, in his present mood, and she decided to forestall him.

'Thank you, Mr Graham.'

'Now, Polly! We are past that stage. You agreed to call me Fraser. Or Charlie, if you would prefer it.'

'Charlie?' she repeated, quite diverted.

'That is my name. Charles Fraser Graham. Take your pick.'

'Charles does not suit you at all. And Charlie is too – too –'

'Too young, perhaps?' he laughed at her.

'I shall continue to call you Fraser, when you behave yourself. Yes,' she smiled back at him, 'it's spiky, like one of your Scottish fir trees.'

'What a beautiful, prickly little flower you are yourself, Polly! So we should be well suited, you and I. I don't suppose you got on half so well with Walter Scott? *He* is far too young for you, of course.'

'I like older men, as I told you,' she agreed as they got up for the next dance, 'and I am so lucky to be working for one!'

'Oh? I understood you to be his sister's companion.'

'He comes into it as well.'

'Ah! I thought he would sooner or later, our little Macaroni!' He laughed out loud, so that the other dancers turned to smile at them.

'Don't tease, Fraser!' Polly gasped. 'I meant that to work for one is to work for the other.'

'And he didn't come tonight?'

'No, he had his night business to attend to.'

'His *night business*! Strange.'

'Not to us. It is quite normal in the Brodie household. But I did see a strange thing earlier tonight. She – I mean it – appeared in the theatre, dressed in black. It gave me a shock, after all the talk there has been in the *Courant* about the ghost of the Royal Mile.'

165

'Oh, Polly! It was not a ghost,' Fraser smiled. 'There are no such things as ghosts. There are no less than three mysterious people dressed in black in the Royal Mile just now. They're all very human, I assure you, and every one a thief.'

'Every one a thief?' Polly's blood ran cold. So Fraser must be suspicious about the Deacon, too. That was why he had tried to stop her working for the Brodies.

'Yes. The MacAllisters and I have been trying to catch them for weeks. We have identified one of them – and you are quite right: one of the other two is a woman. I was following her when she darted into the theatre. That's why I was late.'

She smiled up at him. He was so down-to-earth, dispelling all her fears.

'By the way,' he was serious again, 'Mr Buchanan told me the other day when I was in his shop that you were interested in people called Gray. He asked me if I knew of any.'

'And do you?' she asked, with a great leap of her heart.

'None in Edinburgh, but there *was* a lady in London Lord Braxfield asked me to look for. I never found her.'

'Lord Braxfield? Who is he?'

Fraser laughed. 'Old Braxie, as we call him disrespectfully, is the Lord Chief Justice, the most feared criminal lawyer in Scotland.'

'And this lady he asked you to find – what was her name?' she asked idly, for after all there were thousands of ladies in London she had never known.

Her eyes were on a shadowy figure in the doorway, the same figure, she was sure, which she'd glimpsed at the Theatre Royal. The head was bent and the face hidden, and yet its whole outline so reminded her of someone or something that her stomach was gripped with dread and before he answered she began to feel quite sick and giddy.

'Suzanne Gray.'

Then the music was coming from far away. His face above her swirled in a sickening mist which became thicker and thicker until she no longer saw him or anyone as she sank to the floor.

Fraser Graham, in London, looking for Mama? Sent by the chief criminal judge in Scotland, no less! Three days later she was still shuddering whenever she thought about it, and she could think of very little else. Had they found out about Uncle Philippe in Paris? Were they trying to trace her and bring her to justice? There could be no other explanation.

If only she could go to Fraser then and there, lay her head on his shoulder and tell him the whole story as far as she knew it. But how could she, when she didn't know him well enough and she had no proof of her own identity? Neither he nor anyone else would believe her.

September was changing to October, with a hint morning and evening of the winter to come when the frost bit hard after golden days, and the moon hung high and yellow. Now the people of Edinburgh lit their fires in the afternoons which covered their city with a pall of smoke. It was a race to take the clothes in off the lines by three o'clock.

Usually Margery helped Annie Begbie with the outside work, going down through the wood-yard hoping for a glimpse of Jocky Robertson on her way to the washing lines. Many a time her hands were cracked and swollen, but she reckoned that was a small price to pay for the privilege.

On Monday morning Annie got the washing out first thing, and Miss Brodie and Polly went out to the Luckenbooths earlier than usual. As they walked around the stalls Polly thought if it wasn't for the happy progression of Miss Jeanette's love affair, it would be almost impossible to carry on with her own charade in that house of many charades.

When they came back carrying Miss Jeanette's parcels, the house was in silence except for the sound of Annie scrubbing away upstairs, and looking out of the window, Polly saw that the wind had taken up and the first few drops of a rainstorm were dashing across the panes.

Margery was nowhere to be seen when Polly picked up the basket and raced out into the yard to unpeg the clothes as fast as she could. A giggle from the workshop stopped her. Nobody should be in the workshop at midday. The Deacon would be at the meridian. The workmen would have gone home for something to eat. Everyone was out. So who was in there? She tiptoed up to the window to see.

Jocky Robertson was pulling Margery up from a pile of shavings on the floor. Her face was flushed as she shook down her skirts.

He adjusted his breeches and in that brief moment Polly had time to admire his physique, his strong, muscular legs as sturdy as tree trunks. No, she thought sadly, poor Margery didn't stand a chance against the likes of Jocky.

'The washing's dry. It's ready to come in, Margery,' she said, going into the workshop once she was sure that Jocky was decent again, and looking around the one part of Deacon Brodie's establishment she had never seen so far.

Inside the large shed it was warm, and there was the sweet smell of wood shavings mixed with the pungent fishy smell of glue and the clean vapours of varnish. It was stacked with wood at one end with work-benches around the walls, each with its own rack of tools.

But what caught her eye most was the wall entirely lined with glass-fronted cabinets. They contained rows and rows of hooks, and on the hooks were hanging hundreds of keys, each with its own little label dangling from it.

'Oh, *Polly*!' Margery was scarlet and near to tears in her embarrassment.

' "Inglis and Horner",' Polly read the labels aloud, as if she had seen and heard nothing. ' "Royal Exchange", "Wemyss, goldsmith", "Bruce, hardware", "Plugg, tobacconist".'

'And does any of that ring a bell?' Jocky asked.

'I've heard those names before, yes.'

'You mean, you read them in the newspaper? Places that were burgled?' His eyes smiled knowingly into hers as Margery made her escape to the washing lines.

'It's a good idea, that a man so upright as the Deacon should be in charge of them, you mean? Then if anyone loses a key, they know where to come for a duplicate?'

'You really believe that, Miss Polly?' Jocky laughed strangely. 'Come over here.' He pointed to a japan-black tin that she saw was filled with soft putty when she raised the lid, with a key pressed down in it. She had seen that little black box so many times when the Deacon took it out of his pocket and always thought it to be a snuff-box. 'See, he is taking an impression now. A lot of people have the dangerous habit of hanging their key on a hook behind the front door.'

'You make it sound as if he were doing something dishonest,' Polly said warily.

'And,' Jocky boasted, 'here is something for a lock, a lock he has been unable to obtain a key for.'

They looked at the long thin piece of metal, bent and shaped as though someone had been working on it, clamped in a vice. 'What is it?' she asked him.

'A picklock. With that anyone can open all but the most stubborn locks. And this,' he picked up an evil piece of needle-pointed horn set in a steel mounting, 'do you know what this is?'

She shook her head. Suddenly the workshop didn't feel so friendly any more.

'This has nothing to do with the keys. This is a spur for a fighting-cock. Its own spur is hacked off, and this one is bound to its leg instead.'

'I've seen the vicious things, up in the pens.'

'Oh yes, Miss Polly. The birds fight to the death in the cockpits. There is a Main tonight at Michael Henderson's in the Grassmarket. Those cocks of the Deacon's will be there.'

'You are asking me to believe that a respectable man such as Deacon Brodie would actually participate in such a depraved sport?'

'All right, then. Seeing is believing. Would you like to see it with your own eyes?'

She didn't answer. She couldn't.

When she lifted some of the bunches of keys the label on one of them hidden underneath might just as well have been written in letters of fire.

'Candacraig,' Polly said at last. 'Is that a house?'

'It's a house, all right.' Jocky laughed. 'Miles out in the countryside and huge. It would be a good joke to take the key and go out there some day. But,' his eyes were as impertinent as ever, 'you could never find it without me.'

'Perhaps in the meantime you could help Margery with that sheet she's struggling with,' Polly said coldly. 'Who would want to go into the country in weather like this, anyway?'

'Well, don't forget the offer.' Jocky was unabashed as he left the workshop, and Polly was left wondering when she might be in here again alone. The next minute the key for Candacraig was in her pocket before she went out to help them with the flapping sheets.

'I think it's time to teach Miss Polly about some of Edinburgh's little ways.' Jocky smiled at Margery. 'We could start by taking her to the Main tonight. That might open her eyes.'

'Stop teasing, Jocky! You know it's men only at the cockfights.'

'Nobody would know any better if you were both dressed in mens' clothes. They'll all be too taken up with the cocks. What do you say, Miss Polly?'

Anything, Polly thought, anywhere, if it could only lead to some answers.

'Mr Leslie's coming tonight, Margery,' she said. 'You could leave them a cold collation. Miss Jeanette won't need us. We could say we're going to Candlemaker Row for the evening.'

'I'll arrange everything else,' Jocky Robertson smiled.

At eight o'clock that night Margery arrived in Polly's room panting, with an armful of dark clothes and two iron contraptions in her hand. 'This is a pair of Miss Jeanette's pattens that I managed to smuggle out,' she said.

'What on earth are they for?' Polly eyed the strange clumsy things shaped roughly like shoes on platforms.

'Your slippers are too thin and too dainty to walk down to the Grassmarket now after the gardy-loo. Besides, Michael Henderson's is a stables, you know. You must put your slippers into these pattens and walk in them so that you are lifted up out of all the muck.'

'Put them away, Margery.' Polly dived into her wardrobe and held up a pair of stout black shoes. 'I can do better than that. Don't you remember your mother gave me these when my feet got better?'

'Well, I've got two of everything else from Jocky. Two shirts, two waistcoats, two coats – even two hats.' Margery stepped into one of the pairs of breeches, and the dressing began. They helped each other bundle up their hair inside the hats. 'Now,

Polly, neither of us can possibly breathe in the odours of the night.' Margery soaked two large squares of linen in eau-de-cologne, and handed one over. 'Keep that over your nose and mouth, and when we put on our cloaks we shall be ready to go.'

Every now and then as they ran down the steep incline of the West Bow into the Grassmarket she pushed Polly close to the tenement walls when a shout of 'Gardy-loo' went up, and a pail of filthy water – or worse – cascaded into the street beside them. 'Ugh!' she gasped. ' "The Roses of Edinburgh"! Run, Polly! There's Jocky, waiting for us.'

At first when the three of them sidled into the interior of Michael Henderson's old feed-barn they could see nothing in the impenetrable gloom. The noise of hoarse-throated men all yelling at the top of their voices was indescribable. Fortunately neither Polly nor Margery could make out one word. The language and the shouts of laughter were nothing short of obscene.

At last their eyes became accustomed to the gloom, and they discovered that they were in the back row of the audience with nobody paying any attention to them. Everyone was craning forward to see the stage, which was not raised up as in the theatre, but was a small square pit covered with taut canvas down in the middle of the barn.

Two men squatted opposite each other in front of cloth-covered pens, and one of them was Deacon Brodie, easy to distinguish in his light-coloured clothes. It took Polly a few shocked minutes to realize that this time he wanted to be seen, and that was why he hadn't changed them as usual after the evening meal.

'Is he going tae win, Will Brodie?'

'G'ie us a tip, Macaroni!'

'Is he a killer? Tell us, man!'

The spectators had less respect for the Deacon than for his bird. Jocky Robertson grinned, and Polly was appalled.

The shouting died down to a murmuring, a low excited tension, during which coins chinked and a man climbed on to the tiny stage and announced the first fight. It was about to begin!

There was a great cheer and a roar of laughter when the man tripped on his way off the canvas again. Deacon Brodie and his opponent signalled to their setters-on who brought out the first two cocks, their beaks open ready to strike, and their beady little eyes unblinking and full of malice.

Then the din really broke out as bets were shouted between the owners and the onlookers. Polly clutched Margery's arm when the Deacon leapt to his feet, his eyes flashing, his face burning, all propriety and all decency gone, yelling and cursing with the best of them and dancing in some strange ecstasy with froth on his lips and a bottle in his hand.

She watched, numb with horror, when a yell from the crowd turned into a scream and the released birds hurled themselves at each other, ripping, pecking, lunging with their cruel spurs, and streams of blood spattered on the canvas, soaking it red in minutes.

She had seen more than she bargained for and, sickened, she turned her head away. It was then that a high-pitched, madly screaming laugh echoed through the rafters, and the clamour stopped for a second as if cut by a knife. Polly was paralysed with horror. Even the men there cringed at the sound before the shouting began again.

Oh, God ... It was the unmistakable laugh she had heard first in Paris, then again at the Hornpipe – it had seemed to follow her mother wherever she went. Now it was haunting Polly. She waited and waited, but it didn't come again before Jocky Robertson reckoned they had seen enough for one night and it was time to go.

'But whose bird won?' Margery was asking as he hurried them out.

'Deacon Brodie's,' Jocky snorted. 'He always wins, that little b– oh, I beg your pardon, ladies – that little man!'

Their way was suddenly blocked by a tall figure. Polly pulled her wide-brimmed hat down more firmly over her pinned-up hair, drew her collar close and was just about to skirt around him when a hand of steel fell on her shoulder.

'For God's sake,' hissed Fraser Graham. 'What *is* this?

He pulled her out into the lighter dimness of the Grassmarket and she saw that he was white with fury.

'What do you think you are doing, Polly Buchanan? Margery Buchanan, why did you not stop her? And as for you, Jocky Robertson, how could you allow them to come to a place such as this? Do you not know that they could have been trampled to death? Or attacked – even raped – and left for dead amidst that mob? The men are like wild animals!'

Jocky and Margery slid away into the darkness. Fraser dragged Polly all the way back up the West Bow until they arrived at the Lawnmarket in stony silence. The few times that she dared to glance at him she understood that his displeasure was because she might have been harmed. She longed and longed to have his arms around her. She wished with all her heart she could tell him everything, tell him what she was trying to do.

'What were you doing there, anyway?' she said at last, breaking the silence. 'You're just as bad as all the rest of them to be in that cock-pit in the first place!'

He pushed her through the archway into Brodie's Close, too angry even to reply.

'I can find my own way from here,' Polly said haughtily.

'You will do nothing of the sort,' Fraser said through clenched teeth, and marched her right to the kitchen door. She did not get a chance to bang it shut in his face. He pulled it to, and slammed it in hers.

She cried all the way to bed, and once her sobs died down a bit and she could think of something else, she thought very uneasily about Deacon Brodie. Tonight she had seen yet another side of him that she didn't like.

However, the visit to the cockfight had all been worth it, she supposed miserably. Even if she hadn't spotted the man with that dreadful laugh, she must be on the right track. He had known her mother and he was here in Edinburgh.

15

THAT NIGHT AT the cockfight and its miserable end affected Polly for a whole week afterwards. Each morning now at eight o'clock Margery arrived with Annie Begbie. How many servants had come and gone, even in the short time she'd been here herself, Polly wondered. Mattie and Jess, both gone. Margery would not last long, now that she had a secret life of her own, whatever happened to Annie Begbie with her large, work-reddened hands.

It all added to her own sense of impermanency, of being here only to play a part in some strange drama yet to unfold, and day by day she sensed the tension of it building up tighter and tighter. Some day it was bound to snap.

'Margery, Annie,' she asked them the following morning, 'will you help me to shift a piece of furniture, a writing desk in my room? I don't know why it's there. It won't even open, and it's taking up too much space.'

They shifted the desk into the empty room next to Polly's, a narrow slit of a space with only a skylight in the roof. Annie Begbie set to work at once with her scrubbing brush to clean away the cobwebs where the desk had stood, while Polly went down to the dining-hall to join her mistress.

'Oh, it's so exciting, Polly!' Miss Jeanette's eyes were shining and her breakfast was scarcely touched. 'Mistress Scott is coming to take us over to the New Town this morning at half past nine for coffee. It is a little early, but we are to watch Mr

Vincent Lunardi make another attempt to ascend in his hot-air balloon over the town at ten.'

It was a glorious October day when they entered the Scotts' coach and Mistress Scott spread the rug over their knees because of the chilly breeze. The leaves danced gently in their autumn colours on the trees all over the city, and the Nor'Loch sparkled below as the coach crossed the North Bridge.

Mr Leslie chatted in low tones to Miss Jeanette and Mistress Scott took it upon herself to act as Polly's guide. 'This bridge is like the short bar across the letter H,' she told her. 'One long leg is the Royal Mile, and the other is Princes Street. We are just turning into it now.'

Polly looked along its length and saw Edinburgh Castle from a completely different angle, soaring up on its craggy rock.

'Now this is the New Town,' Mistress Scott continued when the coach turned right. 'This is Queen Street, where we are going.'

'It is all very grand, isn't it?' Walter Scott sighed. 'But I often wonder if any other street in the world could be so majestic and distinguished as the Royal Mile, after all? Certainly, none could be so full of history. The very stones reek of it.'

'Nonsense, dear.' Mistress Scott swept aside her son's nostalgic whimsy. 'Robert Adam himself has consented to design some of the most important buildings. Already it is called the Athens of the North!'

They were certainly very grand, these terraces of houses, all so uniformly and graciously proportioned, and very different from the tall buildings of the Royal Mile so beloved by Walter Scott, the 'lands' of them eight or twelve storeys high, their common stairs dirty, steep and overcrowded.

The carriage bowled along Queen Street, where the windows of the houses overlooked beautiful gardens on the other side.

'Here we are,' Mistress Scott said. 'Number twenty-nine, Fraser's house.'

Polly's heart almost stopped beating. Nobody had said they were going to Fraser Graham's house. She would not have come if she had known, after that terrible night at the cockfight. 'Perhaps Mr Graham meant only you and Mr Leslie to come, Miss Jeanette,' she said nervously.

176

'Of course he didn't, dear.' Mistress Scott was as brisk as ever. 'In fact, he made a point of inviting you as well.'

'Does *all* this house belong to Mr Graham?' Polly asked when the coach stopped.

'Yes. There are no tenement lands here. One house for one family.'

She was deeply impressed. In fact, she was quite awestruck when they stepped up the three wide shallow steps to the very imposing front door, with its brass accoutrements glittering, its iron boot-jacks at either side black-polished, and the fan-shaped window above it of the most elegant design she had ever seen.

Afterwards she had no clear recollection of how she actually crossed the threshold, or who admitted them, or of Fraser coming to receive them – only that he was at her side in the bright square entrance hall, with its floor tiled in a glorious mosaic.

He ushered them into the large drawing-room with long windows all along one side looking out over the gardens. It seemed to Polly that it was full of people sitting in groups of two or three chatting over their coffee. Miss Brodie and Mr Leslie immediately went to join them.

'When I am in Edinburgh this is my one "At Home" occasion in the week.' Fraser smiled. 'All my friends know they are welcome on Wednesday mornings.'

'I see Mistress Sally Henderson over there.' Mistress Scott left them alone to pounce on her crony, and a footman came across the room to whisper something in Fraser's ear. He nodded, and led Polly over to a settee occupied by one large gentleman.

'Lord Braxfield,' he addressed him, 'would you be so kind as to look after Miss Polly Buchanan for me? There is some sort of upset in the hall, but I should not be long.'

Lord Braxfield! Polly wished the ground would open up and swallow her. 'Stay as long as ye like, lad. Dinna hurry back,' Lord Braxfield said. 'And who are you, my lassie?'

She coughed a little, her throat gone completely dry. 'The niece of Mr and Mistress George Buchanan, sir, from Candlemaker Row.'

'Polly Buchanan?' His shrewd dark eyes snapped at her. 'Ye weren't christened Polly, I'll be bound. What's yer real name?'

'Olivia, sir,' she told him, horrified at herself the minute it was out. Why had she told Lord Braxfield, of all people, before she was ready to tell anyone anything? Oh, God, what did he know already? If he knew about Suzanne Gray, wouldn't he also know about her daughter, Olivia? Polly's terror increased as the question came to her – was that why she was here today, in place of her mother?

'Noo then! That's a better combination with a good Scottish name like Buchanan.'

'I come from London, sir. My mother was English.'

'Hm. So ye've lost yer mother, lassie?'

'Yes.' Polly felt her lip quivering, but it was from fear in this dreadful cross-examination.

'Ah weel, lassie, dinna fret.' Lord Braxfield patted her hand. 'It's plain to see she must have been a lady, anyway, to ha'e sic a bonny wee lass as yersel'. I'm verra pleased to meet ye, Polly Buchanan.'

It was so kindly meant and so kindly said by one of the most important men in all Scotland, who obviously knew nothing about her after all, that Polly managed to control herself. She smiled the smile that had captivated other hearts before the great judge's.

'Thank you, Lord Braxfield,' Polly said. 'I am honoured to meet you, too.'

'So ye've come to see this Lunardi chap fly in his contraption, have ye?'

'Oh, I hope he does fly.' Polly could not help smiling.

'My, but ye're a bonnie wee lassie! I aye expected Fraser would choose wisely when it came to a woman. He was never a fool, ye ken, just awfu' unfortunate.'

'Unfortunate? Why?'

'Dae ye no' ken? He's heir to a fortune and more than that, dearie. But he canna prove it in a court o' law. Ay, the law's one thing ye canna dispute. It's a grand thing, the law o' this land.'

'But from what I've heard since coming to Edinburgh, the law is being most seriously flouted, Lord Braxfield.'

'Ay, wi' the burglaries, ye mean. That's verra true, lassie. But the mills o' God grind slow, and they grind exceedin' sma', ye ken. The evil-doers will be up afore me, yet.'

Polly looked at the old man. His was not a handsome face. His nose dominated it, long and at the same time bulbous, but the large brown eyes above it were the sharpest she had ever seen. Now they changed to coal-black, fathomless, implacable.

'Scotland can trust you to be absolutely just, sir.'

'It can that, lassie,' he made no attempt at modesty. 'I'm famed for it, ye ken! Weel, here he is coming back again. Ye ha'e yer problems sorted oot, Fraser?'

'May God preserve me from hysterical women. That was Mistress Ballantyne taking the vapours on account of Mr Lunardi's impending death.'

'She aye was a silly auld besom.' Lord Braxfield laughed wheezily.

'Well, the coffee is waiting over on the side table. Polly, you will have a cup?' He swept her up. 'What about you, sir? Would you rather have another little dram?' Fraser asked, pouring brandy liberally into the judge's glass.

'Ay, lad. That's more like it! None o' yon foreign bitter stuff for me! I'll stick to what I ken.'

'Lunardi should have set off by now from the gardens of Heriot's. Shall we all go out and watch for him?'

'Weel, *you* may, laddie, and tak' this bonnie wee lassie wi' ye. She aye reminds me o' someone when she smiles, Fraser. Who is it?'

'Nobody I know, sir. As far as I'm concerned there is only one like her.'

'It's her smile, and her hair ... ' The judge stared at her. 'I'll get it yet! But I'll just sit here if I may, and watch oot o' yer windows.'

After coffee served with tiny ratafia biscuits Fraser tucked Polly's hand under his arm and led the way to the door. 'He's as sharp as a fox, that old man,' he said, 'and thrawn, and as determinedly Scottish as a thistle. He speaks like that in Court, you know, scorning English. But his mind is like a rapier, for all that. What was he saying to you?'

They went down the steps at the front door and across the street into the gardens which were a long oval, with a path around the perimeter, trees and bushes overhanging all the way.

The whole company followed suit, some walking in one direction, some in another, looking upwards into the sky.

'He was saying that you should have inherited a fortune, but you are very unfortunate. What did that mean?'

'Do you really want to know? Do you care, Polly, after what happened the night of the cockfight?'

'Of course. I realized afterwards you meant it for my own good. Some day I might be able to repay you.'

'That will be a happy day for me. There is a property I hope to inherit, the only one in which I should wish to spend the rest of my life. I lived there as a child with my great-aunt, but we quarrelled and I left.'

'She died?'

'Without leaving a will. None that was ever found, at least. I cannot just assume that the house is mine and go back, so it sits empty,' he said bitterly, 'and going to waste.'

Just then the shout went up. 'Lunardi! Lunardi!'

An apparition like a great grotesque bird floated above them. Polly saw a huge balloon of some light material criss-crossed with ropes which tied it on to a ridiculous basket dangling beneath, and in the basket stood a man.

Was it a man? She shaded her eyes and gazed upwards. Of course it was a man, dressed in a red jacket and red and blue striped trousers, but from down here he looked so silly, so dwarfish, like a tiny mannikin. They could see him waving and hear his faint shouts.

'Oh, it's wonderful,' she said, 'and terrible at the same time. I do not think I really like it. I wish he had stayed on the ground. Men flying are men dying, if they fall out.'

Fraser laughed gently. 'He's not going to fall out. I admire his spirit of adventure.'

'Of course you do,' she said. 'You are a man, and men dare to risk their lives.'

'You are a woman, and it is a woman's instinct to preserve them. *Vive la différence* ... '

She could scarcely bear the look in his eyes, so green, so burning. She forgot that she wanted no one to know that she spoke French, and a blush came to her cheeks.

'Polly ... Polly ...' he said longingly.

180

'So here you are, Fraser! I can just see your head through the trees,' came a familiar voice, and they sprang apart. 'Oh, there you are, Polly!'

'Miss Jeanette.' Fraser's voice was flat as he acknowledged her. 'Jamie.' He nodded at Mr Leslie.

'What a delightful coffee party! Such a success! Was it not amusing, that little man in his hot-air balloon, Polly? Mistress Scott is leaving now, so we must go too. Come along, dear!'

But it had been a very narrow squeak, Polly told herself on the way back to the Royal Mile. That old man, Lord Braxfield, could not possibly recognize her. He could not possibly have known her mother.

'Mr Leslie and I have been invited to my sister's – Mistress Jacobina's – this evening, Polly,' Miss Jeanette interrupted her thoughts. 'So you may have the evening off, dear.'

Polly took a deep breath. An evening off! And she had the key to Candacraig in her pocket! 'Thank you, Miss Jeanette,' she said quietly.

As soon as Miss Jeanette and Mr Leslie went out to visit the Sheriffs Polly helped Margery and Annie Begbie to clear up as fast as they could. Jocky Robertson came for Margery, Annie went with them, and Polly was left alone. The night was young and fine when she put on her cloak, made sure she had the Candacraig key and some money in her pocket, and quietly let herself out of the house to find the best chair man in the town.

She got into the tall old Highlander's sedan chair and looked at Edward Burke's weatherbeaten face with the deepest respect, after all the MacAllisters had told her about him. Edward Burke, the bravest Highlander of them all, who might have gained thirty thousand pounds by a word from his mouth about the Prince after Culloden, but who had returned quietly to his duty as a chair man on the streets of Edinburgh rather than betray him. 'To Candacraig,' she said. 'Do you know it?'

'It will take an hour at least,' he said in perfect English with a lilting Highland accent, his proud eyes upon her face.

Once she would have been intimidated, but not now. She reached into her pocket for the last of Mama's gold coins. 'However long it takes, however much it costs, Mr Burke,' she said offering him all the money.

'Let us get there, first.' He shut the door.

She did not draw the curtains when she felt the sedan chair lift and its curious swaying motion begin. She left them open and watched as the streetlamps flashed by, her heart almost bursting with excitement. At last! At last! *She was on her way to Candacraig.* Soon there were no more lights or even streets, and out here in this strange little moving world of her own she tried to quell her excitement by looking back over all the threads woven into the tapestry of the last few months in Scotland, what she had seen herself, and what others had told her.

June had been a busy month all round in Edinburgh. The town council were debating whether they should lease the cleansing of the streets to a private contractor for five hundred pounds, but they were too slow in deciding it before the General Assembly came and went, filling the town with the ministers of the Church of Scotland from far and wide. Every year it was conducted with the utmost ceremony and splash. This year there had been more pomp than ever.

Then it was the fourth of July and the King's birthday, an occasion well marked in this most royal of Scottish burghs. The street wells and the lamp brackets were adorned with flowers, but none so colourful as the garlands which adorned the statue of King George in Parliament Close, so the Buchanans had told her. It was a holiday. The guns fired a salute from the Castle walls, and at night there were fireworks.

The events in Brodie's Close had made the time pass by like a flash. Next year she would be seventeen, but where might she be by then? Perhaps her whole future depended on what she might find in Candacraig, and certainly if she found nothing she had no future at all that she could see.

What would happen to her? Common sense told her that if all went well for Miss Brodie she would soon be married to Mr Leslie, and would need no other companion but him. Two things were certain – stay on alone in that house with the Deacon she could not, and the prospect of trailing from one lonely lady to another as a companion for the rest of her life filled her with dismay.

Ned Burke had not hesitated when she had asked to go to

Candacraig, and now the chair men were jogging along with the sedan chair at a fine pace. The pitch darkness was not so dense outside Edinburgh, and now she could make out wreaths of mist along the hedgerows. Then suddenly, full and startling in its appearance out of nowhere, the moon sailed magnificently into view.

It lit up the roadside, the bracken and the broom blackened with the recent early morning frosts, and swept the evening mist away contemptuously. The chair men went at a slower pace now, up a hill, and at the top they stopped and looked about them. Then they carried the sedan on to the grassy verge at the side of the road, and Ned Burke came round to speak to her.

'That must be the Edinburgh Fly, very late.' He pointed down the hill. 'It has stopped to let someone out. We will wait here until it passes. Then it is only half a mile to Candacraig, down there.'

The Fly lumbered up the hill towards them, crowded as usual, with the luggage strapped on to the roof and the lamps lit inside. The horses strained up to the top, and when they discovered they had arrived and it was downhill all the way from then on, tossed their heads and picked up speed.

It seemed very quiet after the noise of the coach died away into the night, and the chair men bent to their task once more. For a while they ran along the road ahead and then they plunged on round a curve between two iron gates. Past a lodge, the road opened wide to a long drive beyond. They must be coming to the big house now. Polly's heart beat faster.

At first the road ran straight, and then it began to snake through an archway of trees. The moon in all her brilliance could not penetrate the thickness of the leaves above, and only flickering patches of light came in waves to dapple the path with silver. It was very silent, with just the pad-pad of the chair mens' feet to break the curious stillness.

The silver path became enchanted, winding like a ribbon into the heart of the forest, here and there over little bridges, over streams, and on and on. She wondered if it would ever come to an end, and didn't care if it never did.

And then ahead she saw a clearing, a tiny patch of luminous sky. The trees were thinning and the path became a broader sweep as they turned the last corner of all. There, drenched in the moonlight, lay the dreaming house, a fairy castle, built in a hollow of lawns.

The sedan chair stopped and Ned Burke came round to open the door for her. 'We are here,' he said, 'but there are no lights anywhere. The house seems to be deserted.'

'I have the key.'

Ned Burke raised his eyebrows but he made no comment. Instead he took the night lantern from the back of the sedan and led the way to the front door. 'Let me turn it for you,' he said. 'It's a big door, and a big key.'

He opened the door and while they had their backs turned to look inside Candacraig a man leading a horse out of the stables across the grass suddenly stopped. Silently he backed the horse into its stall again, and keeping to the shadows watched them from the ivy-covered walls.

'Do you wish me to come through the house with you?' Ned Burke asked.

'No. Thank you, Mr Burke, but I can manage alone.'

'Will you take the lantern?'

'I shall not need the lantern, the moon is so bright. Only leave the door a little ajar and then I can get out again when I am ready.'

'We'll wait,' he said, and went back to the sedan.

Then once again Polly had that strange feeling that sometimes came to her, that she had been here before, although it was impossible. She stood still for a moment, and in that moment felt the old house open its arms to her in a rush of music. Yet no music played, and the silence continued.

She did not feel afraid as slowly she moved from room to room, recognizing things she had never known, as though now at last she was home after years and years of absence.

It was in the east wing that she came upon the little jewel of a sitting-room, and knew instinctively that this was where the lady of the house always spent her mornings, writing her letters at the writing desk, making up the menus for her cook, adding up the accounts for her husband's approval.

The moonlight flooded in through the windows and lit up the wall to her left, highlighting a patch where some article of furniture must once have stood, for the wallpaper there was brighter and darker than the rest.

It was furnished with great care, and as with all the other rooms she had visited so far, dusted and polished carefully. Fleetingly she wondered who had done it, before she began imagining how the sun would warm the room in the mornings, how it would look with vases of roses on the mantelpiece, and great bowls of them on the little tables by the sofa. She could see it all in her mind's eye, and tonight the moon made it spring to life as bright as day.

Its moving rays slanted suddenly on the portrait above the mantelpiece and Polly gazed up at it, startled for the first time since she had entered the house, frozen into a statue; for looking down at her was a face she had never expected to see again in this life ... the face of her dead mother.

It *was* Mama! There was no doubt of it. Dressed in the style of nearly a hundred years ago, her hair in jewelled knots, with a little dog upon her lap ... Perhaps she had dressed up like that for a fancy-dress ball. Her eyes were darker and more animated than she remembered them, and there was a strange warning in them. She could almost hear her mother speaking to her. 'At all costs, don't give me away!'

'Mama,' Polly breathed. A footstep sounded behind her, and then a man's deep voice.

'It is Lady Susanna Graham, Polly.'

She whirled around, the moon full in her eyes, and saw Fraser Graham. She didn't understand any of this. The music of the house stopped suddenly, and now there was a buzzing in her ears.

She found herself lying on the floor in the moonlit sitting-room with her head on a cushion. Fraser held a glass of water to her lips. She took a sip and lay back quite still, while the ceiling, the walls and the figure before her took solid shape again. 'What are you doing here?' she said shakily. 'I thought I was alone.'

'I am so sorry, Polly. I should not have startled you like that.'

'I had seen one ghost already.' She glanced up at the portrait. 'My mother's.'

'Perhaps it was a trick of the moonlight,' Fraser said gently, holding the glass to her lips again. 'You mustn't worry. Just lie still. That is not your mother, Polly. It's Lady Susanna Graham.'

She looked again, and now little differences were there in the picture. The eyes were really quite dark, and Mama's had been pale blue, and this lady's expression was livelier, bold and adventurous.

'You still haven't answered my question, though.' Polly sighed. 'What are you doing here?'

'I could ask you the same question, especially since I am in charge of the place.'

'*You* are in charge of it?'

'Erskine Caldwell is the lawyer ultimately responsible, but he allows me to keep a couple of horses here, for getting back and fore to my stables south of the town. Today I rode my horse down there and took the Fly back. Of course, I pay for this privilege. The groom I employ and his wife are caretakers for the house. They live in a separate cottage, round the back.'

'Will they hear us?' Polly shivered.

'If they do I hope they will think it is only me moving about the house. Thankfully you did not take a lantern. Donald MacDonald is a handy man with a gun. But they knew I was coming. I sent them word, and they have seen me already, when I came off the Edinburgh Fly to get one of my horses. All the same, just lie still while I go and reassure them.'

'I can't lie here! The chair men are waiting!'

'No, they are not. I paid them off before I came in through the front door I saw you unlocking. They will be half-way back to Edinburgh by now. So, why would Polly Buchanan want to get into Candacraig so desperately that she even obtained a key, I wonder? You'd better have a good answer ready, my dear, before I come back!'

She lay back and looked at the woman in the portrait again, at her glorious auburn hair. She had made a mistake. Mama's hair was so very fair. Nevertheless, the resemblance was too close for comfort.

While she gazed the rays of the moon moved away from the picture and left that part of the wall dark and empty. Its beams struck the other side of the fireplace this time, and lit up another

186

portrait, the portrait of a man. She tried to sit up when Fraser came back.

'No.' He pushed her back down firmly, and covered her with a rug. 'You look tired and cold. I've brought some dry sticks and logs and the MacDonalds say the chimney is clean so a fire should take up. I've told them I will rest here for an hour or two. Now, I'm going back to their cottage for something to eat and drink, and then I'll hear your story.'

The glow and the sparks from the burning logs woke her some time later, and she saw that he was back in the room. 'I must have fallen asleep,' she said.

'When did you last eat, Polly?'

'Well ...' She considered. She had eaten very little that day, it was true. 'I can't remember. This morning, I think.'

'Just as I thought, so I brought these,' he said, taking the cloth off the basket he was carrying so that the wonderful smell of hot roasted chicken floated under her nose. She found she was ravenously hungry.

'There are herbs in it,' Polly sniffed.

'It is Chicken Rosemary, according to Mistress MacDonald. She gave me this loaf to go with it.' He sat down on the floor beside her in front of the fire. It was glowing now. He tore off a wing of the chicken and handed it to her. 'How does it taste?'

'Wonderful.'

'So now – what is the answer? What are you doing here, Polly?'

'I just felt suffocated in Edinburgh, so I took a sedan chair.'

'But why to Candacraig?'

Polly watched him tossing one drumstick into the blazing fire and taking its fellow. 'I had the key.'

'Well, that's one reason, I suppose. Where did you get it from?'

'Deacon Brodie's workshop. He has hundreds there, all labelled, and I saw the one for Candacraig. I have heard so much about it, I thought it would be safe enough. Everyone said it was deserted.'

'Another crust of bread?' He dived into the basket again and drew out a slim green bottle and two glasses. 'Let's drink to the newly discovered burglar of Edinburgh, shall we? Now that I

187

come to think about it, there have been more robberies than ever since you arrived in town. Have you broken into any other houses lately?'

She shook her head in a daze, and tears sprang to her eyes. 'Oh, Fraser! What will happen now? Who lives here, anyway?'

He poured more wine into her glass, and put his arm around her. 'Nobody yet. Don't worry, I won't give you away. The house has been sitting empty for almost a year, waiting for its new owner who cannot be found for love or money.'

'Why? Who lived here before?'

'Lady Susanna Graham, and me. Before that, Sir John Robertson Graham as well. Those are their portraits up there. They were my aunt and uncle.'

'You mean, Candacraig is the house you told me about? The one you want to live in again?'

'Yes. If only we knew what was in my Aunt Susanna's mind when she died. She had no children of her own. At least …'

'At least?'

'At least, none in Edinburgh that we know about. But there was some scandal about her. She had a lover, long ago. You can tell from her eyes that such a scandal was more than possible. The expression in them is bold and passionate, longing for adventure.'

Polly took another sip from her glass and tried to curb her rising excitement. 'Did anyone find out who she had her adventure with?'

He took the glass gently from her hand and put his arms around her while they sat in the glow of the fire and she loosened the top buttons of her bodice. 'Only me, Polly. I think I know the secret.'

She smiled up at him, languid after their meal, yet with her pulses racing. She wanted him to kiss her.

He put out his hand and touched her neck, lifting the gold necklace she always wore and looking at the ring her mother had given her. 'That is a very unusual ring,' he said. 'Why do you wear it on that chain?'

'In case I lose it,' she said, before they both lost interest in the ring and he kissed her. She wondered after a while if the fire had died down, for she was in darkness, he was in darkness, and there had never been anything before this time and this dark place and his lips on her body.

Later she tried to speak, but his mouth stopped her, and suddenly she felt a wild thrill. It was joy, and fear, and madness and excitement all rolled into one in arms she never wanted to leave. Her arms were round his neck and her lips were trembling beneath his as they explored the darkness again and again. She wanted it never to stop.

But she was quite unprepared for its aftermath.

After the sexual act Mama always appeared as she had been before, cool and unruffled. It had all been a God Bless You, just another natural function.

It was very different for Polly. She sat up and put on her dress again, looking at the lips she had kissed so ardently half an hour ago, and didn't feel cool at all. She looked at Fraser's hands, every bone of them, the shape of his head, the very way his hair grew, and found herself in deep waters she had never meant to get into at all.

'What are you doing?' he smiled up at her lazily.

'Getting dressed. I must go.'

'What are you running away from? From what has just been? You must feel something for me, after that.'

'I do.'

'I love you, Polly.'

'You don't even know me yet.'

And the girl he did know was living under an assumed name, she thought darkly. The daughter of a woman probably wanted for murder.

'I know all I need to know.'

'Don't try to stop me, Fraser! It must be nearly morning. I must get back to Brodie's Close. What's more, I must get back by eight o'clock.'

'What's so important about eight o'clock?' He pulled on his clothes.

'That's when Margery comes to start work. I don't want her or anyone else to know I've been out all night.'

'Do you mean to tell me that you are there alone with the Brodies all night long? I thought Margery Buchanan was always with you!'

'No. I let her out every night at nine o'clock into the company of the MacAllisters or Jocky Robertson, and then I lock the door and go to bed,' she said, swinging her cloak around her shoulders.

Outside it was the dark before the dawn, pitch-black. 'Wait here,' Fraser said, 'until I get my horse,' and five minutes later he helped her up on to the saddle behind him. 'So Deacon Brodie has hundreds of keys?' he asked as they trotted along.

'Jocky Robertson told me that he makes a copy of the keys of every house he works at.'

'Ah! And he was the one who closed up Candacraig ...' he mused. 'Erskine Caldwell did the inventory. The valuables are all in Edinburgh.'

'There's something missing in Lady Susanna's sitting-room. There's a space there, as though some piece of furniture had been removed.'

'I wasn't looking at the furniture, Polly. But that's very interesting. Perhaps Deacon Brodie could not resist it, whatever it was. I wonder how he sneaked it out, right under Erskine Caldwell's nose? Perhaps her will was inside it. If so, he has it now.'

Polly's arms tightened around his waist.

'A will that nobody knew anything about except Lord Braxfield who drew it up.' Fraser glanced round at her. 'He was Lady Susanna's lover, I'm sure of it, and there must have been a child.'

'How do you know that?'

'I'm only guessing, but I do know he desperately wanted to find Suzanne Gray. I believe she might have been that child.'

Polly took a deep breath, thankful that he could not see how her face blanched, then flamed and blanched again. All this was only conjecture. She longed to tell him that Suzanne was her own mother, but she couldn't until she was able to prove the truth.

'Erskine Caldwell gave us her address,' Fraser went on. 'He sent a large allowance to her from the Graham estate every month, but when Lady Susanna died that had to stop for lack of further instructions.'

Polly was silent. The pieces of the puzzle were beginning to fit. That man in London with the dreadful laugh had something to do with it. If only she could find him, she sighed, as they rode up the Royal Mile. Until she did she intended to stay in Brodie's Close, in the very heart of the town, amongst as many people as possible.

It was at the cockfight that once more she had heard that laugh. Any day she might hear it again in the Luckenbooths, or the shops, or the coffee-houses with Miss Jeanette.

'Polly ...' He frowned up at Deacon Brodie's house when they arrived at the close. 'Please come to Queen Street with me.'

'I cannot. At least, not yet. I still have reasons to work on here. So does Margery. We have not been paid a penny so far.'

'This is ridiculous!' Fraser put his hand in his pocket and brought out some silver coins. 'Those won't last long. I'll bring some more for you both. Where do you sleep?'

'Up there.' She pointed to the window overlooking the Lawnmarket.

'It is dangerous to stay in that house, Polly. You know that man is a scoundrel in disguise, and Miss Jeanette is not much of a chaperone, out so often nowadays with Jamie Leslie.'

'There is no need to worry. I always lock my door and bolt it.'

'And you do not think that the Deacon of the carpenting trade could simply take a door off its hinges, if he wanted to?' Fraser lifted her down from the horse. 'I will be waiting in the shadows at the back door when you let out Margery tonight,' he whispered.

She crept through the sleeping house, up to her room and into her bed, falling asleep as soon as she got there. Three hours later, at half past seven, she rose again fresh-faced and radiant, with the kitchen fire lit for eight o'clock.

'What a strange look there is about you today!' Margery exclaimed as soon as she saw her.

'Lack of sleep, I expect. I only slept three hours last night.'

'You should do it more often, then! It suits you. You have a very satisfied look – like a cat after it has had a dish of cream.'

Polly laughed. 'Yes?'

'But watch out,' Margery warned, slapping a rasher of ham on to the frying pan. 'You can get very fat that way!'

16

IT TOOK POLLY until seven o'clock that night to come back down to earth, and then she couldn't believe the force of her awakening. It hit her between the eyes. She should not be entering into a relationship with Fraser Graham or any other man at this stage of her life. For two hours she worried about it, but all her good intentions wavered when the girls' footsteps died away into the Royal Mile and Fraser was at the back door, then evaporated altogether when his arms were around her again.

As one night succeeded the next she discovered another unexpected fact. He was not there only to make love to her. He talked to her, he made her laugh, he stilled her fears and became her friend as well as her lover, always willing to speak about her secret obsession, Candacraig. If any man could unravel its mysteries for her, she became more certain every day that it must be him.

'So why did you quarrel with Lady Susanna, Fraser? Was it very bitter?'

'She has left the whole place fifty years behind the times. That was the sorest argument I ever had with her. That's why I left. I could not bear to see it.'

'Why? What did she think?'

'That it would all go on for ever, the over-cropping of the farms on the estate, with such poor results and such high rents for the workers that they had to work like slaves just to keep alive and bring up their families.'

There was an echo in the back of her mind, an echo from France, about men having to work like slaves and go hungry while their masters got richer and richer. 'So there are farms belonging to Candacraig?'

'Four, and each one more run-down than the last. They will have to be improved. I tried to persuade my aunt to enclose our fields, have a proper rotation of crops, pension off our older workers so that there are fewer, and in better housing. In that way their lives would be worth living. They would take a pride in their work, and so in the end we would benefit.'

'That would mean laying down a lot of money, wouldn't it?'

'That was her objection. Lady Susanna could not see that better farming would yield better results for her in the long run.'

'You sound more interested in farming than in the law, Fraser.'

'I always was. Oh, I could continue to practise! That means all day in the town. I could even stand for Parliament, I suppose. That would mean days and weeks away in London. No, Polly, all I ever wanted was to be back in Candacraig – until now.' He took her gently in his arms again. 'Now, all I want is to be in Candacraig with you.'

Every day now that the month had changed to November the weather worsened, with scarcely a day when the kitchen was not laden with piles of steaming sodden washing. Annie Begbie became tearful and Margery became more and more bad-tempered. She went to Miss Jeanette.

'It would not be so bad,' she told her, 'if we did not have to contend with Master Will's white suits. As it is, there is not a square inch where I can lay down a pan because of all this washing.'

'Mistress Watt, the washerwoman in Libberton's Wynd, always sees to his suits in the winter.'

When Polly followed Margery back to the kitchen Annie Begbie refused point-blank to have anything to do with the washerwoman.

'But there must be five or six suits dirty by this time, Annie,' Margery protested. 'You will never manage to get them done.'

'Bundle them up and give them to me,' Polly said. 'Then tell me how to get to Libberton's Wynd.'

'Oh, I'd better come with you and show you the way! In any case you could never carry them all yourself.' Margery led her out into the Royal Mile. 'Jean Watt, the washerwoman in Libberton's Wynd, is very well known. In fact, she's notorious. That's why Annie is frightened to go.'

Libberton's Wynd was an alley so dark and overhung that it took a long time to accustom their eyes to the gloom, and instinctively they spoke in whispers for fear of someone materializing out of the walls. As it was, Polly did not like the look of the women sitting around silently on their outside steps, ladies of the night by the look of them.

There was one in particular who must be the Queen of Libberton's Wynd. She lounged up against her door, dressed in the finest clothes of her profession, gaudy and tasteless enough to catch any man's eye. A boy of about ten years old stood beside her, staring at the strangers.

'Could you direct us to Mistress Jean Watt?' Margery asked politely.

'That's me,' the woman said.

'These are Deacon Brodie's suits to be washed.'

'Deacon Brodie, eh?' Jean Watt laughed stridently, the boy smiled slyly at her side, and there were titters all around from the other women. 'Och, ay. Hand them over, then. Everyone knows I'll do anything for the little Macaroni – isn't that right, Willie?' She gave the boy a nudge.

'So ye've aye told me, Ma.'

The women joined in the laugh. Then an ugly, ominous silence fell as Mistress Watt took stock of Polly.

'Noo then, Willie Brodie,' she shouted in a loud voice to the boy, 'will ye look at this? Here she is in a' her glory, her that has the cheek tae be livin' in yer faither's hoose! And what may *you* want, madam?' She leered in Polly's face. 'Ha'e ye come to see poor Jean Watt wi' her twa weans?'

The other women got to their feet threateningly and first glared and then laughed at the two girls scuttling out of Libberton's Wynd.

'Mind and tell the Deacon I was asking for him!' Jean Watt shouted after them, amidst howls of laughter.

'Deacon Brodie can take his suits himself the next time,'

Margery panted. 'I'll never go there again. I never thought it would be so bad.'

'She is a terrible woman,' Polly agreed when they reached the safety of the crowded High Street again.

'Is that all you saw? What about the boy, with his short neck, his fair hair – at least it would be if it was clean – and his grey eyes?'

'I saw it all, Margery. The boy was the Deacon's image.'

'You may as well see the rest, then,' Margery said with a sigh. 'Only promise you will never tell Ma and Pa any of this, or else they will take me away from Brodie's Close. It was Jocky who put me wise. We may as well visit Cant's Close while we're at it. It's in here.' She led Polly into another alley, not much lighter and not much better than the one before.

It was long and narrow, no more than three feet wide, and felt eerily like a tunnel. At the very end it opened out into the Cowgate, enough to let a little light and air filter in through the gaps in the grey stone walls, and Polly looked around at the small windows and bottle-glass lights of the close and wondered what she was doing there.

'We'll go into this lobby,' Margery said. 'I hear the sound of a child's voice. Perhaps she will talk to us.'

A little girl, well dressed, sat on the first step. Her head was bent over her top and whip.

'That's a grand top you've got there,' Margery said, 'and a fine whip. Are they new, Jeannie?'

'I got them from my father. He gave me a lovely brooch as well, and he gave Cecil a locket.'

'Did he, now? And what did he give Mistress Grant?'

'Mother? He gave her a necklace with a red stone. A ruby, I think. It has little pearls all around it, and she cried when he gave her it. But I didn't cry, and neither did Cecil.'

'And what is it they call your father, Jeannie?'

The child laughed. '*You* know, Margery! You work for him now. Deacon Brodie, of course, and Mother says he is very rich and famous.'

A tall girl aged about eleven came running down the stair. 'You're to come in, Jeannie,' she said. 'Mother wants you.'

'Och, no, Cecil! I'm playing.'

'Come on, now! You'd better,' Cecil warned, dragging her little sister upstairs.

Polly stared after them. The same short necks, the same little cats' faces. There was no mistaking it; the children were Brodie's.

'There's little Billy, too,' Margery told her as she led her back out into the Royal Mile. 'And there could be another one on the way by this time as well, for all I know. Did you notice their names? They are all Brodie family names. Cecil was the name of Master Will's mother.'

'So he has five illegitimate children ...' Polly said on the way back up to the Lawnmarket. More and more wickedness was piling up against the Deacon.

'The world would come to an end if Miss Jeanette ever got to know,' Margery said gloomily.

'Who would tell her? Thanks to her brother she lives such a closed-in life that she will never find out, either,' Polly said, remembering the conversation one evening at the table.

'I have been chosen by the trial judge to serve as a juror in a murder trial,' the Deacon had told his sister and Polly importantly.

'Dearest brother.' Miss Jeanette sparkled, relief in her voice. 'What an honour!'

She may not *know* very much, Polly kept her eyes on her plate, but she certainly suspected her brother of something. Now here he was, once again laying all her dreads and suspicions to rest, and Miss Jeanette was all too ready to listen and believe in him.

'Fifteen good men and true in the jury box, Jeannie! And all of us substantial!'

In great good humour they tackled their howtowdie, a pullet boiled in rich gravy with eggs and chestnuts. Miss Jeanette refused the claret her brother was pouring. 'Where will the trial be held, Will?' she asked.

'In the High Court within Parliament House. Next week.'

'And who is charged with murder?'

'Nobody from Edinburgh, thank God,' the Deacon said piously. 'It is some soldier who discharged his musket at an angry crowd in the Argyllshire village of Dunoon.'

'Poor soul! Perhaps he was only doing his duty as he saw it.'

'An eye for an eye,' Deacon Brodie said sternly. 'Crime must not go unpunished.'

Polly reflected that his fellow members of the town council and even the scarlet-robed judges of the High Court must all trust in him.

One night Fraser arrived with a rolled-up paper. 'It's the map of Candacraig,' he told her.

'You are very sure you will live there again, aren't you?'

'I am determined, Polly. Now, where can we spread this out? There isn't a table here – there's nothing in this room.'

'There *was* a writing desk until I had it taken out not long ago.'

'Why?'

'It was out of place in a bedchamber, for one thing,' Polly said, remembering the cash register in Master Will's room, and thinking that more than one thing was out of place in this house. 'And it didn't open, for another. There wasn't a key.'

'Oh?' He looked at her with a strange expression on his face. 'That's interesting! Where is this writing desk? Show me!'

They tiptoed into the next room with the night candle. 'My God,' Fraser said.

'What is it?'

'It's out of place, all right. It's the desk from Lady Susanna's sitting-room.'

He pressed something behind it and the top flap and two small drawers inside it were released at the same time, one on either side of the leather-tooled blotter, open and virgin white. Tiny inkwells were ranged behind it, red and black and blue and all stoppered with brass tops, and quills lay ready and sharpened in the groove in front of it.

'This must be the piece of furniture missing from that space I told you about. Oh, how beautiful it is!'

'Yes, it is,' he said, pressing on a panel between the small drawers, and to her surprise a mechanism opened two of the long drawers underneath the flap, for they jumped open a hair's breadth. The bottom one remained tight shut.

'Ah! Is that how they open?'

'You forget I've known this desk since I was a child. All three drawers should open, though. Something must be sticking in the side somewhere. A paper, probably,' he said. 'But you're shivering, Polly. Go back to bed while I fix it.'

She left him the candle and crept to the door. Behind her she heard him pulling out the drawers on to the floor and tugging at the bottom one with a muttered exclamation. Just as she left she turned her head. Fraser's face was white in the light of the candle, his nose pinched, and he was trembling in the grip of some savage excitement as he stared at a jagged piece of paper in his hand before he stuffed it into his pocket.

'Did you fix it?' she asked when he came back to bed. 'Was there a paper?'

'Only a scrap of a document,' he said dismissively. 'Someone must have been in a hurry rifling the papers in that desk and torn off the other half.'

'And who else could that have been except Deacon Brodie?'

'It must be still in his possession, then,' Fraser said, shivering with excitement, though Polly suspected he was trying to hide it. He smiled at her. 'It's too cold through there, anyway. We'll just have to spread out the map on top of the bed covers.'

His eyes were blazing green, but he was not going to tell her any more about the paper. Instead he showed her the four farms on the estate of Candacraig as best he could in the dim light of the candle. 'I'll leave this with you, Polly,' he said, smoothing it out. 'Then you can study it tomorrow in daylight.'

She went back to their previous discussion. 'The older men,' she asked, 'they would not object to being pensioned off?'

'They would be delighted, I should think, so long as they still had a house to live in. None of the workers would object if their linen-cupboards were well stocked, if they had more rooms built on to their houses, if they had chimneys to take away the smoke, if they had slate roofs instead of turf, and wooden or stone floors instead of the bare earth.'

'Of course. It cannot be healthy to live as they do. But Lady Susanna understood none of that?'

'She lived in the past, Polly. But I had felt the winds of change from my many visits to the Continent – new ideas, more dignity and freedom for all, more equality ...'

199

Liberté, Egalité, Fraternité, she thought sadly. The long tentacles of it had followed her from France.

The next morning she went to the parlour. 'Do you want me to go out with you, Miss Jeanette?'

Her mistress did all her shopping and made her small domestic arrangements in the mornings now, and in the afternoons she went out with Mr Leslie in his carriage. Polly wondered how he contrived it, and concluded he must be mixing business with pleasure, for Miss Brodie chattered sometimes about the large country houses she had visited with him, to estimate furniture which had to be reupholstered.

'No. But there is something I want you to see, Polly. Mr Leslie is taking me out again this afternoon.' She smiled, her face pink with excitement. 'I feel the time is coming, dear, when he will ask me a very important question.'

Polly felt a giant hand squeeze her heart. Poor Miss Jeanette must never find out what was going on. Her little face must never crumple up again. 'We will look out your prettiest bonnet, Miss Jeanette. Do you know what your answer will be?'

'Oh, Polly! He makes me so happy, just to be with him! What should I say?'

'Say yes, and name the day.'

'Come along and see my new hat, then.' She laughed breathlessly. 'It will do the trick! Oh, *isn't* it so very up to date, dear? The latest thing?' she enthused, while Polly gazed in horror at her mistress posing before her mirror in the ridiculous Lunardi hat, a huge, round wired monstrosity, like a balloon.

'She will never be able to get into the coach with that thing on,' Margery groaned when the two girls went to see off Miss Jeanette.

'Never mind, Margery,' Polly said seriously as they waved goodbye to the carriage. 'Let's hope Mr Leslie will think it is entirely fetching. Fortunately he is quite besotted with our Miss Jeanette. Thank God for that. With any luck it will not matter to him *what* is upon her head.'

'Do you see where all this is leading?' Margery asked. 'They will be married within a few months, those two – and then you will be all on your own in this house with Master Will every night.'

'No, I won't, Margery. If Miss Jeanette gets married and leaves Brodie's Close, I must leave, too. I am only here to be her companion, you know – not the Deacon's.'

'Well, then! One of the lands above Pa's shop is to become vacant soon. It's only a little room, but it could be a bolt-hole for you. Think about it, Polly!'

'Yes, dearie,' Mr Buchanan said a few weeks later. 'I've got a room to spare upstairs. It would do ye fine.'

'Ye could put some clothes in it, and yer bits and pieces,' Mistress Nell put in. 'Goodness knows there's more than enough furniture down here to spare a bed and a few other things.'

'I'm no' taking a penny piece for it, either,' Mr Buchanan assured her, 'until the Brodies pay yer wages.'

'We'll scrub it out and do it up, you and I,' Margery urged.

'Never mind cooking.' Mistress Nell smiled. 'Ye can always come doonstairs for meals when ye're here. Margery is getting to be a dab hand at it, between cooking for the Brodies and practising for getting married.'

'Come on up and have a look.' Margery dragged Polly out. 'The workers are supposed to shovel up the candlegrease that spills out into this lobby every day.' She frowned as they picked their way over it. 'I'll have a word with Pa about that! But what do you think, Polly?' She flung back the door of the small room.

'What do I think, Margery Buchanan? What did your mother mean? You are getting married? Why didn't you tell me?'

'Jocky only asked Pa last night, and he only said yes after a struggle. You see, the Robertson family live up near the Castlehill, and he is one of eleven children. Thirteen of them live in two small rooms, so there was no chance of us squeezing in there. Jocky and I wouldn't have had a room, let alone a house.'

'What about this one, then?'

'Oh, don't worry!' Margery laughed. 'Ma came up trumps as usual. She's clearing out two old disused storerooms behind the shop. We'll have them all to ourselves! It'll seem like a little palace.'

Every spare minute they got from then on Polly and Margery were down in Candlemaker Row cleaning out the three empty rooms. Sometimes they snatched an hour before the evening meal, and one evening at six o'clock it was pitch-dark and very windy when they left Brodie's Close to run down to Candlemaker Row. They came out into the Lawnmarket and immediately the wind caught their cloaks and tugged at their hair so that they were forced to stop for a minute to pull up their hoods.

On the other side of the street Deacon Brodie backed into the shadows when he recognized them in the light of the streetlamps, and cursed softly under his breath. Where might Polly Buchanan be going, with her eyes sparkling and her cheeks aflame? It could only be to meet a man, and up to now he had not been ready to pursue the little matter of Polly Buchanan himself. It was a perfect nuisance, and him so busy, but it meant that he must follow her, and he thanked God that he was wearing his dark duffle-coat as he flitted after the two girls like a silent shadow.

They led him down to Candlemaker Row. The passage into the Buchanans' house was long and ghostly and very slippery, but they had no fear of it, he saw.

'Ma's sure to have left a candle,' he heard Margery say as they mounted the stone steps to the next landing. 'Did you remember to bring your key?'

Key? Polly had a room here, then? So now he had three women he could visit, if he decided to stay in Edinburgh ... If things went well. Sometimes he wondered if all the things he did, all the really wicked things, were because deep down he wanted to be caught – to be out of the thing for ever. Out of Edinburgh, out of this life, even.

A few days later the two girls were hanging up Mistress Nell's old curtains. The rooms were ready.

'Well, Poison has found a home at last.' Margery took Polly's old perfume bottle out of its paper. 'I've kept her safe all this time. Shall I put her on the dresser?'

'I suppose so,' Polly sighed, staring at the hated brown glass face again.

November continued with the dreaded north-easterly gales. They gathered strength as they thundered up the Firth of Forth, driving the grey seas before them to crash down on Newhaven and all the other small fishing villages around the shores. They howled and battered up against the buildings of Edinburgh, tearing and sucking all before them up and down the closes of the Royal Mile, where they moaned continuously like a vicious, wounded animal.

But Miss Jeanette's latest gown of pale pink satin with its turban to match was in the hands of the seamstresses, the days rolled on calmly in Brodie's Close, and Margery's wedding to Jocky Robertson would take place in her mother's sitting-room the day after Boxing Day. It was all arranged.

Gradually a great calm fell on the town itself, a frosty, icy calm as Christmas drew nearer and nearer. It made the streetlamps, dim as they were, even dimmer in their haloes of hanging, frozen fog.

The smoke from the tall chimneys could not escape. It billowed down into the Royal Mile, where it mingled with the fog, yellow and thick, and made everyone cough. Then Edinburgh deserved its nickname of Auld Reekie.

The Luckenbooths looked gayer and gaudier as a result. Now the countryfolk struggled in over the icy rutted roads from their cottages with their cartloads of bright green holly. Tinsel ribbon glittered, apples were polished until they shone, and fowls hung about the stalls, waiting to be somebody's dinner.

Every time Polly looked at a holly wreath she thought that the berries were like drops of blood against the dark green crown of thorns. She wondered if it was a premonition. Somehow, something was hanging over her ... Or was it that someone or something was following her? She never used to believe people when they said they just *knew* they were being followed. *Now she did*.

Sometimes when she turned round sharply in the street she had the terrible feeling that someone had just darted into one of the closes to hide, but was still watching her. She could not shake off another feeling, even worse, that hands were trying to catch her – brown hands, just like Caramelle's.

Every day Miss Jeanette bought some other little trifle for her Boxing Day gifts. She was very happy, and that made Polly more depressed, for there was still no news of any forthcoming marriage for her mistress to Mr Leslie.

'Isn't it wonderful?' Margery whispered to her in the kitchen. 'The Brodies are not coming to my wedding! Miss Jeanette says they always spend Christmas Day with the Sheriffs. They go to church, and this year they have been invited to spend the festive season with them.'

Robert Burns came back to Edinburgh again, summoned by Mr Creech to oversee his latest book of verses.

'Robbie Burns is coming to the wedding,' Margery told her a few days later. 'The MacAllister boys are bringing him.'

On Christmas Eve the whole Brodie household attended the first of the kirk services at midnight, the Watchnight service, when the shepherds first saw the star over Bethlehem, the star that led them to the Infant in the manger. By that time Miss Jeanette's bags were almost packed and Master Will's lay ready at the front door to go to their sister's house the following day.

'It's not giving you much time to get ready for your wedding,' Polly said.

'A bonnie bride is soon dressed,' Margery laughed. 'The party afterwards is the main thing. Ma's having haggis with clapshot because so many people will be coming, and as a compliment to Robert Burns.'

17

A LARGE INVITED company witnessed the marriage of Margery and Jocky in the Buchanans' sitting-room on the evening of the twenty-seventh of December. The house was ablaze with candles when more guests arrived for the party afterwards, and Polly helped to get them all seated and given a glass of wine or lemonade. By now, it was eight o'clock.

'Those MacAllister boys are never here when ye want them,' Mr Buchanan said just as they arrived with Fraser, ushering in the handsome poet. Robert Burns was not a man to stand on ceremony with the ladies. He smiled at the ones bold enough to ring the piano when he sat down at it, and two or three he kissed lingeringly in a way no married man should kiss another woman. The young girls were almost swooning with delight when he broke into one of his songs, one of Edinburgh's favourites:

> 'Auld nature swears, the lovely dears
> Her noblest work she classes O;
> Her prentice han' she tried on man,
> An' then she made the lasses O.'

That evening over in the New Town William Brodie was bored to distraction. Matthew Sheriff and Jamie Leslie were having an earnest discussion about the new velvet for the covering of chairs, and Jacobina was reciting recipes to Jeanette, since neither of them could read or write. Margery Buchanan's wedding would be in full swing. Everyone in that whole tenement in Candlemaker Row would be at it. It was a golden opportunity to rake through their houses and was not to be missed.

He made his excuses, but his sisters' protests were shrill, Jamie Leslie looked at him strangely and Matthew Sheriff was clearly offended. Somehow he escaped, and once over in the Royal Mile he shed every regret of his conscience and went home to change in to his black clothes. By eight o'clock he was at the entrance to the Buchanans' tenement.

He was standing so still in the silent passage that he heard the faint rustling quite a distance away. It came nearer, but for the life of him he could not see where it was coming from at all. It was not a rat scuttling across the floor; the noise came from much higher up in the air. It drew even with him. It was passing him, when out of the blackness he saw two white eyes moving along and nothing else.

For one frozen second William Brodie was a pillar of fear, until he came to his senses. Two eyes did not move along of their own volition, not in Edinburgh, anyway. There had to be a body attached to them. Curious and piqued that someone else was here, perhaps on the same errand, he followed the rustling up the stairs as quiet as a cat – for was he not the best cat-burglar in the town?

Silently, stalking his prey, and going by his sense of direction, he knew he was following someone into Polly's room. She must have forgotten to lock her door in her haste. Then he discovered he was in the presence of a tall, powerful-looking man. He kept his nerve, but it required all his bravado.

'You're well blacked out,' he observed admiringly, for all that could be seen were the whites of the man's eyes.

A torrent of words burst from the man. The longer he spoke the more words Will Brodie understood from the smattering of French he had picked up on his travels on the Continent, and the jist of them all was that, giant or no giant, the man was absolutely terrified of *him*. At his ease now, the Deacon calmed him down while he lit his night lantern and looked about him with an expert eye.

There was nothing here worth taking. The Frenchman waited

uncertainly. Then Will Brodie dragged him out into the street.

'We could both do with a drink,' he said in the best French he could muster, and the man nodded vigorously and smiled, adding more whiteness – a dazzling row of teeth – to his dark face.

'My God, what a disguise!' The Deacon whistled, and then the truth dawned on him. 'Your face is black enough already! Do you have a name?'

He took him into the first tavern they came to, a small mean place quite unlike John Clark's, speaking his own brand of French loudly and with a flourish. The men drinking there fell back at such a display. The best table was quickly cleared for them, and he ordered brandy.

'Will this do?' he asked jauntily, enjoying every minute. His sharp eyes had detected a bulge in the black man's coat.

Although he was not a drinking man Choco downed the brandy in one and held out his glass for another. He even managed a wan smile when he recognized his benefactor as Monsieur Brodie whom he had glimpsed once in Paris and had heard a lot more about from Caramelle.

William Brodie kept on talking and laughing with him for a while, enough to find out that the black man's brain did not match his body. He watched him relaxing minute by minute and before long Choco began to prattle in the sheer relief of finding someone he almost knew.

'We have been in Edinburgh for eight weary weeks so far, my sister and I. We found a room and it was not so bad to begin with. But then she went off on her own, and where she is now in this rabbit-warren of streets I do not know.'

'So you are lonely, Choco? Lonely for a woman, perhaps?'

The great black eyes swivelled around to the Deacon. 'Not a woman,' Chocolat replied significantly.

'Ah!' What a waste of a man, Will Brodie thought, his eyes travelling over his huge, beautiful physique. 'You do not know anyone here, and you do not know where to look? But I do ... at a price.'

'I have plenty of money.'

'Put it away, man! Not in here! I might be more interested in what you have hidden in your coat. You took it from that room in Candlemaker Row, did you not?'

'It was up on a shelf. It's only an old bottle,' Choco said sulkily.

'Let's get out of here so that you can show me.'

Under a streetlamp they huddled together and examined the doll, lifting up her skirts and finding out that she was made of golden glass. Will Brodie thought he would have a heart attack when he saw it. 'I know this bottle,' he said. 'I gave it to Madame Suzanne in Paris.' Excitement thudded through him. His heart was hammering. How on earth could Polly Buchanan come to have it in her possession?

Choco screwed up his eyes in an effort to work this out. 'Caramelle was angry,' he said. 'She wanted it when Madame finished the perfume.'

'It's not worth much.'

'It might be worth more than you think. If it is old enough it could be worth a lot of money.'

Will Brodie looked doubtful. 'One of her feet is scratched.'

Choco lost patience. 'Very well, then. The bottle for an introduction. Make it fast before I change my mind, and remember I like them young.'

Will took the bottle and put it carefully in one of the deep pockets of his cape. 'Come with me,' he said, and led the black man to a shop doorway in the Royal Mile. 'Some of them sleep here. They have nowhere else to go. Do you have money? They will do anything for money, and nothing without it.'

'I have plenty of money,' Choco repeated.

Will hailed the boys. 'What's wrong with the lot of you? Have you never seen a black man before? He cannot speak our language, but his money is good.' A ripple of interest ran around them. 'Which one of you first?'

'Me!' A sharp-faced urchin of about twelve stepped forward. 'I'm no' caring what colour he is. Are ye sure o' the money first, Macaroni?'

'I'm sure, you cheeky little bugger, and here's another shilling between the lot of you to say you never saw me here tonight, mind!'

'G'wa! We're no' daft!' the boy shouted after him, and held out his hand to Choco.

Will Brodie was too overcome by the events of the evening for once to do anything else but go home. He could not get there fast enough, and up in his room he dug the bottle out of his pocket, gazed at it for a long time and then after a lot of thought went out the back door and down to his workshop to hide it at the back of the stove, his most secret hiding place.

What a lucky, lucky night! He knew without a shadow of a doubt that the bottle was the clue to Suzanne's inheritance. Now all that remained to do was to go over his major plan again, in every single detail. He simply could not afford to fail.

In the Buchanans' large sitting-room the guests balanced their plates on their knees, set their glasses on the floor, and the party was in full swing with Robert Burns in full flow in the centre of an admiring group.

> 'The rank is but the guinea's stamp,
> The man's the gowd for a' that!'

Every man in the room cheered him, and so he continued.

> 'For a' that, and a' that,
> It's coming yet, for a' that,
> That man to man the world o'er
> Shall brothers be, for a' that!'

That message sounded very familiar to Polly, although it had been in a different language the last time she heard it. '*Ça ira!*'

It was easy to see why Burns was so popular with everyone in the room. In a second he had changed their cheers to rueful laughter. 'Ay, lads, and after all that, when we get home we're under the rule of a different kind – the worst one of all! Petticoat Rule!'

'Oh!' screamed the girls, and laughed with him.

'You don't like him?' Fraser murmured in Polly's ear.

'I don't know. He is too bold, perhaps, and his talk is all fighting talk.'

'But all of it true, Polly. The rich always get richer, and the poor get poorer. In Scotland there is no doubt that the poor are oppressed, as he says. Every time I go to France I find it is the same, only over there they are preparing to overthrow the King and the Government.'

'Revolution,' she said.

'Yes, it is revolution, and many Scotsmen support it. I support it myself. I was born into land and riches – an accident of birth – but I believe it is not fair that one man should have more than plenty when the next man is starving. People are what matter, and the governments of the day. Governments can be changed in many ways, you know.'

'How, unless by bloodshed, which I fear Mr Burns will advocate next?'

'By proper representation of all the people, not just the landowners. That's why we are forming societies like The Friends of the People.'

Then, to her horror, he was joining with the other men to sing the song that was still running around in her head, only not in the way that it had been muttered and hummed in the streets of Paris under mens' breaths, but loudly and with conviction.

> '*Ah! Ça ira! Ça ira! Ça ira!*
> *Les aristocrates à la lanterne,*
> *Ah, ça ira! Ça ira! Ça ira!*
> *Les aristocrates on les pendra!*'

She could feel his enthusiasm, see in his burning eyes that he was as carried away as the rest of them when he went to join Robert Burns and the MacAllisters, and after one hurried verse of 'Auld Lang Syne' most of the men filed out of the room and out of the house.

'Where have they gone?' she asked Mr Buchanan.

'Och, it's the end o' the wedding, anyway. Margery and Jocky have gone. The men are awa' to Johnnie Dowie's to hold a meeting of their society. I wouldn't mind going, too.'

'Neither would I.' At that minute Polly would have given anything to be a fly on the wall in Johnnie Dowie's.

'Na, na, dearie. And ye're no' going up to Brodie's Close tonight. Ye'll stay here with us, and that way we'll both stay oot o' trouble.'

But when she went alone to her bed that night no sleep came

to her. It seemed strange and lonely, as though without Fraser only half of her was there in a bed that had got suddenly very large and cold. She tossed and turned and wished he had not gone to that meeting. She could not get rid of the revolutionary jingle that kept running through her head, nor of Mr Buchanan's warning to stay 'out of trouble'. Both brought back unpleasant memories of the past, and made her worry about the future.

The following night back up in Brodie's Close Fraser seemed restless. He made passionate love to her and then an hour later woke her up to make love to her again, so slowly and tenderly that she sensed they were parting. It was a goodbye.

'I love you, Polly, with all my heart.'

'And I love you.'

'I love you, and I want to marry you. Oh, Polly – say you will!'

She wasn't really surprised to see him standing beside the bed in the early morning. Before he ever opened his mouth to speak she knew despairingly what he was going to say.

'No, Fraser,' she moaned.

'It will only be for a fortnight, my darling. We decided last night at the meeting that some of our society would go across to France to find out what will be needed when the time comes.'

'No!'

'It is only for a week or two, I promise. We will be married when I get back. Say we will, sweetheart?'

The next morning was a busy one for Fraser after he left Polly in tears. He could not afford to dwell on her protests. He had to put them to the back of his mind, for before he left to join the society men for France at ten o'clock he had to settle his affairs very fast indeed.

'This cannot wait, Albert.' He strode past old Albert Gow, Lord Braxfield's clerk, when he presented himself at his rooms in Parliament Square and went straight into the inner sanctum and straight to the point.

'Erskine Caldwell's inventory of Candacraig is not accurate, Robbie.'

'What are ye rushing aboot at *that* for – at this time o' day?'

his lordship asked sourly, holding his head. 'Ye're in a hell o' a hurry conseederin' it's only nine o'clock!'

'I am, sir, and it's a long story which I am not ready to tell you yet, even if I had the time. Just take my word for it that Lady Susanna's writing desk, which should be in Candacraig, is at present in the house in Brodie's Close.'

As he intended, the mere mention of Lady Susanna's name captured Braxie's immediate attention.

'Oh, ay? And ye're gey friendly wi' Miss Polly in Brodie's Close.' Lord Braxfield winked in a heavily jocular manner. 'Oh, ay!'

'More than friendly.' Fraser nipped him in the bud. 'I intend to marry her.'

'Weel, I canna say I blame ye. She's a right bonnie lassie.'

'Yes. She reminds you of someone, you told me in Queen Street at the Lunardi coffee party?' Fraser prodded him. 'All that glorious auburn hair?'

'What are ye saying?' Lord Braxfield blustered.

'I'm saying no more for the present,' Fraser fished in his pocket and brought out a crumpled bit of paper, 'except – do you recognize this? It's in your handwriting.'

The judge drew in a sharp breath. 'Where did ye get this?'

'In that same writing desk in Brodie's Close.'

'Good God!' The judge glanced at it and seemed to sag altogether. 'But where's the rest o' it?'

'That's all I know, Robbie. I'm leaving it with you for safe keeping. Look after it, and Polly Buchanan.'

'Why? Where are ye going?'

But Fraser was gone as swiftly as he had come, and Lord Braxfield was left spluttering and staring at the jagged piece of paper, all traces of too much wine last night now gone. He was thoroughly alert when he read it through, although he knew the whole document by heart.

I, Lady Susanna Graham, formerly
Candacraig, Edinburgh, possessed of much sounder mind
me, and considering the follies and
certainty of death, and the
Estate, do therefore hereby exec

lawfully wedded husband Sir John Robertson Grah
his brother Charles Graham, father of Charles Fra
predeceased me.

I leave and bequeath th
to the aforesaid Charles Fraser Gr
hereditary peerage and the titl

The explanati
year 1744 on March fifteenth, t
Robertson Graham, a daughter, the is
me and one who shall remain nameless was born
aforesaid Suzanne, known as Suzanne Gray
the best of my knowledge and belief.

That Charles Frase
in the event of her death, her child, and with hi
inheritors of the house, lands and
inherit from the noble hou

Signed b

Oh God, he thought ... He would never see his daughter
Suzanne in this world now. He had been hoping so much that
something would turn up ... Now here was Fraser Graham with
an inkling that *he* was the one and only remaining heir!
Irresponsible young devil! Where did Fraser Graham rush off
to?' he asked Albert Gow.

'You'd better come out into the Royal Mile like everyone else,
my lord,' his clerk told him. 'The half of Edinburgh is there to
watch! He's away to France wi' the society men.'

'Weel, that's the last time we'll ever see any o' them,' Lord
Braxfield said. 'Stupid young fools! Hot-headed like that
Robbie Burns! This is a' his fault, ye ken.'

He went back inside and locked away Fraser's scrap of paper.
That was the end of everything, now. The end of Susanna, the
end of the Graham family, the end of Candacraig. The house
would just sit there empty for the rest of time, until it too
crumbled away.

Dust to dust, ashes to ashes. It was all gone now.

Early in January the Scottish winter set in with a vengeance.
Every day fresh snow fell on old snow and froze where it lay.

Nobody sensible went out if they could possibly help it except for Miss Jeanette with Polly at her side, combing the almost deserted Luckenbooths for her usual ribbons and trinkets.

Most people stayed at home and crouched over their fires by day and went to their beds as soon as they could at night, but Polly was glad of these little outings, no matter how uncomfortable. Since Christmas the house in Brodie's Close had been quiet and circumspect, and she went to bed every night tired out with her work and the cold fresh air, notching up another day on her calendar – another day nearer to the time when Fraser would come home.

'I don't know how anyone can stay out in this weather,' Margery shuddered one evening. 'It's worse than ever tonight. The fire will be going out in the workshop, too.'

'Perhaps they cannot keep it going in amongst all that wood, Margery.'

'It's not that. Jocky says that the Deacon has been having meetings late at night in the workshop lately. There are bottles all over the place in the mornings. Well, that's his business ... Jocky will soon be here to fetch me, but we would have time to get the hot pigs ready before I go.'

They took the hot bricks out of the oven where they had been slowly heating since the afternoon and wrapped them in blankets.

'I'll take yours and Master Will's upstairs, Polly, if you will take Miss Jeanette's.'

Polly knocked at the parlour door and waited. She seemed to wait a long time before she was called in, and she found her mistress at one extreme end of the sofa and Mr Leslie at the other.

'Your hot pig, Miss Jeanette.' Polly went through to the bedroom beyond and put it in the bed.

'It can't be that time already.' An embarrassed Mr Leslie sprang to his feet and smoothed down his hair self-consciously. 'I must go shortly.'

'Good-night, sir.' Polly smiled at him. She liked Mr Leslie. 'Good-night, Miss Jeanette.'

Margery went away with her new husband and while Polly

banked up the fire and tidied the kitchen for the last time that day she heard Miss Jeanette showing Mr Leslie to the front door, then going back to her sitting-room and a little later the thud of her bedroom door as she shut that too. Silence fell in the house, and taking her candle Polly went through the dining-hall, where she noticed the fire was still glowing, and upstairs to bed.

She locked and bolted her door faithfully as she did every night. Usually she fell asleep within minutes, long ago accustomed to the chimes of St Giles. So why should they wake her tonight? She sat up in bed and listened as the last stroke of the hour, whatever hour had been struck, quivered away into the silence.

Except that it was scarcely a silence. Mens' voices rose and fell somewhere not far away. She tried to distinguish where they were coming from, and as she strained her ears the nameless terrors of the night – the same ones that had visited her the first night she was here in this house – flooded back again.

In the dark she felt her eyes widen with fear. Her hands shook as she pulled on her dressing-robe and tiptoed across the room to listen at the door. The mens' voices were louder now, and one of them belonged to Deacon Brodie. Margery said he kept his cronies to the workshop if they came to visit him late at night. Perhaps because it was so dreadfully cold tonight he had actually brought them right inside the house.

It took some time to relight her candle, to unbolt and unlock her door silently, but then she was out in the passage and listening again, the candle shaded by her shaking hand.

The men were downstairs, in the dining-hall, and the Deacon's voice was the loudest of all. She was amazed at him. Miss Jeanette's rooms were not very far away. What if she woke up and heard this? She would collapse again. That was enough for Polly.

She had better be ready for anything, but to go even to the top of the staircase meant that she would have to douse her candle altogether. Her stomach churned as she edged along the corridor inch by cautious inch until she reached the top of the staircase. Here there was a faint glow from the light of a candle below.

This was the most dangerous part of the expedition, trying to remember and count the stairs that creaked. She crept down the inner side of the treads and suddenly sat down, for below her was a scene which reeked of conspiracy and corruption.

Bottles of Black Cork were scattered carelessly over the beautiful table in the dining-hall, most of them empty and one of them used as a candlestick for a tallow candle. Its yellow flickering light showed up the faces of the four men hunched round it so that they looked like four skulls with great black holes where the eyes should be.

'Now that you've finished complaining about the snow out at Duddingston Farm,' the Deacon said sarcastically, 'I take it you got the coulter? You managed to get it off the plough, Ainslie?'

'A fine noise it made too, and it solid iron with only a stone for the job! Our hands were frozen into blocks of ice, as Smith here can tell you,' Ainslie whined.

'That's right. You might have warned us about the dog, as well,' Smith added his grievance. 'The bloody thing nearly ate me.'

'Well, it didn't, did it?' The third man sneered, and at that the other two turned upon him furiously.

'How is it that Brown always manages to keep his lily-white hands so clean?' Smith asked the Deacon.

'Yes! Why do we get all the dirty work?' Ainslie echoed him.

'You've got to remember, boys, that you are not so unfortunate as Brown here.' Deacon Brodie smiled. 'He *is* a "Wanted Man", after all. One slip from him and he'd be right back inside again.'

How could Deacon Brodie possibly associate with these dirty rat-like creatures, Polly wondered. She turned her attention to the wanted man called Brown, who would have been tall and elegant had it not been for his rags and his shoes which were mostly uppers. He had a particularly large hole at the elbow of his coat which he constantly tried to disguise by leaning on it, and so drawing even more attention to it.

Quite clearly the Deacon's words angered him. It was his turn to be sarcastic now. 'It's a wonder you could not have made something yourself, seeing that you're so famous for it, instead of sending them to get a great coulter off a plough. A key, for example.'

'Oh, I did, Mr Brown,' Deacon Brodie said softly, and in such a sinister way that the hairs stood up on the back of Polly's neck. 'I made a key to the outer door. The key to the inner door is kept by a clerk about his waist. That is why we will have to force it. That is why we need a strong crow ... such as a coulter.'

'And you had nothing yourself that would do the job?' Brown continued to bait him in his English voice.

'My tools are all distinctive, all of tempered steel, which would snap. We need cold iron – in other words, the coulter.' The Deacon still spoke in a tone of suppressed rage, underlined by his patient explanations. 'But if you are nervous, Mr Brown, then maybe you should not join us.'

The tall man glared at the Deacon, furious. 'Me? Afraid?' he snarled, and Polly saw that Brown could be quite a different person from the elegant figure he tried to present to the world. She would not have trusted him an inch. A wolf in sheep's clothing, as Margery would say.

'Gentlemen, gentlemen!' Smith called the meeting to order, and what he had to say produced a silence that chilled the blood of everyone there. 'What about our last job, then? A reward of a hundred and fifty pounds, and now on top of that a free pardon if the informant is an escaped criminal. By God, it's enormous!'

The silence went on and on. Clearly, Deacon Brodie had not seen the notice in the *Courant* after their latest burglary about the reward money going up. Polly could almost touch the distrust and suspicion in the air. It floated above the men and up the stairs like a thick blanket.

After dropping this bombshell Smith stared fixedly at Brown. Brown kept a carefully blank face and the hole in his elbow tucked well out of sight. Deacon Brodie's eyes narrowed to menacing slits.

'Ay,' Ainslie coughed suddenly and nervously, 'that's no' bad.'

'And you, Mr Brown?' the Deacon whispered. 'You would fit into the category of an escaped criminal, would you not?'

'You don't think I would trust them and their promises, do you?' Brown cried, much too quickly. 'I'm still on the run, as you very well know! If I went to inform they would string me up as fast as look at me. There's no dignity in dancing on the end of a rope. No pardon, no freedom there.'

217

'Yes,' Deacon Brodie said. 'That's just what would happen to you, Brown. You'd be a fool to think otherwise. Especially since it would be the new gallows, designed by me. There would be no hope for you on it, and no escape, I promise you.'

The other three stared at him, speechless.

'No,' he went on, 'there would be no escape for any of you, and don't you forget it. Not that the gallows cannot be fixed ... I am the best wright in Edinburgh, so you may be sure that when I invented it I mastered the fixing of it at the same time.'

Smith's face was chalk-white. 'You talk as though you want to try it, Will. For the love of God, say no more about it.'

'Well then, gentlemen, drink up and let us turn to the business in hand,' the Deacon said quite cheerfully, now that he clearly felt he had the ascendancy. 'It has taken me three months to perfect it, for it had to be planned right down to the last detail. It will be by far the biggest job ever undertaken in Edinburgh, and I cannot stress it enough to you – there must be no mistakes with this one. The Excise Office will yield anything upwards of a thousand pounds, perhaps two, perhaps even more than that.'

'Jesus!' Ainslie moaned.

'A quarter share of that could set a man up for life,' Smith said.

'We have wasted enough time in bickering.' Deacon Brodie scowled at Brown. 'Are you all with me, or not?' He looked around, the master of the situation, and they all nodded. 'Then here is the plan I have made of the building.'

They huddled together over the map which Deacon Brodie spread out amid the litter on the table. The guard of the Excise Office was old, he told them. He would present no problem. They would take a rope and tie him up. They would all wear masks.

He, Deacon Brodie, would drop a spur at the scene. Everyone would think it was dropped by a highwayman, especially if men were seen with masks on. Nobody would ever connect the theft with that of Inglis and Horner or any of their other exploits.

They arranged for strong chisels, picklocks and a dark-lantern, and they would carry a brace of pistols apiece. But the detail that impressed the other three most of all was the Deacon's promise to provide a whistle for Ainslie, the look-out man. One blast for the watchman, three for trouble, he said. It seemed to them the final prudent contingency in a masterly and meticulously worked out plan of campaign, and in a silence that was almost awed they held up their glasses to their leader and toasted its success.

'We'll meet again in the usual place the night before for the last run-through, gentlemen. On the fourth.' The Deacon rose to conduct them to the door.

Polly made her way back silently to her room, locked and bolted the door and crept back into bed, her brain so numbed with horror that she could hardly recall the scene she had just witnessed, let alone work out which fourth they meant – was it January or February? Her mind ran round and round on just one theme – trouble ahead.

18

'ARE YOU SURE you are quite well, dear?' Miss Brodie asked her a week later. 'You have not seemed yourself for a few days now.'

Polly smiled wanly. She felt dreadful. She had not had a night's sleep since that awful scene in the dining-hall. The following morning and nearly every other morning she had been sick. It was the worry of it.

'I'll get them to put a little dash of something in your coffee,' Miss Jeanette added anxiously as they sat down to the meridian. 'It works wonders for me when I am feeling low.'

Polly felt too weak to protest. The hot coffee and the burning brandy seared its way down her throat, but after a few minutes she found that it did indeed make her feel a little better, so that she was able to face the rest of the day.

The fourth and fifth of February came and went with no sign of a raid on the Excise Office, and no sign of the Edinburgh men, and now Polly began to be seriously worried and afraid. For weeks she tried her best to keep it to herself, but Margery was not deceived.

'It is because Mr Fraser Graham has gone away, isn't it? Don't worry, Polly. Pa says they will soon be home – they should never have gone – and then there will be an end to all this.'

'An end to all what, my dears?' Deacon Brodie came into the

kitchen smiling. 'You are not too hard-worked, I hope?'

Suddenly it was too much for Polly. He was too much, and too mean.

'Not too hard-worked,' she gave him a look like thunder, 'just very much too under-paid. I have been here six months and more, Margery only a little less, and so far we have not seen a penny-piece for all our work, hard or easy.'

He shook his head and clucked his tongue ruefully, a picture of remorse. 'What a disgrace! You were quite right, Polly, to speak of this. It has been a dreadful oversight, dreadful ... What date is this? The fourteenth of February, is it not? St Valentine's Day, indeed.' He giggled.

Margery nodded. Polly was too angry even for that.

'You see, it is a little late in coming because at the end of March I am to review my workers' wages. They are to go up. You would be better to wait, would you not, Margery – now that you are Mistress Robertson – and then both you and Jocky will receive your additional sums?'

'Oh yes, indeed, sir!' Margery smiled her relief and delight.

'That's all right then, because I have come to ask you if you could manage a very special meal this evening. It will be for family and close friends.'

'I see, sir. How many must I cook for, then?'

'Ten. We should have had a party at Christmas, my sister says. It is her idea to have it tonight.'

'We will have to go to the shops, then,' Polly said, determined not to let him off the hook. 'How shall we pay for it?'

'I'm sure I can leave it in your capable hands, my dear. Just ask Miss Jeanette what it is she would like, tell the shopkeepers to put it down to Deacon Brodie, and they will supply you with the very best.'

It was the afternoon before Polly cooled down, when Miss Jeanette sent for her, very excited.

'It's a wonderful idea, isn't it, Polly? And all Mr Leslie's, to have it on St Valentine's Day! That is the day for lovers, you know. Will you help me to cut out little hearts from this red paper? I thought that would be a pretty decoration for the table.'

Polly smiled at her in exasperation. Miss Jeanette was so childlike, so feminine, so silly and yet so likeable!

By eight o'clock that evening Miss Jeanette was dressed and the table in the dining-hall was ready. The girls had found crystal glasses and washed them. They sparkled on the white cloth in the light of the candles and reflected the oranges and polished red apples they had piled up in bowls, and the red heart place-mats lay between the silver knives and forks.

Mr and Mistress Scott with Walter were the first to arrive, then the Sheriffs and right behind them came Mr Leslie with two friends. Miss Jeanette introduced them to the company as Mr John Stevenson and his wife Mistress Clara Stevenson, from Glasgow.

Half an hour later, after the Scotch Broth, Polly and Margery brought through the goose, roasted to a turn, for the Deacon to carve. He stood up and sharpened the carving knife expertly on the steel. The grating sound brought the whole company to attention, and Mr Leslie chose that moment to get to his feet to make a speech.

'Jeanette and I chose this day to tell you our happy news,' he smiled at them shyly. 'We are engaged to be married on the twenty-fourth day of March in the Canongate Kirk, and afterwards we shall travel to Glasgow where I have been offered a very good position by my friend here, Mr John Stevenson.'

Polly put down the pile of ten large oval plates in front of the Deacon as quietly as she could, and Margery put the gravy-boat at one end of the table and the apple sauce at the other.

'Jeanette!' Mistress Scott was as usual the first to recover. 'My dear! I am so happy for you! Congratulations, Jamie. We all hope you will be very happy.'

Deacon Brodie showed no emotion whatsoever. 'Who would have thought it?' He seemed very amused. 'Our Jeannie! Married at last!' Jamie Leslie looked at him coldly and pointedly, so that the little man recollected himself and his manners. 'Well, we must drink a toast to that.'

'To Jeanette and Jamie!' They all stood up and drank.

'So I am to lose you, Jamie.' Matthew Sheriff looked regretful when he sat down again. 'But you are right, Mistress Scott. We are very happy for them. Is that not so, Jacobina?'

Mistress Sheriff struggled to reply. 'What will happen to our brother, then?' she asked. 'How will you manage, Will?'

'On the twenty-fourth day of March, eh?' Deacon Brodie could hardly contain his amusement. 'By that time I trust I shall be managing very well. Don't worry about me, Jacobina.'

Smiling a little warily at him, the party settled down to their slices of goose washed down with strong cider, and the two girls collected the dirty soup plates and spoons from the side table and took them through to the kitchen to wash them.

'What did I tell you?' Margery said. 'When she goes you cannot stay here alone with Master Will! It's a good job you've got the room in Candlemaker Row to go to.'

So she had only one month left, Polly thought, to try to find out any more clues to the mystery of her background.

'Only the plum duff after this,' Margery said. 'I'll turn it out on its ashet, and you can pour the egg custard into two jugs. Now, the pudding plates!'

They marched through into the dining-hall and laid the pudding on the side-table before clearing the dining table again. Whatever the party had been speaking about in the interval they were back to Deacon Brodie's appearance as a juror in a murder trial again.

'He got his deserts,' the Deacon said. 'He was the first one to be hanged on my new gibbet.'

'In that case, Will,' Matthew Sheriff leaned over and put his arm around his brother-in-law's shoulder, 'we can trust you to see that the same end comes to the ruffians who robbed Inglis and Horner? It could be any one of our businesses next! Oh yes, Will, you'll be the answer to it all!'

'Oh, yes,' Deacon Brodie choked as Polly got the whole pile of dirty plates safely into her hands and Margery opened the door to let her pass. 'Oh, yes,' his voice came out in a strange strangled cry, 'I'm the answer!'

He laughed until the tears ran out of his eyes, and then his laugh mounted to hysteria, to a high-pitched screech that reached the corridor and seemed to corkscrew up the spiral staircases to hit the very roof. It was enough to raise the hairs on the back of Polly's neck and turn her to jelly.

With a crash all ten plates scattered on the floor. She and Margery eyed each other in horror. 'Quick!' Margery hissed and gave her a push. 'They will never have heard! Run and get Annie!

Tell her to bring a cloth!'

The laughing Scotsman was Deacon Brodie, here under this very roof!

'There's only two broken, after all.' Margery got up off her knees with the pieces in her hands while Annie Begbie wiped the floor. 'Anyway, there are another twelve meat plates up on the shelf. Can you see Miss Jeanette counting them all, in any case?'

Already the society men had been away for six weeks instead of the two weeks Fraser promised. Twenty days went past after that, when Polly tried to concentrate on Miss Jeanette's wedding gown, and twenty nights when cold, miserable and distracted with worry she agonized about Fraser. Was he *ever* coming back?

The tension in the house rose to snapping point before the news was shouted abroad in Edinburgh.

'The Excise Office has been robbed!'

And the notice in the *Courant* reported the details faithfully.

'On the night betwixt the fifth and sixth of March, it is reported that some persons did feloniously enter the Excise Office by means of false keys and other implements, including the coulter of a plough, the which has been discovered on the premises. The loss from the Office is not known for sure at this time but seems slight, the criminals having failed to gain access to secret drawers containing, it is reliably reported, more than eight hundred pounds sterling.

Mr James Bonar, Clerk to the Excise Office, discovered the criminals in the very act of theft. Indeed, if he had not fortunately returned to his office, disturbing them, they might have found the great sum of money no matter how well it had been hid.'

Next day there was even more speculation in the city. Brown, the down-at-heel Englishman, walked into the sheriff-clerk's office and informed. How much had he given away to get his free pardon? Rumours were rife in the Royal Mile, running up and down the street like tongues of flame. Nobody knew for sure. Deacon Brodie remained calm and impassive. He considered he had weathered the storm, and later today he was going to inspect the progress of his fighting-cocks.

After Polly told Margery about the Deacon's plot she had overheard, they watched him sauntering into the Tolbooth. 'I wonder why he's going in there, Margery?'

'Jocky says the latest rumour is that Smith is in the Tolbooth. The farmer's dog from Duddingston went for his throat. That's how they identified him.'

'What about Ainslie?'

'They had to let him go. They couldn't prove anything against him, so only Smith is in the Tolbooth. Perhaps the Deacon is trying to see him. Jocky says he will not be allowed,' Margery said. Minutes later they watched the Deacon coming back out of the Tolbooth in a hurry. He was making for home, and his expression was haunted. 'There you are, Polly! They have not let him speak to Smith. Now he does not know where he stands. He does not know what else Brown may have said, or if he said it at all.'

'Where *is* Brown all this time?'

'Gone free. He will be miles away by this time.'

'Margery, I'm frightened for Miss Jeanette. I've made up my mind to warn Mr Leslie. She's such a fragile little creature that she should be miles away if anything happens to her brother, or else she'll go to pieces and never get married, after all.'

'Yes. Go and find him. I'm going down to tell Ma and Pa.'

Two hours later they all met together in the dining-hall; the Deacon having recovered his composure, Miss Jeanette obviously still ignorant of it all, Mr Leslie looking grim and determined, Mr and Mistress Buchanan and Polly, with Margery round-eyed beside her. Mr Leslie seemed to have grown in stature. He was the first one to speak.

'I am taking Jeanette away now,' he announced firmly. 'We shall be at John and Clara Stevenson's house until we are married – in Glasgow.'

The Deacon smiled and nodded absently, far away in very different thoughts.

Mr Buchanan cleared his throat. 'My niece Miss Polly cannot stay here overnight in that case,' he said.

'No,' Mistress Nell chimed in. 'It would not be proper, not at all, without Miss Jeanette for chaperone.'

William Brodie looked around at all their outraged faces. He seemed to come to some momentous conclusion and then he smiled, the same cocksure smile of always. 'Of course! Of course!' he agreed with them all, while a stony-faced Mr Leslie laden with boxes was ushering Miss Jeanette out of the door.

'Oh, Will!' She flung her arms around her brother at the last minute.

'No, no, Jeannie.' The Deacon thrust her off gently. 'Everything is all right! Go on and enjoy your new life – I certainly intend to enjoy mine from now on!'

Half an hour later, a few paces behind, he was following two of his workmen carrying a heavy trunk between them, dressed very unusually in his dark night clothes, for by now he had lost all restraint. His step was jaunty, and it was taking him all his time to keep the grin off his face. Oh, Christ! Soon now, his great adventure could begin ...

'Look at the style o' that!' a passing man shouted disgustedly as they reached the Grassmarket. 'Make way for the Macaroni!' He spat in Brodie's direction.

His friends restrained him anxiously. 'He's a toon cooncillor!' Will heard one of them hissing. 'Watch yer mouth, for God's sake!' and he thrust the man behind him and touched his cap to Deacon Brodie. 'He's drunk, sir. Pay no attention to him!'

Will Brodie swung his cane elaborately. 'We're none of us perfect, my man,' he said, passing on his way to Michael Henderson's feed-barn and trying not to laugh out loud. 'Carry the trunk inside,' he ordered his men who were waiting at the door, 'and then get back to your benches.'

'That little bugger's worse than usual today,' one workman muttered to the other as they turned away. 'I've never seen him all in black like that before, have you? There's something far wrong wi' him if ye ask me.'

'Ay,' the other agreed. 'Dae ye get the feeling that something's coming to a head?'

Inside, in the gloom of the feed-barn, Will Brodie let himself rip at last. 'Oh, Michael! Oh, Jesus!' He exploded into gales of laughter. 'What a life this is! It's all one big adventure! I used to have them only at nights, but now they're spilling over into the days.'

'What now?' Michael Henderson smiled fondly at his hero, small compared with him.

'Let's go around the cock-pens. I've got a lot to tell you.'

'Oh, ay – the pens. I was round them not long ago mysel', and every bird in order.'

'There's no fear of you, Michael. I wouldn't trust anyone else in the world with my cocks. In fact, I wouldn't trust anyone else in the world full stop.'

'That ye can. Wi' yer life, if need be.'

'It might come to that, Michael, if the next stage of my adventure goes wrong.'

'Dinna speak like that, Will, not even in jest.'

'You can take nothing for granted in this world. It's best to have a few alternative plans made. If anything *does* go wrong with me, all my birds are yours, Michael.'

'I couldna! I couldn't take them! They're worth hundreds o' pounds!'

Not for anything would Michael Henderson have admitted to anyone that he had a name for every bird there, all of them the Deacon's. It was his pleasure to tend them with special loving care – Macaroni Blue, Macaroni Red, Macaroni Brown, Macaroni Orange, Macaroni Black, Macaroni White …

'And all for you, Michael, if you make me some promises and do me a few little favours. I'm serious! Now, listen carefully. First of all, that trunk. Hide it, for it contains most of my worldly wealth.'

'Why? Where are ye going?'

'Who knows?' William Brodie giggled. 'But here,' he dug in his pocket and fetched out a gleaming silver tube, 'here is something far more valuable even than the contents of the trunk. In the last resort, it could save my life. Michael, not another living soul must ever set eyes on this.'

The giggling had changed to whining. There were tears in the Deacon's eyes now.

'Nobody will,' Michael Henderson promised, his normally ruddy face pale as he realized he was now part of something desperate. He had never seen his champion in such a state before.

'Life or death, Michael.'

'Trust me, Will.'

William Brodie left a tearful Michael Henderson swearing eternal friendship in the feed-barn and came out on to the Grassmarket again. Everything was going according to plan. He had approached three other men, two white and one black, in these last few busy days, and he believed he had everything covered. It didn't matter that they had only got thirteen pounds from the Excise Office. He was a rich man anyway, with a small fortune set by in the trunk long ago for a rainy day.

He could relax at long last and dwell on the sign sent straight from Heaven, his good luck sign in the shape of the stolen perfume bottle. Suzanne ... The very thought of her reminded him that there was just one more thing to attend to before he left. Miss Polly Buchanan.

Urgent banging on the door of her little room in Candlemaker Row and Margery shouting woke Polly the next morning. For a minute she did not know where she was, and then memory flooded back. She was on her feet and opening the door.

'Polly! Polly! Master Will has gone!'

'How do you know he has gone?'

'He is nowhere to be found, and there is a proclamation out for him. Jocky tore it down from outside the sheriff-clerk's early this morning on his way to work.'

Polly took the proclamation out of Margery's hand.

TWO HUNDRED POUNDS OF REWARD

Whereas William Brodie, a considerable House Carpenter and Burgess of the City of Edinburgh, has been charged with being concerned in breaking into the General Excise Office for Scotland, and stealing from the Cashier's office there a sum of money – and as the said William Brodie has either made his escape from Edinburgh, or is still concealed about that place – A REWARD OF ONE HUNDRED AND FIFTY POUNDS STERLING is offered to any person who will produce him alive at the Sheriff

Clerk's Office, Edinburgh, or will secure him; and FIFTY
POUNDS STERLING MORE payable upon his conviction
by William Scott, procurator-fiscal for the shire of
Edinburgh.

WILLIAM SCOTT

There followed a detailed description of the Deacon which
brought the little man alive, joking and strutting before their
very eyes.

DESCRIPTION

WILLIAM BRODIE is about five feet four inches tall, is
about forty-eight years of age but looks rather younger
than he is, has grey eyes and large black eyebrows, under
the right eye there is the scar of a cut, which is still a little
sore at the point of the eye next to the nose, and a cast in
the eye which gives him somewhat the look of a Jew, a
sallow complexion, nondescript hair, twisted, turned up
and tied behind, coming far down upon each cheek, the
whiskers very sandy at the ends, high-topped in the front
and frizzed at the side, high smooth forehead, has a
particular air in his walk, takes long steps, strikes the
ground first with his heel, bending both feet inwards
before he moves them again, usually wears a stick under
hand, and moves in a proud swaggering sort of style, his
legs small above the ankle, large ankle bones and feet,
small at the knees, which bend as he walks, as if through
weakness. Was dressed in a black coat, vest, breeches and
stockings, a striped duffle greatcoat, and silver shoe-
buckles.

While Polly was reading through the Proclamation Margery,
usually so cheerful, began to cry. 'What are we going to do
now?' she gasped. 'What will happen to Jocky and the other
workmen ... their wages ... *our* wages?'
'Don't cry, dear.' Polly put an arm around her heaving
shoulders and thought fast. 'The sheriff will send his men to
search the house today or tomorrow, there's no doubt of that!'

She pulled her clothes on hurriedly. 'Shouldn't we get there first to see if there's any money left for us? The sheriff will only confiscate it in the meantime.'

Deacon Brodie's house was eerily quiet when they slipped in by the back door. It felt cold and resentful of intruders, affronted that the family who had lived here for so long had simply abandoned it, dropped everything and gone.

'What a mess in here!' Margery held open Miss Jeanette's sitting-room door to let Polly see the litter of news-sheets, stockings, underclothes and rubbish everywhere, and the huge Lunardi hat more incongruous than ever perched in pride of place on one of the chests. 'At least Mr Leslie had the sense to make her leave it behind.' She smiled wanly.

'We'll just tidy up,' Polly said. 'You work your way around down here. I'll go upstairs. Between us we might find some money.'

But she didn't really believe they would find anything. She began at the far end of the upper storey, in the Deacon's room, but search high and low as she might for hours, she found nothing there. The old cash register was empty. His collection of ruffled shirts was gone. With a last lingering look around she went on to the next room, and all the other guest rooms, but she could tell before she began by the undisturbed dust that the answer would be the same.

Last of all, she came to her old bedchamber. Nothing had been disturbed, and she sat down on the bed completely disheartened, the question that had been niggling away at the back of her mind now right out in the open.

Why had Fraser been so secretive about that scrap of paper he'd found in the writing desk? Why hadn't he shown her it? Didn't he trust her? She closed her eyes, pushing away the thought that she might have been too secretive herself ...

With her eyes closed like this she could almost hear his footsteps coming along the passage again as he used to, stopping at the door, and then, unbelievably, he was there by the side of her bed! She opened her eyes and smiled up at him. *But it wasn't Fraser.* To her horror, she was looking straight into the face of Deacon Brodie.

For a second she sat there rigid with shock and

disappointment, gazing at the puckered scar that dragged down the corner of his right eye so horribly. It fascinated her, and filled her with a repugnance which the Deacon clearly would not have believed, he was so very sure of his welcome. He bent over her and fondled her hair. The smile died on her face, and her blood ran cold with terror.

She should have remembered that there was a back way round this upper storey, that half-way there was the staircase down to the kitchen which Margery used every day. He must have entered the house silently by the front door, gone straight up to his room, and then crept round from his room to hers. She prayed that Margery in the kitchen might have heard his footsteps passing overhead.

So he had been in Edinburgh all the time! And now here she was in the very situation Fraser had been determined must never happen.

'Oh,' she said, trying to speak normally, 'you are still here, sir?'

'My dearest girl, you must not pretend with me! You knew I would not leave Edinburgh without you. Yes, I am still here because I have something to give you, and something to say to you.'

'Then it would be better to do it downstairs in a more formal room, Master Will.' She struggled to rise up.

It was a dreadful mistake. Her movements inflamed him to such a pitch that he flung himself down and pressed himself on top of her. His powerful upper body almost knocked the breath out of hers, but she had to keep him talking. 'You have something to give me?' she asked in a strangled voice.

His left arm was under her shoulders, his hand gripping her tight. Now he took his right hand from behind his back where he had been hiding something, and held up the perfume bottle.

She closed her eyes and shook her head. *It could not be Poison*! But when she opened them again it *was* the same bottle, all right. How had he managed to get hold of it? He must have taken it from Candlemaker Row, and she had never noticed because she looked at Poison as seldom as possible. He had been in her room? The very thought of him crawling around it like a slug threatened to make her sick.

232

'I have had it hidden in my most secret hiding place,' he said triumphantly, 'behind the flue in the workshop.'

The workshop. The one place they should have searched and hadn't. 'What is it? Just a bottle? Take it away! I don't want it!'

'Oh, Polly.' He shook his head playfully, and then to her absolute disgust and terror his tongue invaded her mouth. It was making her retch, when mercifully he began to talk again. 'I gave it to Madame Suzanne. Your mother.'

'Madame Suzanne?' Polly asked, her body like ice while her mind was racing feverishly. She did not want to tell this man anything – but her mother was the connection. She had to know. 'Yes, Madame Suzanne was my mother,' she said coldly.

'Was? She is dead? Oh Jesus! Then her expectations will be your expectations now! Oh, what could be better!' He suddenly crushed her lips with his own. 'I have a confession to make, though, Polly. I am not the good boy you always thought me. I have been guilty of taking part in the burglary at the Excise Office.'

She could detect no shame or remorse in the eyes of so prominent and respected a figure in Edinburgh when he uttered these words. Instead, only two glowing imps of mischief. The Deacon was delighted with himself.

'What expectations?' She brought him back to reality.

It was the vital question.

Her whole future depended on his answer, for unless she could drag it out of him there was no other way left open, now that her search had failed – now that Fraser had gone and taken what he knew with him.

'I was led astray.' He ignored her. 'It was a momentary lapse. I had no intention of actually *stealing*.'

'No?' She kept him talking, but he was very irrational, she realized with a chill of fear.

'No. I had been drinking, and always when I drink I am back in *The Beggar's Opera* again, acting the parts. I went along with the others on the crest of the wave, on the spur of the moment, for the sheer excitement of it! You know how I get carried away, Polly! You remember me telling you?'

'I remember.' She tried to judge the distance between the bed and the door. Could she reach it in time?

'Then you will also remember how I always dreamed of running away to sea. It is strange how destiny catches up with you in the end. I am free, Polly! Free at last!'

Free? With all Edinburgh looking for him? Oh, where was Margery? Why didn't she come? Why didn't somebody come? She felt the panic rising inside her.

'Free to go to Holland first, to put them off the scent, and from there to a wonderful new life, perhaps in America.'

'Why are you telling me all this? What has it got to do with me?'

'Because you will be coming with me! Just think, Polly ... We shall have a wonderful life, miles away under the sun somewhere, with your expectations! We have an understanding between us that I have never experienced with any other woman.'

'Not even with Ann Grant and Jean Watt?'

'Oh,' he said, half-giggling like an idiot, 'you mean my little affairs? But I did not marry either of them, did I? You are the only one I shall ask to be my wife. You are the only one to have that honour.'

Now she knew that he was completely mad. Now she knew at last why Fraser had been so fearful for her safety. He could never have dreamed the attack would come during the day, because by day the Deacon was a perfect gentleman. Now, she realized, there was no longer any distinction between the two. The madness of his nights had spread to his days, to make him twice as dangerous as he was before.

'What expectations?' she asked again, almost in tears.

'Ah! I have them well tucked away, dear heart. Nobody will ever find them. Once we are well clear of the law here I'll show you that you have property to sell. A large property, for a large amount of money! Oh, Jesus, this could not have worked out better, Suzanne!'

Suzanne! Now he had her completely mixed up with her mother.

'And you want me as much as I want you, sweet Suzanne,' he babbled, dropping the bottle on the floor with a clatter and flinging up her skirts. 'You remember the sugar candy stick?' He unbuttoned his breeches, grovelled in his underclothes for a minute and finally drew out his pulsating penis. 'You remember?'

'No,' she screamed, creeping hard up against the wall, as far away as she could get, while he came at her, prising her legs apart with his strong arms, straddling her, his fingers all over her, and then ... Crash! Something hit the side of his head and he fell over her, limp.

Jocky Robertson stood at the side of the bed, his arm upraised with the perfume bottle, the first thing that had come to hand, in his grasp. Crash! He hit the side of the Deacon's head again.

'You've killed him,' Polly whispered when the blood started spurting out.

'Not him, the little bugger,' Jocky stated flatly. 'Roll out from under him, and stand behind me. I'll deal with him!'

She struggled out with her skirts still up round her neck. The look on Jocky's face made her somehow more embarrassed than she had ever been with the Deacon.

Margery appeared in the doorway just as the Deacon first groaned, then winced as he felt the side of his head, then rose up and weaved his way drunkenly out of the room.

'Jocky saw him coming into Brodie's Close and followed him. When we heard the clatter and your scream we raced upstairs. Did you see it? His thing is still dangling out of his breeches,' she said in disgust.

'Did we see it?' Jocky laughed. 'Do you mean his stick of sugar candy? That's what he called it, and I thought I'd heard every name for that part of a man's anatomy!'

'Run and catch him!' Polly screamed. 'Don't let him get away!'

They heard his racing feet on the stairs, the slam of the front door, and then she and Margery fell back on the bed together, dazed at first, then almost howling in hysterical relief, and finally laughing until they cried.

'Poison didn't break, anyway.' Margery picked up the bottle and examined it.

'No,' Polly said with loathing. 'I will never be rid of her!'

Deacon Brodie reeled down his own back yard and opened the gate. The handcart was there waiting for him, and so was his faithful friend.

'God, Will!' Michael Henderson exclaimed. 'What's happened

to you now? Let's get him hidden under the tarpaulin, boys —
quick!'

He led the way, and his two sons trundled the cart down to the
Grassmarket. Nobody paid any attention. The Hendersons
trundled their cart about every day.

At the Deacon's house, where Polly and Margery were both still
shakily recovering, Mr and Mistress Sheriff arrived in a coach,
both looking distraught and bewildered. 'I did not expect to see
you here,' Mistress Sheriff told them.

'Margery and I came to tidy the house, Mistress Jacobina, after
Miss Jeanette's hurried departure.'

'She's well out of it,' Matthew Sheriff said. 'Well out of it. I
wish to God we were.'

'Write out a suitable notice, Matthew,' his wife said sharply,
'and go and pin it on the workshop door for the men when they
come in to work tomorrow morning.'

He shambled off and Mistress Jacobina frowned at the two
girls. 'Did my brother leave your wages?'

'We have not been paid since we came here,' Polly told her.

'What?'

'Not a penny.'

'The workmen have not been paid for last week, either,'
Margery said when Jocky came back, shaking his head.

'The sheriff has arrived,' he told them. 'He has started with the
workshop.'

'Oh, God, what a mess! You must understand that we cannot
be expected to pay you. My husband has his own business to run
and his own men to pay.'

Mr Sheriff came back and suddenly asserted himself. 'That will
do, Jacobina. If you are speaking about business there is such a
thing as goodwill. I cannot afford to have any black marks
against my name in this town, not after this, so I will find the
money to pay all the men their week's wages, and I will do what I
can for you, too,' he nodded at Polly and Margery.

'We have to thank you for clearing up the house,' Mistress Jacobina said sadly, 'and now we had better lock it, I
suppose.'

'I will deposit the keys at the sheriff-clerk's office if anyone asks you,' Mr Sheriff said. 'Have you both got your things out of here?'

'Oh, dear,' Margery said as they walked down to Candlemaker Row. 'Did you notice how old they look, just overnight? Poor Mr and Mistress Sheriff! Fancy having to live all that down for the rest of their lives!'

Polly didn't know if she looked older, too, but she felt it.

19

JOCKY ROBERTSON TOLD them the latest rumours the next day. 'Brown got away scot-free. Smith made a clean breast of it in the Tolbooth. He accompanied the officers to Brodie's Close this morning, offering to lead them to some concealed evidence.'

'What was it? Where?' Margery asked.

'You know the fireplace where we melted the glue in the workshop? They found a pair of pistols wrapped in a green cloth in the flue behind it. The night-lanterns were out in the yard with the gamecocks. Of course all those bunches of keys for premises all over the city were taken away for evidence. They were all labelled, as you know.'

'And what of the Deacon himself?' Mistress Nell asked.

'Of him there was no trace. He's escaped all right.'

'They'll catch him and bring him back,' George Buchanan assured them all, 'and then he'll swing. Good God! Who would have thought it? Deacon Brodie, eh?'

Every day Polly went through the newspapers drearily, but there was never a mention of the society men.

'What's wrong, dearie?' Mistress Nell asked her. 'Margery thinks you're missing Fraser Graham, and him away wi' the society men? Oh no, Polly! Forget about Fraser Graham in the meantime.'

Polly's heart sank further and further. As long as Fraser had been there it was all laughter and excitement. Now Mistress

Nell was putting her doubts into words. He should have shown her that paper he found. He should have trusted her. He should not have listened to Robert Burns. And he shouldn't have left her. Although she hadn't told him she might be pregnant when he left, he still shouldn't have gone. 'Perhaps you are right, Mistress Nell,' she said. 'I feel so tired and confused.'

'Your face is paler than usual, too … ' Mistress Nell looked at her anxiously. In spite of binding herself up so tightly that the baby didn't show, Polly wondered if Mistress Nell suspected that she was about five months pregnant. 'Oh, well,' she continued, 'I suppose it's the after-effects of all that uproar in Brodie's Close. Anyway, I've brought you today's news-sheets, Polly. Put your feet up and read them. You should rest while you have the chance.'

Polly waited for her to add 'in your condition', but she didn't. 'Yes, I will, Mistress Nell. Is there anything in them about – '

'Not much. The sheriff's officers have searched the Brodies' house and found nothing else so far.'

When she left, Polly went to gaze unseeingly out of her window at Candlemaker Row. Further up the hill she could just see the Royal Mile, and in her mind's eye the vision came again of Fraser Graham and the society men marching off down it to France. That picture never left her mind day or night. The bitterness of it never left her heart.

He had chosen to leave her. He had volunteered to go.

All day long she brooded over this terrible fact. Every night it haunted her and drove sleep away from her desolate bed, and in spite of trying to occupy herself, time crawled past in Polly's tiny room until she thought she must go mad herself, especially at the sight of Poison still smirking up there on the dresser. In a frenzy of boredom, disappointment and worry she jumped up and hurled her to the far end of the room.

'But no, you won't break, will you!' she screamed at the bottle. 'I wish I'd never seen your face! You're nothing but bad luck!'

Angrily she pushed it with her foot and the stopper came out. Still it wasn't broken. The brown face stared up at her impassively a few inches away from the body.

When she bent down to put the head back on again a vision

of Mama came to her, for after all this time there was still a faint trace of the scent the bottle had contained. Then she noticed that the glass body was a lighter brown than the head. There was something inside. She poked about until she fished it out.

It was a paper all rolled up, and when she flattened it she saw that one edge of it was jagged, as if it had been carelessly torn; undoubtedly it was a document of some sort.

Her heart almost stopped when she read the words 'Candacraig' and 'Suzanne' on it. She swayed as she stood there, drew in a deep quivering breath and then the tears were running down her cheeks.

She had found *something* at last! And where was Fraser to share this moment with?

Flinging about and pacing up and down her tiny room, Polly came face to face with it: Lord Braxfield was the only lawyer in the entire city besides Fraser she had met, and she would have to go and speak to him.

It took the rest of the day to pluck up her courage, and while she was trying to do it she busied herself washing and ironing her grey gown with the white collar and cuffs, then washing Poison's grubby little dress. When she took it off, the gilded black glass of the naked lady was revealed again, and when she held her up to the light she glowed golden, almost living, once more reminding her of Caramelle, once more striking her heart with evil.

On Tuesday morning she set off just as the clock on St Giles was striking ten. 'I wish to speak to Lord Braxfield,' she told his clerk.

Albert Gow looked at her with the utmost disapproval. 'Oh, I shoudnae think so,' he said. 'The judge deals wi' criminals, ye ken, not wee lassies.'

'Please tell him that Miss Polly Buchanan wishes to speak to him,' she persisted, tears not far away.

'Weel, I can aye tell him, I suppose. Dinna let him see ye greeting, though, or he'll eat ye for his dinner.' He smiled, apparently at the picture his words conjured up, and disappeared.

She sat still, prepared for a long wait, but to her surprise Lord Braxfield himself came out of his room to usher her inside. He seated her facing the window and sat down heavily himself on the other side of his desk.

'Are ye well enough, lassie?' he began, noticing at once that she was pregnant. Not that he had any experience of pregnant women in his own life, he thought bitterly, but he had seen women before at the same stage as this, with a slight thickening of the jaw and a faint mottling in the clear colour of the cheeks. 'Ye'll no' have heard from Fraser Graham?' he asked.

Polly flushed to the roots of her hair, following that sequence of his logic. 'No, sir. But I do not want to waste your time with any of that. There is something else.'

'Weel?' he said, quite gently for him. 'Oot wi' it, then!'

'Sir, I was introduced to you as Polly Buchanan because the Buchanans allowed me to use their surname when I arrived from London, and passed me off as their niece. My real name is Olivia Gray.'

'Olivia *Gray*?' His dark eyes bored into her from under his beetling eyebrows.

'Yes, sir. My father's name was Oliver Banks, but he was drowned before he could marry my mother, Suzanne Gray. She was known as Madame Suzanne in London.'

There was a shocked silence in the room. For once Lord Braxfield was speechless.

'Before she died she begged me to go to Edinburgh, to Candacraig,' Polly went on, taking the Poison bottle out of her reticule. Her hands shook, and her fingers fumbled with Poison's little dress, but at last she got it off, twisted off the stopper-head, and drew the paper out from inside the bottle. 'She must have put this paper inside here, Lord Braxfield. At any rate, she said I must never be parted from the bottle, and it was only two days ago that I discovered that it held this secret.' She spread the paper out on the desk in front of him.

'God Almighty!'

'I have come to you for advice, because it looked like a legal document to me.'

'It's a legal document a' right! It's part o' a will.'

'I saw that my mother's name was written on it.'

'This will was stolen,' he said sternly.

'Not once, either.' Polly stared back at him, dark eyes under fine arched eyebrows into the same dark eyes under shaggy brows. 'I cannot speak of the original, before it was torn, but the part you see there was stolen from my room in Candlemaker Row.'

This lassie has spirit, Lord Braxfield thought. 'Ye'd better tell me the whole story,' he said, and sat back in his chair.

Polly decided she would not like to come up before him on the Bench. His shrewd eyes penetrated to her very soul. She would have to tell him the whole truth and nothing but the truth. He would soon know if it was not. 'It sounds like a fairy-tale,' she smiled ruefully, 'and it may take more than half an hour to tell.'

'I'm listening. Ye'd better start at the beginning and dinna stop until ye get to today.'

She spared him nothing – from when her mother took in Uncle Philippe to live with them, the flight from Paris to the Hornpipe in London and her mother's terrible death there, right up through her stay in Brodie's Close and now out of it again.

'Yer throat must be dry noo,' he said after a long pause at the end of it. 'I ken mine is.' He went to the door and yelled, 'Albert!'

'Yes, sir.' Albert appeared. 'Am I to let her oot?'

'It might be a long time before ye let this young lady oot, Albert. We need a refreshment. A glass o' port wine, my dear?' he asked Polly.

'Oh no, sir. Perhaps a cup of coffee?'

'Away and get it, Albert, and ye ken what to fetch me. So yer name's Olivia Gray, is it?' he continued the discussion when the door closed. 'Ye canna prove it, I suppose?'

'No, sir. My mother's perfume bottle is all I have in the world, except for one other thing she left me.' Polly drew the gold chain from her neck and unclasped the ring of little Ss. It rolled across the desk, teetered for a minute, and then came to rest at his hand. 'She said this ring came from her mother in Edinburgh with the money she used to send us. She also said it was worthless because it had no precious stones in it – but I always liked it …'

Her voice faltered to a stop when Lord Braxfield took the ring over to the window without a word and stood there looking at it with his back to her. He stood there with his shoulders hunched for a long time. Then he took out his handkerchief and blew his nose violently, and she saw him wiping his eyes before he turned round again to answer the knock on the door.

Albert Gow came in importantly with a coffee pot, cream and sugar and two cups and saucers on a silver tray. He laid it down on the desk with a flourish and went back to get a bottle and a glass for the judge.

'Ye can shut the door again, Albert.'

'Hoots! I'm no' finished! I've brought some Bawbee rolls and butter, and a round o' shortbread as weel. It's wearing weel on in the morning.' He gave Lord Braxfield a warning glance.

'Tell anyone else I canna see them today, then. I'm too busy.'

'Verra good, my lord.' Albert bowed himself out.

Lord Braxfield poured himself a large brandy, drank it neat and poured out another. 'Ah, my God,' he gasped. 'It's been a shock! Oh, dearie me.' He took out his handkerchief again.

'Then please drink a cup of coffee and eat something, sir. Miss Jeanette used to find brandy in her hot coffee very beneficial.'

'Weel, Miss Jeanette was right aboot that. But your mother, God rest her soul, was wrong. This ring is far from worthless. It came from *her* mother like a message from the grave, for Lady Susanna Graham died soon afterwards. Ay, she was yer grandmother, my dear.'

'Then why were we not told she had died?'

'Before I can answer that, there's something ye should see.' He sighed and went over to unlock a cupboard. Out of it he took another jagged piece of paper and laid it down alongside Polly's.

'Who gave you this, sir?'

'Fraser himsel'. Were ye no' wi' him at the time?'

'Yes, but he did not show me it.'

'He didna ken who the other heir or heiress was, lassie. As ye can see, it is not shown on the part he brought me. All he kent was that without this other person he couldna get back to Candacraig. There's nae doot the twa parts will match ... Ay, look at that! Noo, ye'd better read it, lassie. I wrote it to begin wi'. I ken it off by heart.'

Lord Braxfield pinned the parts together and Polly read aloud:

'I, Lady Susanna Graham, formerly of James's Court and now of Candacraig, Edinburgh, possessed of much sounder mind than any I see about me, and considering the follies and the pitfalls of this life and the certainty of death, and the expediency of the disposal of Candacraig Estate, do therefore hereby execute my last Will and Testament, my lawfully wedded husband Sir John Robertson Graham who left no issue, and his brother Charles Graham, father of Charles Fraser Graham, having predeceased me.

I leave and bequeath the lands and the house of Candacraig to the aforesaid Charles Fraser Graham, along with his right to the hereditary peerage and the title, on one condition.

The explanation of the condition thus: that in London in the year 1744 on March fifteenth, the year previous to my marriage with Sir John Robertson Graham, a daughter, the issue of an extra-marital union between me and one who shall remain nameless, was born to me and named Suzanne. The aforesaid Suzanne, known as Suzanne Gray, is now living with her only child to the best of my knowledge and belief.

That Charles Fraser Graham should seek out Suzanne Gray or in the event of her death, her child, and with him or her to be the joint inheritors of the house, lands and estate of Candacraig and the title they inherit from the noble house of Graham.

Signed by me this day December eighteenth, 1786,
Susanna Graham.'

'Yer grandmother didn't even tell *me* who the "one who shall remain nameless" was, although she sent for me to draw up that will.'

'You were a special friend of hers, sir?'

Lord Braxfield smiled sadly. 'A verra special friend, Polly. Noo, I'm going to tell ye something not another living soul must ken aboot, d'ye hear me?'

'Yes sir,' she quivered.

'I found out only recently that I was this "one who shall remain nameless". I'm your grandfather.' He dabbed at his eyes

245

again. 'I gave that ring to Lady Susanna intending to marry her. But she went and married Sir John Robertson Graham instead. It was years later that I found oot she went to London the year afore she married him to ha'e a child, and that the child could only have been mine. From something she said I believe she thought marriage so early in my career would have jeopardized it – so ye see, in a way yer predicament, and yer mother's afore ye, was a' my fault.'

'But you were not to know, sir!'

'Weel, I ken noo! My ain daughter slipped awa' from me. The same thing canna be allowed to happen to my granddaughter, to you, my dear. To begin wi', yer name is not Olivia Gray. It's Olivia Graham.'

'Graham …?'

'Graham,' he sighed. 'The same name as Fraser Graham. The same family, in fact. He's yer second cousin, ye ken, wi' the same kind o' money – and lands – and privileges! So ye can understand why I was so against him leaving all that and risking his life.'

'Oh!' Polly gasped as her heart plummeted.

'Na, na, dearie.' He poured a dash of brandy into her coffee cup. 'Drink that! Ye've been a brave lassie up to noo! It's his bairn ye're carrying, then?'

'Yes.'

'Noo, there's no need to panic, Polly. We'll just sit here until we work it a' oot. If ye can trust no one else,' he got up and put his arm around her shoulders, 'ye can trust yer ain grandfather, ye ken.'

At that she broke down altogether. The emotions and the shocks of the morning had been too much and Lord Braxfield insisted that she should lie down on his horsehair sofa until she felt better.

In the meantime he sent Albert Gow out again, this time for Walter Thomson. 'He's to ride oot to Candacraig immediately wi' this message to the MacDonalds. When he gets back tell him to bring my coach here.'

'Yes, sir.' Albert scurried away.

So it was not until the afternoon and Polly had recovered that he put her into his coach. 'I'm taking ye home,' he told her.

'I can easily walk down to Candlemaker Row.' She smiled at him.

'We're going to Candacraig, that's where we're going,' Lord Braxfield said firmly. 'That's yer home, noo.'

'The short cut doon Candlemaker Row?' Walter's eyes sparkled in anticipation.

'Certainly not!' Lord Braxfield snapped. 'Not wi' this young lady on board. Ye'll tak' the roonaboot way, Walter Thomson, and gey gently while ye're aboot it.'

'But – the Buchanans?' Polly protested.

'Dinna distress yersel' aboot the Buchanans.' Her grandfather patted her hand as they bowled along. 'I'll attend to *them*.'

So once again Polly travelled through the enchanted lands and over the magical bridges leading to the great house. Once again it held out its arms to her in welcome, and hugged her home.

'Ye've opened up a few rooms, Mistress?' Lord Braxfield asked as he helped Polly down at the portico and Mistress MacDonald flustered down the steps to curtsey to her new employer.

'I've managed the three rooms and the kitchen in the east wing, sir. There's fires going, a bed aired and a guinea-fowl roasting.'

'It's a long time since I tasted a guinea-fowl, Mistress MacDonald.'

'Mistress Jessie, sir, if you please. Well, the redcurrant jelly is ready in the jar. There's just the game chips, the bread sauce and the chestnuts to get ready. Donald's seeing about the claret. I'll dish it up in half an hour.'

'Ah, weel, then! I'll stay, in that case. In the meantime, we'll look over the property.'

Arm in arm they wandered slowly around, starting at the west wing and then moving on to the main body of the house and into the vast entrance-hall where the staircase branched gracefully in both directions.

'Up here,' Lord Braxfield panted as they climbed, 'was yer grandmother's room.' He showed her into a room overlooking most of the estate and out beyond to the spires of Edinburgh itself. 'It has the best view in the house.'

The whole perspective calmed Polly for the first time that day. Edinburgh was not so very far away, after all. 'That cottage down through the trees – whose is it?'

'It's for the grieve and his wife and family, but it looks empty.'

'Yes, I remember. Fraser showed me on the map. And it *is* empty. There's no smoke coming out of the chimneys. Some day I'd like to open up this room again.'

'Why not now?' he asked her as they closed the door and continued on their way down into the east wing.

'It is a room for a married couple, surely?'

'He said he was going to marry ye, Polly.'

'Yes.'

'And ye want to marry him?'

'I said I would.'

'Then,' he stopped on the staircase, drew out the ring of Ss from his pocket and slipped it on the third finger of her left hand, 'let this be yer wedding ring, dearie, for now. The story is ye're secretly married already. Naebody'll argue wi' that, when I say I was the one to marry ye. As such, yer name's no' Olivia Graham any more. It's Lady Graham, wife o' Sir Charles Fraser Graham. Oh, ay,' he simply coasted over her protests and denials, 'I tellt ye I would see ye all right. Dinna argue wi' yer grandfather, Polly! When Fraser gets back here and sees his son and heir he'll soon adopt the title he's scorned a' these years for his sake, wait and see! It'll settle the young devil doon once and for a'!'

They reached the little sitting-room in the east wing, where the fire was burning up and there were daffodils and tulips in the vases on the tables by the settees. Later on, she thought, it would be roses … later, when Fraser was home and their child was born. Oh, perhaps then her life could begin!

She smiled at Lord Braxfield and he smiled back as Mistress Jessie withdrew after serving them with the guinea-fowl. He poured a little claret into her glass. 'Ye ken ye'll ha'e to engage servants, Polly? The MacDonalds are retained here to oversee the house only. He acts as custodian, and she is the housekeeper, but ye'll need a proper cook and maidservants for yersel', and as ye saw there's no grieve here now for the grounds.'

'Do you think Margery and Jocky Robertson would come and live in that cottage? She is the best cook I know, and he can turn his hand to anything. You see, since the Deacon Brodie scandal nobody in Edinburgh is willing to employ his workmen, and Jocky is out of a job.'

'Would they come?' He laughed. 'Of course they'll come! I'm going to see them as soon as I leave here. They'll be here tomorrow. Noo, dinna worry. I'll tell them the whole story – oor version o' it! But ye've reminded me, lassie. There are still things I ha'e to attend to in the toon.'

'Yes, I've taken up your whole day,' she sighed. 'What things?'

'Earlier this morning news came to Edinburgh that Deacon Brodie has been caught. He's on his way back, in chains.'

Polly could not speak. In her mind's eye she saw the little dandy in his lace ruffles with the chains about his wrists and ankles, and tears of pity sprang into her eyes.

'Na, na, dinna cry for the little Macaroni! I aye kent he would be up afore me one day! Noo, Mistress Jessie,' he turned to her as she came in to clear away the plates, 'that was a braw meal, fit to welcome yer new mistress. I neglected to introduce ye to Lady Graham before. Ye're to look after her until her own servants get here tomorrow.'

'Very good, sir. Pleased to meet you, I'm sure, my lady. Donald and I are right glad to see a Graham back in Candacraig again.'

In spite of his very busy day on Tuesday, Lord Braxfield was down in his dining-room early on Wednesday morning. He buried his head in the *Caledonian Mercury* where he found most of the news was of Deacon Brodie clapped in the Tolbooth alongside George Smith awaiting trial.

It seemed all Edinburgh was agog with it, while he himself – who would play such a central part in it – was more concerned with domestic issues. He awaited his wife's arrival impatiently and when at last Lady Braxfield joined him she opened what promised to be a very thorny discussion indeed.

'Where were ye a' day yesterday and most o' last night, Robbie Macqueen? Nae wonder the servants laugh ahint oor backs!'

'They do, do they?' He lowered his newspaper in time to

glower at the slovenly young maid bouncing in to thump his wife's porridge down in front of her. 'Can ye no' keep them in order, woman?' He started to rage, and then seemed to think better of it.

Lady Braxfield looked surprised. She had expected more of an outburst than that. There was something up, she decided, as she pushed the grisly lumps of grey oatmeal to one side of her plate.

'One o' these days I'm going to see aboot them mysel', Maggie, I'm telling ye. That's no' porridge! That's just oatmeal thrown in a pan and never stirred. Christ! I remember in the old days how ye used to make it yersel'. Just like velvet, it was!'

Yes, there was definitely something up. 'Were ye working on the Deacon Brodie case?' she continued her enquiry, but more delicately now.

'Ay, that as weel. But to tell ye the truth I had to work most o' the day wi' a young lassie who came to me for help.'

So that was it. A young lassie. 'Oh, ay?' Lady Braxfield's back stiffened. 'What's her name?'

For a flash he was amused at his Maggie, that she could still be jealous.

'Polly.'

'Weel, what aboot her?'

'She's only sixteen years old, Maggie, wi' no mother or father, and pregnant.'

'Who's the father o' the bairn?' she asked suspiciously.

'She wouldnae tell me, except he's awa' wi' the society men.'

'Ye ken what'll happen to *them* then, in yon terrible place, France! So she'll be alone in the world afore long.'

'Ay ... But she's no' just yer ordinary doon-and-ooter, although she doesnae ha'e a rag to her back.' A ray of morning sunshine lit up his wife's immaculate dark-blue gown, exactly matching her suspicious eyes. 'Ye aye had bonnie eyes, Maggie,' he said in a sudden rush of feeling, 'and ye aye kent how to dress.'

Not only was something most certainly up, it was positively alarming. Undaunted, Lady Braxfield set out to discover what, exactly. 'Ay. I'd never let my man doon, and him the most important man in Scotland, never mind Edinburgh. Ye aye kent that, Robbie.'

'Weel, that poor lassie needs an older, wiser woman to help

her. I can release some o' her money tomorrow to buy something to wear. Dae ye think ye could advise her? Besides, if she's wi' *you* they'll a' jump to serve her wi' the best.'

'Bring her here at ten o'clock, then, and I'll see what I can do.'

'Ye're a grand lass, Maggie.'

Lady Braxfield sighed. 'I aye loved ye, Robbie. Ye ken I'd do anything to please ye.'

The maid came in again with two more plates to set before them, and hastily retreated. On them lay hard dry black objects smothered with eggs that were almost raw.

'For Christ's sake! What's this supposed to be?' Lord Braxfield bellowed indignantly, back to his normal ferocity.

'Smoked haddocks in an egg sauce.'

'I canna eat this muck. I'm going. I'll get something at the meridian.' He marched out of his house and up to his rooms with his hands clasped under his coat-tails as usual, and with a fearsome scowl on his face.

'Deacon Brodie will swing,' the townsfolk whispered when they saw him.

But his thoughts were far removed from the Deacon, if they had but known it. He was remembering the amazement, the consternation even, in the Buchanan household last night when he explained Lady Graham to them, and that she was inviting Margery and Jocky to work at Candacraig.

Lord Braxfield drew his brows down to an even darker scowl, for what stuck in his throat most was the sight of the only dry eyes in the house, those of Jocky Robertson. They were positively sparkling as his pink tongue came out and licked his lips over and over again.

But on Thursday when he went home he forgot all about it.

'Ah, that Polly!' his wife said. 'Sic a bonnie lassie, and sic a fine cratur! I hope she gets on a' right ... Oh, Robbie, I hope her man comes back to her!'

'So do I, Maggie,' he said. 'So do I.'

20

IN THE MIDDLE of May the weather became balmy, and in the
grounds of Candacraig the cherry trees put on their gowns of
deep and paler pink rosettes that swept down to the grass,
swaying with any wayward breeze that shook off yet another
cloud of their dainty petals.

When Polly sat in the window-seat of her little sitting-room
she looked out on the mayflowers dancing in rows, frills of pale
yellow primroses along the banks, and in the distance where the
woodlands began a blue haze of the carpets of bluebells under
the trees.

Most of all she admired the trees, especially the very tall green
pine tree, the king of Candacraig's forest. It was the first thing
she saw when she woke up in the morning and the last thing she
looked out on every night.

'Ah, you mean the Fraser pine, my lady,' Donald MacDonald
explained. 'That's a very old Scots pine, as you can tell by its
height and the girth of its trunk. It has always been known here
as the Fraser pine, after the first Fraser Graham who built this
house and planted so many trees, but it was probably here
hundreds of years before that.'

Inside the gates of Candacraig it was a little world all on its
own, far away from the hustle and bustle of the Royal Mile,
where nothing disturbed the peace and tranquillity of the weeks
flying past, and most afternoons Polly walked slowly and
carefully now, out of the house and down to the tree.

Margery came out of her cottage to meet her, and together they sat under its shade on the soft moss between its huge branching roots while they sewed the silk Lady Braxfield had helped her to choose for her own gowns, and the white cambric for the little gowns for the baby.

'I've brought some lemonade today.' Margery smiled.

'Oh, the lemonade, Margery! Do you remember Miss Jeanette and the lemonade?'

'It all seems very amusing now, when everything has turned out so well for us. Miss Jeanette and her fashions! Miss Jeanette and, thank God, Mr Leslie!'

Polly felt reassured that they were here now, safe in this beautiful place and under her beloved Fraser pine. From the very beginning, any minute of any hour of the day she looked at it, and felt this special affinity. Fraser ... If only he would come home.

'Not long now, dearie.' Margery caught her mood. 'Perhaps another four weeks? Sir Fraser will be home by then.'

'Yes, perhaps only another few weeks,' Polly agreed, with panic in her heart.

She felt irritated and angry at the thought that he might miss the birth of his child when, looking up through the dappled sunlight, she saw Jocky walking up to them.

'My lady,' he greeted them. 'Margery.'

But there was something about that greeting that Polly didn't like. Right from the start Margery had understood that she was Polly just as she had always been, except in company. Her husband made such heavy weather of it that she was beginning to believe he resented her good fortune

'Yes, Jocky?' she said, all her alarm bells ringing. They began to ring in a different way when he replied.

'You've been around the back of this tree, I suppose?'

'No. Why?' Margery asked.

'Come and see, then.' He pulled Polly up, and she felt the strength, the heat, the current from his hand. She felt his fingers clinging longer than they should have. 'Round here.' He pointed to the huge gash across the trunk, a hole overgrown already with moss, and teeming with bright pink brown-spotted toadstools.

'Those toadstools are rank poison,' he told them. 'They only grow in rot. This tree is rotting and dying. One day it will rot right around, and fall.'

'Oh, pay no attention, Polly!' Margery said. 'This tree will still be here when we're all dead and gone.'

The rhododendrons put on their best display in the first week of June, bank after bank of white and pink and mauve all along the avenues of Candacraig. Lord Braxfield did not see them. Instead he sat hunched in a corner of his coach deep in thought, more concerned with the lack of news about the society men than the splendour of the flowers.

Walter Thomson was driving him back to Edinburgh after one of his twice-weekly visits, now that Polly was coming so near her time. Why, he asked himself for the thousandth time, had they and Fraser Graham with them simply vanished into thin air in France? It meant that he must attend to Polly's affairs and those of her coming child himself, and considering what that entailed it could be a sticky business, a very sticky business indeed.

'Ye can drop me off at Erskine Caldwell's,' he told Walter with a resigned sigh. 'I've got some unfinished business wi' that wee mannie.'

God help him, Walter thought, as whistling cheerfully he deposited his lordship at the other lawyer's rooms.

Once inside, Lord Braxfield wasted no time. He pushed past the protesting clerk in the outer office, burst into the inner office and looked at the client sitting there with a stare that had withered many a jury. Immediately the man got up and retreated out of the door.

'No doubt it is something important?' Erskine Caldwell asked icily.

'It's important a' right! Just as important as the last time I spoke to ye aboot it! Ye paid little enough attention, then.'

'What are you saying, sir? I do not understand you.'

'Lady Susanna Graham's will was found, ye ken, after all. And *you* supposed to be looking after her affairs! Humph!'

'Found? Where?'

'Ay, worse and worse, my lad. In her writing desk.'

'What writing desk?' Erskine Caldwell produced a bulky

folder and looked through it hastily for the inventory, glancing over it swiftly. 'There's no writing desk in the inventory,' he said triumphantly, 'and before you come barging in here again – '

'No. That's because it was stolen,' Lord Braxfield cut him off in midflow. 'Stolen by yon William Brodie ye sent in to close up the hoose. Ye couldna see past him, could ye? The very best, ye tellt me! The very best! Well, *noo* see where he's landed – in the Tolbooth waiting to be sentenced to death.'

'Are you saying that Brodie stole the desk out of the house, Lord Braxfield? How do you know?'

'He took the desk and all its contents. It was shown to me by the sheriff's officers last week in the house in Brodie Close when they were doing their search. Of course, I had it returned to Candacraig. It'll no be needed as evidence. There's enough evidence to hang him already, God kens, withoot that.'

'I see.'

'No, ye dinna, Erskine Caldwell. Ye havena even asked who stood to inherit.'

'Fraser Graham, I imagine. There's no one else left.'

'Ah, but there is! Lady Susanna left half to him and half to a lady she knew in London. That lady died, we found out after a conseederable search,' he scowled ferociously, 'which ye neglected to carry oot yersel' – but she had a daughter.'

'Fraser Graham will dispute *that*, of course.'

'I shouldnae think so.' Lord Braxfield played his trump card: 'He's her husband. I married them mysel' before he went wi' the society men. They had no time for a kirk wedding, and furthermore they wished to keep it a secret in the meantime.'

There was a pause while Erskine Caldwell tried to absorb this. 'Highly irregular.' He frowned. 'Highly irregular.'

'Perfectly straightforward, Erskine, lad, and no' as irregular as the slapdash way ye dealt wi' Lady Susanna's affairs! What a disgrace! Christ,' his voice dropped at the sheer awesomeness of it, a tactic he had employed many a time to great effect in his courtroom, 'what a disgrace ...'

When Erskine Caldwell dropped his eyes and his thin cheeks flushed painfully, Lord Braxfield knew he had beaten him, or, as he told himself in his own language, he had him by the balls.

'However,' he said grandly, sitting back now, 'I'm prepared to let that matter drop in certain circumstances.'

'Yes? What circumstances?'

'I'll relieve ye o' the Graham family's business altogether. I'll tak' it ower mysel'. Then nobody'll ask any questions, not aboot them, not aboot you, and certainly not aboot me.'

'By all means.' Erskine Caldwell looked relieved when Lord Braxfield stood up to go. 'I never made much money out of it, anyway.'

'I'll allow ye to see me oot, Erskine. I'll just take Lady Susanna's folder at the same time.'

But Erskine Caldwell had lost what little interest he had ever had in Lady Susanna already. Knots of men, other lawyers, were gathered together and speaking among themselves. 'What is it?' he asked Iley Smith. 'What's wrong?'

'The first two society men came back home this morning, drowned. They were found along by Newhaven where that French fishing boat went ashore on the rocks.'

'Who were they?' Lord Braxfield could hardly speak, he dreaded to hear the answer so much.

'A Gordon Paterson and a James Cochrane. Do you know them?'

'No,' he said. So there was still a chance that Fraser was safe, he thought, but he was very alarmed as he walked unsteadily to his own rooms. 'For Christ's sake, Albert,' he said when he got there, 'fetch me a glass o' brandy.'

The Scottish men lay scattered on the hill outside the Château of Rougemont. The revolutionaries had already stormed the castle, broken down the gates and gone with the marquis and his wife and two sons, alive, stripped of all they possessed and in chains. Some of the soldiers remained inside, determined to fight to the end.

Fraser Graham wondered briefly if they knew what for, before he whistled to the MacAllisters and the others to join him. 'We can't just leave them in there,' he whispered, 'to go down to the village later in revenge and murder every soul in the place. The only way is to smoke them out.'

In their native land the Edinburgh men were well used to

working with the heather that was growing all around on the hillside. They twisted it into long dry sticks, set fire to them and hurled them over the castle walls, keeping their heads well down.

But they were unsuccessful. No flames shot up into the night sky to tell them that the wooden interior had caught. Nothing happened. Again and again they tried, in vain.

'This is no use!' Jamie MacAllister rose up with a burning torch in his hand and dashed through the castle gates. 'Come on, Cameron!'

Cameron was only seconds behind his headstrong young brother, so fast that Fergus MacAllister and Fraser could only watch in shocked dismay when suddenly flames roared up, shot out of the Château in all directions and enveloped the brothers.

Fraser was the first to act. He ran towards the two human torches in a wild bid to save them. At the same time the soldiers, flushed out at last and badly singed themselves, came rushing out firing their weapons. Two explosions, one after the other, felled Fraser to the ground and he rolled over and down with a tremendous thud.

He did not know that he had fallen into a cavity, once an underground store which had been looted of its explosives by the revolutionaries, and he did not know that he lay there dying while the flames scorched and burned the very grass above him, only feet from his head, for the castle now was an inferno.

The world was dark, full of pain and too cold to bear when rough hands dragged him away, and a desperate struggle began. It went on and on, and just as he thought he was almost succeeding, sinking back into the light and peace of another world, he was dragged back into an icy darkness vibrating with unbearable pain.

Someone was dragging him back over and over again until he became angry enough to open his eyes to see who it was. He didn't know her, this woman dressed in blue and white, but every time he opened his eyes she was still stubbornly there, hurting him savagely, and he thought she was trying to kill him. He came to hate her, to dread the sight of her and the agony she always caused.

Bit by bit he tried to locate the pains. There was one in his chest and another, far worse, in his right leg. Every time she touched either one of them he screamed and tried to creep back into that other world again.

He had endured so much of it, and now he only wanted to die. Oh, God, why didn't she leave him alone? One morning he opened his eyes and she was coming at him again with her basins and bowls and cloths.

'Leave me alone!' he thought he screamed, but it only came out in a whisper.

'Ah,' she smiled and spoke in French, 'so you have decided to come back to the land of the living again?'

What that meant he didn't know, and by the time she had attended to him again he didn't care. But every morning after that his eyes opened in curiosity.

'Who are you?' he asked her one morning. 'Where am I?'

'You are in the village of Rougemont, well hidden, monsieur. And I am the nurse, Paulette Michel.'

'What happened?'

'You were shot in the chest and the leg. Our men thought you were already dead when they took you here. It was a miracle that you were not burned to death with the others. But you are recovering now.'

No matter how he groaned and protested every day, from then on she kept repeating it: 'You are getting better. You are recovering,' and forced him to drink her beef broth. 'No,' she insisted, 'you must drink it. It is giving you strength after the loss of so much blood.'

It took two months of her devoted nursing before Fraser came back to life again, and Paulette filled in the gaps of the immediate past.

'You and the other Scottish men set fire to the Château, and the men of this village killed the soldiers. That bloody part of our history you wiped out for us for ever. That's why we have hidden you and helped you all we can.'

'The other Scottish men,' he asked, 'did they get away?'

'No, Monsieur Fraser. As far as we know you are the only one to survive, and we are determined that you shall live. That is why I have had to hurt you so much,' she said sadly.

'How long is it since then?'

'A long time, two months.'

Two months … In Edinburgh he would be believed dead.

It was from Father Jean, the local priest, that he learned what had been happening in the outside world during the eight weeks he had been so ill.

'It is the same as in every war,' the old man said. 'For this will be a civil war before we are much older. Unscrupulous men try to grab what they can. Vagrants from every walk of life are banding together, roaming the countryside, trespassing on the farms by night and cutting the wheat and barley. We all fear for our crops, for should there be such a disaster to this year's harvest then without question next winter we shall starve … And then there are the brigands.'

'Who are the brigands?'

'Militant workmen, armed. The English Prime Minister Pitt is sending hundreds of troops into France to support the aristocracy and chase the brigands into the French countryside to disrupt communications. We are between the devil and the deep already.'

Fraser turned in the bed and winced with pain.

'I am tiring you, my son.' The priest rose to go.

'No, you are not, Father. It is this dammed leg of mine. It is never getting any better.'

'I will pray for you.'

'Pray very hard then, if you please, for it is still very doubtful if I can keep it attached to my body. The wound in my chest is healing slowly, but there is talk about taking my right leg off.' Fraser smiled grimly.

One night the pain in his leg reached such a tremendous height that something burst inside it.

'That's it, at last!' Paulette smiled, with tears running down her face. 'There was something left in your leg, festering away. That was what we were worrying about all this time. Unless it came to a head itself your leg could never have healed, and you might have lost it.'

The poison did not drain away altogether that time. There were other minor relapses after that. The villagers of Rougemont were glad that the Scottish gentleman was recovering at last and proud that it was one of their own who had made that possible. The priest made daily visits now, and Jacques Duval from a neighbouring cottage became a fast friend.

There followed another two months during which Fraser became stronger every day, and was now able to put his foot to the ground. In time the wound healed over and he could walk again, although with a limp.

Fraser spoke to Jacques Duval again. 'I'm afraid my family and friends in Scotland think I am dead, Jacques. By this time they will have heard that no Scotsmen survived the battle of the Château. Is there no way I could get word to Edinburgh?'

'None, unless I take a letter myself to the coast.'

'Then that is out. You have told me yourself it is too dangerous to travel.'

'I said doctors would not travel, Monsieur Fraser,' Jacques said with a smile. 'I said nothing about those of us who might relish such a challenge! There are another two men in Rougemont waiting for an adventure to happen. They will come with me.'

'Who are they?'

'It is better that you do not know. Write your letter today, monsieur. It will begin its journey tonight.'

Where was Polly now? God alone knew, for the news of Deacon Brodie had trickled through to them in France almost as soon as they got there. She would probably be back in London again, if she was anywhere. Would the Buchanans know? In the end Fraser decided to address the letter to Lord Braxfield, and wished to God he could deliver it in person.

Jacques Duval and his two friends came back triumphantly with their mission accomplished, not knowing that Fraser's letter was at the bottom of the sea along with the English fishing vessel they had risked all to put it on.

But Fraser was becoming more and more impatient every day. 'I'm ready to go now, Jacques,' he told his friend one day. 'I've got to get back home, although there will be nothing and nobody worth going home to by this time.'

'I know you can walk, and you can probably ride, but would you be fit enough yet to defend yourself if necessary against an enemy – although the Good Lord only knows who is an enemy nowadays in this country where brother is set against brother?' Jacques asked anxiously. 'But there is one way out.'

'Yes?'

'My wife and I still drive our vegetable cart to the market every day. Everyone knows us, and always help us when the vagrants are about. We will see you to the coast. Will you come tomorrow?'

'I'll be ready,' he said.

With his goodbyes said, the following morning the Duvals hid him in the back of their wagon on a bed of straw. They put straw on top of him, a thick wad above the scar on his leg, and the lightest vegetables on top of that.

'This reminds me of those other two *Anglais*,' Madame Duval told him before she covered his face. 'Only they were escaping from Paris. Madame Suzanne and Mademoiselle Polly.'

'*Who*?' Fraser dashed the straw off his face.

'A Madame Suzanne and her daughter, Polly. Gray, I think they said their name was.'

The nights were still a little chilly in spite of the mildness of the days, and in his study at home Lord Braxfield heaved the rug more firmly around his shoulders, poked up the fire and poured himself another warming glass of brandy. He had plenty of work to do, to study the case of the next criminal to come before him, and he had just settled himself comfortably when the risp tirled on the front door.

'God damn and blast it!' he growled. 'Who could it be disturbing decent folk at this time of the night?' He opened the door and peered out into the darkness, cursing himself for not thinking of bringing a night-lantern with him. 'Weel?' he said unwelcomingly. 'Who is it?'

'It's me, Lord Braxfield. Fergus MacAllister, back from France.'

As soon as Fergus spoke, Lord Braxfield's heart sank like a stone. A terrible foreboding came over him. 'Ye'd better come in, then,' he said, leading the way back to his study. 'In here, where I can see ye ... Jesus, laddie! What happened, for God's sake?'

The last time he had seen Fergus MacAllister he was a bright young man, well-dressed – perhaps too well-dressed, like all the

MacAllister boys – but upstanding and happy. The man in front of him now was the very opposite, ragged, red-eyed, grey-faced and looking easily forty years old.

'The men from the society have come back, my lord. All except three,' Fergus said bitterly. 'I've lost both my brothers. Cameron and Jamie are dead. Nothing will ever be the same for me again. It will kill my mother.' He flung himself into a chair, weeping bitterly. 'I don't know how I'm going to tell her.'

'Here, drink this.' Lord Braxfield pressed a glass of brandy into his hand. 'Tell me what happened.'

'Our assignment was in a small place called Rougemont in the heart of the country, but the marquis there was making life intolerable for the people. He was nothing short of a butcher – a bloody butcher! We killed him, freed the prisoners in his château, and set fire to it.'

Fergus's voice broke again, and he swallowed another gulp of brandy.

'My brothers must have gone back in for some reason. I'll go to my own grave and never know why. They were burned alive. We buried them in the little graveyard of Rougement. Nothing we did after that seemed half so hard as what we had already endured, until it came to getting back home. Everywhere we turned we were blocked by the aristos. We worked our way back to the coast eventually and the French fishermen helped us to get away.'

The little graveyard of Rougement … Polly had described it so faithfully that Lord Braxfield felt a chill of pure horror running down his spine. For some minutes he did not dare to speak, and Fergus brooded into the fire by his side.

'Weel, ye'd better go on home, laddie. No!' He stopped Fergus's protests. 'Of course you won't tell your mother all that tonight, but ye canna stay here. Let her see one o' her laddies safe home again. Let her get *some* sleep, at her age. But ye'll ha'e to tell her in the morning.'

'But that is not the whole story, my lord.'

'No, and I wish to God I didn't have to hear the rest o' it, either,' he said, in tears himself now. 'There was a third man?'

'Yes. Fraser Graham ran in after my brothers, and we never saw him again.'

21

FERGUS MACALLISTER WENT away, and Lord Braxfield dragged himself upstairs. Still weeping bitterly, he sat down on the edge of the bed.

'Robbie! Robbie! What ails ye?' Lady Braxfield sat up in alarm and lit the night-candle. 'Are ye ill? Tell me what's wrong.'

'It's the news o' the society men, Maggie. Fergus MacAllister came to the door just now to tell me. Three men never came back, his brothers and Fraser Graham.'

'Ah ... That poor little Polly. Poor wee lassie. But get into bed, ye'll catch yer death shivering at the side o' it like that.'

He undressed, noticing that her hair was down around her shoulders the way it used to be when they were young and newly married. In the candlelight she still looked quite youthful, and her face was soft with sympathy.

When he climbed in beside her he was grateful that she was not snoring with her back humped up against him as it usually was by the time he staggered upstairs every night. Instead he fell into her outstretched arms and they sank into the depths of their feather bed together.

He was drowning in emotion when he kissed her passionately. She kissed him back just as passionately, as he made love to her for the first time in many months, to give him the comfort and release he needed.

'Oh, Maggie,' he said. 'My wee Maggie.'

'I love ye, Robbie.'

'I ken ye do, sweetheart, and I havena been fair to ye at all. Not all oor married life. I wouldna be so upset if there wasn't a lot more behind this, and it's time I told ye the whole story.'

'D'ye really want to tell me, Robbie?'

'I want to. Ye were right aboot Lady Susanna Graham, although all that was long ower wi' before I met ye. Let me tell ye how she died and why. It's the beginning o' a story that might take a long time to tell,' he warned.

She lit the night-candle again and turned to smile at him. 'I've waited a gey long time to hear it, so tell me now, at last.'

Bunty Gilhooly arrived in the Braxfield kitchen at half past six the following morning, her big feet flattening several cockroaches at a time with a satisfying crunch on her way to open the shutters.

All the other cockroaches scuttled off into their safe retreats in the patches of earth between the stone flags while unconcernedly she shovelled their dead fellows into the pail at the fireside, and the two young maidservants came in, yawning and slatternly.

'Late, as usual,' she snapped. 'Ceelie Clark, get this fire started! And Gladys Watt, go to the pump for the water!'

Having set the household going in this fashion she sat down in the rickety wooden chair by the fireside and set her clay pipe going. She did not present a pretty picture, the pipe just managing to protrude between her chin and her hooked nose, for Bunty was toothless.

'What's for breakfast, Mistress Gilhooly?' Ceelie asked as she raked out yesterday's cinders. 'I'm dying o' hunger.'

'Ay, that's all ye are, ye lazy cow – just a hunger,' Bunty assured her.

'We're supposed to get oor meat.' Gladys came in sloshing water out of her pail all along the floor. 'Her upstairs said so.'

'When I'm ready.' Bunty puffed away. 'When that fire takes up. When that kettle boils.'

'There's only a few slices o' cold mutton,' said Gladys as she explored the pantry, 'and there's mouse droppings all over them. I'm no' eating that.'

'That's for them.' Bunty jerked her head upwards, dismissing the mutton. Presently she rose out of the chair telling them, 'I've got something else here for us,' and before long the smell of ham frying filled the kitchen.

'Och, it goes roon yer heart, that smell,' Ceelie said. 'My mouth's fair watering.'

'And I've got three eggs.' Bunty broke them one by one with agonizing slowness into the pan. 'So?' She smiled confidently and filled her pipe again ten minutes afterwards while Ceelie and Gladys wiped round and round their plates with hunks of bread. 'Those plates'll no' need washing, anyway!'

'It was grand, Mistress Gilhooly.' They sat back, replete.

A noise at the door into the hall made them spin around. To their utter and complete horror Lady Braxfield was standing in the doorway in her dressing-robe, her hair dishevelled and her eyes softly shining. They sat with their mouths open, unable to move or to comprehend anything so unusual.

'Lord Braxfield and I will require our breakfast in bed this morning,' she announced with a strange smile, and withdrew.

'God, how much did she see?' Ceelie asked.

'Or smell,' Gladys added.

'Nothing!' Bunty crashed pans about in a fury. 'I ken what's been going on up there last night! At their age, dirty auld buggers! Ceelie, get that tray ready! Gladys, up ye go wi' it,' she commanded, slapping the cold mutton on two plates.

'It'll take the smile off their faces, this lot,' Glady's said darkly as she set off, and five minutes later she was back down in the kitchen again, hardly able to speak for giggling.

Up in the bedchamber it was a completely different picture when Lady Braxfield coughed nervously, whispered to her husband and he unwillingly let her go. 'It's the breakfast, Robbie. Sit up on yer ain side o' the bed, quick!'

'What the hell's this?' He regarded the tray when Gladys laid it down and fled. 'Cauld stinking mutton? When that bitch doon there kens I hate mutton? Na, na, Maggie!' He dashed the tray against the wall. 'I've had enough o' this! It's long past time to see aboot it.'

'Oh! Oh!' Gladys gasped when back down in the kitchen she stopped giggling at last. 'They were kissing and cuddling! I'm sure he had his leg ower!'

'What?' Bunty Gilhooly's nose and chin snapped together. Once, the master had slapped her backside on his way past. She had harboured high and amorous hopes of him ever since, for everyone knew he and Maggie Macqueen didn't get on. 'I aye kent aboot him,' she sneered now. 'I aye kent he was a horny auld bastard!'

A deathly hush from the two girls made her look round. Lord Braxfield stood behind her. In his nightshirt with his nightcap all askew he was a daunting figure.

'Ha *ha*!' he roared. 'Horny I might be, Bunty Gilhooly! I'm a proper man! But a bastard, no. That's slander, ye ken.'

The cook dropped weakly into the wooden chair, a ladle still in her hand, while from the girls there was a short terrified titter as Lady Braxfield joined her husband, a pinafore over her gown and a leather pouch of household money in her hand.

'But it's no slander, it's the truth, when I tell ye that ye have a dirty mouth, ye keep a filthy kitchen, and yer food's abominable.' Lord Braxfield marched about and came to a halt at the pail by the fireside. 'Oh, ay! Bacon rinds and eggshells, I see! Ye do yersel' proud, Bunty Gilhooly.'

'Caller Herrin'! Caller Herrin'!' came a cry at the back door.

Lady Braxfield opened it to reveal a woman dressed in a white lace-trimmed under-petticoat, with a red and white striped outer-petticoat, and an overdress of pale green muslin looped up round her hips with a string in the hem. She stood leaning on a creel she had taken off her back.

'Fresh herrin', Mistress?' the Newhaven fishwife asked Lady Braxfield, who bought some and put them on a plate under another plate in the pantry.

'Weel, ye're oot o' a job, lady,' her husband was informing their cook when she came back again. 'What's more, ye'll never work in this toon again – and dinna forget that I travel all Scotland. One word breathed aboot this hoose and I'll ha'e any o' the three o' ye up before me. Ye'll get no mercy, I can promise ye that! Clear oot, the lot o' ye!' He threw a few coins out of the pouch in each of their directions contemptuously.

'What did ye do wi' the herrin', Maggie?' he asked when they fled.

'Oh, I'll soon fry the the herrin'. There's oatmeal in the barrel. That's just aboot a' there is.' Lady Braxfield was almost in tears.

'Cheer up dearie. We'll eat a proper breakfast. It'll be the start o' a new life together.'

'Go and dress yersel', Robbie Macqueen. Ye'll get yer breakfast when I'm good and ready. But first I'll ha'e to clean up this kitchen. I canna live among dirt.'

When he came back downstairs again she had the table cleared, clean dishes on it and the herrings in the pan. He watched her every move as she dashed about the kitchen. She had a trim figure, had his Maggie. He told her that she had cooked him the best breakfast he had eaten for years.

'Ay, but we'll ha'e to get new servants noo, Robbie.'

'Next time *I'll* engage the servants.' He pulled her on to his knee. 'Dinna worry yer pretty little head aboot that. We've got worse worries than that to face.' His smile faded and the creases came back to his forehead. 'I'll ha'e to go to Candacraig this morning wi' terrible news for Polly.'

'But not alone, dearie. I'm coming wi' ye.'

Polly had wakened early that morning with pains in her back. Later they got worse, and she felt quite unwell.

'I'm all right,' she told the maid, waving away her breakfast. 'I'll lie still for a little while longer, until I feel better. Go on back to the kitchen, dear. You've plenty to do there.'

Shortly afterwards she realized her waters had broken, and that her baby must be on the way. The pains made dressing a slow and weary business, but holding on to the banister she made her careful, awkward way downstairs and into her sitting-room.

The maidservants had lit the fire although it seemed another lovely day outside. The first thing she did was to go over to the window-seat, content to look out on to the swaying lilacs, until her eyes were drawn inevitably to the Fraser pine.

It could not have listed a little – surely it was only blowing in the summer breeze. Another stronger pain made her forget it and look down the avenue instead. That thing coming so slowly out of the trees at the bottom of the drive looked like a great black crow.

She was not herself today. She knew it when a sudden memory

came to her. She had seen a wounded crow crawling along like that once, its wings down on the ground, flapping along. It had meant bad luck then, that day in Rougemont. It was bad luck now, and with a heart gone suddenly ice-cold she refused to look at it any more. If she blinked her eyes it would go away.

But it didn't go away, and it wasn't a black crow. It was Lord Braxfield's black coach coming nearer and nearer on a Sunday morning, when he always came on Monday mornings and Thursday afternoons. Suddenly she was filled with terror. There was something wrong. Black wings seemed to beat over her head. Angrily she tried to push them away, and the child inside her reacted violently, moving about in painful agitation.

She waited until the coach came to a halt and her grandfather descended, holding out his hand to someone she saw was Lady Braxfield, who had never been here before. Then it was important, and it was bad. Polly went to stand on the top step of the portico while they toiled up the steps towards her.

'What is it? She tried to remain calm, but their sad faces told her all she needed to know. 'It's Fraser, isn't it?'

Lord Braxfield put his arms around her, and held her steady. 'Yes, it's Fraser, dearie,' he said, tears running down his cheeks.

'I think the baby's coming,' Polly said. 'It's coming now,' as the blow of this shock made her reel back and the pains intensify. 'It's too soon, the midwife isn't due to come here for another fortnight.'

'Carry her up to her bed, Robbie,' Lady Braxfield said. 'I'm going to take off her clothes. Go to the kitchen and get the maidservant to boil a sharp knife in water and bring it to me wrapped in a clean cloth.'

In fifteen minutes he was back with the knife and his wife laid it down on the table beside the bed. 'That lassie in the kitchen is terrified,' he told her in a low voice. 'She's never seen a birth. She doesna want to see one noo, either.'

'She'll be no use, then. Tell her to boil plenty of water instead, and ask her where Margery is. Why isn't she here?'

'The lassie says she'll leave pails o' water ootside the door, hot and cold,' he came back to tell her, 'and Jocky and Margery Robertson took the Edinburgh Fly yesterday into the toon. They won't be back until tomorrow morning.'

'Then we're on our own, Robbie. We'll have to help her as best we can oorsel's. I'll stay with her. You get Walter Thomson to drive ye to Newhaven. I ken it's miles on the other side o' the toon, but that's where Beattie Barbour lives, and she's the best midwife in Edinburgh. Just bring her as fast as ye can. She'll come for me.'

'But how will ye manage, lass? Ye've never had a bairn o' yer ain. Will ye ken what to do?'

Lady Braxfield smiled calmly. 'Every woman kens, Robbie. Awa' ye go!'

When he strode off she turned to speak to Polly. 'I'm going to tear up one o' yer bonnie sheets, dearie, but dinna worry. Here it is in strips to bind roon the bed-head. Ye'll need to hold on to something when the pains are bad, and I dinna want yer hands festering wi' the splinters off the wood.'

'Oh,' Polly groaned, 'you're very kind, Lady Braxfield.'

'That's another thing, dearie. Robbie and I were just speaking aboot that on the way here. He's tellt me the whole story. I ken he's yer grandfather, but we'll keep that to oorsel's. The easiest thing is to call him Robbie and me Maggie – like old friends, for if we're no' old friends yet, we soon will be,' she smiled.

'Oh, Maggie!' Polly moaned and gripped on to the bed-head hard.

'That's right, lassie. Hold on. The pains have to get harder and faster all the time, noo that yer little bairn is trying its best to come into the world.'

After that Polly lost all idea of time. The long hot summer day just went on and on in a glare of bright sunshine and hard brilliant pain, while Lady Braxfield sat with her, willing her on and sometimes holding her back.

'Na, na, Polly, dinna push yet! Ye'll only tear yersel'. I'll tell ye when the head's almost down. Then ye can push.'

'I need to!' Polly screamed and screamed.

'Not yet! Not yet, dearie.' Lady Braxfield wiped her forehead. 'Soon. I'll tell ye, dinna worry.'

At the end of six hours Polly was desperate with pain, but at last the head was showing.

'Now, push!' Lady Braxfield said calmly. 'The bairn's nearly here,' and then after an agony which seemed to shatter her whole body apart, 'and another, Polly! One more time for the shoulders!'

This time it killed her, or she thought it had, for there was a silence. There was no baby crying lustily as she thought it would, and Lady Braxfield was no longer at her side.

Then Lady Braxfield straightened up, held up the baby separated from her now, turned it upside down and smacked it smartly. 'Oh, thank God,' she said with tears running down her face when there was a tiny wail. They could scarcely hear it above the noise of coach-wheels on the drive. 'Oh, thank God, Polly! You have a beautiful daughter,' and she had the presence of mind to wrap the child in a sheet before the door opened.

A small, stout woman came in, took the baby out of the sheet and examined her. 'You made a good job, Maggie Macqueen!' She smiled, wiping the baby's eyes and mouth and ears expertly before she handed her gently to Polly.

'Ye're a sight for sore eyes, Beattie!' Lady Braxfield sighed, exhausted.

'And what are you going to call that lovely little girl?' Beattie Barbour smiled at Polly.

'Charlotte Fraser Graham,' she answered and began to cry with great heaving sobs. 'After her father.'

'Go and make yourself some tea, Maggie,' the midwife said, 'while I attend to the mother.'

Born into sunshine, happy and healthy, Charlotte captivated everyone around her that glorious summer of 1788. It was a summer such as few Scottish folk could remember, when even the rain behaved itself and showered down through the nights, so that in the mornings the flowers and the trees were refreshed to bloom on forever.

Polly saw none of it. She looked out unseeingly over the fresh trimmed grass and the formal hedges now so neatly clipped, over the new oval beds created for the geraniums, a bed for each passionate colour of red and flame and shocking pink, and over the walls where the roses climbed, their heady scent pervading all the house.

'No!' she cried when the first great bowls of them were carried into her sitting-room and laid down on the little tables.

'Take them away!' How could there be roses now, or dreams, or any happiness when Fraser was dead? 'Don't bring me roses again,' she commanded the maids, who looked at her sadly and uncomprehendingly, and bore them away.

With a sob she picked up her baby again, removed her sodden little napkin, washed her and then sitting in the window-seat fed her. Each day stretched out interminably, lonely, empty and hopeless. The only small break in the monotony was meeting Margery in the afternoons. Only now there was no sparkle in their conversation. In fact, there seemed nothing to say.

That afternoon Margery had a determined gleam in her eye when Polly took Charlotte in her arms and went to sit under the Fraser pine. In vain Jocky and Margery had repeatedly begged her to sit under some other tree, but Polly had a strange, strong conviction – so strong that it was by now a superstition – that as long as the Fraser pine still stood, she still had something left. The Fraser pine still gave her a trickle of comfort.

'There's a coach and carriage in the coach-house, you know,' Margery told her, taking charge of Charlotte at once and raining little kisses on the baby's face, 'and two horses in the stable. Oh, Polly, let's go into the town! Jocky could drive us, and Ma would so love to see this little darling!'

'All right.' Polly sighed. 'This is Tuesday, isn't it? No visitors come here on Wednesdays, so tell Jocky we'll leave for Edinburgh tomorrow morning at ten o'clock.'

The outside world seemed strange as Jocky drove them as gently as he could over the rutted road into the town and stopped in Candlemaker Row.

'Oh, my! What a wee beauty! Leave the bairnie wi' me,' Mistress Nell took Charlotte in her arms, smiling down at her happily, 'and awa' ye go, the pair o' ye. Ye're only young lassies yet, and young lassies like the Luckenbooths.'

'Where's Jocky?' Margery asked.

'Oh leave him be! Men miss the company o' other men. He'll be awa' wi' his pals.'

Then they were back in the bustling, teeming Royal Mile again, so strange as to be almost alien to Polly now. The crowds pressed in around at the Luckenbooths, and once or twice she fought back a frightened desire to escape for air to breathe, when once she had come here every day and thought nothing of it. She made herself stay and choose some little things for Charlotte.

'Is that all you've bought?' Margery asked curiously on the way back down to Candlemaker Row. 'You've been away from all this for so long, I thought you would have bought a lot more.'

'But I haven't the money, Margery.'

'You haven't the money? How can you say that, now?'

'Lord Braxfield pays your wages out of the estate money. He gives me only a small allowance out of it, too. It may be a long time before the legal settlement is made after Fraser's death.'

'There! Don't upset yourself, dearie. Ma'll have a nice cup of tea ready for us.'

But Polly was very upset, and so exhausted when they came back to Candacraig that Margery was concerned.

'You look so tired, Polly. Charlotte is keeping you awake at nights, I know. Why don't you let her stay with us tonight? We would love to have her! She'll come to no harm with me, Jocky simply worships her, and you would get a good night's sleep.'

Polly hesitated, but the temptation to lie down and forget all the reminders of Fraser's death she would have to face from now on was overwhelming. If only she could sleep and sleep and forget the world ... She watched Margery with Charlotte in her arms and Jocky behind her carrying the crib down to the cottage until her eyes almost closed together, and feeling numb, she fell into bed.

The dawn chorus from the woodland around Candacraig woke her, and for a while she lay still listening to the birds calling to each other. The little porcelain clock on the mantelshelf tinkled out the message that it was four o'clock in the morning, and apart from the birdsong there wasn't another sound.

Instinctively she reached for Charlotte, but there was no baby there, and no crib, and for a minute she knew the first sheer blind panic of her life.

Charlotte ... Charlotte, with her little cries and snufflings ... Charlotte, whose tiny formless features were becoming more like Fraser's every single day ... Charlotte, her beloved child.

Polly burst into tears. Even to herself, she could not explain her feelings at that moment, but she tried to face the truth, that she had been resenting her own baby for living, when her father was dead.

She had not loved her. And yet the very opposite was true, all along. How could she have allowed that tiny scrap of humanity, the only proof of her love with Fraser, to go to anyone else? Her hands were shaking so much that it took her several minutes to dress. For two months she had gazed on Charlotte's face day and night, and yet now, she sobbed aghast, she could not remember a single detail of it.

Then she was down, and banging on the cottage door, and knocking and calling until at last a sleepy-eyed Margery opened it. 'I cannot bear it, Margery,' she wept. 'I need her back. I need my baby.'

'She's here, safe and sound.' Jocky Robertson appeared with Charlotte in his arms. 'She's been good. She slept all night.'

But Polly was gone, half-way up the path, running and running with her child until she was back in her own bedchamber again. 'Oh, Charlotte, Charlotte,' she rained the little face with butterfly kisses, 'I love you. I'll never let you go again.'

It was the turning point for Polly, and it must have been for Margery and Jocky, for at the end of the month Margery told her she was pregnant at last, and Jocky was almost delirious with joy.

'He'll make a good father,' Polly said as he came towards them sitting under the Fraser pine.

'You *will not* sit under this tree any more,' he told them. 'My lady, I'm sorry, but I cannot allow it. It is definitely falling to one side now. Look, it's leaning against its neighbour! It's not safe for you, it's certainly not safe for Miss Charlotte, and not for Margery either in her condition. There is a fine weeping yew over there. You can sit under its branches instead. Come with me!'

Every Wednesday now he drove them into Edinburgh for the day, when Polly took Charlotte to see her 'Aunt Maggie', to Lady Braxfield's delight. Margery clung to her mother, Mistress Nell, and Jocky went off with his friends into the taverns of the town.

They were passing the Tolbooth one Wednesday in September when Margery leaned forward in the carriage, stopped to allow a flock of geese waddle past, and pointed. 'Look, Polly! There's Ann Grant and her children. She'll be taking them to see their father before he dies.'

'Before he dies ...' Before Deacon Brodie was dead ... The enormity of it made Polly clutch Charlotte closer to her breast. 'What's wrong, Margery?' she asked when her friend suddenly writhed as if in pain. 'What's wrong?'

'It's nothing, dear.' Margery smiled, her round blue eyes shadowed in her white face. 'It's just the downward dragging.'

'What downward dragging?'

'I don't know. I suppose it's all part and parcel of it. Didn't you have it?'

'Not until the birth.' Polly frowned as Jocky moved the carriage on.

'Oh, never mind,' said Margery, recovering swiftly. 'The pain's gone now. What's that compared with what poor Ann Grant is suffering?'

Ann Grant came to see the Deacon for the last time along with Cecil, his most dearly beloved child. It was heartrending, the screams of their daughter ringing out long after they said the last goodbye. William Brodie sobbed unashamedly while William Smith rattled in his chains at the other side of the cell and prayed incessantly.

The next visitors came together, all three of them, and the Deacon welcomed them as if into his own sitting-room.

'Michael Henderson, my own dear Michael!' He clung to his hand and turned a little aside. 'You still have the silver tube?'

'I have, Will. This is Dr Degravers who has agreed to do the job, for a hundred guineas.'

'You have the money?'

'Your own, Will, dinna worry, from the cockfights.'

'Oh, God, the cockfights! They seem so far away, now,' he said, turning to his second visitor. 'How are you, Jerry?' He shook Deacon Jeremiah Donaldson's hand. 'Have you got permission?'

'I've seen to it, Will. We were not in the Hell-Fire Club

together all those years for nothing, ye ken. The toon cooncil have agreed that you should be cut doon after two minutes. I persuaded them that it would never do for a Deacon to be seen swinging any longer than that.'

'Good man! Good man! So now, Dr Degravers, it all depends on you.' William Brodie fixed his hypnotic gaze on the purple-faced doctor standing there reeking of drink. 'When I climb up on to the gallows I will bend down, pretending to be coughing. You will thrust the tube down my throat. My coat is all wired up to the hook in the collar so that when hung above the knot my neck will not snap. Do you understand, man?'

The doctor blinked and nodded, but at this the most fraught moment in his life Deacon Brodie was taking no chances. He did not like the look of Dr Degravers. He did not trust him. But only a failure like this one would ever have agreed to try such a job, and then only for the money to drink.

He repeated the instructions several times before he went on. 'For two minutes I will be dead. Then I will be cut down and rattled smartly over the cobbles into Michael's stable. Now, do you understand what you must do next?'

'Oh, yes.' Dr Degraver's eyes swivelled away. 'I must slit your veins to let out the dead blood. Oh yes, sir, I understand.'

William Brodie prayed to God that he did. Next morning, sharp at seven, the barber came to cut his nails and dress his hair. At eight the warders came with porridge, ham and eggs, morning baps and plenty of coffee. Poor Smith vomited at the sight of it, and prayed harder than ever. William Brodie enjoyed his breakfast and welcomed the priest who could do nothing to squash his high spirits.

'George Smith has made his peace with his Maker, Deacon Brodie.' The priest gazed earnestly into his face. 'Are you ready now to make yours?'

'What is between my Maker and me is a very private matter!' William Brodie laughed softly. 'Go and lead Smith out to the gallows. It will cause me no discomfort, I assure you, to watch from here.'

'May God have mercy upon your soul,' the priest droned while the warders carried out Smith, a pathetic figure, behind him.

At one minute past nine all George Smith's worldly troubles were over. He swung, his head snapped over to one side, with his tongue hanging out like a slug.

The warders did not need to support Deacon Brodie to his own gallows at ten o'clock. He walked up the steps himself, humming a tune from *The Beggar's Opera*, as jaunty as ever.

Michael Henderson drove the cart as fast as he could down to the Grassmarket. His two burly sons lifted the body on to a makeshift table covered in white sheets and Dr Degravers began his surgery with trembling hands.

Half an hour later the two young Hendersons laid Deacon Brodie's body in the wagon, Michael Henderson whipped up the horses and drove to Leith at breakneck speed, and there, covered with a reddening sheet, they carried him to the hiding place Michael had sought so assiduously.

'We needn't have worried, Da,' one of his sons said. 'This back alley is deserted.'

'Except by the rats,' said the other.

'Rats don't talk,' Michael said shortly, leading the way.

The two young Hendersons, used as they had been all their lives to the filth, the stench and the degradation of the Grassmarket, were quite unprepared for the room they entered now. It was narrow, no more than six feet wide, and it could only have been ten feet long at the most.

There was no window in it and the ceiling was low and black and cracked. The walls were black too, and running with damp as they saw by the light of the candle burning over the meagre fireplace, although it was still only a little after one o'clock. The furniture consisted of two cot beds and a low shelf beside the door, used presumably as a table.

A figure crouched on one of the beds, his face livid with fear, his eyes rolling in his black face, and when he stood up at their entrance his head came up to within inches of the ceiling.

'For God's sake, Da, he's escaped one coffin only to land in another!' one of the sons exclaimed.

'He'll suffocate in here,' the other agreed.

'There's a vent.' Michael pointed to a slit in the wall. 'They can see out if they put an eye up to it, but nobody can see in. Are ye ready, Choco? Well, get going, man!'

Choco folded down the sheet, now very red, and began to massage William Brodie carefully. This little man had befriended him when months ago Caramelle had deserted him, and over the weeks and months trained him for this job if such a sorry day as this ever dawned. Then, all going well, they would both escape, perhaps to the hot country they both dreamed of. As he set to work with his large capable hands on the small lifeless body Choco was very anxious. This man who was hanged this morning might be his only hope of salvation now, for there had been neither sight nor sound of Caramelle for months.

The Henderson boys struggled back in with a heavy trunk between them and set it down under the shelf.

'It'll make a grand seat in the meantime,' Michael said as he left. 'Now hang on, Will. Dinna give up on me now.'

Will? Who was Will? William Brodie could not remember. All he knew was the agonizing pain stretching from his heart out over his chest. He fainted away. It seemed hours later, at the very gates of Hell, that young voices pierced his ears to cause him even more pain and irritation, enough to bring him back again.

Now his arms were in excruciating agony, and still the children screamed on, playing some game. He thought it was a skipping game. He could hear the beat of the rope somewhere near the vent.

Fading away and coming back, fading away and coming back, every time he was conscious of the beat, beat, beat of the skipping rope – or perhaps it was his heart reaching out, pumping blood back again? Whatever it was, he was almost dead with the pain in his legs.

The children were singing a song over and over again monotonously as they skipped. He made out the first line.

'I'm a braw wee man, a bonnie wee man,' and the old, old song returned him swimmingly ... to somewhere.

'I'm a braw wee man.' Oh, yes!

'A bonnie wee man.' He was!

The children sang it over and over again untiringly, and he remembered that he was going to France when his ship came in.

'Sweet as sugar candy!' a little girl screeched beside the vent, almost in his ear.

He felt the blood rushing to his head. His mouth was smiling again, and to his infinite delight there was a stirring in his stick of sugar candy. Now he knew he would live and love again. But who was he?

'Macaroni is my name –' the children's voices were receding and Choco worked away tirelessly until enough feeling and sufficient understanding came back to William Brodie to realize that he was in a strange room and it was somewhere near the sea. He could hear the boom of it and the seagulls calling. He could even smell the salt in the damp air coming in. The ceiling might be black, but he saw nothing but blue skies above with a few clouds scurrying from left to right in the following wind. He had cheated them all, whoever they were. He was set fair for France.

He smiled. He and Choco would make the perfect team. He had the brains to carry out any job in any country they chose to go to now, and Choco had the brawn to protect him. They could not fail. But he had to have a proper name. What was it?

'Macaroni is my name –' faint screams from the children reminded him.

Of course it was. A macaroni had style. His eyes fell on his trunk. There was plenty of style in there for a macaroni, and plenty of gold for more.

'Macaroni Dandy!' The last sounds faded away.

That was it! That was just right! That was his name! Macaroni Dandy.

When he saw that Brodie had fallen into a peaceful sleep Choco stole out and set off at a run for Edinburgh. Prowling up and down the length of the Royal Mile, he pushed aside the youths who knew him now. It wasn't them he was looking for tonight. He just had to find Cara. She must be in one of the taverns soliciting business while at the same time trying to trace Madame Suzanne. He was sure she hadn't succeeded yet, or else she would have sent for him.

As he was passing Johnny Dowie's a very drunk man stumbled out, followed by a figure he recognized at once with a great leap of his heart.

'Go away, Choco,' his sister hissed. 'Leave me alone. I am nearly there.'

'You mean – you have found Madame Suzanne?' he whispered back.

'Her house, at least. Candacraig.'

'But when will I see you?'

'You'll have to *wait*!' she threw over her shoulder angrily, and hurried away with the man.

Back in the Grassmarket Michael Henderson's sons killed all the fighting-cocks, as they had persuaded their father they must do long ago.

'You've got to put something in the coffin, Da,' they told him. 'Let it be those accursed birds. You cannot be discovered with anything belonging to William Brodie here on these premises now.'

They piled in the dead feathered bodies at top speed and screwed down the coffin, then soberly took it to the graveyard where the gravediggers were getting very impatient. There were to be no prayers said over the Deacon's body, and the Henderson men simply laid down the coffin reverently and drove their wagon away again.

The two gravediggers leaned on their spades. 'Noo then, ye saw that wi' yer own eyes, Frankie,' the older one said as they watched the wagon rolling away. 'Michael Henderson! What did I tell ye? He was aye as thick as shit wi' the Deacon!'

'So ye've been dinning in my lug all morning,' the younger man sighed. Jimmie Wright was an old bletherskite, regaling him non-stop since half past seven this morning with stories about the cockfights, the gambling dens and Christ alone knew what else. 'Let's get on wi' it, then.'

They had dug the grave already. Now they lifted the coffin between them to lower it in. 'It's terrible light, Frankie,' Jimmie Wright said.

'Och, he was only a wee man, remember.'

'Ay, he was wee! He was a cunning wee bastard as well! Cunning enough not to be in here at all. D'ye think we should open it up and make sure?'

'What?' Frankie staggered back an inch or two in absolute horror. 'God Almighty,' he implored his Maker, 'is it no' bad enough to be spending our lives planting dead bodies without

281

having to look at them next?' He started shovelling in the earth as fast as he could. 'This job's turning ye morbid in yer old age, Jimmie Wright, that's what it is. Look at a dead body! And us just awa' for the meridian? For fuck's *sake*, man, behave yersel'!'

22

MARGERY WAS NOT getting any better. Every day her pains grew worse and her afternoon meetings in the gardens with Polly and Charlotte were forgotten, things of the past.

Donald MacDonald sent his wife Jessie over to Candacraig for a few hours a day in this emergency to cook for Polly, and the kind-hearted woman always left some delicacy for her to take down to Margery. Two or three times a day Polly went down to the cottage with a heavy heart, for soon Margery gave up all pretence of eating. Her face seemed to shrink away from her cheekbones and Polly was becoming very alarmed.

'I want you to take the coach, Jocky,' she said. 'Go first to Newhaven and find Mistress Beattie Barbour. Tell her about Margery, beg her to come here and if possible to bring a doctor with her. She is bound to know one.'

'Yes.' He sighed with relief. 'Thank God. This cannot go on.'

'On the way back through the town fetch Mistress Nell. Tell her she can stay here as long as she likes. Margery needs her mother now.'

It was a long sad day after he left, for now Margery was in continual agony. At intervals and in gasps she tried to tell Polly how it felt. 'Thank God Jocky has gone so that I can speak to you,' she said. 'I never wanted to speak about it to him. He didn't want to listen anyway. He is so impatient, and so disappointed.' She was lying on her side, knotting herself up into a tight ball every time a fresh pain struck. 'There's

283

something not right with my baby, Polly,' she wept. 'Our little son.'

'Ho,' Polly tried to coax a smile, 'how do you know it will be a boy?'

'It's Jocky Robertson's, isn't it? Of course it's a boy! It couldn't be anything else.'

Margery was as certain about it as Polly was uncertain that there was a child coming at all. It was not as a pregnancy should be, or any that she had heard of. It could be some other trouble, but Doctor Finlay Smith – who arrived late that night in his own coach with Beattie Barbour and Mistress Nell in Jocky's – pronounced it most certainly was a pregnancy, after a long examination of Margery in the bedroom.

His face was very grave when he explained it to them in the living-room of the cottage. 'The foetus is ten weeks developed, as far as I can judge,' he said, 'but unfortunately it is not developing in the womb. It has lodged itself in one of her tubes instead, swelling all the time. This is the reason for her severe pain, of course.'

'Will the baby be all right there?' Jocky asked. 'Will he grow?'

Dr Smith hesitated for a long time, clearly hating the answer he must give. 'Yes, it will grow,' he said, 'but I am afraid it will not be all right. And neither,' he looked sadly at Jocky, 'will your wife.'

Mistress Nell began to cry quietly in her chair.

'Can nothing be done?' Polly cried. 'Can you not remove it for her?'

'Perhaps I could, if it had been in the womb,' he said. 'But where it is we should have to cut into her to remove it. If only we were that far advanced!'

'No,' Mistress Nell cried again, 'not the knife! I will not have it,' while at the same time Jocky broke down and sobbed. 'Nobody ever survives the knife!'

'Unfortunately it may be years before we know enough about surgery to perform such an operation,' he told them. 'We are only beginning to learn, in the new Royal College of Surgeons. In the meantime, I will leave you some laudanum.' He looked at Beattie Barbour significantly. 'You understand, Mistress Barbour?'

Polly understood. Margery was going to die. The doctor was going, because there was nothing more than that he could do for her.

'Indeed, I do, although I have come across it only once before. Thank you for sparing the time, sir.' Beattie Barbour smiled her bright nurse's smile as he left. Then she took charge. 'We will have to make up a rota,' she said. 'She will require two of us with her constantly, and I will need plenty of pads and clean linen.'

Margery endured almost another three days of mortal agony before she died. The deathly hush afterwards, after her terrible screams, was the most shocking of all. It was as if the very air was screaming and quivering still, screaming on and on. Beattie Barbour roused them gently. 'I think you should bring Mr Buchanan here now,' she urged Jocky. 'There are all the arrangements to be made.'

Three days later Polly wept in the window-seat as the little procession moved slowly away from the cottage and down the drive, the black horses with their nodding black plumes pulling the hearse, the Buchanans and Jocky with their heads bowed in the coach behind. She was glad that ladies did not go to the graveside to see their loved ones lowered into the ground. She would rather remember Margery as she had been, pretty, full of life and laughter, her best friend, living on for ever in her heart, and in Candacraig.

Jocky Robertson was never likely to come back from Edinburgh. Day after day Polly expected to see him, but after a week there was still no sign of life in the cottage.

'Gi'e him time,' Lord Braxfield advised on one of his visits. Nowadays he was always accompanied by his wife, for in Lady Braxfield's opinion Charlotte was almost her own child since she had brought her into the world. 'Sometimes men do queer things in a case o' that kind. Nae doot he'll be lying drunk somewhere in the toon.'

'Drunk?'

'Ay, drunk, Polly. It's called drowning yer sorrows, poor laddie.'

Ten days after the funeral Jocky came back to Candacraig and straight to see Polly, very contrite. 'I'm sorry, my lady.' He hung his head and offered no other explanation. In spite of that she was quite relieved to see him.

The mournful autumn changed imperceptibly when its mists turned to frosts and the winter nights of late October came in dark and cold with a high yellow moon over Candacraig. It lit up the Fraser pine which was leaning alarmingly sideways now. Polly sat in the window-seat as she loved to do every night no matter what the season, and could no longer deny it herself.

Perhaps Jocky was right and it should be cut down. Jocky ... it was the drunken list of the tree that made her think of him. What had he been doing all that time in Edinburgh? He could not have been drinking all day and all night. A tiny suspicion entered her mind: another woman? But he could not have recovered so soon after his bereavement – and then, uneasily, she recalled one of her conversations with Margery.

'I cannot understand why I have not been expecting a baby long before this, Polly.' She blushed. 'He wants me every night. Sometimes he comes home during the days as well ... He is very demanding. I hope you will not mind me speaking to you like this, especially after Fraser, but sometimes I am worried.'

'Why should you be worried, dear? He is your husband.'

'You do not know him. Often he takes one of the horses and gallops off into the town at nights. He always comes back in a bad temper.'

'What are you trying to tell me, Margery?'

'I think he goes with other women. One is not enough for him.'

'No! I cannot believe that. He will be with his friends, that's all, in one of the taverns. You know he has never been so happy as he is now, since he met up with them again.'

'That's true, but I don't know these friends. I don't know what company he keeps in Edinburgh.' Margery was not to be comforted.

Polly sighed and got up from the window-seat with one last glance outside. Jocky Robertson was there, right under her window, looking up. She drew her curtains hastily and then stood on her bedroom floor and wondered why she had done it. She still had all her clothes on, she argued with herself. It wasn't that. But somehow, it was wrong.

Then every night he kept coming and just standing there, just looking up, until her nerves were jangling. What was he doing it for? Why, she asked herself? She made up her mind that she would ask him, as soon as Charlotte's cough got better, and watched over her baby all night instead. Jocky Robertson was in the kitchen the following morning when she went to fetch some warmed-up milk. 'The baby, is she ill?' he asked, eyeing her tired face, genuinely concerned.

'She has a cough,' Polly told him, all thoughts of tackling him about his visits under her window gone with her worry.

'I'll get you something.' He went off and came back with a jar. 'It's goosegrease mixed up with something else,' he said. 'It has a horrible smell, but my mother always made me take it. It cured all our coughs.'

'What do you do with it?'

'Rub it on her back and her chest, and then the cough will loosen up. I'll come back and see how she is tonight.'

The goosegrease worked, and that night he was back in the kitchen again when she went down with Charlotte in her arms for more milk. 'Is she any better?' he asked anxiously, and at the sight of him Charlotte stopped grizzling and smiled. 'Ah! Give her to me, the little darling! Have you been missing your Jocky, then?' He took the baby in his arms and his fingers brushed Polly's accidentally for a second – at least she thought it was, until later when she was back up in her room and she realized it had not been accidental at all.

He had touched her at last, and when he did a flame of desire shot through her whole body. Now she knew that right from the start in Brodie's Close she had been unwillingly attracted to him. Now she knew that he knew it, too. Deliberately, she stopped sitting in the window-seat at nights. It was too dangerous, and besides she didn't even like Jocky Robertson. She told herself she would far rather be with Charlotte, who by this time had not a shadow of a wheeze and had discovered a new game to play with her mother.

Whenever Polly laid her down on the floor she heaved and struggled until she rolled herself over on to her stomach, and then began to creep along the mat.

'She's away to crawl.' Mistress Jessie laughed. 'She won't take long to learn.'

287

Before November was one day old the snow began to fall. Polly opened the window and allowed the fat white flakes to fall on Charlotte's little outstretched hand, and the child screeched and laughed in the excitement of it. It was a great adventure for Charlotte. The snow would keep Jocky Robertson inside his own house at nights, too. Polly willed him to stay at home, and perversely wanted him back under her window again. But he didn't come. Her own small excitement, the racing of her blood, was over. She was a fool.

The following night, sighing and accepting her lot of widowhood, she undressed soberly and put on her nightgown. Almost casually she went over to the window to look out before she drew her curtains. He was there again, his powerful figure outlined against the snow, his face pleading in the moonlight, and at the sight of him she caught her breath in the sudden racing of her heart.

He made a gesture towards the kitchen door. In spite of herself Polly raced downstairs and unlocked it. Then she was in his arms, their first kiss desperate in their need for each other.

The desperation mounted with every kiss, with every touch, until there was a trail of clothes marking their slow progress upstairs into her bed, and into ecstasy together.

'It was always you I wanted,' he panted once during the night of passion. 'You know that, Polly. You always knew. I saw it in your eyes. I saw that you wanted me just as much. And oh, Christ! I'm greedy! I want you again.'

Even that first night the arrogance of his words hurt her. Margery was forgotten. Fraser was forgotten. Jocky Robertson was the master now, and her weak flesh could not stop him. Throughout the day he swaggered around Candacraig. Throughout the night he mastered her, and although she despised herself for what was happening, she was powerless. Besides, she told herself weakly, he was so good with Charlotte ... But when he disappeared the following Friday night she fretted and worried while her whole body yearned for him.

Jocky was in Johnny Dowie's, where he had been going ever since Margery's death. At first it was for drink to blot out the memory, and for the dice to cheer him up when he won, as he often did. Unlucky in love he might be, but Lady Luck stayed with him at the tables. Now there was a different reason altogether, and when she came in dressed as usual in her long black cloak the whole tavern fell silent in a wildly expectant hush.

Along with all the other men Jocky prayed as he pocketed his winnings that she would tip back her hood. She had only done that once before, and it had become the talk of the town. Now she did it again, and while the men sat glued to their seats, just staring, the blood rushed to Jocky's head. He went over and sat beside her. 'Pardon me for speaking to you, miss. We can see that you do not belong here. None of us would like you to feel strange. Can I buy you a drink?'

'Brandy.' She nodded unsmilingly.

Jocky raised his eyebrows, but went to fetch it. 'You are visiting friends?' he tried to press on with the conversation.

'No.'

'What am I to call you, miss? You have a name?'

'No doubt Edinburgh will find a name for me before long.' She smiled bitterly, and just for a second there was a flash of very white teeth.

'I am afraid it will, if you keep coming into the tavern, miss. Men will think – if you will excuse me – that you are …'

'For sale?' She threw back her head and laughed. Her skin glowed like gold, and her black eyes glittered. 'Then they would be right. I *am* for sale. At a price.'

'You mean that you are looking for work?'

'That's a new way of putting it, Mr – ?'

'Jocky Robertson.'

'And who are you, Jocky Robertson? What do you do? Where do you live? It cannot be in the town, for you are not here every night.'

Ah, Jocky thought. So she had noticed him before. 'You are quite right. I am a jack of all trades now, although I used to be a carpenter, and I live in a cottage on a large estate south of the town, called Candacraig. My wife worked for Mistress Polly – or should I say *Lady Graham*, as she is now.'

For an endless minute Caramelle sat absolutely stock-still, seeming hardly to breathe. Could it be that she had found Polly and Madame Suzanne at last? She spoke again, turning her large liquid eyes full on him. 'I meant what I said. I need look no further for work, but my price is high.'

'How high? A guinea, perhaps? I can pay that.'

'For you, ten guineas.'

'Jesus Christ!'

'That's what you won tonight, is it not? Pass them under the table.'

'Where?' Jocky asked in a fever. 'Where can we go?'

'I have a room. There is plenty of time. I will drink another glass of brandy first, Jocky Robertson. I want you to tell me more about your estate before we go.'

On Monday morning Jocky turned up again in Candacraig, contrite, sorry, bitterly ashamed, even more than before. Only it was not quite the same this time, for Polly. Absence had made her heart grow fonder, for one thing. For another, Jocky stunned her with what he had to say. 'I need money, Polly,' he told her. 'I have been very foolish in the gambling dens.'

'How much?' she asked.

'A hundred pounds.'

'*A hundred pounds* ...?' Her breath was taken away.

'Have you got it?'

'Of course I haven't got it.'

'I've got to get it,' he said desperately, 'or else they'll come out here, the men I owe it to. They are violent.'

The next morning she dressed herself and then Charlotte and summoned him into the house. 'Get the coach ready,' she told him. 'Take me into the town.'

'But the snow, Polly ...'

'You want the money, don't you?' she asked bitterly. 'And when other people are likely to overhear, my name is Lady Graham. I would rather not risk Charlotte's life with some evil thugs threatening this house. Did you never think of that when you were getting yourself into all this trouble?'

'A hundred pounds, Polly?' Lord Braxfield asked, surprised. 'Ye dinna usually spend so much.'

'Charlotte is growing at such a rate that she needs new

clothes. Besides, is not the money only an advance of what is mine, anyway?'

'Of course it is, dearie,' her grandfather said hastily. 'I'll let you have two hundred, shall I? Only I must keep a check, ye ken.'

'Yes,' Polly said unhappily. 'Let me have two hundred, Robbie. I may need more yet.'

Outside she got into the coach again and went to Covenant Close. 'I shall stay here an hour with Lady Braxfield,' she told Jocky. 'Here is the hundred pounds. See that you pay off those men before you come back for us.'

'It is done?' she asked him when he returned.

'It is done, my lady,' he answered sullenly, like a small boy who had been caught out doing some mischief.

She sighed her relief. 'Polly.' She smiled.

'I can come tonight, then?'

'Perhaps.' But they both knew she would welcome him back.

Their reconciliation was short-lived. Before long Jocky was missing again. Before long he was asking for more money, and more and more until the second hundred pounds were gone too. Besides that, his visits became more and more infrequent, and Polly realized sadly that she had only been buying what had passed for love.

Love? She groaned. It had never been love. It was only lust, and she had been as guilty as he. Only with Fraser had she ever known true love, and after this terrible incident in her life she missed him more than ever. She was weighed down with guilt and remorse, and on her dressing-table the evil Poison bottle seemed to gloat.

The weather did nothing to help her or anyone else. The snow lying dourly on the ground froze hard. It was no longer a virgin white, but grey and yellow with here and there twigs of last summer's flowers poking through blackly to give it all a dirty, unkempt air.

There was something else to worry her more than any of that. The house itself was not happy any more. Gone was its music, its calm happy atmosphere. Instead doors banged in some unexplained draught, windows cracked, and the whole house creaked and groaned interminably. Polly watched and listened.

The house was objecting to something, but what it was she didn't know.

Then food began to disappear. She was sure Mistress Jessie had left almost a whole chicken under the gauze in the pantry when she went down hungry one night. It was gone, and there was only enough milk to feed Charlotte in the morning. She noticed bread was disappearing at an alarming rate, and there was always less cheese than she remembered in the dish. One day Mistress Jessie asked her what had happened to all the eggs. She had brought a dozen only the day before.

'It can't be mice,' Polly said. 'There's no sign of them, and they can't carry away a dozen eggs in the middle of the night.'

'Well, there are collops waiting to be heated through in a pan and a butterscotch tart, my lady. I'll get Donald to bring more milk and more eggs.'

'Yes,' Polly smiled. This time she was determined to keep an eye on the pantry, for it seemed to her that it must be a human hand that was taking the food away. But whose? Not Jocky Robertson's, surely? In any case, how would he get into this locked house? She remembered the first time she had ever come here, with a stolen key. Did he have one too? After all, he had worked in the den of stolen keys, in Deacon Brodie's workshop.

Polly was not afraid, not in Candacraig, and she took no lantern or candle with her that night when, after she put Charlotte down, she went on another voyage around the house. She had already made one in the afternoon, and apart from open doors which she closed, there seemed nothing amiss. She began in the pantry. There was nothing missing yet; the collops were still there, and the butterscotch tart.

Room by room she went round in the dim light of the moon which shone fitfully beneath racing clouds. The doors she had closed this afternoon were open again, and frowning she went right into the rooms and looked around. But nothing was wrong. The house seemed to be lying in wait for something, but she could find nothing.

Then when she approached the door leading to the west wing, the wing that was still disused, she hesitated. Someone or something was willing her on, but her hand lay on the handle for a long time before she turned it.

292

Leaves rustled ahead of her along the dark corridor. A window flapped, and made her jump. The leaves must have blown in sometime during the autumn, she thought, for no one had been here to sweep them up.

Just then the capricious moon chose to come out from behind a cloud and she saw that there were no leaves at all blowing along the corridor. What she had heard was the rustling of long black skirts, and she was face to face with the ghost of the Royal Mile.

23

THE WHOLE HOUSE of Candacraig behind Polly seemed to join forces with her, to close in around her and protect her as she stood there paralysed with fear; its creaks and growls were now menacing.

The moon disappeared briefly, and when it flickered out again for a faint moment she saw that the corridor was empty and the ghost had gone.

Somehow she got back to her room and straight into the little room next to it to see Charlotte, but the baby was sleeping soundly and undisturbed. All that night she shook and trembled, and knew now what the old house had been objecting to so bitterly that it had almost spoken to her.

Even Jocky Robertson's company would have been better than this. She could have told him about the ghost. But he was away again, he had not been seen for days, and she was alone with only the detested Poison to share her room. Every time she glanced across at the perfume bottle its glassy smile seemed more evil than ever.

'I always thought the door to the west wing was locked, Donald,' she said wearily the following morning.

'So it is, my lady.'

'It was unlocked all day yesterday, and all last night. There was no key in the lock.'

'I'll go and see. I've been thinking that one or two windows along there will have to be looked at, anyway.'

Later he came back to report. 'You were quite right, my lady. The door was unlocked and the key gone. How that has happened I do not know, but I have done some temporary repairs in the meantime. The windows are now boarded up, and I have put a new lock on that door. Here is the key for it.'

With that done she felt happier, and all day she devoted herself to Charlotte indoors, playing with her to take the child's mind off not being able to go for her usual walk in the fresh air. Charlotte was a child of the outdoors. It was her favourite place to be, but Polly feared for her in the intense cold, the forerunner of more snow to come.

In the evening, when she laid the child down to sleep and the darkness came down again, the moon came out to sail across clear skies. Then Polly herself was seized with a great longing to be right outside in the crisp cold air, and making sure that Charlotte was sleeping peacefully in her crib, she put on her cloak and slipped out of the back door for a few minutes.

The air was like chilled wine when she breathed it in, in great gulps. It stung her face and sparkled her eyes with the tears of frost. She could not stay out here for long, and was turning to go back when she saw a light flare for a second inside the cottage. Someone was in there.

Silently she ran down over the snow and reached the cottage wall, flattening herself beside the window when she heard voices inside.

'What is the use of this? There's no food, the place is freezing because you will not light a fire, and you never have any money.'

'I've given you all my money! Christ, I've given you two hundred pounds in the last few weeks! What have you done with it?'

'That's none of your business. You knew I was expensive when you brought me here. If you want me, you must pay. There is nothing for nothing in this world.'

'Pay, for God's sake? I've done nothing but pay, pay, pay ever since I met you!'

'You told me you could get your hands on plenty of money. That's how you persuaded me to come here. But what do I find? Nothing! No money and no food, unless I steal it – *and* she nearly caught me at it last night.'

'She will never catch you, or me. She suspects nothing. She has no idea that I have made a key for every door in the house. They never found the Deacon's japan-black tin with the putty in it.'

'You are wasting your time searching that house! She keeps no money in it. I've told you so a thousand times. I've also told you two ways you could get it for yourself, through her. You could marry her, for one thing.'

'I don't want to marry her now. I love you.'

'You've played your cards no better with her than you've done in the card games in Johnnie Dowie's tavern! Love, what is that? You do not have to love her to marry her. But there is always the other way.'

'No! I cannot do it!'

'Jesus, you're a lily-livered fool! I will not stay with a fool any longer. This is no way to live! I was better off in the town, and tomorrow I'm going back on the Fly.'

'No, please … please don't leave me! I can't live without you, now … All right, then, I'll have one last try! One last try at Johnnie Dowie's. If that doesn't work we'll do it your way.'

'One last try at Johnnie Dowie's won't work. My way is the only way, believe me, and in the end I'll go ahead and do it myself if I have to. I mean it, make no mistake.'

'Give me one last chance. One more game. I'll get the money this time, I swear it.'

'Do you promise?'

'I promise. I love you. Oh, I want you! How could there be another woman after you?'

Polly stole away, sickened. It was little wonder that Jocky Robertson had not come to her bed for a fortnight. He had another woman hidden away in his cottage all that time. A woman who could come and go at will in her house. A woman determined to steal more than just food from Candacraig. A woman unscrupulous enough to do anything for money. A woman who had a murderous plan of some sort, one that Jocky clearly wanted no part of.

There was never a ghost; Fraser told her long ago there were no such things as ghosts. She should have listened to him then, and she should have listened to a lot more he had said besides.

Then she would have understood why he had given his life for something he believed in so passionately.

Of course the ghost was the woman in black, the same faceless woman who had haunted her in the theatre, in Fortune's and in the Royal Mile. But who was she, and why had she singled her out in some sort of twisted revenge? Polly fell asleep wondering, and next morning she was not surprised that the minced collops had gone and half the butterscotch tart as well. A lock and key were no protection against that woman and Jocky Robertson in collusion, she saw that now.

There was no doubt about it, he would have to be dismissed. But this was only Tuesday. It would be Thursday before the Braxfields were back, and then only if their coach could travel the roads.

Fraser Graham travelled north from London on the Edinburgh Fly as far as his own stables just south of Edinburgh. There he descended as he had done so often before in more carefree times to find everyone overcome to see him. 'We thought you were dead, sir,' his head groom said shakily. 'Everyone thought so.'

'Almost, but not quite, George. I'm surprised after all this time to find the stables intact. One of my great dreads was that the horses would have been sold – scattered all over the place – after all the hard work it took you and me to select them.'

'Oh no, sir! I dreaded it too, but thank God Lord Braxfield would not allow it.'

'So old Braxie's been looking after things!'

'He's a changed man, sir. He's mellowing in his old age.'

'Well, George, I'm in a tearing hurry. I'll be back to see you in a day or two. In the meantime give me Courage. I need a good horse with a heart like his tonight.'

Twenty minutes later he overtook the Fly with a wave of his hand to the drivers and galloped on into the Royal Mile, over the North Bridge and straight to Queen Street. 'Yes, it's me, Alistair!' He clapped his white-faced footman on the back. 'A bath and a change of clothes! No, I will not require anything to eat. I have to go out again as fast as I can.'

His entire staff were assembled in the hall when he came down again, refreshed. 'Oh, Sir Fraser, sir,' he heard his housekeeper crying. 'We're that pleased to see ye! But ye're no' going oot again on a night like this?'

'I won't be long,' he promised.

'Ye said that the last time, sir,' Alistair said severely. 'Not without yer greatcoat, then.' He held it up and Fraser struggled into it. 'There'll be more snow tonight, and that before long.'

'I'll be back,' he promised, and leapt onto Courage again in the searing, desperate cold. Alistair had been quite right. It was now sharply colder, and the east wind never absent from Edinburgh for long was blowing straight from Siberia. Over the bridge again and back down the Royal Mile as far as the High Street, he got no answer at Covenant Close. He tied his horse to the bar outside it and for a while marched up and down, clapping his arms about him smartly as the temperature lowered further and further. He *had* to see Lord Braxfield tonight! Then a coach came down the High Street, stopped, and Lord and Lady Braxfield shivered and shuddered out of it. 'Don't collapse,' he implored them. 'It's me, Fraser Graham, back from the dead.'

Between the cold and the shock the Braxfields were speechless, ushering him into their house. After a brandy all round and a poking-up of the fire in Lord Braxfield's study they all three thawed out a little, and Lady Braxfield left the room.

'Maggie hauled me oot to this bloody awful soiree o' hers,' the judge told him. Fraser smiled. His language hadn't changed, anyway, no matter what George said. 'And to add insult to injury the cold collation was non-existent! She's awa' noo to see what she can rake up to eat. Ye'll ha'e a bite?'

'I would be delighted, sir, but I do not have the time. Just tell me – where is Polly Buchanan? Is she still in Edinburgh? Oh, God, I have to find her!'

'Weel, ye've come to the right place, laddie,' Lord Braxfield said as the first hard-driving scatter of snow and hailstones battered on the windows. He poured out another glass of brandy for them both. 'Here, drink this, ye'll need it. To begin with, she was never Polly Buchanan. She was never Polly Gray as she thought she was all her life.'

'I found out about Suzanne Gray and her daughter Polly quite by chance two days ago in France, sir.'

299

'Gray wasn't their name, either. That was Lady Susanna's idea. Suzanne was her own child, and she tried to disguise it by calling her Suzanne Gray. And Polly isn't Polly. She's Olivia Graham, and the other heir to the Candacraig estate.' The judge got to his feet and took two bits of paper out of his bureau. 'Put these two together, and see.'

'Where did you get the other half of this will?'

'From Polly hersel'. Her mother had hidden it inside a perfume bottle. She found it after you left, and before she had the baby.'

'The baby?' Fraser felt the room beginning to slip sideways.

'Take a sip o' that brandy, lad! Ye may as well get all the shocks in one go. Ay, the baby. A wee lassie. Her name is Charlotte Fraser Graham. Noo then, Fraser, what does that tell ye? Na, na, dinna greet! Are ye a' right? Yes, Polly was the missing heir all along, only she never even knew it hersel'.'

'Have any o' ye looked ootside?' Lady Braxfield asked them half an hour later. 'It's thick! It's smooring! Fraser, ye canna go oot o' here tonight. *No*! Ye're just no' going, even if he *has* told ye aboot the baby, and I can see he has! That wee bairn's father hasna come back from the dead by some miracle just to be lost in a snowdrift. We canna allow it, so come down to the kitchen. It's warm and there's a fine dish o' stew waiting.'

'Ye'd better do what she says.' Lord Braxfield smiled. 'Besides, we still ha'e a lot to talk aboot.'

At midnight, with the blizzard worsening, they decided to bed down in the study. Lord Braxfield lay back in one easy chair. Lady Braxfield lay in the other. 'And ye'll stretch oot that leg o' yours on the settee,' she insisted. 'We'll take it in turns to watch the weather.'

'I'll take the first turn, then.' Fraser was adamant, and by five o'clock in the morning he had never had the heart to waken either of them. The storm was easing. 'I'm going now, sir.' He touched Lord Braxfield's shoulder. 'Don't worry. I'll go round to your stable and get my horse myself.'

But his horse couldn't make much speed through the deep snow, soft now in a sudden thaw brought by the south wind. As they plunged on Fraser had plenty of time to try to come to terms with all that Lord Braxfield had told him, and at least keeping the road was easy in the bright white light.

So he and Polly had been the joint heirs to Candacraig all along! In spite of all his principles, would he ever have gone to France if he had known that? He doubted it. And once in France would he have raced back at this exact moment if he had not heard the names of Suzanne and Polly Gray? He doubted that, too. But one thing was certain. If he had known that Polly was having their child he would never have left her side.

He tried to dispel an uneasy feeling at the back of his mind. He couldn't be turning superstitious now at his age, and yet as he rode on that windy morning he became more and more aware of danger.

Charlotte Fraser Graham – and he had passed the very gate where she was last night, he cursed as he rode back towards it. With all his heart he longed to see Polly and his little daughter, both of them together, both of them alone and defenceless in this wretched wilderness of snow.

The wind from the south freshened with every mile he rode, tearing great white avalanches off roofs, bending and snapping little trees with too much weight of snow on them, and suddenly Fraser was seized with a nameless fear for the two he loved best in all the world, a fear he couldn't explain and couldn't shake off.

'Maggie, Maggie!' Lord Braxfield woke his wife. 'It's half past five in the morning. Fraser Graham has gone to Candacraig.'

'Then we'll follow. Go and rouse Walter. One poke and the kitchen fire'll be bright again. We'll ha'e a tassie o' tea afore we go.'

For almost four months now Michael Henderson had been ferrying supplies of food, drink and candles to Leith in his wagon, for Choco wouldn't budge outside during the daytime, and William Brodie did not dare. For half of that time Brodie remained so confused that Michael was in despair. Even now, with his condition vastly improved, Michael seriously doubted if the Deacon's mind would ever revert to what passed for normal – for William Brodie, even.

But at the first signs of recovery in his little friend, Michael had undertaken an intense, difficult and very delicate task of

301

diplomacy. First he had to find a skipper, French if possible, who could be relied upon to keep his mouth shut whether in French or in English, for the sum of money he was prepared to invest in the last adventure.

As if that wasn't difficult enough, next he must be assured of a definite date of departure on a reliable vessel to a very busy destination, so busy and cosmopolitan that one small man accompanied by a tall black man would go unnoticed.

And finally there was the horrendous danger of actually transferring Will Brodie and his trunk out of the coffin-room and on to the ship unrecognized, for Leith was only a stone's throw from Edinburgh and there would be a thousand eyes watching day and night. But at last these arrangements were all accomplished, and now on Wednesday he was going to warn Will of them. 'Christ,' he muttered to himself on the way, 'how could Will ever have taken up wi' that black fool?' Why could not Choco's character have matched up with his undeniably beautiful ebony face and his magnificent figure?

For Choco was a coward, and there was no denying it. He was still refusing to go out of the dark room to buy food. The butchers, the bakers, the grocers were shut up long ago and the fish-stalls of Leith trundled away before Choco would venture out on his nightly excursions to the ships lying in the dock to look for young sailors of the same inclination.

Michael arrived at the coffin-room, threw down the few supplies he had brought with him on to the shelf beside the door, and was surprised and delighted to find his friend so much further improved over the last week. It had been a long, hard struggle. He knew that Will would never be the man he was, but this was his best yet. He paid scant attention to Choco, lying as usual on his narrow bed looking agitated.

'Yer ship's coming in at last, Will,' he said. 'Tomorrow morning. She'll be ready to sail on the turn o' the tide at eight o'clock in the evening for France. Ye'll be ready to go?'

William Brodie doubled up as if in some dreadful agony, but it turned out to be an excess of ecstasy instead. 'Oh, Jesus Christ!' he gasped. 'Oh, Michael! It's really coming tomorrow?'

Michael Henderson grasped the Deacon's hands and tried to calm him down. 'Yes, Will, it's coming, don't worry.'

But his own feelings were very mixed. In one way he was relieved and happy to be engineering the final escape, but in another he was sad beyond belief to be saying goodbye soon to such an unforgettable man, for Michael was convinced that Edinburgh at least could never forget Deacon Brodie. He found that tears were running down his cheeks the same as they were running down Will Brodie's.

'There's only one snag.' Will glanced across at Choco bitterly. 'He's got wind of something out at Candacraig. What it is he will not tell me, the stubborn brute. But you can see for yourself, Michael, he's desperate to get there. He won't leave the country until he does. He'll be no use to me if we don't get this problem resolved before we go.'

Together the two friends glowered at Choco. Michael pondered for a moment before he spoke. 'That only leaves tonight, then. Whatever happens ye canna be seen, especially at this stage of the game. And to think that ye're safely here, Will, only a minute away from the pier! Christ!'

He gave Choco a look that would have sunk any of the ships in the port of Leith, wrinkled his brows and thought again, clearly annoyed at this upset to his carefully laid plans. 'Well, there's an ancient coach at the back o' the stables. It's never been used since my wife died. I'll get the boys and we'll see if we canna get it moving. What time?'

'The very early hours of tomorrow morning, Michael. What about five o'clock?'

Five o'clock in the morning! The very time had an ominous ring to it. Michael Henderson did not like it at all, going all that way in a coach he could not guarantee, as far away as Candacraig with the sky blackening and descending threateningly minute by minute until it seemed to be down right above their heads. No, he didn't like it at all. It was unlucky. It was dangerous. But for Will's sake he tried to sound cheerful and encouraging. 'Five o'clock it shall be,' he promised.

After Fraser got out of the Edinburgh Fly and rode on ahead to Edinburgh, the stagecoach stopped at the gates of Candacraig and an old woman, the widow of a forrester, got out, hirpling and groaning all the long way up the drive, past the big house and on to the MacDonalds' cottage.

'It's me, Mamie!' She battered on the door. 'Open up! I've something to tell ye.'

A good five minutes later Mistress Jessie MacDonald opened the door a fraction. 'What is it, Mamie? D'ye no' ken Christian folk are in their beds at this hour?'

'I ken it's ten o'clock. The Fly was late because of the snow. Let me in, for the love o' God! I'm freezing.'

'Well?' Mistress Jessie asked their visitor. 'What is it, then?'

'Were ye away to make a pot o' tea?' Mamie eyed the kettle singing quietly over the banked-up fire.

'No, I was not.'

'Weel, ye'd better! Ye'll need it, when ye hear what I have to tell ye. And get Donald MacDonald up at the same time. It's important. He'll need to know.'

Donald trailed through irritably. 'What is it now, Mamie? It had *better* be important.'

'It is. I've just come off the Fly, Donald MacDonald, and who d'ye think was on it?'

'Well, here's a cup o' tea anyway, Mamie.' Mistress Jessie yawned, filling the teapot from the ever-ready kettle.

'Ah, that's fine, Jess. Thank you.'

'Come on, then! Who was it?' Donald pushed away the mug his wife had filled for him, his eyes hooded and glazed with sleep.

Mamie delivered her bombshell: 'Sir Fraser Graham! As large as life! He got off at his stables and rode past the Fly not half an hour ago, heading for the toon.'

Mamie got her reward. The MacDonalds sprang awake immediately. Donald grasped the mug he had pushed aside minutes ago, drank the scalding tea and became alert as if by magic.

'Now then, Mamie,' he said, 'what ye're saying could be very serious – if it's only a story.'

'It's the God's truth.'

'Are ye sure it was him?'

'I saw him and he saw me. He waved at me. Of course I'm sure.'

'So he didn't speak to you?'

'He couldn't. There were far too many folk on the Fly by the time I got on it, and he was at the other end. I told ye, he got off at his stables. Why don't ye go down and ask John if ye don't believe me?'

'I'll see ye hame.' Donald got his storm lantern and put on his overcoat, and fifteen minutes later his wife heard his horse galloping past the window and going on down to the stables in the perishing cold.

'Now for it, Jess,' he said when he came back. 'Ye'll have to come with me. I've got a terrible bad feeling.'

'I know. There's an evil feeling about the whole place tonight. All this snow and misery! And Lady Graham's going to get a terrible shock to add to it all.'

Forced to remain indoors with Charlotte, Polly had found Tuesday interminable and now Wednesday was dragging past with no smoke coming from the chimneys of the cottage and no sign of any movement in it.

She was exhausted when she went to bed. These last two days had felt more like two weeks, and now the snow was falling heavily again. Thick flakes of it were scurrying across her window panes when she drew the curtains shut and blew out her candle that Wednesday night. But Candacraig seemed to be more settled now, in spite of a rising wind, with only an odd rumble from the chimneys, a rattle of tiles on the roof or a creak of floorboards when she fell into a light sleep.

It couldn't have lasted long before loud bangings on the back door and voices woke her again, and she sat up on one elbow to listen. The voices belonged to the MacDonalds. If she didn't hurry up and go to them they would waken Charlotte next, and it might be hours before she settled the baby again.

Half an hour later Mistress Jess was applying cold cloths to her forehead while Polly kept repeating the same thing over and over again. 'But why didn't he come here first?'

'Perhaps he didn't know you were here, my lady.'

'But he went right past the gates!' Polly wept. 'Why didn't he come in?'

Of course Fraser couldn't know that she was at Candacraig, but it was the bitter disappointment of it ... He went right past the gates when there was so much mystery and fear inside them. She could not believe the irony of it.

'He's never seen the bairn yet, has he? He's bound to come back.'

'He doesn't even know about Charlotte. He was away before we knew she was coming, long before she was born.'

'He'll soon find out, in Edinburgh.'

'If he goes to see Lord Braxfield. But the snow will stop him. The snow will stop the Braxfields as well.'

'No, it won't, Lady Graham. D'ye not feel it a lot milder already since this last fall? The frost has lost its grip. It'll a' melt away tomorrow, you'll see. You go back to bed now, so that ye're rested for when Sir Fraser comes again.'

'I know you're right, Mistress Jessie.' Polly pulled herself together, but she knew she wouldn't shut her eyes again. 'Besides, you and Donald have had a shock, too. Please go back home now. Charlotte and I will be all right.'

Back in bed she heard the whinnying of a horse outside. For a wild minute she hoped it was Fraser, but that hope soon chilled and perished in the cold light of reason. By the time Fraser had reached Edinburgh he would have been prevented by the storm from turning around and coming back. This rider must have flown before it.

No, the horse in the grounds could only mean that Jocky was back from his gambling game. She prayed to God that he had won a lot of money, that even now he was going down to the cottage with it, that the woman would be satisfied with it, and then perhaps they would go away together – far away, out of her sight for ever.

Minutes later her door burst open and Jocky Robertson stood there swaying, as drunk as a lord, so that he was unable to speak. He flung himself down, soaking wet, on top of the bed beside her. The next minute he was out to the world, breathing stertorously, and she could not move his dead weight.

Terrified, she tried to edge away from him and the stink of his breath. How could she ever have admitted this man into her room, into her bed and into her body? Sobbing, she was forced to lie there while light edges crept around the curtains. Another day was coming, and perhaps her grandfather would instruct Walter to try to get through, as usual. But what might she have to endure before that? Oh, how could she get out of this whole terrible mess?

24

WITHIN HALF AN hour of Fraser's departure from their house in Covenant Close the Braxfields were dressed and Walter had got the horses and coach ready. They were almost on their way when Lord Braxfield went back for a book, and at the last minute Lady Braxfield remembered something she had bought recently and came back out slipping it into her reticule. Then they really did set off.

'What d'ye think, Walter?' Lord Braxfield pulled down the window and shouted up.

'It's deep, but it's soft,' Walter told him, 'and freshening all the time. It's not underfoot we have to worry about, so we'll get through, dinna worry. The danger will be from above our heads. This wind could blow some trees down wi' all that snow on them.'

Lord Braxfield settled down again and took his book out of his pocket.

'The Bible, Robbie?' his wife asked him.

'Well, Fraser Graham's back, isn't he? And where is he headed for?'

'Yes.' Lady Braxfield said, her face pale. 'All roads lead to Candacraig today.'

'What does that mean?'

'It's just a queer feeling I have, Robbie. I hope Fraser gets there safely and all is well.'

'Of course he'll get there safely. He might even be there by now. Oh, Maggie,' he squeezed her hand, 'they're in love! There's the bairn to prove it. They'll ha'e to be married noo.' He held the Bible out in front of him at arm's length. 'And I'm the verra man to do it. I'll just make oot their lines wi' a little mistake in the date. I'll make it 1787 instead of 1788.'

'Oh, Robbie!' She sighed. 'Ye canna see that wee printing, can ye? Here, take these and put them on yer nose.' She took out the pair of spectacles she had bought only yesterday from her reticule.

'What's this?'

'There's a new Luckenbooth opened up. A wee man was selling them. They're magnifying glasses for my eyes.'

'What's wrong wi' yer eyes?'

'I canna see so well to read nooadays, Robbie. We're a' getting older, ye ken.'

She was in a strange mood this morning, putting the fear of the very devil into him, he thought, as he peered into his wife's blue eyes. They looked just the same to him, but to think that any part of his Maggie was deteriorating was now a matter of extreme concern. 'Ye canna *see?*'

'Try them on.'

'Na, na! There's nothing the matter wi' *my* eyes!'

'Robbie Macqueen! I've surely seen ye in every shape and contortion by this time! There's no one else here in this coach but us. Nobody will see ye. Now, put them on!' Unwillingly he settled the spectacles on his nose. 'Well, what d'ye think?' she asked him.

'By God, that's amazing! I can find the marriage service mysel', nae bother. Christ, Maggie, I canna get ower it!'

'Yer eyes are bound to be strained wi' the reading ye ha'e to do, dearie. Keep them. I'll get another pair the next time I'm at the Luckenbooths.'

'Ay, weel ...' He sighed, and put them in his pocket along with the Bible.

He could no longer concentrate. Whatever Maggie was feeling was infectious. Lady Braxfield sensed that the nearer they got to Candacraig the more agitated her husband was becoming. Now Walter was making the awkward turn in through the gates. Then he knocked down and Lord Braxfield opened the window again. 'There's been another coach and horses here before us, sir. Look at their marks in the snow!'

'So who could that be?' he bellowed. Who *could* it be, coming all the way out here at this time of the morning in a coach? They trundled on slowly until they came to the trees around the big house. 'Where is it, Walter? Can you see it?'

'I can see something, sir, in amongst the trees over yonder.' Walter pointed. 'I think it's a coach. It's hiding.'

'Then don't take another step until we see what they're up to!'

'Calm yersel', dearie.' His wife patted his hand, but as they sat waiting in the coach half-way up the long driveway they were both as anxious as each other.

So it was that they all arrived around Candacraig within minutes of each other. Michael Henderson pulled his old coach, green with age and neglect, back into the shelter of the trees. William Brodie sat inside amongst the puddles from the holes in the roof and smiled happily, quite unconcerned, thinking his own thoughts and dreaming his own dreams beside Choco.

Fraser saw the old green coach. He tied the bridle of his horse to the trunk of a tree and went forward on foot. Then he caught sight of the Braxfield coach hovering in the snow.

What *was* all this, he wondered, in the dawn's first grey light. Why were they all sitting or standing in a ring around Candacraig in this terrible silence, like an audience at some ghostly play waiting for the curtain to go up?

The old house stood proud and majestic, crowned with white. From time to time the wind loosened a fan of snow off the gables and corbels so that it spread like a lacy cobweb over the whole structure, and gave it an eerie and unreal air. The windows were closed and blank. Candacraig was giving away none of its secrets, and for a few long minutes there was no movement to be seen. However austere Candacraig appeared in the eerie half-light outside, inside fear quivered through every stone and sinew and nerve of the old house. It rippled along the floorboards and transmitted itself to Polly, so that after a few minutes when she must have dozed off that Thursday morning her eyelids flew open again.

Before her horrified eyes Jocky Robertson was now naked and back in the bed beside her. There was a little more light in the room, enough to let her see that his face was rough and unshaven. His breath still stank, but he was perfectly sure of his welcome. She pushed him away as hard as she could.

'Get out! Get out! I don't want you here,' she cried.

'How can you say that, Polly, after all that we've been to each other? I want us to be together always. I want to marry you. It would be the perfect solution for us both, you a widow and me a widower.' He was uttering the words, but it was the woman in the cottage speaking. 'And then,' Jocky was continuing, 'there's Charlotte ...'

At the mere mention of the child's name he stopped and lifted his head, and somehow Polly knew that he was instantly sober again when suddenly he rolled off her and stood up listening intently. Then he pulled on his breeches from the sodden heap of his clothes on the floor and dashed into Charlotte's room.

There were no little noises from her baby, and Polly got up in alarm. Jocky rushed back across the room, tore back the curtains, threw open the window and gave an agonized cry.

'No! No! *That black bitch!* She's got Charlotte!'

The flinging back of the window and Jocky's shout echoing around the grounds signalled the beginning of the end. No one doubted who the black bitch could be.

Michael Henderson scowled and cursed. So it had all been for Choco's whore of a sister?

Deacon Brodie vaguely remembered a lady in Paris who had a beautiful coloured girl for a maidservant, but he did not understand why Choco was so rigid at his side.

Lord and Lady Braxfield had pieced together most of the story long ago and discussed it – but how could that woman from Paris be here in Scotland, in Edinburgh even – let alone in Candacraig?

Fraser Graham remembered the last time he had seen her, insolent and clever at the door of Madame Suzanne's apartment, evading every question.

A thousand memories chased through Polly's head when she looked out of the window herself and saw the woman in black running in the direction of the trees with a bundle in her arms. Her mouth twisted in bitterness. She should have suspected it all along.

Jocky was out of the room in a flash. She heard his feet taking the stairs two or three at a time and then she was behind him, running. She could not keep up with his giant strides through the snow. She floundered behind him.

But he was catching up with the woman, and she was heading towards the Fraser pine, which was creaking and cracking terribly in the wind with the weight of fresh snow on its branches, coming to the end of its life.

'No! Watch out!' Jocky yelled and flung himself on top of the woman, who was still clutching Charlotte just as the Fraser pine began to was topple.

It swung backwards and forwards, backwards and forwards for a dizzying few seconds, and then with a roar that echoed far and wide it crashed down on top of all three ... still vibrating, still snarling in its death-throes.

The horror, the shock and the noise of it froze everyone there into total immobility while the ghastly vibrations went on and on.

'Oh, God! Oh, God! Oh, God!' Polly screamed and sobbed as the crashing of the tree made the snow splash up in a huge spume. It spattered all over her and blinded her, icy cold and wet through her thin nightgown and chilling her to the bone.

It didn't stop her. Nothing could have stopped her. She plunged on towards the tree and came upon the body of Jocky Robertson first, his blood seeping out and staining the snow bright red.

Then she found the woman. Her cloak was dragged off her somewhere beneath the tree, and there was no disguise now for Caramelle's dark face and her sightless black eyes. In one hand she clutched the head of what had once been Poison, and the golden splinters of the rest of the bottle gleamed on the snow.

Caramelle. A fraction of Polly's mind was registering as she searched frantically for her baby. Caramelle, who must have been following her for over a year, all the way to Edinburgh, all the way out here to Candacraig, all the way into her bedchamber to steal the Poison bottle. Caramelle, who envied

311

everyone everything, even the bad things, who had wanted everything for herself.

Around the other side of the tree Polly heard a tiny wail and before her disbelieving eyes Charlotte was struggling out from between the branches on her hands and her chubby little knees, blue with cold. Her own little Charlotte, still alive.

Polly snatched her up and hugged her, still sobbing and shaking like a leaf, and that seemed to be the signal for everyone else there to move all at the same time.

'Oh, my God! Did ye see all that, Maggie?' Lord Braxfield gasped.

'They'll need us now,' she told him as Walter moved the coach on.

Michael Henderson did not believe the Deacon even heard the tremendous crash of the tree. He sat still and smiled while Choco gave a great cry, loped over to it, and after a minute shambled back in tears.

And so in the end it was Fraser who raced towards Polly and the baby, his own living flesh and blood, lifted them up in his arms and carried his small family safely into their home of Candacraig.

POSTSCRIPT

WHILE THE DEACON smiled foolishly out of the windows of the old coach and Michael Henderson strained every sinew to trundle it back to the coast as fast as he could, Choco sobbed on.

How could Cara have come to this? She had not been clever at all, bringing them to this freezing hell-hole called Edinburgh and then betraying him, leaving him – dying on him, even!

His sobs dried up in the bitterness of it all ... But then, Cara was a woman, and when had he ever liked women? From now on he would trust only his own kind, like this little man snoring gently and happily beside him, a man who was heading south now, into the sun where Choco had always wanted to be. It showed how sensible the Deacon was, and apart from that he had cheated Death. Very few men accomplished that.

Long before they came within sight of Edinburgh Choco was smiling down at his small guide and mentor and trying to shield him from the rain now pouring in through the green and porous roof.

'There she is then, Will,' Michael Henderson said when they arrived in Leith, sweating after his exertions and the terrible worry. How it had ever been achieved after all that he would never know to his dying day. 'There she is, *La Brilliance.*'

'*La Brilliance*? My God, Michael! What a lucky name! It's a sign of good luck! Oh, you've done well! You've done

313

well to the end!' William Brodie slapped his friend on the back and shook his hand, standing for a moment on the pier. Choco at his side seemed perfectly calm now.

Then the Deacon called Michael his dear old friend and hugged him for the last time. Michael's heart was nearly breaking as the little man, whom he was convinced would go down in history, walked up the gangway.

As the dawn broke William Brodie was stepping out of his past and into his future, bound for foreign climes where there was nothing but blue skies by day and bright and brilliant lights by night.

Just before the ship cast off and he went below with thoughts almost too triumphant to bear, he stood for an instant on the deck with Choco by his side, waving goodbye to Michael Henderson, waving goodbye to the desperation of Edinburgh, waving goodbye to the last dim flickerings of the morning candles where it had all begun, in Candlemaker Row.